NEW BEGINNINGS

Patti Ann Bengen

Book Worm Publishing

For further information, contact the author at:
Book Worm Publishing
P.O. Box 759
Shoreham, New York 11786

Book design by:
Arbor Books
www.arborbooks.com

Printed in the United States of America

Patti Ann Bengen
New Beginnings

1. Author   2. Title
Library of Congress Control Number: 2005909075
ISBN: 0-9774059-0-7

New Beginnings

To people all over the world
who want to be free from abuse.

Angie, to a special friend . . .
and to think it was all your idea.

For Laurie, Cathy, Sondra, Vaughn, Maria
and all my friends who have been so supportive.

Chapter One

*H*eather, did you fucking hear me? Listen to me, bitch! I don't give a fat rat's ass for you or anything you want!"

The hurtful words echoed in her ears. Heather listened to herself being badgered. There was no end to John's verbal abuse. Suddenly he bolted toward her. She jumped up and, quickly looking around her, realized that she had fallen asleep in her bedroom chair and had been dreaming. Well, having a nightmare was more like it! She took a deep breath and relaxed. How she wished it were only a dream and not the past haunting her. She shivered at the sound of John's voice still ringing in her ears. It was so real, so present! Making a deliberate effort to relax and banish the voice, she stretched her legs and looked around her. She leaned her head back and listened to the still quiet. What a contrast to the dream!

She'd come a long way in the past year. Her nightmares were less frequent and she was busy with many new adjustments in her life. So much had happened in such a short time. Changes came quickly after she was offered the position at Hargrove Electronics as an executive assistant. At that time, it had represented a fresh start . . . possibly a new beginning. She

was a different person now, not the person who had married
John and had allowed so much ugliness to follow. So much
had happened so quickly.

She sank into the velvety softness of the mauve easy chair,
settling further into it, curling her feet up under her. She leaned
back and remembered . . .

She had been so happy! She was so much in love with
John she couldn't think about anything else. John Langdon
was tall and slender, with dark blonde hair and deep blue eyes.
He was back from Viet Nam for three months when she met
him. He had been a blue-collar worker for a short while at
Hargrove Electronics before going into the service and he
resumed his position when his hitch was up. She and John had
fallen in love so quickly and completely they decided not to
wait to get married.

Heather's parents were concerned because it had happened
so fast; they didn't know anything about this man their daughter was so in love with. But they also knew this was what
Heather wanted and that her mind was made up. But her parents couldn't shake their misgivings. After all, Craig and
Peggy Hilton wanted their daughter to be happy; it meant
everything to them. When she had come to them, she was five
years old. They had given up hope of ever having a child, so
Heather was the greatest thing that could have happened to
them. She was their gift from heaven. They had waited so long
for that moment and then, all of a sudden, she was a part of
their family. Forever.

Craig and Peggy saw to it that Heather had everything
she could possibly want, but there seemed to be a part of her
they could never reach. When the adoption came through,
there wasn't much information about their new little girl
except that the mother had been killed in a car accident.
There was no father in the picture. The Hiltons wished they

had had more information but there was nothing else. They had paid an exorbitant price for this adoption and did not want to risk losing their precious daughter now that they had her.

For the first few years, Heather suffered recurrent nightmares, screaming awake nightly, sending Peggy and Craig running to her room. They blamed these episodes on Heather's fear of the car crash and her mother's death and were always there for her, trying their best to make her feel loved and secure. By the age of ten, the nightmares had ceased. But she was still haunted by a dream that was always the same but which she could never quite remember. Heather struggled with an inner conflict she couldn't define or identify but she was happy growing up with the Hiltons and loved them dearly. They were the most important people in the world to her until John came into her life. He swept her off her feet and, before they knew it, they were at the altar.

What a wedding! It is so true that you relive that day through pictures because for Heather the entire day seemed like a dream; it was over so quickly and they were off to the Bahamas. Ah, the joy of having ten full, wonderful days with only each other!

John carried Heather over the threshold of their honeymoon cottage. It had a heart-shaped bed in the center of the bedroom, which shared a fireplace with the living room. They were awed by the gigantic bathroom, complete with a small jacuzzi. They wasted no time peeling off their clothes and lowering into the silky warm water.

Heather slowly shook her head as she remembered how much in love they had been. It seemed like a lifetime ago. They had gone water-skiing, kayaking, bowling, dancing and swimming. They had dined out every night. For ten glorious days they did it all. Then, just as quickly, it was over.

*   *   *

They were almost home. It had been a long, bumper-to-bumper drive during rush hour on the highway from the airport. Heather was tired of driving. John had lost his license for driving while intoxicated before the wedding and was not legally allowed to drive for one year. It had bothered Heather that she had to drive on their honeymoon, but she didn't want to wait until he got his license back. It was a dull, cold December day and snow had been forecast to start late in the afternoon. As if reading her mind, John suggested, "Let's stop off at Mario's on the way home, Heather."

"Okay. Want to pick up a pizza there? I'll be glad to get off the road and be anywhere that has a little girls' room!"

As they got out of the car they noticed the first flakes of snow flutter down around them. Heather twirled around and said, "I hope we have a blizzard!" As she spun around she caught sight of their friends Tracey and Vito coming around the side of the building. Vito saw Heather and John and shouted, "Hey, newlyweds!"

"Hey, it's the big V!" John bellowed back. "How's it goin'?" The two women hugged in greeting.

"Tracey, you're looking good," Heather commented, at the same time noting the complete opposite. Tracey looked tired, drawn and pale. But she didn't ask if anything was wrong; she knew Tracey would tell her when she was ready.

"Hey, check out the old married man!" Vito teased. "Let's go in and celebrate!"

The two men had met by chance at Mario's after returning from Nam. Vito was in the Navy while John had been in the Air Force. Tracey was a senior in college. Vito, a construction worker, always appeared bronzed and weathered, and had a stocky, muscular build. He was five-ten with light brown hair and deep blue eyes. He seemed rough but had a heart of gold, and was a mush when you got to know him. Tracey was the complete opposite. She was only five foot two and a size three. She had long auburn hair that fell down to her waist, tremendous dark brown eyes and a peachy-cream complexion. She looked like a little doll. Tracey seemed so quiet the first few times the couples went out together, almost to the point of being withdrawn; but once she got to know them, she opened up and was a ball of fire. She had been dating Vito steadily for three months then and things seemed to be serious between them. The happy couple was talking about marriage, but Vito's ex-wife was giving him a hard time about the divorce. There had been no property or children in the marriage, but Julie was still being miserable.

The waitress brought over four glasses and the famed pitcher of beer.

"Why don't you and Vito come to the house next weekend for dinner?" Heather asked Tracey.

"Let me talk to him and see what he wants to do. I'd love to come, you know that." Then Tracey barely whispered across the table, "Maybe I'll come up and see you earlier. I need to talk."

Keeping Tracey's confidence, Heather said casually, "Why don't you call me tomorrow? John's working days. Do you have classes?"

"No. Tomorrow's a light day so I'm cutting. Why don't we meet at the diner?"

"That's a good idea. I have to drive John to work so if you want, I'll pick you up."

"Sounds great," Tracey replied, and furtively sighed in relief. She loved Heather and they shared everything. Now she needed to not only share but to ask for advice as well. "What time?"

"Oh," Heather thought for a moment. "How about seven-thirty? Is that okay?"

"Sure." Heather wondered what was going on. Not much seemed to bother Tracey, so something must be up.

They all sat in the booth and finished three pitchers of beer while they discussed John and Heather's reception and what they'd done on their honeymoon. As Vito suggested getting one more pitcher, Heather glanced at John and rose from the table. She could tell that John was already feeling no pain. She announced that she had to leave now or wouldn't be able to drive home. But she was really afraid of John having more to drink. She was exhausted from driving, but couldn't wait to get to her new home.

They would be living forty minutes from the city, up by the river. It was quiet in winter, but a busy little town during the summer months. They had looked high and low for a reasonable apartment and finally found this furnished place. It was a private home split into two separate apartments. The living room was long and narrow and had the only closet. There was a hole in the ceiling that housed a light fixture at one time. That hole bothered Heather's mother more than anything else. The bedroom followed the living room but you had to step over the bed to get to the bathroom. The main entrance was through the kitchen. Heather's favorite spot was the big picture window in the kitchen which overlooked the river flowing approximately twenty-five feet below an embankment. It was a cute apartment and Heather had fallen in love with it immediately. She had worked hard to get it to look the way she wanted. She had bought contact paper to put on the walls in the kitchen, with matching curtains and accessories, and she did the same in the bathroom and the bedroom. She had spent much time trying to find the right drapes, furniture throws and all the accessories. She was proud of her new home but now, with the wedding plans and packing and all the other preparations over, she wondered how she would start to fill her days.

Chapter Two

Heather, did you hear me? Where were you then?" John noticed that Heather drifted a lot like that. He wondered if she had some problem she hadn't told him about. But she'd always say she was deep in thought. After all, that was what she believed.

"I'm sorry, John. What did you say?"

"I said it's time to carry you over the threshold." They both jumped out of the car, Heather trying to race ahead of John to the front door. Everything was pitch-black and they were both feeling a bit of a buzz. But John quickly caught up with her and swept her into his arms as she giggled, "John, please, the neighbors will hear us!"

"Oh yeah? Well, let 'em listen, because this is nothing to what they'll be hearing in a few minutes!" And with that his mouth found hers and his kisses told her that she was his and that he wanted her, now.

John reached into his pocket for the key while balancing Heather in his arms. He unlocked the door and pushed it open. He gently put Heather down and held her lovingly in his arms, bringing her face to his. "I love you, Heather, and I'll never, ever let you go. I want you so much."

"Oh, John, I love you desperately! I could never imagine a day without you by my side," Heather whispered breathlessly as her hands slid caressingly down his back. John turned and, grabbing Heather by the hands, led her into their bedroom for the first time. Throwing her onto the bed, he glided his body over hers as they quickly undressed each other. Hungry to be fulfilled, they pleasured each other again and again until they rolled over, exhausted, and fell into sleep.

The alarm awakened Heather first at five-thirty. "John, my love, wake up or I won't let you get up." Heather hesitated, not quite sure whether she should once again call out to him. She carefully pushed herself up off the bed to get a better look at him, and as she did, John quickly turned, grabbed her and pulled her on top of him. Heather giggled. "John, there's no time for this." But as she said it she felt his need for her against her body. She realized on her first morning home as a married woman that time didn't matter.

"Heather, I have to have you now," he said, as his hands searched down her back and drew her closer to him. Heather laughed playfully, as she met his demands once again.

* * *

Heather sounded the car horn in front of Tracey's house. It was just seven-thirty. It was bitter cold, but the sun was shining brightly and she had hoped for a great day. The front door opened and Tracey stuck her head out and waved. Heather carefully watched Tracey as she got into the car. "Tracey, what's wrong? Are you feeling all right? You sure don't look it."

Tracey moaned, "Well, maybe I'll be better after coffee." This was strange, Heather thought. Tracey was always cheerful and she never looked away as she spoke, yet this morning Tracey hadn't met her eyes once.

"Okay, Tracey, how about the Early Bird Diner, is that okay with you?"

"Heather, this morning I don't give a shit where we go." As Heather pulled into the diner's parking lot, she glanced toward the passenger seat and thought she saw a tear at the corner of Tracey's eye. Pulling the parking brake, Heather blurted out, "Okay, let's have it. You're like a keg of dynamite ready to explode. What's wrong?"

"Everything is wrong. Heather, I'm so scared. I don't know where to begin."

"Why not say the hardest part first?" Heather suggested. She watched as Tracey drew in a deep breath and started.

"Well, you know how Vito and I have been talking about getting married. You also know we can't because his divorce still isn't final." She started to cry and Heather handed her a tissue.

"Yes, but you know that you'll both be together once it's all over with."

"Oh, I know that. Under normal circumstances you know I'd be okay with that. After all, what could we do about it? And we haven't known each other for that long, and I'm still in school. I wish it had stayed that simple. But now, to complicate matters, I think I'm dying." Heather sank back into her seat as Tracey sobbed.

"Tracey, what are you talking about? Dying?" Heather was at a loss.

"I…" Tracey mumbled through her sobs, "I found a lump in my breast. Oh, Heather, I don't know what to do. I can't tell my mother. I can't concentrate on school, and Vito and I can't get married now. He'll end up a widower."

"Tracey, honey, I honestly don't think you're dying. Try to calm down a little and let's go inside and have some coffee. We'll think of something. Here, take more tissues and wipe under your eyes. You know, that's why I'm here this morning. I saw you last night and I knew something was wrong. I hope you know I'll do anything I can to help you. Are you in pain?"

"No. Well, I ache. I'm sorry, Heather. I don't mean to dump on you like this, but you're the only one I can talk to."

"That's what good friends are for. Now, come on, calm down and give me a hug. God only knows how much you need one right now."

Fortunately the diner wasn't crowded. Heather asked for a booth in the back corner and a pot of coffee to start. "Please give us about fifteen minutes before coming to take the order."

As they slid in, Heather faced Tracey and began. "Okay, Tracey, the first thing you have to do is get to a doctor."

"But I don't know any doctors except for my mother's and I don't want to go to any of them. I can't tell my mother."

"You don't have to, dummy. I know several good doctors you can go to, and you can even go to mine. In fact, we can call from here and make an appointment. Look, the office opens at nine. We'll call from here."

"You know," Tracey moaned, "I can't look at my mother. She'll automatically know that something is wrong. I want to be with Vito more than anything. I really need his strength and support right now. What am I going to do?"

"Tracey, look at me. I will help you all I can and John is there for Vito, and you know that things have a way of working themselves out. We'll get through this and someday we'll be sitting here drinking coffee, looking back and laughing at the terror we felt over this situation." She reached for Tracey's hand. "It's going to be all right, trust me. Now, let's order some breakfast then you can call the doctor's office and see what they say."

Once Tracey started to eat, she realized how hungry she was despite being so upset. She counted her blessings for the day Heather came into her life.

When they finished eating, Heather suggested that Tracey go to the telephone and call the doctor's office. She rummaged through her pocketbook for her address book, found the page with Dr. Annan's number on it and wrote it down on the napkin. "Here's the number. Take this change. Now go call the office and tell them I referred you and that you need an appointment as soon as possible."

Heather watched as Tracey methodically got up, taking the napkin with her and disappearing through the back door of the diner to the pay phones. She took a deep breath and turned to stare out the window as she wondered what would happen to Tracey.

"Heather, are you asleep? I was talking to you and I don't think you heard a word I've said."

Heather laughed quietly. "I'm sorry. I guess I kind of got lost in my own thoughts. What did the doctor's office say?"

"The office wasn't open yet, but the nurse was in and I spoke with her. She made an appointment for me to see the doctor at one o'clock on Thursday."

"Good. Now at least you started the ball rolling. You can't do anything until you find out what's up."

"Thanks, Heather. I appreciate it. I don't know what I would do without you."

"I think that works both ways, Tracey. We wouldn't know what to do without each other." They smiled at each other with a silent nod of acknowledgement.

"I'll see if Vito can take off from work and take me on Thursday."

Chapter Three

$\mathcal{H}$eather smiled and her heart started to race as John approached the car. "Hi, hon, how was your day?" he asked as he got into the car.

"Good for my first one at home as an old married lady." On the way home, Heather filled John in on the details of her day with Tracey. As John put the key in the lock, the phone rang. He reached for the phone on the wall. "Hello? Hey, Mark what's happening? Great, great." Heather could hear him as she brought up the rear carrying packages and a bag of groceries through the door. As she put the bags on the counter, she looked out the kitchen window at the river. It reflected a bright orange glow in the dimming afternoon light. The ice that had formed close to the river's edge glistened. It's beautiful, she thought.

John broke through her thoughts, "Hey, Heather, it's Mark, our best man. What about having them come over Saturday night?"

"Sure, I guess so." Her thoughts slipped back to Tracey and Vito, hoping they would come on Saturday, too. "Do they want to come for dinner? I'll make Italian."

"Hey, Mark, why don't you and Linda come and join us for dinner? Great! About seven-thirty okay?" Heather looked at John as he paused for Mark's reply. "Great! See you then." He hung up the phone and walked over to Heather. He put out his arms, wrapped them around her and gave her a big hug. "When's dinner going to be ready? I'm starving. I don't know. She's married for ten days and it's down the drain already!"

Heather was trying to wiggle out of his tight grip, laughing, and said, "Guess we don't eat then. The cook didn't show."

With that John picked her up and took her over to the stove. With his head nuzzled in her neck, he teased, "Cook, woman, or you'll be forced to pay the consequences."

"And just what might those consequences be? I may take my chances."

"Oh, then let me waste no time!" John said, and swept her off into the bedroom.

"Now, Mrs. Langdon, I will fully illustrate the consequences." He yanked off her jeans and pulled off her tank top. He found, much to his amazement, she had nothing else on. "This is just the way I'm going to keep you." And he kissed her, caressing her in his arms. He listened to the warm sounds of pleasure that he loved to hear coming from her. She was a kind, loving woman, he thought. He was lucky to have found her. John was filled with love. He wanted to possess every part of her, body and soul, and devour her! And he did. He lost himself and, once again, she was his.

They fell asleep in each other's arms, content. John was the first to wake. It was nine o'clock and the house was in total darkness. He looked over at Heather, who was sleeping peacefully. He decided to get up and call out for pizza to be delivered and save Heather the bother of cooking. When it arrived, Heather woke up, hearing the commotion at the door.

"John, what's up?" she mumbled, half asleep, as she grabbed for her robe, struggling to put it on as she walked out into the kitchen just as John was ripping off a slice of pizza. "Umm, what a good idea!" She was pleased that she didn't have to cook and that John had been so thoughtful as to order food in. "John, I think Tracey and Vito might be coming up this weekend, too." She reached above in the cabinet for two plates, a knife and some napkins. "Want anything to drink?"

"A soda will do. I'm taking the pizza into the living room." John didn't acknowledge her comment but, as she thought about it, everyone got along and maybe it would be good for Tracey and Vito if more people were around. No one liked Mark's girl, Linda, but as long as she kept that big, loud mouth of hers shut, things should be okay. They watched some television but, before too long, they were back in bed for the night.

* * *

Heather was walking out the door on Thursday afternoon when the telephone rang. "Hello?" Heather answered breathlessly from running back into the kitchen to get the phone. It was Tracey crying on the other end.

"Heather, I just got back from Dr. Annan's office. He said that everything's all right, although he wants me to have a scan and keep a close watch. So I'm not going to die."

"Oh, Tracey!" Heather felt her heart pounding. "Be ready in forty-five minutes. I'll drop John off at Mario's . . . where's Vito? Is he at Mario's already?"

"Yes, he came with me to the doctor and then he dropped me off at my house."

"Okay, then let's do that, and we'll spend some time together. Tracey, I am so relieved. We have to celebrate somehow. I'll see you shortly, okay?" She hung up the phone and was out the door. She didn't want to be late picking John up. There was nothing more he hated than waiting for a ride. But when Heather pulled into the parking lot, she could see John waiting by the lobby door. As he got into the car, he reached over for a peck on the lips.

"Hello, my number one wife. How was your day?"

"It was good, John. I went shopping and I bought the tiniest little turkey. Wait until you see it."

"Heather, turkeys aren't small. Maybe you got the breast and not the whole thing." John was smiling to himself but Heather was insistent.

"Well, this one is tiny, believe me. It even says 'Turkey' on it."

"So, what else is up? Did you talk to Tracey today?"

"Yes. In fact, she called as I was walking out the door and she was crying. After the doctor examined her, he said it is not cancer. Vito dropped her off at home and I want to go see her. Vito is at Mario's and I think he needs someone now, too. How about if I drop you off and I'll take Tracey for the scan and meet you back there?"

"Jesus, Heather. I don't believe this. I mean, I think it's great that Tracey's all right but they should be together." She was still concerned for Tracey because the doctor wanted to keep her close. But she was also thinking about John. She pulled in front of Mario's as John slid over by her. He brought her face to his, kissing her while his other hand was sliding, teasingly, up her skirt. But Heather protested.

"John, please don't start here."

"I only want to start what I'll be finishing later." He could see Heather was serious. "Okay, okay, Heather. I love you and I'll see you both later."

"I love you, too!" She hugged him tight. Then John was

out of the car and she was on her way to pick up Tracey. Her thoughts drifted.

She knew that by the time she and Tracey got to Mario's, they would have two drunk men on their hands. But that wasn't the worst part. There seemed to be a darker side to John, a part she didn't know that much about, and that scared her. Heather never knew what to expect when John had too much to drink. But she tried to toss it off, hoping it would be different this time. After all, they were married now and if he loved her, as he said he did, there would be nothing to worry about.

* * *

Tracey was waiting outside when Heather pulled up. They had to be at the x-ray appointment in thirty minutes.

By the time they made it back to Mario's, it was two hours later and the place was jammed.

The restaurant was small and not well-decorated, but they made the best pizza and heroes around. Tracey and Heather walked into the restaurant. People were wandering around and all the booths were filled with people sharing a good time and laughing. The women walked to the back and looked over at the bar. John and Vito were in a game of pool. Heather swallowed hard as she took one look at John and knew exactly what state he was in. She could instantly tell how much he had to drink.

She had hoped things would be different now that they were married but, at this moment, things didn't look any different at all. She had hoped he would start to relax more and try to put Viet Nam behind him and get into life here and now. But it didn't seem like he would; not tonight, anyway. She had even hoped that after they were married his drinking would at least slow down; to stop altogether seemed to be too much to ask for. She never knew what to expect. Sometimes he would be happy and full of life and other times he would seem depressed and miserable. At least she didn't have to worry about John driving, she thought and she waved to a couple of guys who she knew. Tracey started to tug at her sleeve.

"Come on, Heather. Let's sit down and get something to eat. It's almost nine o'clock."

"Unbelievable, Tracey! They're both ripped!" Heather flipped her fingers through her hair as she shook her head. Then she distracted herself. "Listen, think about it and see if Vito wants to come over for dinner on Saturday. I know I asked you a few days ago, but in light of everything that's happened I'm sure you haven't had a chance to mention it to Vito. I'm cooking Italian." She could see Tracey starting to laugh. "Don't laugh! As the saying goes, you don't have to be one to cook like one, right? Anyway, Mark and Linda are also coming by. Try to make it because John starts a three-to-eleven shift on Sunday."

"I'll talk to Vito but if he works on Saturday, he might not want to go."

John and Vito came over to the booth and joined Heather and Tracey for a bite to eat before they all took off for the night. The evening had gone without incident and was actually fun. Heather was relieved.

The rest of the week went quickly for Heather as she shopped and prepared for her first moment as hostess. She busied herself at home cleaning and rearranging everything until she felt it was perfect. It was Saturday afternoon and she wanted to take a nap to feel refreshed before everyone arrived. She took a final look around the house; everything seemed in place. John was getting a ride from work and would be home by four o'clock. It was the perfect time for a well-deserved rest.

When she finally opened her eyes it was dark outside. It was already after six o'clock. She looked around the house, but John wasn't home yet. That was strange. He knows we're having company tonight and was looking forward to everyone coming over. She quickly dressed and then began to fuss with her hair and put on her make-up.

John walked through the door just as she put the finishing touches to her hair. He explained that he had stopped off with the guys on the way home. Heather didn't think too much of it because he had accepted a ride home and was somewhat of a captive audience, although she would have preferred if he had come straight home. But John was in great spirits and Heather was excited about having their friends over. The moment was tucked away.

The evening was wonderful. Heather was pleased that the lasagna came out perfect. Linda was pleasant the entire evening, and Vito and Tracey were able to make it. The parfaits she made were a great hit. The only problem was the coffee. It came out so strong that the spoon could actually stand straight up in the cup. But they had a great time. Mark brought his guitar and they sang, laughed, relaxed and enjoyed themselves. Vito and Tracey decided to stay the night. Heather felt so excited and pleased with herself. John was proud of her and told her so in as many ways as he could. He held her in his arms and declared his love to her.

Chapter Four

On Sunday morning they all went out to breakfast and talked about the good time the night before. Vito stated he had something extremely important to share with them.

"In three weeks, after graduation, I plan to take Miss Tracey Lucci to be my wife," he proudly announced. He hugged Tracey as he continued. "Now, in order for this special event to take place, I need to have a best man. John, will you take the job?"

"Yo, V, I would be honored. This is great, but what about the divorce? Did it come through already?"

"Well," Vito started, "I spoke with Julie and explained what Tracey has been going through, you know. She said she understood and that she likes Tracey and doesn't want to be the cause of any further problems or heartache to her. So she contacted her attorney and the divorce should be final in two weeks. That'll give us the extra week to plan the vows, right, sweetheart?" He kissed Tracey affectionately. "The only hurdle is speaking with Tracey's parents and we plan to do that this week."

"Oh, Tracey! Vito! I am so happy for you both!" Heather exclaimed.

"Well, Heather," Tracey said, "that brings me to a question that I have to ask you. Will you consider standing up for me and being my matron of honor?"

"You don't even have to ask! I would love to. I've never stood up for anyone else before and I would love it!"

"Good, then," Vito intervened. "Now that we have that out of the way, I have to make an appointment with the Justice of the Peace. We have to go down to Town Hall to register and then I'm going to take my bride away for a few days."

"That's wonderful," Heather beamed. "But you guys have to have a wedding cake." Heather's wheels were turning.

The rest of breakfast was spent in heavy discussion of the planned event, graduation and the honeymoon. Vito and Tracey didn't have any place to live or even to stay. John let them know that they didn't have to worry about a roof over their heads as long as he and Heather had a place. Heather chimed in that it would be wonderful to help them out any way they could. It was all exciting. Heather started making mental lists about the things she would have to buy in order to prepare for her friends' wedding. They needed a wedding cake, so she would make it. She'd have to get the pans and whatever else was needed; she really had no idea what it entailed because she had never done anything that involved before. They'd need a wedding album and she had to remember to get film because they had to have wedding pictures . . .

The next two weeks were busy and happy. Heather was relieved that Vito and Tracey would be staying with them. It practically consumed every discussion each day. Heather searched for the things she needed and now she had everything necessary to bake the cake. Things were quiet with John and

those next two weeks were romantic and a flurry of activity.
Vito and Tracey were spending more time at their house
because they had nowhere else to go. Tracey's mother was
furious when they went to tell her the news and told them she
didn't want anything to do with them; then, in the next breath,
she suggested that they speak to Tracey's uncle about renting
a house nearby. Everything seemed to fall into place for them.
The divorce came through as Julie had promised. They were
actually ready to get hitched without a hitch!

* * *

The week of the wedding arrived. There was so much to be
done and little time to do it in! Heather had ordered corsages
and a bouquet for Tracey. She ordered those little lapel things
for the guys, boutonnieres, she thought they were called.

Money was tight for Tracey and Vito so Heather suggested that she make a special dinner for them at the house before
they left for the Poconos. Vito managed to get enough money
together to pay for the three-day venture to one of the honeymoon spots. Tracey was elated, and even though her mother
did not plan to participate in the festivities, she gave Tracey
money for things she needed.

Heather and Tracey shopped. The most important item on
the list was a wedding dress. Tracey couldn't find anything she
liked. They had already gone through a dozen dresses, but she
kept trying them on. She was upset because she thought she
looked fat in everything she tried on. Heather couldn't understand how anyone wearing a size three could feel fat! Tracey
decided on a cream-colored silk swing dress with a long-
sleeved bolero jacket to wear over it. Heather thought she
looked beautiful. They found shoes to match and bought a delicate comb decorated with pearls to wear in her hair. It took all

day to finish the rest of the shopping but it was easy to get so much done because they had few time restraints living together.

John had accompanied Vito on his shopping expedition and they managed to get everything he needed. Vito and Tracey already ordered the rings and planned to pick them up.

On Wednesday afternoon, while John worked and Tracey and Vito were out to pick up the rings, Heather baked the three-tier wedding cake. Her landlady gave her a recipe for a wine cake. While it was baking in the oven, the aroma was overwhelmingly delicious. She held her breath, it seemed, for the entire time she was baking and decorating it. But she was thrilled with the results, considering it was a first attempt. When the cake was completed, she took it over to her neighbor's house so that the bride and groom would not see it until after the ceremony. The only thing left was to place the little bride and groom on the cake and she would do that when she brought the cake back and set it up on the table.

The next job was preparing the dinner. She marinated the filet mignons and defrosted the shrimp she had purchased the other day. That was all she could prepare until the next day. She stored all the food at her neighbor's so the dinner would be a surprise to them. She gathered everything else she would need to decorate and set the table, the tablecloth, candles, silverware, napkins, champagne, cups, and set it all in a box in the closet. Then she pulled out the shopping bag filled with the wedding things. She had purchased a wedding candle, the bride and groom topper for the cake, the bride and groom champagne glasses. Ah, she found the little blue furry garter for Tracey to wear and set that aside. The small photo album and two rolls of film were the last of the articles in the bag. She was pleased that she could do all this for them. She busied herself until she heard John come home with Tracey and Vito right behind him. They brought pizza so Heather didn't have to cook and two bottles of champagne to start celebrating. They were all talking at once and the evening passed quickly as they shared their anticipation of the next day and the planned honeymoon trip.

On Thursday morning, the men rose early and left right away. Vito drove them over to his sister's, where they were planning to dress. They would meet the girls at the town hall at two o'clock. Besides, the groom couldn't see the bride on the day of the wedding, Heather insisted, so she made sure they would not be around.

Tracey and Heather took turns using the bathroom to get ready. While Tracey showered, Heather opened the table and set it and got everything ready for their return from the little civil ceremony. She realized as she was setting the table that Tracey would see everything ahead of time, but there was nothing she could do about it. It had to be done now as part of the surprise for later.

The table looked beautiful. She went to the neighbor's, making several hasty trips, and brought back all the food and the wedding cake. She set the cake on another table, placing the bride and groom topper on top. Yes, the finishing touch. Then she placed the bride and groom champagne glasses on both sides of the cake, with the wedding album in front. She arranged the knife next to the cake and put the candle in the middle of the table for Vito and Tracey to light when they returned to the house. It would be the first thing they would do as a married couple. Heather stepped back from the table to take in the whole scene. It looked magical! Heather was elated because all of her planning had worked out and everything was falling into place.

Tracey had to call her mother. She knew she had to but procrastinated until the last minute. Her mother had finally accepted the idea of her daughter marrying Vito, but she wasn't happy about it. No one from either her family or Vito's family was meeting them at the town hall. When Tracey got off the phone she was crying. Heather hugged her and reassured her that everything would be okay and that her mother just needed time. After all, Heather reminded her, her mother had come through by calling her brother to see if Tracey could rent his house. He had explained that the present tenants were still there but would be leaving within thirty days. John had insisted that Tracey and Vito stay with them.

As Tracey dried her tears, she looked around and saw the table, then her eyes riveted to the wedding cake. She could not believe that Heather had made and decorated it herself. It was a real wedding cake and one that she had not expected to have at all. With white piping all around and pink and white flowers, it was magnificent. Tracey began to cry again. This time Heather joined her, in part because she felt bad that no one in Tracey's family would partake in the festivities. She could feel Tracey's pain.

The flowers arrived at one o'clock and soon Heather and Tracey left for the town hall. They talked and laughed the entire ride down. When they pulled into the parking lot, the groom and best man were already there. John was rearranging his tie and Vito was pacing back and forth along the side of the car. When he saw Tracey and Heather park, he ran over to the car and helped Tracey out, hugging her and giving her a big kiss. "Hey, babe, this is our special day. We'll remember it for the rest of our lives! I love you so much, Tracey."

"Vito, I love you, too! I can't believe that in fifteen minutes I'm going to be Mrs. Vito Perilli!" John came over and grabbed and hugged Heather.

"Okay, baby, are you ready to take your vows again?" Heather giggled and told John how handsome he looked. Before they knew it, they were all inside waiting nervously for the Justice of the Peace.

The ceremony took all of five minutes, but Heather managed to cry anyway. Afterward, they all hugged each other, went to their cars and honked their horns all the way home. Heather and John were happy for the newlyweds. Then the real celebration began! Heather made sure John took lots of pictures. It seemed like a mini-reception. The food was delicious and the champagne was flowing. Heather had bought four bottles to make sure there was enough. Tracey and Vito had planned to stay the night and leave at six the next morning. That way, they would be in the Poconos by ten. But John surprised the newlyweds with a hotel room for the night. He had called earlier and charged it on his card. So Mr. and Mrs. Vito Perilli packed what they needed for three days and were off to the hotel with another full bottle of champagne.

It turned out to be a day of love all around. Heather and John were relieved that all their plans had gone smoothly. Exhausted, but pleased with themselves, they shared in wishing the newlywed couple a lifetime of love and happiness. They turned in early, holding onto each other.

Chapter Five

Heather shifted in her plush winged chair as she smiled to herself, remembering the happy times. Throughout that year, the two couples had done everything together. Then John got his license back and slowly things started to deteriorate. John would be an hour late coming home, and soon he was arriving late at night. He would stop after work for a few drinks with the guys and forget to come home.

Heather remembered how she blamed herself for John's not coming home. She thought maybe she hadn't cooked well enough, or maybe she wasn't a good enough wife. She figured that it had to be something that she was or was not doing. But deep down she loved being married and truly enjoyed her wifely responsibilities.

But John started to change as he drank more. He had a way of making it seem like it was her fault. For a long time she said nothing, but as they planned evenings with friends, John wouldn't show up. It was frustrating as well as embarrassing, and she was becoming more upset until she had to speak up about it, which only made John angry. And so the nasty altercations began. John would verbally pound her down and she would withdraw into her shell. After each argument, she would try harder to be perfect so that John wouldn't be able to say anything. She would clean more, cook more, and try to look prettier. She tried to be flawless, but her efforts were in vain. No matter what she tried, nothing made a difference. How she had wished that it would all go away. She didn't know what to think. At times, she felt he resented her or didn't love her anymore or maybe he wanted a different life from what they had. The confrontations became worse until John would storm out of the house after his late return and stay out, which made Heather frantic. She felt scared, alone, abandoned and betrayed. They only had one car so she couldn't go anywhere or do anything by herself. Tracey and Vito were still renting the house from Tracey's uncle but that was forty minutes away. She felt trapped, and she was beginning to feel desperate.

One night John came home drunker than usual at about three o'clock in the morning. Heather was beside herself. She had been afraid for hours that he was dead or hurt in a car accident. In the argument that ensued, John announced he was leaving. Heather was miserable and couldn't comprehend what was going on. Hers was a horrible situation. She had no money to speak of, no car and no job. She was devastated. Her mother and father tried to get her to leave John, but she wouldn't go. She felt it was her responsibility as a married woman to play this out. It was her place to stay. She felt she had to find out what was wrong. Maybe she wasn't doing something right. She had to make it work, somehow. She remembered how upset her parents were as they left her there, miserable and alone. Her father had told her later that he was almost on the verge of hiring someone to bring her back home. He felt she was in a dangerously vulnerable position and couldn't see it. But he knew she would only go back to John. It ultimately had to be her decision.

Heather had to do something. She had no money and practically no food. She refused any help or money from her parents.

John had been staying with his parents but they had only made things worse. His father wasn't as much to blame as was his mother. She had gone as far as to tell Heather it was her fault and she was no good for her son. That was the last straw. It bothered her that his parents knew about their whole situation. It annoyed her that they knew she had no transportation, job or money. It drove her crazy thinking that they were helping him. Oh, sure, she thought, he does need help, but not the help Mommy and Daddy were giving. She knew it was time and she had to do something.

First on the agenda was getting a job and a car – not necessarily in that order. One of Heather's neighbors knew someone up the road with his own repair station. She explained to Heather that he frequently attended car auctions and brought back cars to sell. There was hope! So she asked this neighbor to go with her. The guy at the station had no reason to believe or trust her, but for some reason he did. She liked him instantly. He was probably in his fifties, not married and had kind eyes. She told him that she had to get a job in order to pay for the car. She couldn't believe it when the guy told her they would work something out. He didn't have any cars in, but he was planning to attend an auction in Boston that weekend and, if there was anything worthwhile, he would let her know by Monday. He jotted down her number.

Next, Heather started arranging job interviews. She was a lady not without valuable skills and abilities. She managed to line up a few interviews for the following weeks and called her parents to tell them the news. Of course they wanted to send her money, but more than anything they wanted her to come home. They told her she always had a job in the garment industry. But they knew she wouldn't come home and she wouldn't work for them, either. She was quite head-strong. She was going to work this out by herself. Besides, though she couldn't understand why all of this had happened, she didn't consider her marriage over yet. How could it be? What went wrong? She felt bad because John had pulled away from all of their friends and, little by little, Heather felt herself becoming more isolated. At first, no one wanted to get involved. Then, it was always couples getting together and she was no longer part of a couple. She missed Tracey and talked to her on the phone but she still felt very much alone.

On Monday, the man with the repair station called and told Heather he had a 1968 Buick. He wanted eight hundred dollars for it. She wanted to see the car first so they went out for a test-drive. It seemed all right. After all, the guy was making arrangements with her to pay for it. She told him she had job interviews set up for the rest of the week and she would get back to him. This man was so nice that he would let her take the car for the interviews. He told her to come back the next day to pick it up after he registered it at Motor Vehicles and cleaned it up for her. She thanked him over and over and he smiled back at her. She was stunned by so much kindness and would be eternally grateful.

She went to all the interviews and ultimately landed a job in the city as a dental assistant. She didn't have any dental training but her nursing school experience would help with chair-side assisting. The pay was pretty good for a forty-hour week though she wasn't thrilled with the dentist because he seemed like a real meathead. But she needed the money and would do the job to get by, starting work the following Monday.

She'd been working for about six weeks and had made one car payment and paid the rent. It didn't leave her much money for anything else, but that didn't matter. She was pleased that she was able to pay for the car and keep their apartment.

* * *

But Heather missed John. Sometimes she would cry herself to sleep. It seemed that as time passed, all the bad memories melted away and she could only think about the good times they had shared.

About six weeks later, John showed up out of the blue. He was sober, loving and attentive. He asked Heather if there was a chance that they could get back together. Heather started crying and asked him why he had left. He told her he was having problems at work that he couldn't work out and then all hell broke loose and he lost it. He told her that he had wanted to tell her everything that was going on, but he was too ashamed and she had been angry with him for staying out so he didn't say anything. He told her he would do anything to make up for what he had done. So Heather, still in love with John, took him back.

Things were going well between them. With both of them working, they were able to save money quickly and buy a house. Vito and Tracey had been looking all over and said there was a small house for sale nearby them and they should come to look at it. They did, and ended up buying it. Another new beginning.

Moving into that house was the most important thing in the world to them. They tried to save every penny they could to put more money down on it.

By this time, Heather had had enough of the meathead she worked for and started looking for another job. On an interview at the Bryant Todd Medical Clinic, she was hired on the spot. Her nursing background enabled her to get an administrative position in nursing care and she was thrilled. The money was a lot better and it wasn't that far from the house. She was proud of herself. John was proud of her, too, and had been extremely supportive of her efforts. That night he brought home a bouquet of flowers and took her out to dinner to celebrate her success. It was a romantic evening and the new start she needed. It had been a heady six months but their happiness didn't last.

John started the same routine. He came home later and later. Heather didn't know what to do this time. She did not want to end up alone again. He claimed he tried to talk to her, but she was always angry. So she kept her mouth shut and endured. At least Vito and Tracey were two streets over to visit. But that didn't fill the emptiness in her heart, the dread she felt each night waiting for John to come home, the secrets she was keeping from everyone by pretending that everything was all right. She threw herself into her work and into painting and fixing up the house. She was relieved when she was by herself or with friends; it gave her some breathing space and a little time to build up some strength. She tried to be satisfied with that.

She decided it was not emotionally safe to look to John for anything. Depending on John's mood, whatever she tried didn't work and her acceptance of her situation as well as her silence sometimes worked against her. She had noticed that he was starting to get suspicious of her. Whenever she went out, by herself or with friends, she would get the third degree when she came home. That hurt even more because she had never done anything in their marriage to give him cause to suspect her. But his behavior didn't make any sense.

Chapter Six

There were several employee functions during the year that they attended for John's job. Heather didn't know too many people he worked with. Sometimes he talked about them, but most of the time he didn't have much to say. The couples were nice, but Heather noticed that most of them kept their distance. She couldn't understand why because she was always nice to everyone. Maybe it was because most of the women were so close, having known each other for years and living close together. But it didn't really bother her because she spent such a small amount of time with them. Yet . . . she couldn't shake a nagging feeling of uneasiness. Maybe it was because they knew more about John's behavior than she realized.

The last Christmas party was the worst. Heather and John were ready to have a good time. The company was known for the extravagant parties it gave for its employees. This particular event started off great, but then John got drunk. She couldn't figure out how it happened so fast. He began talking loudly and making inappropriate remarks. The other women at the table could see how upset she was and tried to take Heather's attention off her husband. But, feeling embarrassed and humiliated, Heather left the table. She made her way to the ladies' room to hide for a couple of minutes and catch her breath. She never realized she was being watched closely. She had been too absorbed with John's behavior to realize that someone was trying to catch up with her.

She made it into the ladies' room, where she regained some composure. She fussed with her hair and applied fresh lipstick. She knew she was only stalling for time. She hated the thought of having to go back out there but she had no choice. Maybe John would be in better shape by the time she returned to the table. But as she left the safety of the restroom, she felt her confidence slipping. Heather had reached the foyer entrance leading back to the banquet room when someone gently touched her arm.

"Excuse me. I'm sorry if I startled you. My name is Brian Hargrove." Heather was taken by surprise as he held onto her arm, forcing her to move backward against the foyer wall. She immediately recognized him as one of her husband's big bosses.

"Yes, Mr. Hargrove. I do believe we have met in the past . . . maybe on several different occasions. Is there something I can help you with?" She almost laughed in his face at the irony of her situation. She was actually making an offer to help someone else? She figured she must be losing her mind. By this time, Brian Hargrove had Heather pinned against the wall.

"You see, Mrs. Langdon, I have been watching you all evening. In fact, I can't take my eyes off you. I've wanted to ask you to dance, but I could see that your husband has been keeping everyone at your table entertained. I would consider it an honor if you would join me for a drink." Heather tried to brush his arm away.

"Really, Mr. Hargrove, I am flattered but that's it. As you know, I do have a husband and I must return to my table before he realizes I'm not there."

"But why would you want to go back to that?" Hargrove's hand was gesturing toward the bar inside the banquet room. "Please reconsider. Kindly join me for one drink and I promise I'll let you go." Flustered, Heather excused herself and ducked under his blocking arm back to the restroom.

After peeking around the door, she left the haven of the ladies' room once again. On her way to the table she saw John with three other men at the portable bar. Five minutes after she sat down, John was in a fight and the bar cart toppled over. It was a mess! To their credit, everyone at the table tried to comfort and calm her.

John had quickly been restrained and taken out of the room. Although Heather was humiliated, the worst was yet to come because John was so drunk. As he walked over to the table he signaled to Heather to get up to leave. On the way out, Heather asked him for the keys but he wouldn't listen.

Brian Hargrove quietly observed. He couldn't understand how a beautiful woman could tolerate such horrendous behavior. He signaled to someone standing by the entry, who immediately responded to Hargrove's call. "Follow that couple and make sure they make it home in one piece." The attendant wasted no time in following them to their car. Brian Hargrove was still watching from the balcony overlooking the parking lot.

John opened the door for Heather and roughly pushed her into the car. Heather could see how drunk he was and tried to talk him out of driving but to no avail. She was petrified. He was quick to pick up on her fear, asking if she was afraid of crashing with him behind the wheel. But before she could answer he pushed down hard on the accelerator. The last time Heather dared to look at the speedometer, it read over ninety miles per hour. She was scared to death and started screaming for John to slow down! He was totally out of control and she was afraid for her life. If she ever believed she had an angel looking over her shoulder it definitely was that night. By some miracle they made it home unharmed. But now Heather was even more aware and fearful of John's dark side.

The next day, John tried to make up with her but she realized that she was afraid of him. She was *not* at that party with John and she did *not* come home with him, either. *Where* was the John that she loved and *thought* she knew? *This* John was unpredictable and she *couldn't* trust him. Yet, still she stayed with him, hoping he would change.

Their lives would be peaceful for about six months and she would start to relax, thinking that things were getting better. She even started to feel a little happy but then all hell would break loose again – and so it went nightmarishly on and on, crystallizing in a definite repetitive pattern for the next three years. By the end of the third year, John's personality took still another sudden change. His personality switched overnight and the John she married was gone forever. She was fearful of this new intruder.

John came home one day, talking about taking a transfer and starting over someplace else. Heather worried because she loved her job and she knew that it stabilized her existence. She never knew what was going to happen in her relationship from one minute to the next or what she would find when she came home. Was John at work or was he out somewhere getting drunk? Her personal life had become unmanageable.

She tried even harder to make him change. She assumed more responsibilities around the house. There must be a way, but at this point she didn't know that John's behavior had nothing to do with her. She wanted to be happy, enjoy her home and go to work. She was so easy to please. John couldn't even see that. She doubted whether he appreciated anything about her. Her feelings toward John had changed and she saw nothing positive ahead for them. She didn't want to let anyone down, especially her parents. She wanted them to be surprised and relieved that her marriage was a good one. But it was at the point where she couldn't hide the truth from them anymore. Since she could see no way out, she felt that she was a failure.

Late from work one afternoon and in a quandary about what to cook for dinner, Heather stopped at the store. She rushed into the house, wanting to change, get dinner going and sit down to relax a little before John came home – if he did come home. Her rushing around was a habit. Thinking about it for the first time, she wondered why she continued to do all this because she knew deep in her heart that John wasn't going to come straight home anyway. Why should tonight be any different? In fact, she knew she would be out looking for him; if she waited for him to come home on his own he would be horribly drunk.

She decided to take her time and relax for her own sake, resigned to the reality and the inevitable. But this evening, John was home at seven o'clock. He bounced in the front door feeling no pain. Those blue eyes looked as if they were going to pop right out of his head.

"Heather, I've made it! My application for the research and development division was approved."

"That's wonderful! When will you start?" Taken by surprise, Heather felt hope rise within her – again.

"Well, that's just it. I'm not sure." He shifted his feet and then walked into the kitchen to get a beer out of the fridge. Heather followed him.

"I don't understand. How, if you have accepted the position . . .?"

"Well, it's not that simple." He sank down on the sofa. "You see, it also involves a transfer...to Manhattan." Just as quickly, she felt her anxiety rise.

"What are you saying? Do you mean to tell me that you accepted this position and didn't come home to discuss it with me first before making a decision?"

"Oh, Heather, come off it. You're telling me that you wouldn't be happy to move to Manhattan? You can get a job anywhere. Besides, I made up my mind. I *have* to do this. You're *my* wife and it's *my* job that's most important. The opportunity is too great to pass up!"

Heather stood in the middle of the living room in stunned amazement as John walked past her and up the stairs. As she heard the music blaring from the stereo, she still could not believe what she had just heard. She thought about what her own job meant to her and wasn't ready to give it up. She stomped up the stairs. "John, that's not fair. You've been looking locally, but you never said anything to me about considering a big move. What about the house and my job? It's taken me all this time to get where I am. How can you treat this so lightly? You just throw this at me and expect me to accept it!"

"Look, Heather, don't give me that now. You're the one who always wants to go to New York. Now you've got the chance and you're going to fuck it up. You even said that I needed to make a change and, now that I am, you're moaning and complaining. I can't make you happy at all!"

"John, don't give me that line. You must have known something was up or you wouldn't have applied in the first place. We should have been discussing this all along." After her last comment, John picked up his beer and, with his finger pointed, started walking menacingly toward Heather.

"So what if I did make this decision? It's none of your fucking business. You are my wife and you are supposed to obey my wishes. Look at the reaction I get! You're a bitch, Heather!" And with that he stormed down the stairs and out the front door. Heather ran to the front window as he got into the car and took off.

She was angrier and more upset than she'd ever been. She thought about how much they had poured into the house. And, of course, there was the job that she loved, despite its demands and her never having enough time. Tears of frustration burned her eyes. Then she thought about how John manipulated, yes, he had manipulated this entire situation. He always set himself up. But why, she wondered. She knew it was useless to speak to him at times like this when he was irrational. He seemed to have something else on his mind even now when such a major change could upset their entire lives. Oh, God, "upset" barely expressed it. It was no use thinking about it since nothing made much sense right now. And yet, the thought kept nagging her…what was she going to do?

Chapter Seven

She walked through the darkened living room into the bedroom and plopped herself onto the bed, tears rolling hotly down her cheeks. The same thoughts came back to haunt her. All she had wanted in life was to be happy. She never asked for much. She worked hard, especially in the last few years to make whatever she could to get to where they were now. John was not a saver. In fact, he was quite the opposite, and money seemed to burn a hole in his pocket. That confused her because John's behavior always seemed to contradict itself. He also worked hard, sometimes with long overtime hours, yet he could spend money faster than he could make it. She could rarely go out at night, especially if she wanted to see her friends, because John did not believe that she should be out by herself. Heather believed John held her captive so she wouldn't tell anyone what was going on in her life. For a long time, it seemed easy to deny what was going on. As her anger mounted, her frustration was becoming unbearable yet she was afraid to say anything to anyone. At least she had some freedom by having her own wheels. It took her time to get used to it. She wasn't stuck at home and could do some things whenever she wanted, whether he wanted her to or not. She made it a point while shopping to find time to see one of her friends.

But as Heather became secretive about her unhappiness with John's drinking, she withdrew from many of her friends. She found herself turning down invitations because she was afraid to be embarrassed by John's behavior. So she spent most of her free time alone, while John was either out with his friends or alone drinking at one of the local gin mills.

There had been a turning point in their lives, in 1978, when she lost the baby . . . she didn't want to think about that right now. But that year marked the beginning of extramarital affairs for John. Yet for some crazy reason, she kept hanging on. Where was this leading her? And did she really even care anymore? Maybe the entire situation had become a sick habit. She thought about all the accidents, the indiscretions. The humiliation was unbearable. The downright vulgarity was demoralizing. Even his friends had made a point of stopping by from time to time, knowing that John was *not* home and looking for the opportunity with the lonely wife! Just a signal would have been enough for any of them. Ugh! But, as unhappy as she was, this was her marriage; it was sacred, indissoluble, and eternal! There had been many occasions when the temptation was almost too great to resist . . . to chuck it all and have her vengeful flings. But she knew she didn't want that kind of attention, however good it felt at the moment. She knew if it led to anything more she would be disappointed in herself later. Besides, it wouldn't make a difference, and mere unhappiness was definitely no justification. Not unless she was ready to make the final cut. But she knew she *wasn't*.

John could confuse her easily. She found herself sinking lower into the pit of depression. Each time she felt less strength to fight back. This drove her crazy and she would end up saying the same thing, "I don't understand why."

*   *   *

Tracey had similar problems, but not as severe as Heather's. If it wasn't Vito acting out, it was John. They would laugh wryly, at the most awkward situations, telling each other they'd take turns. They were so glad they had each other.

But thank goodness Tracey was such a good friend and lived so close, within walking distance, if necessary. Especially on nights when John took Heather's keys and forbid her to leave the house, and then *he* left. She could always walk over to Tracey and Vito's so she didn't have to spend the evening alone. Once their three kids were in bed, they sometimes took out a bottle and played cards for drinks or pennies. She managed to make it home before John did because she didn't want to pay the consequences.

Except for the night when Vito's friends came over and they had such a good time she didn't realize how much she'd had to drink or what time it was. It was ten o'clock when Vito dropped Heather off, and John was waiting with one hell of a buzz on. He had left the door unlatched and Heather, in a rush to get into the house, practically fell through the door. When she looked up, John was standing over her.

"Hi, hon," she managed. She could see by the look in his eyes that he had been drinking quite heavily. But Heather noticed something else . . . a tone that sent chills down her spine. Heather was by no means drunk. A couple of drinks over the course of the evening were more than enough for her. She was one of those people who could not drink. She felt her nose getting numb after only one drink then she would feel tired. So she didn't enjoy drinking much and she didn't feel it did anything for her anyway. She would admit that, at times, it had calmed her down and allowed her to get to sleep but her parents had been strict about alcohol throughout her childhood. So with John's look, it didn't take much for Heather to realize that she was entering a potentially dangerous situation, and she was scared to death.

"Don't you fucking 'hi' me! Look at you! Get the fuck up!" He yanked her arm, practically lifting her off the floor in one heave.

"John, you're hurting me," she protested.

"What else were you up to, Heather? Out fucking around? With who? You bitch! I work all day and I can't even go out without you pulling this shit. You whore!"

"John, that's not true. You don't know what you're saying"

John screamed, "Shut up! I know what's going on." He became more physical as he yelled at her.

She knew enough not to say a word. John grabbed her again, pushed her toward the sofa and shoved her down onto it. Her mind raced, wondering if she should make a run for the door. How else could she escape from this man? But even as she sat there, she knew she was in as much trouble with silence as if she retaliated.

As if to affirm her thoughts, John yelled in her face, "What the fuck are you so quiet about? Think if you're quiet it's going to help you?" Heather could feel herself trembling. That definitely was not just drink talking. She thought maybe she could lock herself in the bathroom and get out a window and get back to Tracey's for the night, but that would only bring their troubles to Tracey and Vito and they already had enough of their own.

She nearly jumped out of her skin as she heard the honking of a car outside. "Well, well, a bit edgy, my dear? How come? Is that your fuck for tonight coming to pick you up?"

Heather made a move to get up and John shoved her back down. "Don't bother looking. It's for me. I'm getting the fuck out of here, but your ass better be in bed where it belongs when I get home." As he started to walk to the door, he moved toward Heather and she knew . . . his arm came up, catching her hard across the back of her head and knocking her off the sofa. "Remember what I said. That's just a taste of what you'll get if you're not in bed when I come home. In fact, it's less than you deserve for all your screwing around." With that, he stormed out the door.

Heather pushed against the sofa to help herself up. She was seeing double from the blow but managed to get to the front door and throw the bolt. She turned with her back up against the door and just leaned. But she felt herself sliding down until she was planted on the floor. She stayed there for a long time, in shock over what had happened and at the same time relieved that he was gone. It was about two hours later when she finally lifted herself off the floor and went to the back door to let the dog in. Out of habit she took a shower and crawled into bed. She was exhausted and didn't want to think; sleep seemed the perfect escape. But sleep didn't come immediately. Instead, she tossed and turned, thinking of where John was going and when he would be coming home until, finally, her restlessness settled down enough for her to drift into a troubled slumber.

It was four forty-five in the morning when she woke with a start. The house was in total darkness and there was a loud silence. She rolled over onto her back and pulled the covers up to her chin as she laid thinking about what had happened and wondering if John had come home. Her head hurt. Maybe he was asleep on the sofa.

She quietly slipped out of bed and peeked into the living room. As her eyes adjusted to the darkness she found the sofa.

Her eyes drifted over it, but she only found the outline of the cushions lying in place. She walked into the kitchen and opened the cabinet for a glass. She let the water fill the glass and took it into the bathroom with her. She turned on the light over the sink and gazed into the mirror at her reflection. She didn't see any visible signs of the blow but her head pounded as she opened the cabinet and took the aspirins out. She opened the bottle, shook out a few and tossed them into her mouth. As she closed the cabinet door, she washed them down with the water, and studied her reflection in the mirror. Aloud she commented, "Heather, you are an asshole. Haven't you had enough?" There was no answer. Feeling defeated, she turned out the light and walked back to the bedroom. She placed the glass on the bedside table and slid back under the covers.

The early morning air was chilly and she snuggled under the covers hoping for a little more warmth and a bit of security beneath them. In just two hours she had to get up for work and she was exhausted. She wondered how she would get through this day, especially if John didn't show up before she had to leave. She knew she would keep wondering where he is and what he's doing, or was he in jail some place? But she needed her job, especially now. This was not the time to take off from work for any reason though how she wished she could.

*   *   *

Heather awakened with a start to the sound of her alarm clock belligerently buzzing in her ear. How annoying; almost an insult to wake up to. It was six forty-five and she knew she had to get going or she would be late. She lingered under the covers a few minutes longer, watching the sun coming up in the sky. Despite the sun's warm glow, it was cold. As she lifted her head off the pillow, she winced at the throbbing she felt coming from the back of her head. As she rubbed it, she sat up with a start. Had John come home? She grabbed her pink terry robe and put it on as she walked out into the living room. The dog was happy to see her and ready to go out, but no John.

Well, what now? Was his boss going to call? Did he make it to work? Oh, God, she thought, this is awful. She looked at the clock as she wandered into the kitchen and then gasped out loud. "The car!" She ran to the front living room window and looked out. It was there. "The keys!" She ran back into the kitchen and opened the drawer; no keys. She checked her jacket hanging in the closet; no keys. Nearing panic, she checked her pocketbook; no keys. She sat down slowly at the dining room table. He must have taken the keys with him, she thought. "How am I going to get to work? I had better call Jenny before she leaves or I'll never get in today." Feeling strangely calm, she made a pot of coffee and took a moment to enjoy the fresh brew and collect her thoughts. She picked up the phone and dialed Jenny's number. She prayed quietly, waiting, hoping that Jenny was still at home.

Jenny. Jenny was one of the most delightful people Heather had ever met. She was a powerfully positive person and sure of herself. They worked together at the Clinic. Heather knew the first time they met they were going to be good friends. Jenny, the petite, adorable, long-haired brunette with the bluest of sky blue eyes and the happiest laugh she had ever heard. The patients absolutely adored her. She was the most genuine person Heather had ever met, because she didn't like it when people put on airs. There was nothing artificial about Jenny. She always told you just the way it is. She was so cute and had a beautiful figure, but she sometimes worried that she was not thin enough. She would be starving herself one minute and then walk into Heather's office with a box of crackers, any crackers. She loved crackers. She loved life. Her spirit was contagious. They grew close and shared a lot at the Clinic. They had hit if off right away and no matter what, Jenny was always there for Heather but on a completely different level than that of Tracey.

Heather had a deep respect for Jenny and the way she lived her life. To Heather, Jenny had the perfect life with the perfect husband. She had everything. And she was happy for Jenny. Heather could only feel that way since Jenny brought joy to everyone she knew.

Jenny lived with her husband Frank in the upper suburbs, literally on top of a mountain in a two-story colonial. She loved it up there and they were meticulous about the care of their home. And it looked it. It was like a castle and lacked nothing. But, that was Jenny. She lived for today. If she saw something she wanted, she would get it. She believed in living life to its fullest and experiencing everything. She was a strong influence on Heather's life.

"Hello?" Jenny's voice startled Heather back to the present.

"Oh, Jenny, it's me. I'm glad I caught you before you left."

"Yes, you caught me as I was heading for the garage. What's the matter, sweetie? Is everything all right?"

"Yes, I'm okay, but do you think you can pass by on the way to work and pick me up?"

"Jesus Christ, Heather, what's that son of a bitch done now?"

"I don't know, Jenny. The car is here but the keys are gone. He must have gone through my pocketbook because all the money's gone, too."

'Well, we'll talk when I get there. As long as you're okay, that's all that matters. I'll be there in a bit."

"Thanks, Jenny. You're a sweetheart," she said gratefully and hung up the phone.

Within the hour, Jenny was there and they were on their way to work. They decided that, given a reasonable work load, they would go out for lunch and discuss what had happened.

Heather's days began with a bang and ended with a deep sigh because it was virtually impossible to accomplish all she had to do in one day or even in one week. There were so many people with so many needs, from all walks of life and all ages with all different ailments. A part of her was already concentrating on the patients scheduled for the day. The other part was trying not to pour her heart out to Jenny.

Heather knew only too well that Jenny could not stand John. But Jenny respected Heather and did not push her to open up. She knew Heather would when she was ready. They had reached the Clinic and walked quickly past the front desk. Jenny could see she had patients waiting for admission.

"And what are you thinking about, lady?" asked Jenny. Heather looked over to her, gradually leaning forward in her desk chair and bringing her thoughts back to the present.

"Oh, nothing. What did we say we were doing for lunch?" Heather's stomach churned at the thought of any food entering her mouth. But if they went to that one little place she liked she wouldn't have to eat. She could have one of those delicious Black Russians she liked so much. Even if it was only lunchtime, she needed something to calm herself down.

They were interrupted as Elaine from Physical Therapy stormed in. "I need these reports typed up right away! My secretary's out and I'll need coverage." Jenny rolled her eyes, turned on her heels and tip-toed out of Heather's office as she heard Heather answering Elaine in her ever-patient way. How Heather put up with everyone's shit she would never understand.

She knew Heather was hurting this morning, but she would have to wait until later to hear about the latest catastrophe. She hated to think of all the catastrophes, and she was

especially afraid to think of the one to come, the big one.
Heather was playing with fire, but she knew that Heather
couldn't see it. She blamed everything on love – or the lack of
it. And as time went on her fear mounted for her dear friend.
She became more afraid for Heather as she continued in her
delusions. She knew she would, but Jenny didn't want to get
that phone call someday. She had never liked John, but toler-
ated him for Heather's sake. She tried to include them in every
function she had at the house, but usually Heather declined her
invitations and she knew why. She knew Heather would be at
every party she had if she could. But she realized only too well
that Heather was afraid of John and not just because of his
drinking. Heather could not see that John was a mean and
spiteful person. He had no respect for anyone. Jenny felt there
wasn't a warm spot in his entire body. And that's why she worried so much for Heather's safety. She had talked to Heather
many times about John's behavior. But Heather always made
excuses for him. So after a while Jenny stopped trying to con-
vince and worried, silently.

Finally lunchtime came and, as always, found Heather and
Jenny enjoying each other's company despite the circumstances. It wasn't the food that made it, but the conversation.
They never lacked something to talk about. It always amazed
Jenny that their friendship was like that from the start. They
shared so much, and that's what scared Jenny. They told each
other everything – almost – and always said exactly how they
felt about things regardless of possibly offending each other.
So of course they had their disagreements from time to time,
but nothing serious. Their lunches were treasured times and
helped them get through the rest of the busy afternoon. She
cherished their relationship and wanted to see Heather happy
– and in one piece.

Chapter Eight

*H*eather was nervous about going home that night. Jenny dropped her off after work but didn't stay for coffee. She said she had shopping to do before she went home. When Jenny – and her warmth and strength and safety – pulled out of sight, Heather cautiously let herself into the house. John was not there. In nervous relief she decided to take a shower and pick up around the house a bit before starting dinner. She hugged and kissed the dog before putting him out, and then hopped into the shower to unwind.

Heather was at the kitchen sink preparing dinner when John walked through the door. She felt panicked, like she was going to throw up, when she heard his footsteps. She had to concentrate on what she was doing to control her fear. He walked right over to her and put his arms around her as if nothing had happened and said, "Baby, I love you so much." Heather cringed at his touch. She could smell the alcohol. His movements were sloppy. She closed her eyes, pretending she wasn't there. She was too afraid to confront him. She literally felt sick to her stomach and wanted to push him away with all her might, but she was too scared. Yet she would not show it in her voice.

"John, come on, what's up?" Heather didn't know whether she should question John about where he was the night before or drop it. But he was definitely high again tonight.

His voice, oily and low, sounded innocent as he asked, "Hey, hon, you're not angry because of last night, are you? So I got a little hot and blew off some steam at you. You aren't going to hold that against this loving guy, are you?"

Heather sought for words, but none came. After all, what could she say to make anything better or worse? "John, please stop. I want to be serious for a minute."

"Well, that's all you've got is one minute before I wrap you around me like a snake and take you for the most unbelievable ride," he countered, forcefully planting kisses all around her neck. He turned her to him and finally silenced her protests with his mouth on hers. Heather figured there had to be another way. She couldn't fight this.

Afterwards, John rolled over and slept. Heather looked the other way and, trembling, lit up a cigarette. She got up and went into the kitchen to make a cup of coffee. On the way she saw her keys dangling out of John's coat pocket and something snapped inside her. Without another thought, she grabbed some clothes, make-up and a few other necessities and was out the door. She made up her mind. "I'm leaving! I can't take this anymore! But where am I going to go where he won't find me?" She thought for a moment and then spoke out loud to herself, "I can't go to Tracey's; not Jenny's. I could stay at a hotel. That's what I'll do. It's only eight o'clock. It's early yet. I'll keep on driving and driving." But she didn't. She did end up at Tracey's, finding that she needed the warmth and safety that she would find there. She rationalized that she'd have to work tomorrow, so how far could she really go? She felt trapped.

But Tracey was out shopping. Vito was home and greeted her at the door. He knew a lot more than Heather could ever have imagined, though he wouldn't say anything. He knew the kind of person Heather was. She was a good wife; didn't go out or cheat on John and she didn't have any habits, no drinking or drugging. He didn't spend any time with John anymore. John seemed to be on a different road with a different crowd. He had even heard that John was using cocaine. He worried about Heather. "Hey man, what's up, Heather? Come on in. Tracey should be back in a minute." Heather smiled and pecked Vito hello on the cheek. He could see by her expression that she was upset.

"Hey," Vito said, teasingly as he looked at the clothes and stuff Heather was carrying. "What's up? Are you visiting or are you staying? Man, I don't know if I can keep the both of you happy and satisfied!" But as much as he tried to tease her he couldn't get a smile out of her. Things must have gotten a lot worse since he had seen her the other day. He put out his arms and Heather walked into them as he hugged her and she cried.

"Heather, come on into the kitchen."

"Thanks, Vito."

When Tracey came in soon after, the three sat at the kitchen table going shot for shot in a game. Later, as Tracey cleaned up the kitchen, Heather made her bed on the high riser in the narrow living room. Her head was spinning from the shots and her thoughts about John were all over the place. As she slid between the sheets of her freshly made bed, she thought for the trillionth time, there must be a way to work all this out. After all, John keeps saying how much he loves me. But if he loves me, he wouldn't keep drinking. So what am I doing wrong? Her last thoughts were about the transfer that John had accepted and what she would do about her job and their home. Her thoughts finally melted away into the peaceful darkness of sleep.

*   *   *

John woke with a start. He looked next to him and realized that Heather wasn't there. Maybe she was in the kitchen, he thought. "Where the hell . . . Heather, got any coffee ready?" His only answer was silence and the dog's panting in an urgent plea to go out. "All right, let's go out." He got out of bed and headed for the back kitchen door. He couldn't believe he had slept through to morning, but then again, after the night he had, he needed sleep. He felt great. "No note, no coffee," he said to no one in particular. She probably had an early meeting …but then…that bitch! Did she sneak out on me last night? If she did I'll…no, I won't. I'm going to make good and sure she wants to move with me. I'll find out if there are any openings at Hargrove in Manhattan for her. Then she'll have to keep her ass in gear with me around. Yeah, that's a great idea, and she'll never know I had anything to do with it. I'm pretty sure Brian Hargrove asked Heather if she wanted a job at last year's Christmas party. Maybe the offer still stands. I should kick her ass on general principle since she's not here, but if this plan works I'll have total control.

Heather returned home the next day after work. John was extremely courteous and said nothing about her not being home the night before. Heather was confused and filled with a nagging dread. She spent the rest of the week frustrated and depressed. But much to her amazement, the remainder of the week was uneventful. John remained pleasant and on his best behavior. Preoccupied with the opening of the cardiac rehab section at the Clinic, a welcome distraction, she didn't want to think about John at all. She didn't even want to think about her life outside of work anymore.

But the following Monday morning her secretary left a message on her desk. It was from Brian Hargrove and the message stated he would be in touch with her later that morning.

John had followed through with his plan. He had spoken with a friend who worked in personnel at Hargrove. This person was sworn to secrecy and had faxed over information to the Manhattan office about John's transfer and the availability of his wife for a possible position in Manhattan.

When John spoke with his friend, he was advised that there was an executive assistant opening in the top offices of Brian Hargrove. Perfect, John had thought, a challenge that Heather would not be able to turn away from. John was pleased with his undercover work. He figured that the groundwork was completed. Now all he had to do was sit back and watch the plan go into action by itself. He wanted total control and felt he was on his way. He didn't know that Brian Hargrove had pursued Heather after that last Christmas party. He had no idea that Brian Hargrove thought he was an idiot.

Heather walked into her office slowly and looked over the surface of her desk to see if she had any urgent messages to respond to before starting her day. She looked and then looked again. Brian Hargrove? What does he want? Without taking her coat off, she sank into her chair and picked up the message, staring at it. It was definitely for her and it was from Brian Hargrove and it was in Millie's handwriting. Didn't she say enough to him at the Christmas party to deter him from any further advances?

"Oh, no," she said out loud, not noticing Jenny had come into her office.

"Oh, no, what, sweetie? You looked shocked. Has something happened?" While Heather handed Jenny the message, she reviewed the Christmas party in her mind. Brian Hargrove had liked what he had seen at the corporate event and continued to pursue Heather at work with invitations, phone calls, messages and flowers. He had continuously tried to involve Heather in a romance. He had even gone as far as to tell her to get rid of the asshole and live life with a real man. But Heather refused to acknowledge any of his advances and with Jenny's help managed to avoid his calls. Now this. She had never mentioned any of Hargrove's antics to John. She knew John had been so drunk he wouldn't remember. Besides, he never would have believed her. "What do you think he wants now, Jenny?"

"I don't know, doll. You'll have to wait and see how this one turns out."

Heather started thinking about John's transfer. Yes, maybe that was it. But why would Hargrove call her? She hadn't told Jenny about John's transfer to Manhattan yet. "Yeah, I guess you're right," Heather answered thoughtfully. She knew she had to say something to Jenny soon, but how? They had shared so much and they worked closely for so long. But she didn't feel she could share this; now was not the time. All she could think about was Brian Hargrove and what he wanted.

Jenny interrupted her thoughts. "Are you planning on seeing any of the patients waiting outside today?"

"Oh, no. I forgot about the poor patients. Very funny, Jenny." She left Heather's office laughing. So Heather's day started, and kept up its hectic pace until she heard herself paged to her office. Her heart started to pound. What if it was Brian? She knew he was someone she could not trust. She glanced at the clock down the end of the hall showing eleven o'clock. She entered her office moments before her secretary buzzed on the intercom. "A Mr. Brian Hargrove is on the line. And, Heather, he said that he insists on speaking to you and he said, and I quote, 'I'll wait as long as it takes.' Will you take the call?"

"Thanks, Millie. Pass the call through." As the phone lit up and buzzed, Heather drew a deep breath, sat back in her chair and picked up the receiver. "Hello, Mr. Hargrove. It's been quite some time."

"My, my, my, Heather, why the formality? I'm sure you haven't forgotten that my interest was of a more, shall we say, intimate nature? Please, at least give me the courtesy of Brian."

"All right, Brian. But surely after so long, you couldn't possibly . . ."

"Heather," Brian interrupted, "I'll never stop giving you time, my dear, to realize all I have to offer you. I simply do not respond well to, uh . . . rejection, and have given you some time to reconsider your options. But that's not the reason for my calling you at the moment."

Heather hesitated, feeling her conscience twinge a bit; maybe someone in his family was ill and needed a referral or assistance. "It isn't? Well, what can I do for you? Is someone in your family ill?"

"No, Heather, just me: ill with lust for the sight of you." Heather sat forward in her chair and gulped hard, trying to think of something to say to shut this man off. Why is he doing this? What does he expect her to do, dump John and run to him?

"Heather, are you still there?" His voice interrupted her thoughts.

"Yes, yes, I'm sorry," she said, trying to think of an excuse. "My secretary just needed my signature. Please go on."

"Well, your husband's name came across my desk. I understand that he is transferring to Manhattan to research and development."

"Yes," Heather barely managed to get out.

"Well, I would assume that John is ready to start as soon as possible. How about you?"

"What about me? I don't understand."

"I know that you're still with John, although God only knows why, but what are you planning to do about your job?" Heather shifted uncomfortably in her chair. How dare he delve into her personal life! Brian had put her on the spot and she didn't quite know how to get out of this situation.

"Really, Brian, why are you so concerned about what I'm doing?"

"I told you. I have a special interest and I am going to protect that interest."

"But surely that can't be the reason for your phone call."

"No," Brian laughed as he continued to toy with her. "I won't beat around the bush any longer. You're too smart for that. That's what I admire so much in you, Heather. But I happen to have an opening for an executive assistant to work closely with me. When I saw John's name I thought it was the perfect opportunity for me or, shall I say, for you."

"Brian, please. That would be absolutely impossible. You know how I feel."

"But, Heather, in the end I *always* get what I want." Heather tried to remain calm. She didn't know what to say to this man. After all, he was a big boss in the company her husband worked for. She couldn't hang up on him. She also found herself wondering what it would be like to be so loved. Her life was hell but she didn't want Brian to know that.

"You're asking the impossible."

"Heather, I never ask the impossible of anyone. No, you definitely are an ace at what you do and you will be well-rewarded as an employee of Hargrove."

"Brian, I . . ."

Brian cut her off. "I think we should meet for lunch to discuss the details. After all, this job is right up your alley. I couldn't see you doing anything less."

"Well, that's kind of you, Brian, but I simply cannot accept your offer. I am pleased that you thought of me for such a responsible position and I am truly flattered."

"Heather, please think about this offer before giving me an answer. When you really sit down and think about it, you have much to consider."

"I have only my pride and my self-respect, Brian. I need not reconsider that."

Brian was trying not to lose his patience. He had his mind set on Heather. His decision was made. Now it was just a matter of time before she would see things his way. After all, he was Brian Hargrove and he had the power. "Well, Heather, let me give you a little food for thought, in case you need it to help you come to a decision. Let's see. John is scheduled to begin here in sixty days. A lot could happen in sixty days."

"I think I'm missing something. Exactly what is it you are trying to say to me?"

"Well, you know how much this job means to John." Heather was silent. Her blood ran cold at what he was implying. "I can tell by your silence, Heather, that you have decided to at least consider the implications. Good. That's a start. Now I want to formalize my offer to you in writing through the office and have my secretary send it out to you in the mail, to your home address, of course. Now, I'm planning to be near you a week from today. I strongly suggest that we meet on Monday at the Valley Hilton at, say, one-thirty for lunch. How does that sound to you?"

"I don't know why you're doing this. I can't . . ."

Brian's voice had become persuasively stern as he cut Heather's objection short. "My dear lady, this offer gives you much opportunity but little choice. Meet me, Heather. You won't regret it. My secretary will call you on Friday to confirm our meeting. I'll arrange to have my limousine pick you up at your home and take you to the hotel. I can't discuss this any longer. Goodbye, Heather."

He was gone. Heather wondered what had just happened. She couldn't believe what he had said. If she didn't take Brian's offer, John would lose his job. What was she going to do? Maybe she should tell John. No, she thought, she simply could not do that. He wouldn't believe her anyway. If he doesn't get this job…. She paced in her office, trying to think.

Jenny had popped her head in the door and was leaning up against the wall watching Heather. With a quizzical expression she asked, "Heather, should I even begin to ask what you're doing?"

"Nothing," Heather answered, embarrassed that she was caught in her thoughts. "I. . ."

"Listen, Heather, it's already noon. Lunch, remember? I have to be on time because I have four patients to admit for one o'clock appointments. Do you still want to go?"

"Oh, Jenny, I'm sorry. Of course, I'll be right there." She turned and as she grabbed for her pocketbook in the desk drawer, she glanced once again at the message from Brian Hargrove. What he had wanted had not yet become a reality. Then she thought about lunch and telling Jenny what was going on. Jenny already knew about Brian's initial phone call. She would have to fill her in on all the details. But before that, she would have to tell her about John's transfer. What a lunch this was going to be! They had better go to their favorite little place where there was lots of privacy.

As Jenny drove, Heather set the stage. "Jenny, something's up. I was hoping not to have to deal with it, but not only *do* I, I'm also going to need your help to get through it."

"Wow, sounds serious. Don't tell me: you're going to give John up! I'm sorry, Heather, but you know there's no love lost there."

"Jenny, no. Be real," Heather pleaded.

"I was and you know it. I love you and I worry about you, your bruises – and what's going to happen to you one of these days if you continue to live with that man!"

"I hear what you're saying. I do. I can't deal with that yet."

"Okay, sweetie. I'm always here for you. I hope you know that."

"Yes, Jenny, and I love you for it."

Jenny parked the car and they went into the restaurant. Heather could already feel a tear burning the edge of her eye in anticipation of telling Jenny she would be leaving. After the hostess seated them, the waitress came over reviewing the specials of the day. Jenny asked for coffee and Heather interrupted, "Jenny, let's have a drink."

"Well, I was just going to have coffee."

"Believe me, Jenny, you're going to need it."

"All right. I'll have a Bloody Mary and I know that she's going to have: a Black Russian." The waitress walked away. Jenny leaned over the table to Heather. "I'm concerned. We can't keep drinking at lunch. Maybe after work is okay, but we shouldn't be doing this during the day, doll."

"You're right. But I think you're going to agree that I need this to talk to you and you need it to hear what I'm going to say." The waitress was back with their drinks. They placed their orders and she disappeared. Heather stirred her drink and began.

"Jenny, there's no easy way to tell you this, so I'm going to come right out with it. John came home a couple of weeks ago and announced that he had accepted a job transfer. I didn't think too much of it because we both knew he was trying to get out of repairs. Well, I was happy for him." She continued to let her story unfold. She watched Jenny closely as she spoke and could see that no more words were necessary. The message came in loud and clear to Jenny. It all seemed so unfair. Heather couldn't imagine not working with Jenny. It was Jenny who finally broke the silence.

"Heather, you never said anything before."

"I know, I know. He never said anything to me, either. I guess I assumed he would accept a transfer to a local place, at least. Or that he gave up and decided to let things stay the way they were for a while. That's what the fight was over. But it really wasn't a fight. You see, John came bouncing into the house announcing the transfer and that it would happen within two months. When I protested, he blew up."

"But, Heather, why didn't you tell me when I picked you up that day?"

"I don't know. I didn't know if it was going to happen. But as it turns out, he starts his new job in sixty days. I found that out today when I spoke with Brian Hargrove."

"Oh, my God! Heather! I can't believe it. I don't want you to go. I don't believe this is happening. Je-sus! What did Brian have to say? I can't believe how much you're dealing with."

Heather had thought about what she was going to say to Jenny regarding Brian's phone call. "Brian offered me a job at Hargrove today. John's name came across his desk and so he took it upon himself to call me and offer this position to me."

"Oh, my God! What are you going to do?"

"I don't know yet. Everything's happening so fast. I don't even have time to procrastinate! I need more time to think. John already accepted his transfer, so the move is imminent. Now, about me, I'll have to give notice as soon as possible so Kevin has a chance to replace me. I don't believe all of this either, Jenny. It's too much to take in at once. Then I'll have time to decide about Hargrove."

Jenny listened to Heather explain the entire phone call and the plans to meet Brian at the Valley Hilton. She said, "You know, Heather, I care about you very much and you know how I feel about John. He *doesn't* deserve you. Now, I don't know anything about Brian, but my goodness, he sure knows how to go after what he wants! What can be so bad about that? You'd better do a lot of thinking." As always, Jenny offered to help in any way she could. Heather sipped her drink and felt tears stinging her eyes. The rest of their lunch –as well as the rest of their working day– was quiet. Heather mentioned that her parents were leaving for England. She cooed about how romantic it was that they were reliving their honeymoon and even taking the bus to the airport, as they had done the first time.

On the way home, Heather wondered what she should say to John. She hadn't told him about Brian, so she couldn't tell him now, and she certainly couldn't tell him about his phone call. While she prepared dinner, she decided that she would tell him that the personnel office at Hargrove had called and advised her that a position was open that she might be interested in, given the fact that her husband had already accepted the transfer to Manhattan headquarters.

She thought about Hargrove Electronics and Brian's offer. John's co-workers and their wives always had juicy tidbits about the Hargrove clan. And of course, there was always media coverage. The electronics business was prosperous and she surely did have a future if she could learn to deal with Brian's "lust."

Chapter Nine

$\mathcal{B}$rian Hargrove was Vice President of Hargrove Electronics Corporation; his main office was at corporate headquarters in Manhattan. Along with his stepfather, Alec Hargrove, and his two brothers, Winston and Bob, Brian maintained complete control over the company's operations.

Alec Hargrove, the company's patriarch, had removed himself from the daily operations but remained Chairman of the Board. He was available for consultation but usually from a distance since he and his wife Alicea traveled regularly.

Distinguished, still noticeably handsome, and an impeccable dresser, Alec had a way of drawing people to him. He would stop by each of the secretaries' desks to inquire after their well-being. People swore that he had a photographic memory because he never forgot anything someone said no matter how trivial it seemed. It was believed to be one of his secrets to the success of his company. He made wise, solid business decisions and was never hasty. He was driven.

Of the three sons, Brian was hungry for total control. He was commonly known as the "power monster." He could not be trusted. In his twelve years with the company, he had developed a reputation as ruthless, cold and indifferent to others except when he needed or wanted something. He was like an animal waiting to pounce on its prey at precisely the right moment. He never failed to attract the ladies . . . and neither were they safe as long as he was around. Yet Brian had remained a bachelor. Although he was not handsome, there was an adventurous, alluringly reckless and carefree way about him, an almost irresistible magnetism. He had dark brown hair brushed lightly back and deep brown eyes that could seem like two brown stones, cold as ice – and then as quickly could change to soft brown pools overflowing with affection. He dressed conservatively and as impeccably as his stepfather. He favored three-piece suits, tailored for him. He lived in a condominium in the Towers across from the Plaza Hotel, with a beautiful view of Central Park. He owned a silver Porsche, but his distaste for driving combined with the convenience of a chauffeured limousine left it rarely used.

Winston Hargrove had quite the opposite of his brother's reputation among the staff. At thirty, he was known as an adept and caring manager. His lean build crowned with blond wind-swept hair and shy blue eyes against tanned skin made him especially attractive. Although he had only been working for three years in Manhattan, he had developed a style all his own and people liked and trusted him. But these very attributes enhanced the friction and jealousy between him and Brian. He lived in the Village in a loft apartment that he and his girlfriend had redecorated. Winston, too, was always well-dressed, but his style was more casual, sports jackets and slacks. He had moved to Los Angeles to pursue a career in writing but found himself working two and three jobs to make ends meet. He finally decided to move back east and join his brothers and stepfather at the electronics firm.

The third Hargrove brother, Bob, was harmless, though a worrier. At thirty-seven, he carried the weight of the world on his shoulders and was always covering up Brian's schemes. He was excellent at handling the books and was responsible for the entire financial operation. With his thick glasses and hair that had already turned almost entirely gray, he appeared to be walking around in a fog. Corporate staff trusted and respected Bob, his work and his business ethics. His clothes were usually rumpled and looked as if they could use a good pressing. But he was soft-spoken and, like Winston and their stepfather, caring. He was the only one of the three brothers who had married. He and his wife had three children. But Bob and his family rarely attended any of the company functions.

Heather's parents were familiar with the Hargrove family and had filled her in on their tragedies and triumphs. Her mother had served on several fundraising committees with Alicea Hargrove and spent quite a bit of time with her. Heather had met the entire Hargrove family on different occasions. It was usually the Christmas season when dinners were given and bonuses and awards were presented. Heather had met Alec Hargrove only once, at an awards dinner, and she liked him then. She immediately felt his warmth and caring and she felt drawn to him. She had heard others express the same sentiment about him. But for her there was something more than that. She had heard many stories about his first wife and child. As it was told, Alec Hargrove's first wife, Monica, had taken their three-year old daughter, Melissa, to France. While in France, they were involved in an auto accident. Monica was burned beyond recognition. Melissa, the daughter, was never found, and was believed to have fallen out of the crashing vehicle, down the cliff to the ocean below.

Alec Hargrove had been grief-stricken, a broken man. He had been devoted to his wife, and he had worshipped the ground little Melissa walked on. He had lost all joy in living and practically abandoned the business in the process. But he rallied and buried himself in his work, building his business into an electronics empire.

During one of his business trips several years later, he met the woman who would become his second wife. She was breathtakingly beautiful with wild, jet-black hair, deep sea blue eyes and delicate features set on ivory skin. She was tall and slender with long, shapely legs. He couldn't take his eyes off of her. He first saw her at a dinner party. She was dressed in a black gown, long and flowing. He could not stop staring at her. He had felt a stirring that he had thought was gone forever.

Alec made it his business to find out the other places she frequented in Manhattan and planned one night to be where she was. There, she was as beautiful as the first night he saw her in Chicago. Sitting alone, she took his breath away and he boldly walked over and introduced himself, ordering a bottle of champagne then engaging her in conversation. Fortune smiled on Alec; Alicea also found herself attracted to him and welcomed his company that evening.

He pursued her ardently, sending her flowers and notes and invitations to dinner, the opera and the theater. Alicea was reserved at first, but Alec was persistent and charming, so she finally agreed to dinner. Within a very short time their relationship blossomed.

Alec had his private investigator, Lou Martucci, find out everything he could about this woman. Her name was Alicea McCallum. She lived in New Jersey about twenty minutes over the George Washington Bridge, which made it fairly convenient for Alec to set up his plan of pursuit, since he was living in Manhattan at the time.

Martucci had done his homework and by his first dinner date with Alicea, Alec had quite a background on her.

According to Martucci, she attended the opera and frequented one of the local clubs for the wealthy in Manhattan. He also learned that she had been married before to an English diplomat, with whom she had had three sons – Winston, Brian and Robert. When he wanted to return to England, Alicea had refused to give up her citizenship and live in England. She won custody of their three sons but the agreement stipulated that they were to attend a military boarding school; failure to do so would render custody back to the father. As the three boys approached school age, Alicea reluctantly made the arrangements to place them in such a school. It broke her heart to send them away, but she had no choice in the matter. She was inconsolable the day they left. She pleaded with her husband to change the education clause in the custody agreement, but he would not be dissuaded. Alicea worried about them and made frequent visits. She felt very alone without her children and lived to see them on their vacations.

The three boys had been her entire life and she was lost without them. Following her friends' advice to travel to take her mind off them, she began to make the most of her new-found freedom. Alicea made sure the boys were able to join her during vacations and semester breaks, wherever she was. She had a handful with Brian, who was difficult and seemed to take after his father who was headstrong and competitive. Bob, as he liked to be called, was more withdrawn, quiet and pensive. She worried about him. She felt closest to Winston, a warm and loving child.

Alec continued to pamper Alicea and take her to special places and events, always planning surprises for her. Her heart almost broke when he shared his tragedy with her. To make it worse, he explained that, strangely, he received occasional letters from France saying that his daughter was alive. When he got the first letter, he packed his bags and flew off to France in hopes of finding her – any small but miraculous hope. He found nothing but dead ends. Each successive letter brought with it only pain. Finally, he ignored the letters, throwing them away unopened. Alicea wanted to wipe the sorrow from his heart and free it with her love. So, after a romantic courtship, they were married but not without complications.

Alec hated leaving Alicea on Sundays, when the boys regularly visited their mother, to return to his condominium in New York, but he insisted that they take the time to let Bob, 17, Brian, 15, and Winston, 13, get used to the idea. Alicea expected them to fall in love with Alec as she had and to instantly become a family. But Brian was not so easily persuaded. "I don't want another father," he insisted.

Winston, on the other hand, was happy for his mother and supportive of her developing relationship with Alec. He enjoyed Alec's company. Bob was also fine with the idea: he had never liked the fact that his mother was alone. She was the world to him and he felt she deserved to be taken care of just like she had always taken care of him and his brothers. Though was busy with his studies, he told his mother that whatever she and Alec decided, they could count him in. But Brian remained the problem.

"Brian, I'm not asking you to accept Alec as your father, but as a friend and someone that I have grown to love. You already have a father and no one in the world will ever take his place."

"Mother, you don't need anyone else. I'll take care of you."

"My love, I know you will, but soon you'll start your own life. Wouldn't it be nice to see your mother happy and secure?"

"I guess…but I won't give one inch. I'll build an empire and you won't have to worry about anything ever again!" Alicea hugged her son.

"Brian, let's take one step at a time. I love you and that will never change." The phone rang. She knew she was not getting through to Brian but that somehow she would have to.

"I'll get it, Mom. It's probably for me." But it was Alec.

"Hi, Brian. Is your mother around?"

"Sure, Mr. Hargrove. Hold on and I'll get her for you." Brian handed the receiver to Alicea without a word and then made his escape. He only knew one thing: he had to devise a plan to stop Alec from marrying his mother, and get it into action fast, or else. There must be some way to build an empire for his mother. He had to give it some thought but right now he was off with his friends.

They planned the wedding for late August, which kept Alicea busy all summer. They were going to be married on Alicea's magnificent estate. They felt it would be better to remain where the boys were comfortable. But in June, after the boys got out of school and were getting ready to spend a month with their father in England, they got the bad news. Their father had died suddenly of a heart attack two days before they were to meet. The young men were all upset, but Brian was devastated. He was angry and irritable and blamed everything that went wrong, including his father's death, on Alec. Alec let him vent his anger since nothing else could be done. At first Alicea thought they should postpone the wedding but, after talking it over with Alec, she realized that whether the boys' father was alive or not was immaterial to their plans. They had to go on with their lives.

Brian was furious when he found out his mother was going to marry Alec anyway. He tried to think of a plan to thwart it, but couldn't. Besides, he was beginning to understand that if he wanted to build a good life for himself, he needed to seize the opportunity to get involved with Hargrove Electronics.

For the rest of the summer until the wedding, Brian became more tolerant of Alec. He started to spend a little more time with him, asking him questions about the company and fishing to see if there would be a place for him in the network.

Alec, of course, was pleased and took time to explain the entire operation. He decided to adopt the three boys and give them his name, especially since they all showed an interest in his company. It would be wonderful to have three more Hargroves eventually involved in the business. But he decided to wait until the honeymoon to bring up the subject.

The wedding was exquisite. The grounds were covered with trellis and garlands of flowers. The ceremony was held outside on the south lawn with a grand reception, catering to over five hundred guests and making the society pages of all the papers in the tri-state area. Alec and Alicea were joined by Brian, Bob and Winston at the altar, making a handsome family. Alicea and Alec felt it important to include all three boys in the ceremony. But, as always, the wedding day was over only too quickly and Alicea and Alec were off to the British Virgin Islands.

Toward the end of their honeymoon, Alec introduced the idea of adopting Alicea's sons. She was hesitant at first because of Brian. But she was touched and thought it a wonderful idea. She spoke with the boys one morning after she and Alec returned and was completely delighted to find there was no objection from any of them. When Alec came home for dinner, the boys surprised him with their unanimous decision to be his sons. It was more than he could have hoped for. Emotion rendered him speechless. They were moved to see Alec's reaction as he wept. Regaining control, he thanked them. He promised it would in no way affect the memory of their father. In fact, he didn't even expect them to call him "father;" "Alec" would be fine. Then he shared the story about his own little girl and how he lost her. As he listened, Brian felt a bit sorry for him but reasoned that with the last name Hargrove, Hargrove Electronics would someday be his.

The next day, Alec went to see his family lawyer to start the paperwork for the adoption. As far as he was concerned, it couldn't happen soon enough! By the time Halloween rolled around, they were officially the Hargrove family. That first year flew by: Brian was off to Harvard, Bob was in his last year of Yale, finishing early, and Winston, at fourteen, was very much into girls. Alec and Alicea basked in the happiness of their newly united family. But before they knew it, all the boys were out of the house.

Chapter Ten

*H*eather didn't have to stop off at the market; she knew what she was going to make for dinner. As she entered the kitchen, she remembered that her parents were leaving on vacation and felt happy for them and touched at how romantic they were. She had to call them but wanted to shower and start dinner first.

John couldn't wait to get home that evening. He figured that his plan must already be in motion and wondered if Heather had heard from Hargrove. This was definitely the best idea he had ever had so he decided to celebrate his ingenuity by stopping off for a few before going home. But his mind was set on being home by seven tonight since he didn't want to miss one minute of action.

John didn't make it home until eight-thirty but, the way he looked at it, that was close enough. Time just seemed to go too quickly for him. Heather was busy in the kitchen. She had made veal parmesan and was placing mozzarella cheese on top when John walked through the door.

"Hi, hon. I'm home – and do I have something for you!"

"Hi, John. Dinner's almost ready. Do you want to wait or eat now?"

"Well, I could go for something sweet myself, but I don't think it's on your menu."

Heather knew, as always, that he had had some drinks on the way home, but why was he in such a good mood? Oh well, she thought, might as well take advantage of it while I can.

"Oh, really, and what do you have in mind?" Heather teased along. John held out a bouquet of flowers he had been carrying behind him. She exclaimed, "Oh, John, they're beautiful. Thank you. But what's the occasion?"

"Nothing special . . . except to celebrate a new beginning with Hargrove in Manhattan!" Heather listened as she fought off a guilty twinge, almost giving in and telling him what was going on. He was so happy about this transfer that she was afraid to spoil his mood.

"Well, thank you. They are absolutely beautiful." She turned toward the sink to put the flowers in water. As she did, John was standing in front of her. He took her face in his hands, pushed aside her long curls and kissed her with such force that Heather lost her balance. As he caught and steadied her, he pulled slightly away, looking pointedly into her eyes, and said, "I got you, baby, believe me, and I will *never* let you go." He meant every word he said, and thought he was on the verge of total control. He took her into the bedroom and placed her on the bed, sitting beside her. He leaned over and kissed her again, this time very gently. But as he started to unbutton her blouse, Heather moved to get up. He gently but firmly pushed her back, his hand in the middle of her chest.

"Heather, just lie there. I'm going to undress you and look at you before I make wild love to you. I don't want you to move. Do you understand me?" John had never acted this way before. As he continued to unbutton her blouse, he kissed down the front of her neck and caressed her breasts, bare under her blouse. She began to turn away. "Don't move," he commanded.

He pulled down the zipper and slipped her pants off. She had a tiny pink lace bikini on. Propped up on one arm, he stroked his wife from her neck down the middle of her breasts, to her stomach, just to the beginning of the pink lace. Heather drew a deep breath as fear crept up from deep within. Her heart began to race. At the same time, what he was doing felt so good. Yet something was wrong; she tried to roll onto her side to face him, but his hand on the flat of her stomach prevented her. "Just lay back, Heather. I'll take it from here," he whispered. At this moment, his feeling of control over this woman was heady, and he intended to make it unquestionable. The thought of his plan and the sight of Heather helpless and at his mercy was almost too much for him. He threw off his clothes then stretched out on his side, his eyes never leaving Heather's. He continued to caress her as he rose over her and, without further preamble, forcefully entered her. Heather gasped at the harsh suddenness. Her fear was momentarily supplanted by surprise, anger, and panic. What seemed like his old passion suddenly changed into this brutal assault. Without acknowledging her, John finished and raised himself off Heather. He said in a self-satisfied tone, "Let's go, hon. Time for dinner."

Heather was shocked and humiliated about what had just happened. She got off the bed and dressed as fast as she could. She went into the bathroom and looked in the mirror. Holding back tears, she felt sick to her stomach, matched by the physical pain he had caused her.

"Let's go, Heather. I'm starving!" She walked into the kitchen and distractedly finished dinner, fighting back tears the entire time.

"What's wrong with you?" John asked in irritation, as he popped the top of a beer.

"I have a headache," she said flatly.

"How could you have a headache after that brilliant performance?" he demanded.

"John, please." Heather made a motion with her hands to keep him away from her. "It wasn't brilliant. You really hurt me."

"You bitch!" Before she could say another word, John came at her, hitting her head with the beer can. He grabbed her arms as she tried to shield herself and swung her against the wall. She hit it hard and fell down the three steps leading to the back door. He came at her with the beer can again and smashed it across the other side of her head. He kicked her in the stomach twice. "Get up, Heather! Get the hell up!"

Heather was whimpering, too scared to move or cry. She felt blinded by the blows she had taken to her head but instinct told her not to stay in one spot because he might kill her.

Before she could move, he yanked her to her feet. "I hurt you?" he yelled into her face. "Why are you going to work with no bra and lace panties? Who's at work, Heather?"

She was shaking and could taste the blood dripping past her lip. She didn't have the strength to break free from his grip and blood was blinding her eyes. He was out of control and she thought for a clear moment that she was going to die like this, too weak to save herself. The pain in her chest and abdomen was more intense than anything she'd ever felt. He went to get another beer out of the fridge and she tried to steady herself. "John, please calm…"

"Don't tell me to calm down. You never dressed like that for me!"

He came at her again, shoving her against the wall so hard that she fell to the floor in a final heap as he kicked her several times.

"Whore!" He grabbed her arm and dragged her across the kitchen floor. He struck her again but let her go at the same time the blow hit. She lay crying hysterically on the floor.

"Please, stop. Why are you doing this?" As suddenly as his rage came, it was gone.

"I'll be back later," he said. "And you better be home or I swear I'll kill you." He walked out the door, never looking back to see how badly he had hurt her. Heather lay in a crumpled heap, sobbing too frantically to call for help and hurting too much to move.

A long five minutes went by when she heard the door open and Tracey's voice. Heather tried to get up but Tracey already heard her crying as she came into the kitchen.

"Heather! What happened? My God, you're bleeding! Are you okay? Let me help you. I'll call Vito." Heather tried to protest but Tracey was already on the phone.

"Get over here right away. You have to help Heather. He beat her and she's in bad shape." She was back at Heather's side, "Come on, let's get you up."

Heather sat up sobbing as Tracey held her. They hadn't changed positions when Vito came running into the house.

"Oh, God, Heather, what happened?!" He ran water over a kitchen towel and tried to clean off some blood to see how badly she was hurt.

"I didn't do anything…but he thinks I'm seeing someone at work." While Heather explained, Tracey brought clean face cloths and towels from the bathroom.

"Here, sit still and let me wipe your face. Hold this towel on the side of your head. Vito put ice cubes in it." Her distressed friends continued to clean the blood from her wounds. Vito wanted to call an ambulance but Heather wouldn't hear of it.

"Did John say where he was going? I'm gonna go look for him," suggested Vito.

"No, please don't leave me! I'm scared," Heather cried. Vito and Tracey talked apart from Heather, trying to decide how to handle this. They went over to Heather and checked her head; the bleeding had stopped.

"She may need stitches," Vito observed. Standing on each side of her, they tried to lift her by her arms. She cried out in agony, slumping back down. Tracey knelt and carefully raised Heather's sleeves. Bruises were already forming on both arms. Vito gathered her up into his arms like a broken doll and carried her into the bedroom. Tracey followed saying, "It's okay, Heather, we're with you now." Tracey smiled weakly.

"I still think we should call an ambulance and get you to the hospital. I think you need medical . . ."

"No." Heather said, gasping and clutching her side. She didn't know which part of her body hurt most. "I'll be all right. Just let me catch my breath and I'll be all right."

"It's against my better judgment. But you rest for a while and if you're not better we're taking you to the hospital." Heather nodded.

As soon as Vito felt Heather was calm and in no danger, he took off in search of John, leaving Tracey with instructions to call for an ambulance if Heather started to worsen. He didn't know exactly what he'd do. He wanted to kill John. There was no reason for ever hitting a woman. What an asshole, he thought. He had loved John. They used to be really tight. But he crossed the line Vito was ready to stand up against him and protect Heather.

Vito looked in Mario's and asked around in several other places but John was nowhere to be found. Finally, Vito headed back to Mario's hoping John would show up there sooner or later. It was a nasty night to be out and Vito thought it wouldn't be long before the roads froze up. It was bitterly cold and raining hard. He decided just to wait.

John left the house in such a fury that he drove around aimlessly. Then he thought he'd try and find Mark. He caught up with Mark at some dumpy gin mill in the valley. They headed out to a place that Mark knew to play some pool, have a few drinks and blow off some steam. John knew that he had lost control, but he'd never admit it to Heather. He had wanted to control her but had lost control himself. But she deserved it for messing around on him!

John didn't think he had hurt Heather too badly. He couldn't recall the specifics nor did he want to. He had been feeling good when he got home earlier in the evening, having mixed a few lines with a few beers and adding a few more at home. But he lost it. He decided not to mention anything to Mark.

It was eleven o'clock when Vito decided to leave Mario's. He was tired and anxious to get back and make sure everything was all right. As he entered the house, he heard the telephone ringing and Tracey's voice.

"Yes, this is the Langdon residence. Who's calling?" Vito snatched the phone out of Tracey's hand before she could say anything more.

"This is Vito Perilli. How can I help you?"

"This is Sergeant Martin at the Eighth Precinct. I'm looking for Mrs. Heather Langdon."

"Well, yeah, she's here . . ." Vito paused, wondering if Heather should try to speak on the phone. "Let me get her for you." He signaled to Tracey to get Heather right away. Tracey ran into the bedroom and woke Heather, but while they made their way to the kitchen Tony was saying, "Sergeant, is everything okay?"

"We have her husband, John Langdon, down here at the precinct with a friend. They were arrested for armed robbery of Jillian's grocery store in Montford. They were apprehended after a chase. I need Mrs. Langdon to come down to the station to make a positive identification and we have some questions that we would like to ask her about this evening."

"She's gonna be very upset about this. I guess I better bring her." He turned to look at the two women, Heather already inquiring about who Vito was talking to.

"That'll be fine," Sergeant Martin continued. "When you come into the precinct, ask for me."

After hanging up the phone, Vito turned to face a pale and drawn-looking Heather. She had dark circles under her eyes that could have been bruises. Her long brown hair had been wiped but there were still traces of blood. She looked like if he touched her she would fall over. She sure didn't look like she could take much more. She was in no condition to go anywhere.

"Heather," Vito said as he put his arms around her gently, "we have to take a ride. John is fine, but he was picked up tonight and is at the precinct."

"What?" Heather half-whispered. "What does that mean?" Tears were streaming down her face once again. "I can't go anywhere like this. Everyone will know."

"Look, Heather, we gotta go. They're waiting for us. C'mon, Tracey, fix her up a little." He turned around and ran his fingers through his hair in nervous frustration. He knew Heather was in no shape to go anywhere except a hospital. He felt he was doing the wrong thing by listening to Heather's protests against medical help.

Heather limped her way into the bathroom to change. She was mostly numb but could feel a sharp cramp in her lower abdomen. When she breathed, felt a lot of pain where John had kicked her in the ribs. But the rest of her felt as if she didn't exist anymore.

Tracey checked on her, "Are you doing okay?"

"Yes. But I can't understand what John's doing." Heather finished dressing with help from Tracey but it was too painful to get out of her jeans. Heather tried to brush out her hair, but her head hurt so much and she was afraid it would start bleeding again. She stared at herself in disbelief then began to apply some make-up to cover the bruises on her face, which hurt so much and was starting to swell in spots. Nothing was going to help.

"Here, Heather, let me help you." Tracey delicately placed a hat on Heather's head. She put some mascara and a little blush on Heather's battered face then helped her out of the bathroom. But, suddenly and most dramatically, Heather slithered down the wall before Tracey or Vito could catch her. When Vito reached her side, he realized that she passed out. He lifted her and brought her to the sofa.

"I'm calling the ambulance right now." Tracey, placing cold cloths on her friend's forehead, watched as Vito grabbed for the phone.

"I have an emergency here and a woman is unconscious. She needs help fast." Vito hung up then dialed the phone again.

"Who are you calling now?" Tracey asked.

"I have to call that Sergeant back and let him know not to expect us." But Vito was surprised to find out that the police department had already received notice of an unconscious woman and Sergeant Martin was on his way over to the house.

As soon as the police arrived, the couple filled them in. Sergeant Martin stared at Heather. He recognized something about her. Why did she look so familiar? Where had he seen her before? And then it hit him. He had seen a picture of her with some guy. It was a coincidence, but one of his friends, Chris Hurley, had been working a security assignment at a gala Christmas party. That's where the picture was from. He thought about it a second longer and made a mental note to call Chris later.

Tracey held the door for the medics carrying the stretcher into the house. When she returned to Heather's side, she looked at her in horror. "She's bleeding again! Oh, Heather! We're here with you. Hold on, just hold on! Vito there's something really wrong with her!" She held Heather in her arms, crying out hysterically for someone to help. Vito grabbed Tracey to get her out of the way so the medics could work on Heather. Within seconds she was on a stretcher with oxygen and IV tubes. Vito followed them out.

"Hey, what hospital you going to?"

"Brookville Central," one of the medics hollered back. Officer Hill had been assigned to Heather until further notice and would ride in the ambulance with her to the hospital. Sergeant Martin said he would follow the couple over to the hospital and get their statements. Grasping Tracey's hand, Vito helped her to their van and they were on their way.

Martin would have to check with Officer Hill to see if Heather had regained consciousness or spoke. Very pretty lady, he thought, but she won't be pretty for long if she continues to live like this . . . if she's fortunate enough to make it. He shook his head. Unfortunately, he saw this almost every single day of his police career. He wanted to give his friend Chris a call. It was late, but Chris was a night owl and bound to be home unless he was working a case. "Hey, Chris, it's Jack."

"Hey, Jack! I didn't think I'd hear from you before Saturday night. What's going on that you're calling this late?"

"I thought I'd give you holler for what it's worth. Remember that job you did around Christmas last year?"

"I'll never forget it. That job changed me financially. Every job should be that good. I told Brian Hargrove I'm *always* available for him. Why?"

"Yeah, that's the name. I couldn't remember. Hargrove. Well, remember the pictures you showed me from that event?"

"Yeah."

"Do you remember one specific picture with Hargrove speaking to a very pretty lady?"

"Let me think a minute. Yeah, I remember. I took that picture because he had her leaning up against the wall. I wasn't sure what was going on. Later on, when Hargrove saw the pictures, he had me make him a copy of that one. So what brings this up?"

"I thought you might like to know that I was expecting that same lady at the precinct this evening but we got an emergency call from someone at her address. By the time I reached the house she was unconscious."

"What's the story? Is she a collar?"

"No, her husband is. She was in bad shape, badly beaten. She's at Brookville Central with a uniform assigned to her."

"No kidding. I remember her husband. He was a real loser at that party. He caused a lot of trouble…drunk and out of control. In the end, Brian Hargrove had me follow the happy couple home to make sure they got there safely. He is a bad accident just waiting to happen . . . on or off the road."

"Well, he may be in bigger trouble this time."

"Thanks for passing on the information. I owe you one. Guess I'll see you at the game Saturday."

"You bet."

Chris slowly put the phone down. This was an interesting turn of events. Of course, anything of interest to Hargrove Electronics was also of interest to him. It means dollars, and many of them. He thought he'd give Brian Hargrove a call. *He* sure was interested in this lady. He looked up the number and dialed.

"Good evening, Hargrove residence."

"Yes, good evening. I'm sorry to call so late. My name is Chris Hurley of Pro-Secure Services and I'm trying to reach Brian Hargrove. It's very important that I speak with him."

"Please hold on for one moment and I will check." Chris wondered what the attachment was between Hargrove and the Langdon woman. Although, he thought to himself, he wouldn't have hesitated to go after the woman himself if she weren't married.

"Brian Hargrove here," he answered with an annoyed tone. Brian was testy about being called so late by someone not presently working for him. "Mr. Hargrove, this is Chris Hurley. I did some security work for you, including that fantastic Christmas party."

"Yes, of course I remember. I assume your calling at this late hour means that you have some information that you would like to tell me. It must be pretty heavy news."

"Yes, it is. I'm sorry about the hour, but I thought you might want this information without delay. I just found out myself."

"Well, Chris, let's have it."

"I just got off the phone with a friend, also a cop. He said an arrest was made this evening, John Langdon. He also informed me that he was sent out to an emergency call at the Langdon residence."

Brian felt his entire body tense as Chris spoke. "Go on; there's evidently more you want to tell me."

"Well, apparently Langdon was taken into custody earlier tonight, and Mrs. Langdon was called down to the precinct. It is my understanding that she was in bad shape and passed out in her home. She had cuts and bruises on her head and face and was transported by ambulance, still unconscious, to Brookville Central."

Brian held his breath as he listened to Hurley. It was beyond all comprehension. He didn't dare wonder if his conversation with her earlier in the day had anything to do with her current situation. His beautiful Heather! It took all he had to continue in command of the situation.

"You did the right thing. Consider yourself in my employ again. The first thing I want you to do is to find out everything you can for me. I want to know exactly what happened to Mrs. Langdon and whether she's all right. Then, I want all information regarding her husband. Do you have that?"

"Sure thing, Mr. Hargrove. Your requests are in capable hands."

"Good. I'll advance you ten thousand, which will be in your business account by nine in the morning. I will give you my direct number so you can reach me at any time. Any questions?"

"No, Mr. Hargrove. I'll get right on it and be back in touch with you within a couple of hours." Ah, Chris thought, business was sweet.

Brian gave Chris his direct line and hung up. He wanted to go directly to the hospital but he thought he had better not. Yet he had to know what was wrong with her and exactly what had happened. He had worked so hard to get her to meet him at the Hilton, and now this. He sunk back into his leather chair and opened a drawer in the round mahogany pedestal table next to it. He pulled out a frame with the picture of Heather and him at the Christmas party. The very same picture Chris had taken and the same picture Sergeant Martin had seen.

He became lost in thought as he stared at the picture. He alone should be the one to possess this woman. She should be his. He felt he was the only one who could make her happy, protect her from life's cruelties and give Heather what she wanted out of life. Now he didn't even know if she would live. Did John do this to her, he wondered. Maybe she had told John about their conversation that day. He would never forgive himself if he were the cause. He knew he had the power to make Heather his, but she had to have the will, the will to want him in her life completely. He must make her need him. Once he knew she was okay, he would devise a plan to make her need him. He had to entice her away from that loser she thinks she loves. He slid further into the soft, enveloping cushion and closed his eyes, ruminating about how he would win Heather.

Chapter Eleven

$\mathcal{T}$he Perillis were sitting in the emergency room waiting area. Heather was already in the treatment room with Officer Hill at the door. It seemed like they were taking forever. Sergeant Martin had already taken their statements and informed them that he would be in touch with them if he needed more information.

Chris Hurley walked nonchalantly into the emergency room. He was glad to be inside; it was bitterly cold outside and had started to sleet. He scanned the emergency room for anything he felt would be helpful. It wasn't that crowded yet, but if that weather kept up they were in for one hell of a night. There were two nurses at the station; a child was being wheeled on a stretcher and an older man was in a wheelchair, hunched over and holding his head with his hands. But there was no sign of Mrs. Langdon. He casually walked over to the beverage machine and got a cup of coffee. He thought his best bet would be to stand as close as he could to the nursing desk without appearing too obvious and listen for any information about Mrs. Langdon. Just as he started to sip his coffee, a dark-haired nurse called out to a couple he had seen sitting on a sofa in the waiting area, "Mr. and Mrs. Perilli." The exhausted twosome jumped up and flew over to the desk where the nurse was standing. They nodded anxiously to the nurse, who continued, "The doctor will be out in a minute to speak with you about Mrs. Langdon. Please wait over there."

"Thank you," Vito said, and led Tracey to an enclosed area next to the waiting room on the other side of the nurse's station.

Bingo, thought Chris. He slowly worked his way around to the far side of the cubicle and stood there leaning against the wall, sipping his coffee as if he were waiting for someone. Tracey was saying, "Vito, what can we do?"

"Tracey, you have got to calm down. Let's wait until the doctor comes in. We can't do anything until he tells us . . ." He placed his arm around her shoulder and squeezed.

"Mr. and Mrs. Perilli?" a voice interrupted. "I'm Dr. Holden. I'd like to brief you on Mrs. Langdon's condition. First of all, did you know that she is pregnant?"

Vito and Tracey looked at each other in amazement. "No," they answered at the same time. Then Tracey added, "I doubt *she* even knew. She lost one baby and she's been trying for quite some time. I know she would have been excited. She would have told me right away."

"Well," Dr. Holden continued, "the pregnancy at this stage is definitely threatened. Mrs. Langdon is hemorrhaging. She's in shock. She's unconscious. She's being prepped for surgery as we speak, and time is of the essence. At this time, we do not know if we can save the baby until we assess the damage. The cuts on her head have already been stitched. There are multiple bruises all over her arms and it appears that she was kicked several times; at least three ribs are broken. At first I thought she was in an accident, but finger mark bruising is present over her arms."

"It was no accident." Tracey said angrily, "Her husband did this to her!" and broke down in tears.

"I want you to know that we will do everything we can to try and save the baby and prevent a hysterectomy. If you're going to stay in the waiting room, I'll be back down after the surgery to let you know how things went. I have to get back to Mrs.Langdon. She is in critical condition right now and anything can happen. I'm just preparing you for the worst scenario. I don't want to scare you but she's in pretty bad shape."

"We'll be right here," Vito replied. They saw a stretcher coming out of the room. Tracey jumped up and brushed past the doctor before anything more could be said.

"Heather, Heather," Tracey said softly, as she reached the stretcher. The attendants didn't stop so she kept moving along with them. Heather looked deathly pale and she had a surgical cap on her head. She looked so helpless! Tracey squeezed Heather's lifeless hand as if she were trying to squeeze life back into her. Then the elevator doors opened and Heather was gone. Tracey felt the tears falling down her cheeks. Heather was all that was good in this world. She cried as she leaned against the wall, feeling guilty: maybe if she had called an ambulance earlier? What if she never sees Heather again? She sobbed harder. Then she felt a pair of familiar arms around her. She turned and buried her head in her husband's chest, continuing to cry softly. "Vito, what if she doesn't make it?"

"It's okay, baby. Heather's a fighter. She'll come through this. You'll see. Come on, let's get some coffee," he soothed as he led Tracey down the hall and back to the waiting area. Vito looked up and saw the female cop sitting at the nursing desk. Langdon's in big trouble, he thought. He had no idea what John was up to lately.

Chris was satisfied with the information he had collected in a relatively short period of time and was anxious to get back to Hargrove. It seemed as if the phone didn't even ring.

"Hello?"

"Mr. Hargrove, it's Chris. I have some information for you."

Brian sat straight up in the chair in anticipation of what Chris had to relay. "Well, get on with it."

"I'm in the hospital parking lot. But I've been inside and overheard the doctor's conversation to a couple, apparently good friends of Mrs. Langdon." Brian tried to sit back as he listened to the nightmare his Heather was going through. He could feel his nails digging into the palm of his hand as Chris explained how she had been beaten and kicked. But he wasn't prepared for his total loss of breath when he heard the word pregnant. He dropped the phone for an instant and could hear Chris calling him and asking if he were still on the phone.

"Just a moment...Okay, please continue."

"Well, according to the couple, the Langdon woman probably doesn't know of her condition. I did hear the doctor say that they were not optimistic about saving the baby. There's a female cop assigned to Mrs. Langdon for protection. I haven't spoken with her."

"Good work, Chris, keep on it. Try and find out what's up with the husband."

After Brian hung up, he paced his bedroom. Heather, he thought to himself, you have to make it. First thing, he would contact the hospital administrator and arrange for the best care possible for her; she should want for nothing. That miserable excuse for a human being sitting in a jail cell! That's where he belongs. Yes, Brian thought, that's exactly where he belongs.

Vito and Tracey were stretched out and dozing on the sofa in the waiting room. Vito heard voices in the distance and opened his eyes. He looked around but didn't see anyone. He swung his feet down onto the floor and looked at the clock. It was four o'clock in the morning. Just as he turned his head to check on Tracey, Dr. Holden came through the double elevator doors, still dressed in his surgical greens.

"Mr. Perilli, I see your wife is catching a bit of sleep."

"Yes," replied Vito, "we both were nodding on and off."

"Well, Mrs. Langdon . . ."

"Wait a second," Tracey interrupted. "I want to hear this."

"Yes, of course...Now, Mrs. Langdon gave us quite a scare in the operating room. Unfortunately, she lost the baby and, due to the damage to her uterus and the internal bleeding, we had to do a hysterectomy. She has lost quite a bit of blood. She has three broken ribs. It was most fortunate that those fractures didn't penetrate her lungs. She is presently being taken to Surgical Intensive Care where she will remain until her condition stabilizes. She will be monitored closely until we feel she is out of danger. Then we will consider a transfer to a surgical floor. I am hoping for no further complications, but it's too early to tell. We have to see how she comes through the rest of the night. Now, do either of you have any questions you'd like to ask? Also, is there anyone else to be contacted? Does she have any family?"

The couple exchanged looks. "Well, her parents," Vito answered, "And her husband was taken into custody earlier this evening. Her parents left tonight, in fact, for England."

"Can we see her?" Tracey asked.

"No, not at the present time. I suggest you both go home and get some rest. It's okay, Mrs. Perilli. Mrs. Langdon is in a deep sleep and should stay that way throughout the night. Good night." As the doctor turned to leave, a blonde nurse called to him saying he had to be on emergency stand-by because there was a big accident coming in. Vito stood, shaking his head, then reached for Tracey, who was softly crying, and held her in his arms.

"It's going to be okay, darlin'. Come on, let's go home and get some rest." As they were leaving, they watched the staff preparing the emergency room for the highway crash victims. Their thoughts were on Heather but also on getting some sleep, planning to be back at the hospital by mid-afternoon.

They drove home in silence. There was nothing to say. Once home and in bed, they held each other until they both fell into a deep sleep.

Chris had come back into the emergency room and overheard the discussion the doctor had with the Perillis. Now he needed to get some information about John Langdon, but he decided to go home and catch a couple of hours before he followed up on that subject.

Chapter Twelve

$\mathscr{B}$rian's alarm went off at seven o'clock. He turned over to shut if off and got up and into the shower. When he came back to the bedroom, his breakfast was set on the table by the picture window. He walked over to the table as he continued fluffing his hair with the towel and poured himself a cup of coffee. He flicked on the television to get the news as he sat down to his morning brew. While listening to the local news, a SPECIAL BULLETIN flashed across the screen. He watched as the newscaster announced that a bus traveling south on Interstate 95 was involved in a fatal accident during the early morning hours. Apparently, the bus swerved on the icy roadway to avoid a truck that was out of control. The bus went off the highway and rolled over down an embankment, where it had burst into flames. Brian shook his head in disbelief and flicked off the television. He was anxious to start his day. He was anxious about Heather. He had not heard any further news from Chris. He picked up the phone and called Ralph Duprey, administrator of Brookville Central Hospital. Brian, his brothers and stepfather were major contributors to the hospital and two years prior had financed the expansion for a cardiac services wing.

"Mr. Duprey's office. May I help you?" said the female voice.

"Good morning, Lisa, it's Brian Hargrove. Is Ralph around yet?"

"Good morning, Mr. Hargrove. Yes he is. He arrived about an hour ago, because of that crash on the highway."

"Yes, that's right. I just heard about it myself. It's terrible."

"Yes, it is. We are on crisis stand-by but there may not be any survivors. But hold on one moment and I'll transfer you."

The next voice was Ralph Duprey's. "Brian, good to hear from you. I was watching the news. So, what can I do for you this morning?"

"An acquaintance of mine was brought to the hospital emergency last night." While Brian spoke, Ralph was already reviewing the night admissions and activity report, and although it seemed to have been a quiet night, four admissions and three emergency surgeries had been performed.

"I see. I'm looking over the activity report now. What's the patient's name?"

"Heather Langdon."

"Oh, yes. I see it. Emergency OB-GYN surgery."

"Yes, I know. I don't know the extent at this point, but I want her to have the very best, Ralph, whatever she needs. And please get her round-the-clock private nurses starting immediately."

"Of course, Brian. But as far as the report indicates she was placed in Surgical Intensive Care last night after surgery and she is still listed in critical condition."

"My God! Is there any way you could find out if she's still there? How critical is she?"

"Brian, Brian, relax. I'll check everything out for you and call you back with all the information. Many times after surgery patients are placed in Surgical Intensive Care because they need extra care and supervision. But I will also get the private-duty nurses and anything else she might need. Is there something else?"

"Yes, I need to know the surgery that was performed, her current medical condition and the surgeon and the attending, if possible."

"Okay, let me check it all out and I'll call you back shortly."

"Thanks, Ralph. I appreciate it. Remember, whatever she needs."

"You've got it. Talk to you shortly."

Brian hung up the phone and sat at the table pouring another cup of coffee and happy that his requests were being met. But he was extremely worried about Heather. He flicked the news back on, only half listening. "At this point," said the newscaster, still reporting on the bus accident, "there are no known survivors."

Dr. Holden was reviewing Heather's chart. Her vitals were dancing around and indicated that she was unstable and therefore still critical. But he felt that she was in a deep sleep and resting comfortably. When he went back to the nurses' station to write the orders, the head nurse handed him a requisition they had just received from the Administrator's Office. Heather was to be placed in a private room as soon as her physician deemed it safe. Dr. Holden read on, "round-the-clock private-duty nurses to begin immediately upon transfer orders." There must be a lot of money behind this one, he thought.

"Nurse Davis, I want to be notified as soon as she seems to be coming around. At that time I will assess if she is to be moved out of SICU. The police officer is to remain outside this door until further notice. I do not want any officials trying to get in here and bothering her for any reason whatsoever." He quickly reviewed what he had written. "I will be in the hospital for a few more hours and I am sure that she will be awakening before then. I repeat, I want to know immediately."

"Yes, Dr. Holden. I'll advise Mr. Duprey that Mrs. Langdon is to remain is SICU."

*   *   *

At the precinct, one of the detectives in charge of the case was preparing for a line-up. The grocery store owner, Nick Ashton, had come in to identify the intruders. Detective Joe Hawkins, had been assigned to the case.

"Okay, Mr. Ashton, we are going to present a line-up of possible suspects and you have to see if you can identify any of them," Hawkins explained. He had been on the squad for some time and had an excellent record with the department. He was a tall, well-built man with salt-and-pepper hair and green eyes. He was generally liked because of his

soft-spoken and patient nature. He concentrated on Mr. Ashton as he explained what they were going to do, but he wondered if he was getting through to this elderly, balding man with the thick Italian accent.

"Well, I will do my best," replied Mr. Ashton nervously. Hawkins spoke through the intercom. "All set…bring'em on in."

Hawkins and Mr. Ashton were in a large room with a one-way mirror so the victim could try to identify the suspects without being seen. Hawkins further explained to Mr. Ashton that he could call out to any of the numbered suspects and have them step forward for a better look. He explained in detail how he would go through the line-up once and then on the second time around, he would ask Mr. Ashton to speak up if he could make a positive identification.

As Ashton reviewed the second line-up of men, he leaned over towards Hawkins and spoke quietly, "I think that's one of them."

"You must be absolutely sure, Mr. Ashton. Let's finish the line-up and see if you recognize anyone else." They went through the process once again.

"I'm pretty sure that Number Four is the one, but I can't be definite. It was dark and everything happened so quickly."

"Take your time, Mr. Ashton."

Number Four was John Langdon. He could not believe what was happening and, even worse, he could not remember anything from the night before. He knew he had gone to work but after that he didn't remember a thing. He only knew he needed a lawyer because it appeared that someone was about to nail him for something. Where the hell was Heather, anyway, and why didn't she come to get him the hell out of there?!

"Yes, the way he just moved. I believe that is one of them that came into my store to rob me last night," Mr. Ashton stated anxiously.

Detective Hawkins pushed the button on the intercom instructing the officer by the line-up to take Number Four back to the holding cell.

"Bring in the next group," he ordered. He explained the entire process again to Mr. Ashton. This time he positively identified the first male, John's friend Mark.

Chapter Thirteen

*H*eather stirred and the private-duty nurse called to have Dr. Holden paged immediately.

Heather was opening her eyes and trying to focus. She could not fight the sleepiness. She could feel stinging tears but it hurt too much to cry. The nurse was by her side, holding her hand and stroking her forehead, reassuring her that she was all right. Dr. Holden came in seconds to her bedside. He reached out and gently touched her arm, "Heather, I'm Dr. Holden. How are you feeling?"

"What happened?" she asked groggily. She tried to move and, in pain, grabbed for her stomach. "Oh, my God, did I . . . what happened to me?" She felt the bandaging on her abdomen.

"Heather," Dr. Holden said, "look at me." She dutifully complied. "Now try to relax and take as deep a breath as you can. It will hurt when you try to expand your chest because you have three broken ribs." Heather obeyed, wincing again as her cracked ribs sharply limited her intake. Still, she made the effort. "Okay. I will explain. But what's most important to me is how you are doing right now." Heather gave a little nod.

"Please understand that you are going to be all right. You are doing fine. Do you remember anything about last night?"

Heather started to remember . . . Tracey and Vito helping her. She focused on the doctor, "How did I get here?"

"You were brought to the emergency room late last night because you collapsed at your home. Your friends, the Perillis, were with you and stayed with you almost all night." Heather watched him and listened.

"When you came in, you were unconscious and had two bad cuts on your head, which we stitched up. But you were also bleeding. Did you know that you were pregnant?"

"No, I . . . oh, God . . . please don't tell me I . . . pregnant . . .?"

"I know this is *very* difficult for you, but I want to be honest with you so you can have trust in me." Heather nodded. Dr. Holden continued, "You were in the very early stages of pregnancy but, due to the extent of your injuries, we were unable to save the baby. You were hemorrhaging and you had sustained damage that we could not repair, so we had to perform a hysterectomy."

"Oh, no," Heather tried to scream out but only managed an animal whimper. "A hysterec . . . what happened?! Where's John?" Despite the pain, Heather began to cry hysterically, gasping for breath. Dr. Holden sent the nurse for medication to sedate her while the private-duty nurse increased the liters of oxygen flow.

"It's going to be okay, Heather," Dr. Holden soothed. "The oxygen will help to ease your breathing. I am your doctor and I'm going to do everything I can to help you." But he realized there was no calming her. She fought with him and the private-duty nurse. While the nurse injected the sedative, Dr. Holden checked Heather's abdominal bandage and could see seepage. "Heather, you have to calm down. You don't want to go back to surgery for resuturing." As the medication was taking effect, he watched Heather open and close her eyes with a startled expression. It must have been a horrible beating. She was reliving it now. He tried to comfort her as much as he could and reminded the nurse that Heather was not to be questioned by the police until he gave the okay. Heather was sleeping quietly now. He changed her abdominal bandages and advised the nurse to notify him of any changes, no matter how slight. "Check her blood pressure every fifteen minutes. I'm worried about a bleeder." The nurse nodded her head, "Yes, Doctor."

At the nursing desk he signed an order to have Mrs. Langdon placed in a private room by two o'clock that afternoon unless her condition took a turn.

* * *

Chris Hurley had been waiting at the precinct during the line-up procedure. He paced back and forth wondering what was taking so long. Finally he saw Joe Hawkins come out of the observation room, but the detective had seen Chris first. "Chris! What are you doing down here? Long time no see!"

"I'm doing all right, Detective. I understand that you're working the Langdon case, and I was curious how things were going."

"Well, right at this moment, the store owner identified John Langdon and Mark Smyth as the men who attempted to rob him last night."

"Is that so?"

"That's about all I can tell you for the moment. Langdon's also charged with driving while intoxicated, and the District Attorney is considering pressing charges against him for spousal abuse, but they haven't been able to speak with Mrs. Langdon yet. If you want, I'll keep you posted. But why the interest?"

"I have a client who has an interest. Here's my number and my pager if you need to reach me. I was over at the hospital last night when Mrs. Langdon was admitted, and she's in pretty bad shape. She still has a blue assigned to her. But I guess I'll see you on Saturday night." Chris handed him the piece of paper with his contact numbers and flew out the door. He wanted to get back to the hospital and find out how things were doing and he also wanted to take a ride to the scene of the robbery.

Heather opened her eyes. She looked toward the window, not fully comprehending her surroundings but trying to sort everything out. It hurt too much to move or breathe. She felt like she'd been hit by a train.

Her thoughts were interrupted by a red-headed nurse who introduced herself as Anne and explained that she was her private-duty nurse until three o'clock. Heather didn't say anything, just gave the nurse a weak smile and nod. Still she winced with pain. Nurse Carr told her that she was going to put some pain medication into her intravenous. That's nice, Heather thought, but private-duty? She would have to try to understand later, because she felt herself being pulled back into the darkness of sleep.

Chapter Fourteen

$\mathcal{V}$ito and Tracey stopped by Heather's house on the way to the hospital to let the dog out and make sure that everything was all right.

It was about one o'clock by the time they got there. Tracey was grateful that her sister was able to take care of their three children. As a construction worker, Vito didn't have his regular work load during the winter season, only repairs and an emergency here and there. So, while checking out the house, he listened to the answering machine for messages while Tracey picked up a bit.

"[Beep] You have five messages. [Beep] . . . Hello, Heather, darling. It's Mama and Dad. We're about to leave to catch the bus to the airport. We're sorry we missed you. We'll call you tomorrow when we get settled. We love you, dear… [Beep] . . . "Mrs. Heather Langdon, please contact the Vantage Bus Line Service as soon as possible at 555-2121. Thank you… [Beep] . . . Mrs. Langdon, this is Peter Albright at the Brookville Medical Examiner's office. Please contact my office as soon as possible at 555-3737. Thank you. It is imperative that I speak with you as soon as possible… [Beep] . . . Heather, where are you? You didn't show up for work. No one is looking for you yet but I am *very* worried. If I don't hear from you soon I'll take a ride over to the house. Do you hear me? I'm getting *really* upset, Heather! ... [Beep] . . . Mrs. Langdon, this is Peter Albright again, please call as soon as possible…"

"What are those messages from a bus company and from the medical examiner's office? Examiner of what?" Tracey looked from the blinking machine to her husband.

"I took down the numbers and I think we should call them. Heather's going to be in the hospital for a while and we don't know what's happening with John yet."

"I think that's a good idea." As he dialed the first number, Tracey heard someone coming to the front door. She looked out the living room window. It was Jenny. She ran to the door to let her in. "Hi, Jenny, come in. We have a lot to tell you."

"Oh, my God, what happened? Where's Heather?" Tracey grabbed Jenny's arm and led her to the sofa.

"Listen, Jenny, a lot has happened since last night. Heather's in the hospital and John's in jail." Jenny sat back for a moment. There was a ringing in her ears as she realized that her biggest fear had come true.

"I can't believe this. Is she all right? I mean . . ." Jenny covered her mouth to stifle her sobs. But Tracey took Jenny's hand in hers as she explained in detail while Jenny sat in utter disbelief and horror.

Vito called the bus company first. A recording came on: "All our lines are busy at the moment. Please hold on for the next available crisis representative."

He had heard about the bus crash. In fact, everyone was talking about it but it didn't occur to him what was about to unfold. "Vantage Bus Lines. This is Carol speaking. How may I help you?"

"My name is Vito Perilli and I'm calling for Mrs. Heather Langdon. A message was left on her answering machine to contact this bus company."

"Mr. Perilli, I need to speak with Mrs. Langdon personally."

"I'm sorry, but she's in the hospital right now. She had emergency surgery early this morning and she's still in Intensive Care. My wife and I are the closest people to her aside from her parents, so if there is something we can help with, please tell me."

"Mr. Perilli, I have some very bad news for Mrs. Langdon. Apparently, her parents, Mr. and Mrs. Craig Hilton, were on a bus out of Brookville very early this morning. I am afraid there has been an accident and we need to notify the immediate family."

"Wait a minute. Are they okay?" Tracey and Jenny listened intently as Tony's voice lowered and took on an anxious edge.

"I'm sorry, there is no easy way to say this, Mr. Perilli, but there are no survivors from the crash."

"Oh my God! How am I going to tell Heather?"

Vito slowly hung up the phone. By this time, Jenny and Tracey were hovering over him. "What is it? What is it?" they both chanted.

He turned and looked at the women. "This is horrible. You know how Heather's parents were going to England?"

"Yes," Tracey said. "They told her they were taking the bus to the airport like they had done years ago. That was one of the messages on the machine."

"That bus accident on the highway this morning involved Heather's parents. The woman explained to me that there are no survivors." Tracey and Jenny put their hands to their mouths. Tracey tried to speak but no words would come out; she fell into the chair close behind her.

Jenny couldn't believe it. It didn't seem possible and it was so unfair to Heather, of all people. All she could think about was going to Heather but she had to go back to work. She had left the Center out of concern for Heather. But she would go to the hospital as soon as she got off work. "What are we going to do?"

"I don't know, but I don't think Heather can handle any of this right now. Should I call the medical examiner's office?" Vito asked.

Tracey answered, "Yes, I think you should. We better find out everything." Vito paced between the kitchen and the living room thinking of what he had to do next. Too many things were happening at once. They wanted to protect Heather and they wanted to make the right decisions to help her.

He punched a number into the phone. Immediately there was a voice at the other end, "Brookville Medical Examiner's office. May I help you?"

"Yeah, I think so. My name is Vito Perilli and I'm calling for Mrs. Heather Langdon. She is presently in the hospital recovering from surgery and I'm the closest thing she has to family. I just called Vantage Bus Lines and spoke with someone at the crisis center. So, please, be honest with me about what's going on."

"Just one moment please, Mr. Perilli. I will connect you with Dr. Albright."

"Mr. Perilli? This is Dr. Peter Albright. I left the message for Mrs. Langdon. I am supposed to speak directly to any immediate family, but I understand there is a problem?"

Vito briefly explained the situation to Dr. Albright, adding that he was told Heather's parents died in the crash. "Is that what you were calling about?"

"Yes, Mr. Perilli. I'm going to need someone from the family to identify the bodies, but apparently that's not going to be possible at this moment. I'm sorry to have to do this, but if you are handling this situation, I'll need you to get back to me as soon as possible." Vito responded, "We're heading over to the hospital shortly. I'll call you from there. I think I have to find someone to help us with this."

Vito hung up the receiver and turned to look at Tracey and Jenny. "Well, the medical examiner's office confirmed it. And now they need someone to identify the bodies."

"Look, guys," Jenny said, "I want to be able to help but right now I have to get back to the office. I'll let our boss know and he might be able to lend a helping hand. I get out of work at four and I'll come right over to the hospital. The way I see it, with more of us there, it's better for Heather and the more support we can give each other, too."

"We'll wait for you at the hospital. There must be someone there who can help us," Tracey suggested.

It was settled then.

Chapter Fifteen

It was three o'clock by the time Vito and Tracey arrived at Brookville Central. They had been discussing the bus accident on the way over, but Tracey could think of little else but Heather. They walked to the front desk for information. The desk clerk advised them that Heather had just been transferred to a private room, #222. She handed them passes and told them that there were private-duty nurses assigned to Mrs. Langdon on all three shifts. As they got in the elevator, Tracey thought she was going to bust. "Vito, did you hear that lady say Heather had a private room and private-duty nurses with her day and night?"

"Yeah, I don't know how that happened, but it's good news."

As they approached Heather's room, they saw the police officer. An elderly nurse and the red-headed nurse were standing at the door, exchanging a few words. After the younger nurse left, the other nurse turned to face them. "Hello," she said, "I'm Nurse Katie Hamilton. I'll be Mrs. Langdon's private nurse until eleven o'clock tonight."

Vito extended his hand to Katie. "This is my wife, Tracey, and I'm Vito Perilli. We're friends of Heather. Another friend, Jenny, will be coming here as soon as she leaves work."

"I noted on the chart that you both came into the emergency room with Mrs. Langdon last night."

"Yes, that's right," Vito said.

"Mrs. Langdon was transferred here about an hour ago. She has been having a tough time. But, apparently, the doctor felt confident enough about her progress to transfer her to a private room. Her condition remains guarded, though. When Dr. Holden spoke with her this morning, she took the news badly, whatever she could comprehend. He had to sedate her and she has been sleeping most of the day. She did wake up a little while ago and was given some pain medication, but has been sleeping since. Per the doctor's order, she will continue with sedation and pain medication until he feels he can cut back without jeopardizing her condition."

"May I see her?" Tracey asked. "I'll be quiet. I need to sit by her side just in case she wakes up. Then she'll see me there with her."

"Yes, of course, my dear. Go right inside. Call me if you need anything."

"Uh, Katie, I need to talk to you for a minute . . . away from the door."

"Of course, Mr. Perilli . . . Let's go down the hallway a bit. Is this better?"

"Yeah, thanks. Nurse, we have quite a situation on our hands and I need some advice on how to handle it because it all directly affects Heather."

"Okay, Mr. Perilli, anything I can do to help. That's the reason I'm here," she replied.

"Well, first of all, you know that Heather's husband is presently in police custody?"

"Yes, I do. I don't know any of the details, but I know he's being held and there has been no contact at all between Heather or the hospital and Mr. Langdon today."

"The situation has become even more complicated. Heather's parents were going away on vacation to England. They took a bus to the airport . . ." Katie interrupted before he could finish his sentence.

"You mean that bus . . .?" She put her hand to her mouth in disbelief.

"Yeah, that's right."

"Oh, that poor dear! How horrible! Mr. Perilli, I would suggest that you speak with Ralph Duprey. He's the administrator of the hospital and he will be able to help you. In the meantime, I think it best that nothing be said to Heather. I'm sure the doctor will want to be advised of anything regarding Heather, especially something like this."

"Okay. Where do I find the administrator?" he asked.

The nurse directed him to the administrator's secretary. "She will connect you with Mr. Duprey. Go now, because he's probably still there. I'll let your wife know where you have gone."

"Thanks. I appreciate it." Vito headed for the elevator. Katie walked back to room 222. She exchanged a few words with the officer at Heather's door. When Katie went inside, Tracey was sitting by Heather's bedside, holding her hand. Heather was sleeping peacefully.

*   *   *

Ralph Duprey looked at his watch and could not believe it was already three-thirty. He pushed the button on the intercom and asked Lisa to get Brian Hargrove on the phone. He sat back, continuing to review Heather's chart.

"Mr. Duprey, Mr. Hargrove is on line two."

He explained to Brian the extent of Heather's injuries, the baby she lost, the hysterectomy. Brian held his breath and let the words sink in. The intercom interrupted Duprey's litany.

"Sorry, Mr. Duprey, but I have a gentleman out here stating he is a friend of Mrs. Langdon. He said it's important that he speak with you."

"Show him into my office. Brian, something else has just come up in connection with Heather Langdon. Let me see what's going on and I'll call you right back. Oh, and Brian, take it easy. Everything possible is being done to help this woman."

"I'll be waiting for your call."

After the introductions, Vito broached the topic tenderly. "It is difficult for my wife and me to see Heather this way. At least she's holding her own, but I have more bad news."

"I see. Is it about her husband?"

"No, I wish that was the *only* thing." Ralph sat up in his chair when began to mention Heather's parents, the bus service and the medical examiner's office. He knew Peter Albright, he knew the crash was real. Yet he could not believe what was happening to that poor woman. Yes, indeed, she needed all the help she could get because she was incapable of handling anything to do with this horror. Ralph scanned the passenger list they had received at the hospital. Sure enough, there it was . . . "Mr. and Mrs. Craig Hilton."

"You mean *The* Mr. and Mrs. Craig Hilton? The garment industry's Hiltons? Good heavens! What were they doing on a bus?"

"According to my wife, Heather said they were reliving a romantic event."

"I'm absolutely amazed that the papers haven't gotten hold of this yet. You mean to tell me that Heather Langdon is their daughter?"

"Yes. But I'm supposed to get back to the medical examiner's office with information because he said someone from the immediate family has to identify the bodies."

"Mr. Perilli, do you happen to know if Mrs. Langdon has an attorney?"

"I'm sure she does but I don't know who represents her."

"Let me think about what is the best course of action to be taken. I also feel, given Mrs. Langdon's condition, I need to get in touch with the surgeon and the attending physician assigned to her case. Once I've spoken to them, I'll come to her room to see you."

"Thank you, Mr. Duprey," Vito replied with much relief. "You know, Heather is such a good person. I hate to see her going through all this pain."

"I understand, and I certainly concur."

After Vito left, Ralph pushed the intercom button and asked Lisa to get Brian Hargrove back on the phone.

"Brian, sorry this took so long." He pushed the intercom button again, "Lisa, see if you can get Dr. Holden for me."

"Brian, I'm sorry. This situation is becoming worse by the minute."

"What do you mean, Ralph? Heather hasn't taken a turn for the worse, has she?"

"No, relax. Her condition remains unchanged at this point. But her friend came to see me…" Duprey explained the sad circumstances surrounding Heather's family. He added, "We have to make sure their names are not released and that the press doesn't get hold of this information. At least, not yet."

"You mean to tell me that her parents are *The* Hiltons?"

"Yes, Brian. But you have to remember . . . past tense. As horrible as it sounds, they *were* the Hiltons. Well, that's all I can tell you at the moment. I'm waiting to hear from the surgeon to find out how he plans to handle this. The medical examiner's office needs immediate family to come down to the office to identify the bodies. It's most unfortunate there are none other than Mrs. Langdon."

"Well, surely Heather is in no condition to deal with this. Can't they wait?"

"I'm planning to call Peter's office now and find out more. I'll be in touch with you later." As he finished the sentence, Lisa was on the intercom with Dr. Holden holding on line one.

Brian fought back the rage growing within him. That detestable animal she was married to . . . ! How dare he lay a hand on her! He needed to speak to Chris Hurley. He needed to know what was going on with John Langdon. He needed the entire picture at this point. But his thoughts drifted back to Heather. How he wished he could hold her in his arms and make her feel safe. Just the thought of the pain she was already in and the emotional pain she would feel over the loss of a child and the loss of her parents…the Hiltons! She is going to need a lot of help; especially getting her away from John. He had a lot of work to do, and quickly.

*   *   *

Ralph Duprey pushed the button on his phone. "Dr. Holden, I am so glad I could reach you. I have quite a situation developing with one of your patients, Mrs. Heather Langdon."

"What's wrong? I haven't heard from the floor so I assumed her condition is still stable."

"It is but a grave situation has developed that directly affects Mrs. Langdon."

"Well, then I'm glad you called me. Her health can't be compromised." After Duprey relayed the tragedy, the doctor was ready to advise. "I do believe that we must tell her what happened. But I'd like to speak to Josh Stein. I'm sure you're familiar with his reputation. He's not affiliated with Brookville Central, if that's okay with you?"

Ralph grunted a bit as he replied, "Well, there are no restrictions on the cost of her medical treatment here. But the conditions for non-participating physicians still stand. I strongly suggest that you work through our own psychiatric department. We cannot afford to step on anyone's toes."

"Okay, I'll call Abe Sutter first and arrange it through him. Then I'll talk it over with Stein to see how he would like to handle it. Between you and me, I feel that I should be the one to tell her. I don't want to but as her physician I have had the closest contact with her."

"You're the professional."

"But I think I should run it past Josh first and see what he feels is best; especially since there really is no 'best' in a situation like this."

"Okay, Bruce. I'll hold off getting back to Peter until I hear from you."

Holden contacted Dr. Abe Sutter and relayed the situation to him. Sutter said he had no problem with Josh Stein taking the case. In fact, he said he looked forward to working with him. Holden set up a time, around ten o'clock, for them to meet with Sutter the next morning. Since he was still at the hospital when he received Holden's call, Sutter decided to go downstairs and peek in on the patient.

In the meantime, Holden contacted Dr. Josh Stein. Stein was at home and happy to hear from him. Holden discussed the case with him, and after a few "uhms," Stein said he was interested. But he cautioned it would be difficult. He did not know what kind of response to expect from the patient since he had no background data on her about her childhood. But he was in agreement with Bruce that she be told about the death of her parents. He arranged to meet with Bruce and Sutter at ten o'clock the next morning and asked if anyone could give him some background information on Mrs. Langdon.

"As a matter of fact, Ralph explained to me there are two of her friends with her now. Why don't you call the floor and one of the nurses can get them for you? This way you'll have a bit more information to piece together before tomorrow morning."

"That's a good idea. I'm also thinking that someone from the medical examiner's office should be at the hospital room with us. This way we can show Mrs. Langdon the pictures of the Hiltons while we're together and plan for her reaction. She should have a friend, someone close, who will be with her when she is told." Stein explained that he would take it from there and call Sutter right away to confirm their plan of action.

Holden called Duprey to tell him the arrangements. Duprey thanked him for his assistance and quickly dialed the medical examiner's office to explain the identification procedure to Peter Albright. Everything was set, so he went to Heather's room to speak with her friends.

Jenny had arrived and the three of them stood waiting by the bed for Heather to awaken. Vito was relieved to see Duprey walk through the door. Duprey nodded back out to the corridor and they all walked outside. Vito introduced Tracey and Jenny to the administrator and, once the formalities were over, Duprey explained the doctors' plan of action. Heather's friends were apprehensive, but said they would be at the hospital without a doubt to help in any way they could. Duprey reassured them that everything would be fine; she had the best working for her.

Duprey took a deep breath as he walked to the elevator to return to his office. Now, the last step is to contact Brian and fill him in.

Brian was on the phone with Chris Hurley, who was fill-ing him in on what had transpired at the police station. He explained that the store owner would not sign a statement until he was completely sure and that John Langdon had no recol-lection of the events that took place on that night. Langdon had called home to his wife and got no answer. Then he had placed a call to an attorney, Andrew Price, who would contact Langdon's parents to find out where Heather was.

Price came to see Langdon and advised him that his wife was in serious condition at Brookville Central Hospital and could not be questioned; Langdon was probably facing assault charges.

While Chris was filling him in, Brian thought that he should go and see Langdon but then realized that was a bad idea. To make him an offer surely was no guarantee that he would stay away from Heather. Maybe he should visit the store owner. If Ashton could not make up his mind, then Langdon and Smyth would be released. He could offer dam-ages to Ashton if it guaranteed getting Langdon out of the pic-ture. As he thought further, he decided that he would have to wait for this to play itself out before he made a move.

Chapter Sixteen

$\mathcal{J}$ohn sat in the holding cell. How could everything have gone so wrong? His freedom hinged on if this jerk could identify him. He thought about Heather in the hospital but couldn't remember it having anything to do with him. Assault charges? What had he done? It was like that night was totally erased from his memory. He left work and stopped with the guys for a few drinks. Nothing else.

He got more worried when his attorney told him that Heather was not pressing charges, but the District Attorney's office had taken over. So even if he's not identified, he could still be in a lot of trouble.

John's parents came to see him. They told him not to worry about anything but they had not been up to the hospital to see Heather because she wasn't allowed any visitors. The doctor left orders that no one other than Heather's three friends were to be in that room with her without notification. John could not understand this.

When his attorney got back to him, he explained the extent of Heather's injuries. Price told John to listen carefully to what he was about to tell him; the damage to Heather's body seemed unreal to John until Price made sure he understood that there were finger mark bruises all over her arms and that the rib fractures were most probably due to having been kicked. And then there was the baby.

The words rang in John's ears, but he could not make any sense of it. He cried out and his parents tried to comfort him, but his pain was so deep no one could reach him. He couldn't believe that he had done this to Heather. It must have been someone else. But his attorney explained that the police report was explicit, that friends had found Heather on the floor not five minutes after he had left the house. Still a complaint had not been filed.

His attorney told John to hold tight and he would try to arrange for bail, but until John was arraigned, he could do nothing. What a bunch of bull shit, John thought. He would lose his job, lose Heather! Maybe what they were saying was true. How could he know?

Detective Hawkins felt that John wasn't sorry about what he had done, even if he didn't remember doing it, but he was sorry that he had been caught. He knew from years of first-hand experience that this attitude is common in the criminal personality. He believed that John Langdon was an alcoholic and a drug abuser and had no exposure to rehabilitation at any level. And he understood why John had so many problems after he had spoken with John's mother. Hawkins knew that she would protect Langdon and blame everyone else rather than taking a good look at her son and helping him to deal with it, get help. But, typically for alcoholics, abusers and bullies, Langdon could not see any of this; he blamed everything on everyone else. He was angry to the point of belligerence and he had his mother to back him up. He had been on the job for many years and had seen this scene numerous times before. He felt sorry for the victim lying in the hospital bed who now had to deal with radical things she never had to deal with before. He hoped that this would be the end of this relationship for this woman, and he hoped that she would get enough help to realize it was a dead-end.

He had already been up to see Mrs. Langdon and was unable to get in, but he spoke with the uniform outside her door. He didn't like what he heard. He had to go see John Langdon and notify him that his wife's parents had been killed in the bus crash. When he walked into the visitor's room at the precinct, Langdon's parents were still there. He approached Langdon to speak with him in private.

"Anything you have to say to me can be said in front of them. Say what you have to say or get out of my face."

"Mr. Langdon, we just received official word that your wife's parents were killed in a bus crash early this morning. I am sorry to have to tell you this now. But I must notify you of the situation."

"Does Heather know?" John asked quietly. Hawkins felt for just one fleeting minute that he could actually hear some emotion in that voice before it turned stone cold again.

"No, not yet."

"Well, I don't know what difference it would make to that cold, cheating bitch. She doesn't even care enough to call me in here and try to help me. What do you want me to do about it in here?"

Joe Hawkins bit his tongue, as he always did when prisoners lashed out. It was nothing personal, but their attitudes were brutal and sometimes, depending on the circumstances, it took everything he had to hold back. "This doesn't mean you can be released. You're facing serious charges, but we are to alert you to anything drastic that happens." Hawkins was not shocked at Langdon's attitude, but he could not believe how cold the parents were. Talk about dysfunctional! "I am required to let you know and if you had any doubts, worries or requests, I came to offer my assistance."

"Well, aren't you Mister Nice Guy. If you want to do something then get me out of this rat trap. Don't go making up stories about my wife and her family. I'm the one with the big problem right now and I don't see anyone running in here to help me."

That was enough. Hawkins checked with the detaining officer and left the room. He was going over to the hospital again to see how Mrs. Langdon was doing. They still had an officer assigned to her for protection, and just maybe, the uniform would let him take a peek at the victim.

* * *

Heather slept. She woke up from time to time but never for long. The doctor felt she was doing well receiving nourishment through a feeding tube and fluids and medications intravenously. Her blood counts were steadily improving and they had just removed the last empty unit of blood. She was building strength and healing. God knew she needed it for what lay ahead of her.

When Detective Hawkins arrived, he exchanged a few words with the officer on duty. He looked inside the room and saw a man and two women sitting at Heather's bedside. He got their attention and motioned to them to come out into the hallway. He made a mental note of how she appeared to him.

He put out his right hand and said to the small group, "Hi, my name is Detective Joe Hawkins and I am assigned to this case."

Vito took the detective's hand and shook it. "My name is Vito and this is my wife, Tracey Perilli. This is Heather's other friend Jenny Trafarri. We understand that she is not to be questioned, according to the doctor."

"I didn't come over here to question Mrs. Langdon. I stopped by to see how she's doing. How *is* she doing?"

"Well, she's had a tough go of it," Vito began. "She seems to be sleeping peacefully, but the doctor is keeping her sedated. She doesn't know about her parents, and she hasn't been awake long enough to even voice an opinion about John."

"I see. Well, I'm glad to see that she's not alone and that she has good friends with her to help her along the way. I'll tell you what…" Hawkins reached into his pocket and pulled out his business card, handing it to Vito. "…If I can be of any assistance, please give me a call."

"Thank you, Detective," Vito replied, accepting the card. "We would do anything to erase the last forty-eight hours. She doesn't deserve such misery."

Jenny intervened, "I was afraid this was going to happen. In fact, I had warned her, again, the other day at lunch. I could see it coming, but not Heather. Even if she did she would have tried to toss it out of her mind so that John could have another chance." The three friends nodded in agreement.

"She must be very special. Remember what I said." After saying good-bye he was on his way, shaking his head. He could not erase her face from his mind. There was just *something* about her. He wanted to open her eyes to him. Strange, how people can affect you. He would wait for any further news in the case. The district attorney's office was hot to get in there and get ready to file charges against Langdon. It wasn't a matter of if the D.A. was going to file charges, but when. He lit a cigarette as he left the back entrance of the hospital and was on his way to the precinct, the pale face on the pillow haunting him.

*   *   *

"Mr. Duprey, you have Mr. Hargrove on line one," Lisa announced.

"Lisa, would you tell Brian I'll get back to him shortly."

"Mr. Duprey, it's not Brian, but Alec Hargrove for you."

"Okay, I'll take it. Alec, how are you?"

"I'm fine, Ralph, fine. I thought I would give you a call and see if you're free for lunch one day this week."

"Well, I don't know. It's been pretty hectic around here. The bus crash had us all off schedule in preparation and your son has been keeping me busy with a friend of his."

"And which son might you be referring to?"

"Why, Brian, of course. Apparently a female friend of his was admitted through emergency early yesterday morning and he called me first thing this morning to make sure she would get the best of care. So, I have been busy working things out for him. We still aren't out of the woods yet."

Alec listened quietly as Duprey spoke, wondering what he was talking about. When he mentioned Brian's name he still had no idea but, knowing Brian, he was possibly involved in something he shouldn't be. Brian had a knack for schemes but in this situation, it certainly seemed out of character. No one knew anything about his friends or any of the women he dated and Duprey's professionalism kept him from revealing this one's name. There were always rumors but Brian never allowed himself to get caught. Something was definitely up but Alec diplomatically covered, "Of course, Brian mentioned it to me earlier today. Is everything okay?"

"Alec, this is one mess of a case." Duprey let the facts unfold.

Alec listened in utter amazement, wondering what his son had gotten himself involved in. Who was this woman and why was she so important to him?

"It sounds like you are doing the brilliant job that you always do, Ralph. I'm sure things will work out. With you at the head, I know they will."

"I hope so. This is a lot for one person to swallow at one time. I hope she's strong enough to handle it all."

"Yes," was all Alec managed. He didn't dare allow himself to think that Brian had made the dreadful mistake of placing his security in jeopardy by fathering her child. He couldn't even begin to imagine that that was Brian's style. Preoccupied with everything Ralph had just divulged to him, he shook his thoughts free to finish speaking.

"So, what about lunch?"

"Let's see. How about Friday?"

"Friday's okay, so far. Our usual?"

"Sounds good. See you then." Alec Hargrove hung up and sat back in his chair. He placed a call to Brian's office but the secretary said that his son had not been in the office for the last two days. Alec asked if there was anything going on that he should know about.

"It seems," the secretary started, "an employee was going to be transferred to corporate headquarters in the R&D division. But this person has been arrested for armed robbery."

"I see. What does his name happen to be?"

"John Langdon. His wife Heather appeared on the list for an administrative assistant to Brian."

"Okay, thank you. You don't have to mention to Brian that I called. I will be in touch with him myself." He hung up the phone. Why did that name sound so familiar? Was Brian somehow involved with this woman? It had to be something serious because Brian was too ambitious to stay away from the office. Determinedly, Alec contacted his own private investigator. He left a message on Leo Martucci's machine. Martucci called him back within fifteen minutes.

"Sorry, Mr. Hargrove. I was out of the office. What can I do for you?"

I want you to investigate someone. Find out everything you can on a John Langdon who's presently at the Eighth Precinct, and his wife, Heather, a patient at Brookville Central Hospital. When you have some information, please get back to me. I don't care what time it is."

"Sure thing, Mr. Hargrove. I'll get right on it."

"Good. I'll talk with you later, Leo, and thanks." He hung up the phone and was out the door to see Brian.

Brian was busy. He had driven himself crazy all day trying to figure out how this scenario would play itself out to get Langdon out of the picture. He was not willing to get into trouble. That was not his style. Instead, he decided to focus on Heather. He wasn't ready to visit her in the hospital yet, risking rejection. So he finally decided that he would buy her a house. It sounded crazy but he figured that she needed a place to live. He contacted a realtor who was preparing a list of homes presently on the market that fit his list of specifications: a large home, fairly new, though he wasn't quite sure what else he wanted . . . The doorbell rang. He opened the door to find his stepfather standing on the other side.

"Hi there, Alec. What a nice surprise. I know that you weren't just in the neighborhood, so it must be something important."

"Not really. I called the office to say hello and your secretary said that you've been out for two days. I found that somewhat unusual for you, so I decided to stop by and make sure you're okay."

"Well, as you can see, I'm okay. Why don't you come in and have a drink? How's Mom?"

"She's just fine. She's attending some fashion show this evening. But getting back to you, Brian, why don't we go out for dinner together?"

"That's nice of you to ask, but I'm waiting for an important phone call and don't want to leave the house."

Alec noticed that Brian appeared to be on edge, very odd for him. He had always been good at hiding things, but Alec felt that Brian *was* involved with this woman at the hospital; he didn't know how or to what extent. He wanted to come right out and ask but, with Brian, you could never do that. Especially if he was afraid he was going to get caught. You had to find out what he was up to first and deal with it later.

"Alec, you seem as if you have something on your mind that you want to talk about," Brian was fishing. It was very strange that Alec would show up unannounced. He couldn't possibly know anything that was going on…

"No, I was concerned but I can see that you are all right. I don't want to keep you from what you're doing so I think I'll go home and wait for your mother. You know how I'm lost when she isn't around."

Brian smiled in acknowledgement. After all, he had grown to love Alec, in his own way. He knew that Alec truly loved his mother and had treated her like gold as long as he had known him. But Brian was stubborn about his relationship with Alec and would never accept him totally. He was pleased that his mother was married to a good man, but he had also been relieved to finally leave the house and start out on his own.

Alec felt bad over the years that he could never develop a strong relationship with Brian. He tried to be supportive and friendly, but Brian was not always accepting of what Alec had to offer. Just as now, Brian did not try to stop Alec from leaving; he would much rather be by himself. So Alec shook Brian's hand as he said his final good-bye. Brian added to send his love to his mother.

As Brian closed the door, he wondered what that visit had been about. He had learned one thing about Alec, and that was not to underestimate his astuteness. Brian would have to be careful about what he was doing. He did not want any repercussions.

Back in his office, the realtor had faxed over the listings he had been waiting for. Whatever the reason for Alec's visit, Brian was sure that he could be ten steps ahead of him. So he dismissed the visit and concentrated on the listing of homes in front of him.

Alec rode home anxious to get word from Leo Martucci. Of course, Brian was a grown man, but Alec wanted to be sure that he wasn't placing himself or the business in jeopardy. Brian had always been a hard worker, a super-achiever, but due primarily to greed. Alec tried to stay one step ahead of Brian, just to keep him in line.

Alicea was not due home until about eleven. Looking at her picture over the mantel, Alec thought about his love for this woman. His entire existence revolved around her, but it wasn't one-sided.

The phone ringing interrupted his reverie. The housekeeper came in the room to announce a call. It was Leo, who in the last two hours felt that he had accumulated enough information.

"Hello, Mr. Hargrove. I have some information for you."

"Fine, Leo, let's hear it."

"The man, John Langdon is one of your employees. Langdon was taking a transfer to corporate headquarters in R&D. He's married to the woman in the hospital. He apparently spoke to Personnel and submitted Mrs. Langdon's name for any possible opening at Hargrove. Mrs. Langdon is a patient care coordinator over at the Bryant Todd Clinic and has built quite a reputation for herself in the community by helping people through the clinic."

"According to record, thus far there are three separate charges against John Langdon. The first charge is formal and is a DWI. The second charge, which isn't formal and may never come to be, is for armed robbery of a grocery store with another male. At this time, the store owner can't make a positive ID, so Langdon might be released tomorrow. The third charge is through the district attorney's office for assault on his wife. But that charge has not been verified yet because of Mrs. Langdon's condition."

Leo gave a detailed report regarding Heather Langdon from the time she entered the police station to the present. "She has a uniform at her door. She is heavily sedated and her condition is still listed as critical. She also has another close friend from the clinic by her side."

"She has three shifts of private-duty nurses and a private room, ordered by Brian Hargrove. There is a private investigator by the name of Chris Hurley doing some work over at the hospital. At this point, I would have to believe that he's working for your son."

"Another horrendous part of this case, if it could get worse, is the fact that Mrs. Langdon's parents were killed in that highway bus crash." Martucci let the details unfold. "That's all I have. Do you want me to stay on it?"

"Yes, I do. In fact, I want you to keep surveillance on my son Brian. I want to see what his involvement is with this woman. Her name seems familiar to me, but I cannot place what she looks like. You are doing a great job. Keep in touch."

"Thank you, sir. Yes, I will."

As Alec hung up the phone, he leaned back in his chair and pondered over the information he had received. He felt sorry for this woman, whoever she was. She was in a horrible situation. It appeared that she had a good reputation but what was she doing with that Langdon man? The tragedy of her situation brought back the loss of his daughter and wife and the indescribable pain and the sense of loss he continued to feel to this day. It was a part of him that never seemed to heal. And he still wondered sometimes if his daughter did survive the crash and grew up to live her life some place, not even knowing she had a father who would give anything to see her. Yes, he knew what this poor Langdon woman was about to go through.

Martucci had done an excellent job of compiling so much information in such a short time. But what should he do with it? There seemed that nothing could be done, at least not yet. He didn't know enough yet. He still did not know why Brian was paying the woman's hospital expenses. Brian was so greedy; he never spent a penny he didn't have to. So why would he set no limit for his woman? He wondered if he should mention it to Alicea and then thought better of it. He figured that he should wait until he had the rest of the story. He knew too many important people in the community and didn't want to arouse suspicions or let the press get wind that there might be a story here.

He envisioned the woman lying in bed, not knowing what was going on all around her. It seemed silly, he didn't even know her, but he felt compassion for her and what she would learn the next day. Yes, he thought, Duprey was right; he also hoped that she would be strong enough to endure. The housekeeper announced that his dinner was ready and he methodically raised himself out of the chair, but his thoughts were still with this woman and her pain and where Brian fit into all of this.

The nurses were wonderful with Heather. She would only awaken for brief periods, but was starting to take some fluids, a little water or juice, and a smile at the nurses before falling back to sleep. It was as if she were not aware of what had happened to her. She drifted in and out of a world that she needed protection from.

Chapter Seventeen

Dr. Abe Sutter had come to Heather's room to check on her and review her chart in preparation for the next day. His compassion was aroused as he looked at her lying there helplessly. It was good she was resting so well, because she was going to need it. But he also wished that she were more alert so he could get to know her. He wondered what secrets lay within her. He wished he had more information of her background than he was able to retrieve from her friends. But he was thankful he had at least that to work with. He heard footsteps behind him and turned to find Josh Stein smiling at him.

"Hey, Josh, you ol' son of a gun. It's good to see you!"

"Same here, Abe. You have a place we can go to talk?"

"Sure, let's go upstairs; I have some Chinese food coming, in case you're hungry."

"Sounds good to me." As Josh stepped back, he took a good look at Heather. She was lovely, even with all the bruising and cuts to her face and head. She had the complexion of a porcelain doll, with dainty facial features. She looked as if she had a good upbringing. Her hair, hands, nails all looked well taken care of. "Well," he thought aloud, just above a whisper, hoping the sleeping woman could hear him, "I'll be here for you, Heather. That's why I am here. I hope we'll be able to work well together to get you through this. I want you to trust me and to have faith in me and together we'll walk that painful path to recovery." As he followed Sutter out, he thought about his own wife with a smile on his face. She always said she loved him so much because he showed so much compassion for his patients.

The two psychiatrists headed for the elevator that would take them to the twelfth floor, where Psychiatric Services was located. By the time they got to Sutter's office, they smelled the Chinese food and Stein realized just how hungry he was.

They sat down and filled their plates, bringing each other up-to-date on families and practices. They were good friends, but didn't see that much of each other because their professions were so demanding. So when circumstances brought them together they had a lot of catching up to do. Afterward, they cleared off the table and worked out their plan of action for the next day.

Sutter briefed Stein regarding the patient's physical condition; that he had met with Heather's three friends, trying to obtain some background information about her. At first, they appeared somewhat reluctant, but once they understood what he was doing they were more comfortable and were eager to be of assistance. The information they contributed would also be helpful in deciding how to approach Mrs. Langdon's treatment.

"Well," Stein cut to the chase. "Let's have it. Does she have an unhealthy background?"

"No, Josh, it's not that her background is unhealthy, but there is so little of it. According to her friends, Mrs. Langdon was adopted. There is little information about her mother and none about her father, who apparently is not even in the picture."

"It seems she was adopted at the age of five. Her mother was killed in a fatal car crash. One of her co-workers, Jenny, stated that Mrs. Langdon complained to her of a recurrent dream, a dream she said she couldn't quite get the grasp of but which was always the same. Another friend, Tracey, said that Mrs. Langdon had confided in her that she had nightmares for the first five years she was with the Hiltons. She would wake up screaming. She said that her parents were wonderful to her and they were always there for her, but the nightmares wouldn't stop. Then, one day, she said they just went away and all that remained was the vague dread of the dream she could never remember.

"While she was growing up, the Hiltons made sure Heather had everything she wanted, and they loved her dearly. But once she was old enough she wanted to make it on her own. It seemed too easy to her to just ask for it. Of course, there were the occasional arguments. But later on, the bulk of their disagreements were about John Langdon. It seems the parents were not happy about their daughter's marriage to Mr. Langdon after only three months of courtship. As most parents are, they were anxious about the relationship because they knew so little about this man she was in love with. But according to her friends, Heather had always been very headstrong and, though they tried, the parents couldn't persuade her to postpone the wedding. They were absolutely furious that their daughter had to do all the driving on their honeymoon, as well as the entire first year of their marriage. Apparently, Mr. Langdon had lost his license a few months prior to the wedding. Mrs. Perilli explained that their marriage started to fall apart as soon as John got his license back. He evidently started drinking heavily and didn't come home until late. He had pushed and shoved his wife in the past, but nothing more severe happened, to her knowledge, that comes close to the severity of this incident. Jenny had chimed in at that point stating that only the week before Mr. Langdon had taken his wife's keys and left the house at night, not returning. She knew this because the patient had called her for a ride to work."

"Jenny had explained further that she was always worried that, as she put it, something like this would happen. She said she had expressed her fears to Mrs. Langdon, because, according to her observation there were many other incidents that were apparently leading up to this one, but Mrs. Langdon would not leave her husband. She said that Heather told her she felt it was her responsibility as his wife to try to make things work. But her friend noticed Mrs. Langdon getting more and more depressed."

"Well, Abe, that certainly sheds some light on the subject. I wish we had more information about her birth and her biological parents, though. You know, it amazes me how this continues to happen in adoption cases. There's nothing to hide anymore, yet people are so reluctant to give up information that could help the child in the future."

"I agree, but based on the information we have, what do you feel is the best approach to take?"

"One thing's for sure," Stein declared. "She will definitely have to be sedated. She is still in too weakened a condition to sustain such an emotional shock. We really could expect any type of reaction, even becoming despondent."

"You're right. There's a very distinct possibility that she will be unable to absorb the news about her parents. In light of that, there's not much we can do for her except daily treatment until she is ready."

Both psychiatrists were quiet for several minutes as they thought about the implication of their shared information. Then Stein continued, "I would have to say that this is the scenario we have to look at: she's already loaded with emotional pain over the abuse from her husband, physical now, but also the mounting emotional abuse over a period of time. That abuse now culminated in the loss of a child she didn't even know about and the hysterectomy that was performed. So she may bury all that once she has knowledge of her parents' deaths."

"Yes," Sutter picked it up after a pause. "Unfortunately, I would have to agree with that bleak outlook. She's got old abandonment issues and new ones. How are we going to deal with it? A good question! I think we have to prepare her some-how, but then as I think about it, there can be no preparation. There is no preparation for the acceptance of death. The best thing that can be done is for her friends to be there so she'll feel a little less threatened. But I definitely feel that we can do nothing to prepare her for this. I agree with you that she should be medicated and medication should be at the bedside with the nurse to inject IV, if need be."

Dr. Stein regarded his colleague thoughtfully for a few sec-onds and said, "Yes, that sounds realistic to me. I mean, once she's told this news, there will be nothing we can do. I cannot believe how helpless I feel in this situation. We are usually able to work with our clients toward a goal, but in this case we can't. She's going to have to work through this herself."

"I don't think we can go much beyond that point tonight," Sutter rejoined. "We have to wait and see what the reaction is going to be. We need to know from Holden just how long he thinks she'll be in the hospital. Then we'll have to decide if she's better off here or if she should be transferred to some other care facility."

"It is my understanding that there is no ceiling on the cost of Mrs. Langdon's medical care. She is to receive the best. Her parents were the well-known Hiltons. It's most fortunate for the young woman, no matter how it comes about."

They finished for the evening, adding a few more notes, and went their separate ways. They would get some input from Holden in the morning before they went downstairs to the patient's room.

Chris Hurley was about to call Brian Hargrove, when his phone rang in his hand. He recognized Jack Martin's voice. "Chris, I figured I'd better give you a call and let you know what's going on. At this point, there's a good chance that Langdon will be released. The store owner decided that he couldn't make the identification. He felt there was too much doubt and couldn't commit."

"Wow, no kidding. That's a lucky break for our Mr. Langdon. Well, what are you expecting?"

"We've notified Detective Hawkins because if Langdon is released, it's the general feeling that he'll head right for the hospital. Wait; let me put you on hold for a minute." As he put Chris on hold, John Langdon was being brought out for release. He was being escorted to the property room to pick up his belongings. Martin heard the processing officers reminding him that the district attorney was still looking to press charges. They also reminded him of his upcoming court date for DWI.

"Hey, Chris. What we just talked about has already happened. He has a court date for the DWI and the D.A. is letting him go, but they'll pick him up later, when they're ready. I better hang up, but I thought you should know. Oh, by the way, they're still keeping the cop with Mrs. Langdon."

"Thanks, Jack. I appreciate your call. Let me go; I have some work to do." He hung up the phone and pushed for a dial tone automatically. He had to get Brian and let him know.

Brian was still sitting in his office at home looking through all the home listings. "Hello," he answered, absently.

"Yes, Mr. Hargrove, it's Chris Hurley. I wanted to give you a quick call and let you know that John Langdon is being released as we speak."

"What? How is that possible?"

"Well, from what I understand, the store owner withdrew the identification. The District Attorney can't get to Mrs. Langdon for the information they need to make the charges stick. He was seen for the DWI and got a court date, but they had no choice but to let him go."

"I don't believe this! That woman is lying in a hospital bed because of that bastard and they're letting him go! Her life will never be the same. But he's going to head straight for the hospital. Is the officer still with Heather?"

"Oh, yes. I forgot to mention that. They're keeping her at the door. It's the general consensus that he'll get loaded and head to the hospital."

"Thanks, Chris. Keep me posted. I'll be at home tonight but tomorrow morning I'll be at the office."

Brian hung up the phone in disgust. That miserable piece of garbage! How could they let him go?! He thought about John trying to get in to see Heather; his stomach lurched. There was nothing he could do now; he knew that the police would not lift the guard from her room. Heather was at least protected from Langdon for the moment. But he wondered what Langdon's next move would be. He would just have to wait it out.

He was furious but he also felt helpless. He knew he had to get busy and decide which house he was going to buy. Though this "plan" was weak, it had to be ready so that she had a place to go when she left the hospital. He had narrowed his choices down to three homes. In the morning, he would contact the realtor and go see all three. He wanted to make a decision at that time and push the deal through as quickly as possible.

Chapter Eighteen

$\mathcal{T}$racey lingered at Heather's bedside. She didn't want her to be alone without anyone close there with her. But she was also afraid that she would awaken and ask what was wrong. Her facial expression would not be able to hide the morbid news from Heather. They knew each other so well they could tell when something was seriously wrong just by looking at each other. She would have to wait until the morning.

Tracey and Vito nervously talked about the next day through dinner into the rest of the evening. They tried to picture what tomorrow would bring until they finally exhausted themselves and turned in for the night. Fitfully, Tracey fell asleep in her husband's arms.

Jenny had gone back to the clinic to let their boss know where Heather was and what was going on. He told Jenny to take the time that she needed to be with Heather and to call him if she felt he could help in any way.

When Frank came home, Jenny had cried and filled him in on everything that had happened. He sat in disbelief as he listened to the sequence of events that unfolded. He thought about John and remembered a night he had come to a party they had given. John was so drunk there was no way he could have driven. Jenny was thrilled when Heather and John decided to stay the night and had prepared her famed "Green Goddess Room" for them to stay in. But something had gone very wrong during the night and Heather was downstairs on the sofa when he and Jenny came down in the morning. When Jenny saw her that morning, she could tell by the expression on her face that something bad had happened. Frank had sensed there were bigger problems, but never said anything. Heather wouldn't discuss what had happened and made up some excuse as to why she was sleeping on the sofa. Frank had felt sorry for her. She was a special person and he knew how much his wife loved her. Hopefully, he thought, things will work out for her – although, he knew, not without a lot of pain ahead of her. He got up and went over to hug Jenny, who was still crying softly. He turned her around and led her out of the kitchen turning off the light on the way out.

Chapter Nineteen

$\mathcal{J}$osh Stein was early at the hospital. He stopped at the cafeteria to get a cup of coffee. But Abe Sutter was already in his office upstairs. Stein made his way back up to the twelfth floor. Bruce Holden was finishing up a dressing on a patient. Ralph Duprey needed to finish reviewing the night's activity report. Technically, Duprey did not have to attend once he set the wheels in motion but, with a special interest in the case because of Brian Hargrove, he wanted to make sure that the wheels turned smoothly. It was a little before ten by the time they all gathered together. They sat down at the conference table and Abe Sutter took the floor.

"Gentlemen, let me quickly review the information available to us and the plan of action that we decided on. Bruce, we'll need your input this morning on the patient's condition." Dr. Holden nodded. Sutter continued, filling everyone in on the details of the meeting from the night before. Then Sutter gave Holden the floor.

"I saw Mrs. Langdon this morning. She is awake and alert, still under the effects of the sedative, but not responding very well. She smiled at me and recognized me. She had very little to say. Her vitals are stable and her wound is doing nicely."

"On the emotional level, I feel she's in for a rough ride. I would have to agree with you that she is not capable of accepting any more bad news, much less the death of her parents. I honestly wish, for her sake, that we didn't have to follow through with this at this time. It's not in her best interest. I have no problem with her being heavily sedated. But I think she should only receive minimal medication prior to your telling her. Then, have meds bedside to administer if need be, right after she receives the news. I understand that she is the only living relative and this I.D. process must fall her way, but it is against my better judgment to subject this young woman to such an ordeal at this time."

"Dr. Holden," Josh asked, "do you feel it's too early to be able to indicate how long she would be in the hospital for the surgical recovery?"

"Well, I would estimate at least another five days. That is just for recovery, yes. I find it difficult to assess what her overall condition will be after this morning. I would have to say we wait and see."

Since there was no more to discuss, the group left the room to meet with Peter Albright from the medical examiner's office. They also wanted to brief Mrs. Langdon's friends.

Everyone was waiting for them in the conference room. Introductions were made and then it was agreed that Jenny, Vito and Tracey should go into the room and spend a little time with Mrs. Langdon. The friends would have about fifteen minutes to visit before the session. Peter Albright would stand by the door, where he could hear what was going on, and come into the room as his name was mentioned.

The trio of friends left the conference room. Heather saw them coming through the door and gave them all a big smile.

"Hi, there, you guys," she said weakly. "I'm happy to see all of you. Thank you for coming to see me," she said breathlessly. Jenny felt a lump in her throat and wanted to run from the room because she doubted she would be able to carry it off. Tracey was absolutely stiff; Vito had her elbow and was almost pushing her into the room. But once Tracey saw Heather smiling, she walked right over to the bed and hugged her gently.

"Gee, Tracey, I guess I wasn't too lucky this time. Jenny, I have to say you were right. At this moment, and you are all my witnesses, I never want to see that man again."

"It's okay, Heather," Jenny replied, giving her a hug and a kiss. "The most important thing is that you are going to be okay. We love you and we want you to get better and get out of here. We've been so worried about you. Sleeping Beauty has nothing on you the last couple of days!"

Heather glanced over at Vito, who was very still. "Vito, are you feeling all right? I must say I have never seen you so quiet. Is anything wrong?"

"No, Heather, I'm okay. But try to get one word in whenever the three of you are together!"

"Well, I guess John has gone and done it this time. I can safely say that our life together is definitely over." She started to cry. "And not only that, but now I'll never have any children of my own. There is so much to cope with I don't know what to cope with first. How am I ever going to tell my parents?"

"Heather, please don't do this. The first thing that you have to think about is getting better," Tracey said. Heather nodded, as the nurse handed her a tissue.

"You know," Heather stated, wiping her eyes, "I don't understand where all these wonderful nurses came from and how I got into a private room. I can't afford all of this. The insurance company will definitely not pay for it. Do you know how this happened?"

"Ah, and how is my favorite patient this morning?" Holden asked as he entered the room. He did a visual of his patient and was pleased to see her looking and acting as well as she was. Maybe it was because of her friends and maybe it was all an act. He didn't know and only wished he had more time to find out. But she seemed like a delightful young woman.

"Hello there, Dr. Holden. I think I'm coming back to the world of the living."

"Well, that's mighty good news to hear. I like to believe that it's my wonderful bedside manner that makes my patients so happy and eager to get better." He chuckled and Heather smiled at his little joke. Then Holden made the move.

"I hope you don't mind, but I have a couple of my colleagues I want to introduce to you. This is Dr. Abe Sutter and this is Dr. Josh Stein."

"How do you do?" Heather asked. "I think it's so kind that all of you have chosen to visit me. You have no idea how much I appreciate everyone coming." Stein noted that she was smiling and talking, but her voice was flat. She was putting on a show. He had been listening to her conversation with her friends and he thought she did well in the verbalization department. But he wondered if she actually realized the serious implications to her future or was she in denial?

Dr. Holden came around to the side of her bed, put the side rail down and gently sat on the bed. He patted her shoulder as she winced in pain from the slight movement of the bed. "Heather, I have asked these people to be here this morning because we have some news that will be difficult for you to hear."

Instantly Heather stiffened and paled, the forced smile gone. "What is it? Has something happened to John?"

"No, it's not about John," Holden continued. His mouth was dry and he searched for words. "When you were brought into the hospital the other night, the weather was bad and the roads were icy. There was a bus accident."

Heather asked guardedly, "What are you talking about? What bus accident?" Suddenly realization came. She stopped talking and drew a quick breath. "Oh, my God, it's my mother and father, isn't it? They're okay, though, aren't they? Oh, mon dieu!"

"Heather, there is no easy way to tell you this, but no, they are not. There were no survivors."

Desperately, Heather appealed to her friends. She was trying to sit up, trying to get out of bed, fighting with the intravenous tubing. "I don't believe it. They were only going on vacation." She saw tears well up in Jenny's eyes as she shook her head. Tracey blanched, eyes wide and staring at Heather, watching her for signs of being needed. Vito stared at the foot of the bed as he steadied Tracey. Dr. Holden continued.

"Heather, listen to me. I know this is difficult for you, but you have to be brave and look at some pictures from the medical examiner's office. Do you think you can do that?" Heather was shaking visibly. She looked at Dr. Holden with panic. She couldn't breathe; sharp pain stabbed her abdomen. Albright walked into the room. Dr. Holden nodded to Sutter to have the medication ready.

"I can't! I just can't! How did this happen? Where are they? I want to go see them. I have to be with my mother and father! You don't understand!" Albright was already at Heather's bedside. Holden nodded at him to go ahead.

"Mrs. Langdon, I am Dr. Peter Albright, the Medical Examiner. I know that this is going to be extremely difficult for you. I am sorry to put you through this. I have two pictures that I need you to look at." Heather, wracked with pain and shock and heartache, had become stiff. She turned her head and tried to nod at Albright in acknowledgement. The nurse was on one side of Heather and Dr. Holden was on the other. Albright slowly held both pictures up in front of her. Heather looked at them and screamed, "Momma! Poppa!" Albright took that as recognition and pulled the pictures back immediately. Sutter was already putting the medication into the IV, while Heather continued to scream despite the pain of her broken ribs. Then her screaming stopped suddenly and she was silent, just staring blankly ahead. She dropped back onto the pillow over Bruce Holden's arm. The nurse softly stroked her head. It was all over. Sutter and Stein examined the patient. Everyone was as silent as Heather. The three doctors continued to work over her and began to whisper among themselves. No one knew exactly what to do. Jenny and Tracey wept softly, and Vito was trying to comfort his wife.

Peter Albright had slipped out of the room. He was relieved that it was over and even more relieved to be out of there. His job was never an easy one and there was no easy way to break news like that to anyone.

Suddenly there was a loud commotion outside the room in the corridor – coming their way. As the occupants turned their attention to the disturbance, they could see the officer at the door restraining a man. The distraught group of friends stiffened, recognizing John Langdon.

"What do you mean I can't go inside?! That's my wife and no one is going to fucking stop me from going in there to see her!" Langdon continued to push forward, fighting with the police officer.

"I'm sorry, sir," she responded, blocking Langdon from entering the room. "But I have my orders. You cannot go in there. Now calm down, sir, or I'll have you escorted out!"

Dr. Holden motioned for everyone to stay where they were. He signaled to Sutter to close the door. Langdon was screaming so loud that Vito suggested he go outside and try to calm him down. But Sutter and Stein shook their heads, explaining to him that it was better for him to stay out of the way. There were tears in the friends' eyes as they looked mutely at each other, all choked up. The three physicians opened the door and tried to assist the officer in restraining Langdon. Sutter, Stein and the officer struggled to gain control over Langdon.

The floor clerk had called hospital security, and they were running down the hall to further restrain Langdon, who was now yelling obscenities at the three doctors. The security guards took him, still kicking and fighting, to the elevator and down to the security office. The doctors relaxed a bit, walked back over to Mrs. Langdon's door, opened it and looked in. The nurse saw them and signaled back that everything was okay. Dr. Holden advised her that he would be outside in consultation for a few minutes. Heather was beyond responding.

Holden was already speaking to Sutter and Stein at the nursing desk. "Well, I guess we've had our formal introduction to Mr. Langdon. Rather a subdued chap, don't you think?" They all laughed wryly because it had been a potentially dangerous situation which they were relieved was over. They returned their attention to the patient. "What do you think?"

Stein offered his observations first. "Well, that was a tough scene to play out. No one could have done a better job, Bruce. But before the medication took effect, I thought I observed a despondent stare. What do you think, Abe?"

"Yes, I think you're right. I would have to think that she is going to come off this medication just as she went in: despondent. We should know a bit more within the next twenty-four hours."

Stein advised his colleagues that he would be staying for a while to see that everything remained calm. Holden announced that he was heading for surgery and would check in later. Sutter also had to start his rounds. As they headed for the elevator, two police officers got off, walking toward Heather's room. The hospital had strict regulations and had probably called the police immediately. The officers spoke with the guard at the door then went back downstairs to the security office.

Stein went back into Heather's room and to her bedside. He held her wrist as he took her pulse to assure himself that she was all right. It was slow and steady. Good, he thought to himself. She was in a deep sleep. But he was worried that she would experience a long recovery from what he saw before the medication took effect. He thought about the smile on her face when she first saw Holden. There probably was evidence of denial of the events to a certain extent at that time, but then the news brought her over the edge. There was no telling what state she would be in when the medication wore off, but he knew he wanted to be there when it did. He wondered about her mother's car accident. Had she possibly been with her mother? Had she been physically hurt herself? Was she French or did she just speak the language? She had yelled something out at the end before the medication. There were so many questions. But there was no question about her husband! Holden was right that he should be kept away.

Chris Hurley had dressed as a maintenance worker on the floor and had witnessed the unruly scenario. He swept himself into a closet, ripped off the maintenance uniform and flew downstairs to the security office. The door was closed, but he could hear jumbled and angry voices inside. Before he knocked, he thought it was best that he contact Brian and let him know what had happened. He found a pay phone and quickly dialed the number.

"Mr. Hargrove's residence. Mr. Hargrove is not in at the moment." Chris hung up the phone and searched in his pocket for the other number Brian had given him for his car. He dialed it and Brian answered.

"Yeah, Mr. Hargrove, I'm at the hospital and I wanted to bring you up-to-date."

"Good, Chris, I'm glad you caught me. I'm on my way to the office."

"Well, it's been quite a morning at Mrs. Langdon's room." Chris quickly let the details of the drama unfold. "Later, I heard the doctors talking and they aren't too hopeful about her mental state when the medication wears off."

"What does that mean?" Brian asked impatiently.

"I heard them discussing what had happened and the one psychiatrist, Josh Stein, brought up the fact that she seemed in some kind of non-responsive state before she went under. At this point, they don't know what to expect until she comes around. But there was quite a commotion when her husband showed up at the hospital drunk and demanding to see her. He made some scene and hospital security has him in the office right now waiting for the police to come. Apparently, the hospital may press charges. What do you want me to do?"

"I think we'll have to sit back and watch this one unfold; there's really nothing we can do. Langdon has just created another disaster for himself. Keep on it but keep your distance and keep me informed."

Brian had to think about this. He had to call the shop foreman to find out if John Langdon had called in to work at all.

When Brian reached his office, he called his secretary in. She briefed him on messages that had come in while he had been out, then he instructed her to call the shop foreman and find out what was going on with the Langdon matter. She came back in to report her findings, telling Brian that there had been no contact between work and Mr. Langdon since the last day he had reported in. He thanked her and dismissed her.

So, Brian thought, Langdon didn't even bother to call in. Well, we'll cancel his transfer and then make it permanent by firing him altogether. Yes, that's the best thing to do. He called Personnel and advised the administrator of his decision and to set all the paperwork in motion. He was adamant that he wanted the paperwork sent out by messenger today. He knew that, legally, there wasn't a problem; he was within his bounds as employer. The company might have a bit of a problem with the union, but nothing they couldn't handle.

That out of the way, his thoughts turned to Heather and what she must have gone through this morning. His poor, sweet Heather. How he wanted her to awaken and be herself again! But he knew that wouldn't happen. He had met with the realtor earlier in the morning and picked one of the three homes. He thought to himself, just for a second, that he must be absolutely crazy but he couldn't help it. Well, the closing would take place in five days and he would set title for the house in her name as a gift. She would have a place to live, a beautiful place. He would hire a housekeeper to live at the house as soon as possible. He leaned back in his desk chair and looked at the city below him, thinking about Heather in her new home.

Together, Jenny, Tracey and Vito left Heather's room, heading for the cafeteria. They knew she wouldn't be awake for hours. They were upset and exhausted by the experience and felt helpless. It was a horrible situation and there was nothing any of them could do to make it better. They agreed that, however the private-duty nurses got there, it was a blessing they were there with her. They were grateful that she was medicated and sleeping.

Chapter Twenty

$\mathcal{L}$eo Martucci had also arrived at the hospital just in time for the entire scenario as it unfolded. He was seated in the hall to the left of the emergency room, not too far from the security office, waiting to find out what would happen with John Langdon. The security office door swung open and he saw two police officers taking Langdon out in handcuffs.

"Settle down, Langdon. You agreed to do this. If you do, you won't go to jail and you won't face charges for disorderly conduct and disturbing the peace. Just come along with us now." Martucci listened intently, wondering what Langdon had agreed to and where they were taking him. Langdon appeared to be drunk. Martucci decided to hang by the security office door to see if he could find out any more information. The guards were still inside talking.

"Yeah, well I didn't think he was going to go quietly, that's for sure. He's one nasty son-of-a-bitch."

"Hell, yeah! I thought we were definitely gonna tangle. But the administration is strict, and I'm glad they are because they back up whatever we do. He was fortunate that the administrator was willing to deal."

"Definitely. He would've been pretty stupid not to accept time at Hillsworth Rehab instead of jail and charges. But I've seen this before; I don't know if it does any good, you know what I mean? It sometimes prolongs the inevitable."

"Well, no matter what, he got a second shot at it, and if he has one ounce of brain matter left, he'll give it all he's got."

The two guards continued talking and laughing, but Leo had what he needed. He felt as if he hadn't been to bed all night. In a way he hadn't because he had been over at Brian's since five this morning. He wanted to see how he was going to start his day and what he was up to. He had a lot to tell Hargrove. He couldn't wait to get to home. He was beat and it sure would feel good to catch a couple of hours of sleep. He drove home thinking about the case. It never ceased to amaze him how people could screw up their lives.

Once at home, he opened the door and there was his five-year old golden retriever, Skipper, wagging his tail happily as Martucci slid through the door. He let the dog out, grabbed the phone and dialed Hargrove's number.

"Hello?" Alec answered the phone himself. "Leo, Good to hear from you. What do you have for me?"

"Well, Mr. Hargrove, it's been a busy morning. I've been at your son's since five. He met some realtor at eight and he looked at a couple of houses. He decided to buy the last one. I confirmed that when I called the realtor and she advised me it had just been sold. So I would have to assume that Brian is the buyer. He headed straight to the office after that."

Alec shook his head in amazement. "Please continue, Leo."

Martucci was so excited over the detailed information he had to give to his client. He couldn't wait to spill it all out. He stopped at intervals to catch his breath and to make sure that he didn't leave anything out. "That's what I have for you boss. Is there anything else you want me to do?"

"Yes, I want you to maintain your watch on Brian and look out at the hospital for Mrs. Langdon."

"Okay, I can do that. I'm just gonna get a couple hours sleep and then I'll be back on it." The conversation ended. Leo prepared himself some breakfast and then headed for the bedroom to get some shut eye, with Skipper at his heels.

Alec pondered over this new information. Puzzling that Brian would want to buy a house; what was he up to, anyway? He was at the office but what else was he doing in connection with the Langdon woman? His thoughts were interrupted as Alicea walked into the room and put her arms around her husband, sat on his lap and kissed him good morning. What a wonderful way to start a day, Alec thought.

* * *

Stein spent most of the day in Heather's room. He left only to get something for lunch and to call his office and see how things were going there. Then he immediately returned to Heather's room, hoping there would be a change. He brought one of his latest journals to read, but he found himself watching Heather as she slept.

It was about six o'clock in the evening. He must have dozed. He awakened with a start as the nurse called for him to come to the bedside. Heather's eyes were open, but they were fixed, and she stared straight ahead with a blank expression on her face. Stein called out her name but there wasn't even a twitch. He waved his hand in front of her eyes and she didn't blink. Damn, he thought to himself. She had shut down emotionally. The death of her parents *had* pushed her over the edge and she was emotionally unable to absorb or deal with any further pain. This was not good, he thought, and was what he was afraid might happen. He pushed the bedside intercom and asked the desk clerk to page Dr. Sutter, stat. As soon as Sutter heard it, he knew it was for Mrs. Langdon. He came right down and found Stein and a nurse by Mrs. Langdon's bedside.

"What is it, Josh?"

"Look. Our worst fears confirmed. There's absolutely no response from her." Sutter came closer to the bed and started to examine Heather. Stein was right. There was no response. She was like a wax statue. Sutter touched the woman's shoulder and whispered close to her ear, "Heather, you take all the time you need. We'll be here waiting for you when you are ready." Then to Stein, "Let's step outside for a moment, Josh."

The two psychiatrists walked down the corridor in silence, both thinking of what the best approach might be. Stein was the first to speak. "I think we should transfer her to the twelfth floor as soon as we can get a medical clearance from Bruce. She has a private-duty nurse who we can work with so she has a better understanding of what to do and what to look for in a patient in this condition."

"Yes, I think you're right. She'll need total care while she's in this state, and I think we should begin a course of pharmacological treatment as soon as possible."

"Abe, let me call Bruce and see what he has to say. He'll be on rounds shortly. In fact, let's check with the desk clerk and see if he's already in the building." She advised Sutter that Dr. Holden had already signed into the hospital. Within minutes, Bruce was on the second floor and saw the physicians waiting for him.

Bruce signaled for them to follow him as he went behind the counter and opened a door to a small conference room. "I thought we would have a little more privacy in here. I just got out of O.R." He was still in his surgical greens. "So, what's up? I went to see Heather a few hours ago, but she was sleeping soundly."

"Well, there has been a change in her condition. Stein was in with her most of the afternoon but the nurse awakened him with the change. We think you should come with us and see her now." They headed for Heather's room, Stein leading the way. Heather was half sitting up in bed, but with the same fixed, blank stare. Bruce walked up to her and examined her and did the same things Stein and Sutter had done. It was really an automatic reaction. He flashed his hand in front of her face but she didn't bat an eyelash. He snapped his fingers in front of her eyes and she did not blink. He hit the intercom button and asked the nurse to come in with Heather's chart. Meanwhile the private-duty nurse confirmed that Mrs. Langdon had been sleeping most of the day, with a little movement, but she had made note in the chart of the change in her condition about six o'clock that evening. All three doctors returned to the conference room, taking Heather's chart.

"Well, what do you think is our best course of action?" Holden asked.

"We've talked it over," Sutter started, "and feel it would be in her best interest if she was moved to Twelve where we could work with her and monitor her closely until she comes out of this. But, of course, that all depends on your okay for her to be moved from the surgical floor. Do you think she's stable and out of the woods yet?"

Dr. Holden thought for a minute as he looked through her chart for her newest blood gases and values. "Well, I have my reservations, although she appears to be coming along as well as can be expected for the injuries she sustained. I am not pleased with the amount of drainage on this dressing and her blood pressure seems to be lower than it should be. She might have to go back to repair some of the internal sutures if this drainage continues." He thought for a moment.

"I have no objection as long as she has private-duty nurses. I can follow her just as easily upstairs. But by all means do what you have to do. Right now, it's most important that you both have the access to her and that there be close monitoring. So if that's your recommendation, I'll sign the orders now and we can get the ball rolling." Stein and Sutter nodded in agreement.

At once Bruce signed the order and Sutter called the nurse to advise her that Mrs. Langdon would be immediately moved to Twelve. The ward clerk called for transportation for the patient.

The two psychiatrists knew that they had a limited time to work with her and hoped that within the thirty days there would be some change in Mrs. Langdon's condition. If not, she would have to be transferred to another facility. But they had time to deal with that, if they had to. At this point, Sutter and Stein did not know what to expect, but they wanted to start working with her right away.

Once their patient was settled in her new room, Sutter and Stein took the private-duty nurse outside by the doorway and explained to her what they expected her to do. She was instructed to talk with the patient as if she were awake and conscious, to read to her, reassure her that she's not alone and to give her personal care as if she were alert. She was to let the patient know she is protected and going to be fine and to keep telling her to take her time and that we are all here for her when she is ready to come back to us. The nurse nodded in agreement.

Dr. Holden ordered physical therapy twice a day to get her out of bed and start her walking and sitting in a chair so that she would gain strength and there would be no ill effects from prolonged bed rest. As far as her physical condition went, they reassured the nurse that the patient was ready, and that under normal conditions Mrs. Langdon would have started to ambulate already. The nurse said that she under-stood the instructions and would pass on this information to the next shift that came on at eleven.

It was already nine o'clock in the evening by the time Heather was settled in her new room. They assisted the pri-vate-duty nurse to reinforce patient care and stayed with Heather while one of the floor nurses showed the private-duty nurse the necessities on the floor.

Sutter and Stein talked to Heather and explained to her what they were doing, that they had changed her room and that they were getting her out of bed to get a little exercise. Heather did not respond. They watched her closely for any reaction, but there wasn't any. But they completed everything with her that they had set out to for the evening anyway, hoping to bring her back to the land of the living. It was a start. For Heather, it would be another new beginning.

Chapter Twenty-One

*J*ohn was taken to Hillsworth Rehab. He was furious! He tried to call his parents, but they didn't answer. They were on their way over to see him. Unfortunately, he refused to understand that he was not allowed any visitors for the first two weeks. It was about three o'clock in the afternoon by the time his parents arrived. They brought a letter for him from Hargrove Electronics they had received by messenger. John's mother was beside herself that John had been placed in a Rehab Center. She sat fuming while she waited for the counselor to speak with them. Finally, the door opened and a tall man with dark hair, a short beard and glasses came into the waiting room.

"Hello, Mr. and Mrs. Langdon. My name is Bobby Brighton and I've come to speak with you to explain what is going on and what you can expect. Why don't you come into my office where we have more privacy?" Bobby wasted no time escorting them.

"I want to see my son. I do not want to waste any time speaking with you," insisted Meredith Langdon.

Bobby realized that he had a problem mother here. He was used to family members' resistance to the situation and their ignorance of rehabilitation. Prior to the Langdon's arrival, he had received information from the police department and from the hospital on the complaint that brought Langdon to Rehab. It was specifically stated on the form from the district attorney's office that Langdon had made the choice of coming to rehab instead of going to jail. This way he avoided sentencing for the charges brought by the hospital. Bobby would have to explain all of this to Langdon's parents.

"I understand how you feel, Mrs. Langdon. But you must also understand that your son has been placed here on a court order. He would have gone to jail if he had not accepted this offer, so . . ."

"I don't care what anyone says! My son did nothing wrong. Why isn't anyone listening to what I have to say? It's that woman he's married to that should be here. She's the cause of this whole situation."

"I hear what you're saying. But whether you believe what I say or not, these are the facts the way they stand at this time. You can choose to work with me and help your son or not. I need your assistance."

Calmer and more reasonable, her husband urged, "Meredith, listen to what the man is saying."

"Oh, be still, Tom! I know what I'm talking about!"

Bobby decided to go ahead with the orientation. "Okay, now. John will be here for sixty days. During that time he will receive therapy and he will be in interactive group sessions with other adults. You cannot see him for the first two weeks of his stay here. That is mandatory and we cannot make any exceptions. You cannot see him and you cannot talk with him on the phone. After the initial two weeks, he will be allowed scheduled visitors and he will be allowed to receive and make phone calls during a certain time schedule. Are there any questions about this?"

"Well, this is ridiculous! I have never heard of such a thing! I demand to see my son right now or . . ."

"Mrs. Langdon, please try to understand. As I said before, your son is here by a court order. I can do nothing about that. If you work with me on this, it won't be that long before you will be able to see him. He is in very capable hands and will be well taken care of. You must hear what I am saying. He has no options. It is either here or jail. Now, if you think about it calmly for a minute, where would you rather him be?"

Mrs. Langdon was momentarily speechless. Then she remembered the special delivery letter that came to the house. Surely they would let her give it to him. She said to Brighton, "Well, I have this letter for him that came by messenger."

"Fine, I will take it and give it to him." He continued right on so Mrs. Langdon would not have a chance to interject. "Now, John is going to need five changes of clothes. Is it possible that you could get back here and drop them off by tomorrow, at the latest?"

Tom Langdon pre-empted his wife. "We will do that. If we can, we will drop the clothes off today. Is there anything else he'll need?"

"You can bring personal items such as deodorant, toothbrush, toothpaste, comb or brush, shampoo. But no razors, mouthwash or anything with alcohol in it."

"Okay, we'll get that stuff to you as soon as we can."

"Great. Thank you. Now I would like to get some information from you about John. Please remember, we are not being nosey. The more information we have about John, the more we will be able to help him, which is the reason he's here. I am sure within a couple of weeks that John will be able to start to communicate his problem to you himself, but until that time, we need every bit of information you can give us."

The rest of the interview flowed without further outbursts from Meredith Langdon. But she thought about Heather with daggers. How she could have done this to her son was beyond her. John was such a good boy, she thought. She should go right up to that hospital and give Heather a piece of her mind. She thought she just might.

* * *

It was Friday morning. Ralph Duprey arrived at his office late. One of the kids needed a ride to school, and he had started talking to the teacher, and well, he was late. Noon would be here before he knew it and he had a lot of ground to cover before then. He rushed into his office and immediately called for the stat sheets; then he wanted to check on the Langdon case. Lisa brought him a fresh cup of coffee which he enjoyed while he reviewed the stats from the evening and night shifts. He dictated a few memos and a couple of letters and he was off to see Mrs. Langdon. He knew from the stats that she had been transferred. He scooted straight on up to Twelve only to find Stein and Sutter in deep discussion at the front nurse's station. They saw Duprey, waved him over and briefed him on what had transpired the day before and the facts that brought them to the decision to bring Heather onto the psych unit. Then the trio slowly walked down the hallway to the patient's room.

Outside each room was a mirrored viewing station so the patients could be observed without anyone entering their rooms at any time during the day or night. The men walked to Heather's viewing station. Duprey looked inside. Heather was seated in a chair by the window, but she was expressionless. She looked like a statue to him. She didn't even look as if she were breathing. He shot a glance at Sutter and Stein and then looked back at the patient. Stein finally broke the silence.

"It's hard to say how long she'll be in this state. It's up to her and when she'll be ready to face everything. It was too much devastating news on top of her physical trauma, and she literally shut down emotionally. But it is important that we continue to talk to her as if she were fully awake. From what we can understand about this condition, the patient is aware of what is going on around her, but later will either have no recollection or will remember almost everything, though at the time she was unable to respond to external stimuli. At this point we have no way of knowing what to expect. The patient will be the one to fill us in once she decides to return to us."

"I see," Duprey answered. "But she will come out of it? This is only a temporary state?"

Abe answered this time. "We certainly are looking into that point. There is no telling how long someone will remain despondent. You have to watch them closely and wait for any small indication, no matter how minute."

"The poor woman. I feel terrible and I don't even know her. She has gone through more than any person should have to endure and in such a brief period. Her entire life changed in those twenty-four hours. Well, I trust that the both of you will keep me posted, and I will be up periodically to see how things are going. If you need my assistance for any reason, let me know. It doesn't matter what it is, just give me the word."

The three went their separate ways. Stein was back in the room with Heather. Sutter scurried off to his rounds. Duprey looked at his watch as he walked through the exit doors to the elevator; it was already eleven-thirty. He had just enough time to get to the golf club for lunch to meet with Alec. As he drove over he thought about the Langdon woman. He could not get her out of his mind. It could be his daughter . . . anyone's daughter.

Alec had arrived early and was talking to a few acquaintances who had come in from a round of golf. He saw Duprey enter the restaurant and went to meet him. The two men greet-ed each other and shook hands. They were seated at a table facing the golf course where they caught up on all their fami-ly news; Duprey filling Alec in on their recent vacation and their oldest son starting college. They spoke of the upcoming charity ball for the hospital and how many would attend this year in comparison to last year and how much they hoped to realize in donations. The hospital board was planning a new rehabilitation wing. They stopped to order their lunch and the waitress brought their drinks. Once she left, Alec decided to bring up the Langdon matter.

"So, how are things going in the Langdon case?"

"Oh, Alec, that is a sad case. Honestly, I have never seen anything like it. They have moved the patient up to the Twelfth floor to be near the psychiatric offices. I observed her with the psychiatrists this morning. She just sits there staring. She doesn't look real. The physicians are in agreement that she shut down emotionally. They've started her on some medica-tion and are hoping that she will be stimulated into coming back."

"Does anyone know how long she'll be like that?"

"No, they're hoping to pull her out of it, but there are no guarantees. They're going to use everything they can to get her back. It's a shame. She's such a lovely young woman."

Alec found the case intriguing. He found himself thinking about it all the time. Maybe he was so intrigued because of Brian's interest, but whatever the reason, he wanted to see this woman. "I would like to have a look at this patient"

"Why, Alec, I didn't know that you had an interest also. I thought Brian was the one in the family with the interest."

"No, I have no personal interest, but I must say I find the entire situation with Brian intriguing. You know that I would never ask you . . ."

"Alec, it's no problem. Really. When we finish lunch, if you have time, we'll go back to the hospital and I'll take you up."

Alec felt foolish, thinking his curiosity had gotten the best of him. But he needed to see this woman who had stolen Brian's heart. He knew it, whether Brian did or not. It was the only explanation possible.

They enjoyed the rest of their lunch together, talking over the planning of the new rehab wing of the hospital. There was so much to be done before ground was broken.

Back at the hospital, they took the elevator to the twelfth floor. The head nurse acknowledged Duprey as they passed the station. When they entered the viewing station and Alec got his first look at Heather Langdon, it took his breath away. He watched her as she stared, lifelessly, it seemed, but he remembered her face. He remembered her from the last Christmas party. He had noticed that Brian hung around her like a bee around honey. Her husband had been drunk and had ended up making quite a spectacle of himself. It all came back to him. She was lovely, but more than that, he felt he knew her. There was something about her eyes. There was something familiar about her, even in this state. He felt bad for this strange woman, and was reminded, once again, of the horrible pain in his heart for the loss of his former wife and daughter. In fact, he thought, his own daughter would probably have been about the same age. He sighed deeply.

Dr. Stein was in the room with Mrs. Langdon, talking to her as if she would respond to him. Of course, that's what he was hoping for, trying to provoke some kind of reaction.

Alec thanked Duprey for the favor and they left the department. Alec was on his way to Brian's. He thought it was time to speak with his son then he planned to go home and talk to Alicea about what was going on.

Tracey and Vito hurried to Heather's room. Dr. Stein had stayed true to his word and had called them and advised them of what was happening with Heather. They wanted to see her as soon as possible. Stein told them it was fine and, in fact, a good idea for them to come and visit. Tracey had called Jenny at the clinic to let her know what Dr. Stein had relayed to them. Jenny said she would be over as soon as she finished admitting her afternoon patients. Dr. Stein was coming out of Heather's room as they reached the door.

"Dr. Stein, how is she doing?"

"Well, there has been no change since I spoke with you. I explained to you that we do not know how long she will be like this. It is important that you treat her as if she were awake and carrying on a conversation with you. Do not hold anything back because you are afraid to say it. I'll be in the viewing station watching so you won't be alone even if she happens to come out of it. Don't be frightened by her appearance. Remember that she can hear every word you say but she has shut down in responding to anything."

Tracey went right over to Heather, who was sitting in the chair, and hugged her and gave her a kiss. "Hi, Heather, it's Tracey." She felt a big lump building in her throat and she suddenly felt hot, but she was determined that Heather was going to be okay. "Heather, everything is going to be all right. Vito's here too. We came to spend some time with you. You don't have to say anything if you don't want to. After all, you know me. I'm never at a loss for words!"

"Yeah, Heather, this is the 'very quiet' woman you first met when I started dating her. Real quiet, isn't she?"

As she studied her friend's face and stroked her hair, Tracey saw a tear appear in the corner of one of Heather's eyes. She quickly motioned to Stein in the mirror. Immediately he came into the room.

"What is it?"

"Look," Tracey pointed to the tear. "I think she's starting to cry. Oh, Heather, if you want to cry, you go right ahead and cry. We're all here for you. You're not alone."

But that was it: that one tear that slowly trickled down the side of her face until Tracey caught it with a tissue. Stein felt hopeful. It was a sign that she was still with them, that she was not completely gone. He had to make sure that she was continuously stimulated – as he had been doing most of the day. The sooner they could bring her back the better. He wanted to make sure that the couple clearly understood the importance of verbal stimulation. He once again explained the urgency of this phase of Heather's treatment.

Tracey and Vito stayed for about two more hours. Just as they were getting ready to leave, Jenny walked into the room. She was not prepared for the way Heather looked and had to leave the room to regain her composure. Tracey followed her out to tell her what had happened since they had been there. She explained that, although there had been no other signs, Tracey and Vito had continued to talk to Heather as if she were alert and in full conversation with them.

"Come on, Jenny. I'll go back inside with you. Just talk to her normally, as if she were the same old Heather." Jenny nodded, wiped her face and blew her nose. She straightened and took a deep breath, then walked back into the room. But she could not get her emotions under control. She felt so horrible and helpless; she couldn't stand to see her best friend in this condition. But she also wanted to help Heather come back to them, so she steeled herself, walked over to Heather and touched her shoulder.

"Heather, it's Jenny and I'm here with you, sweetie. I don't know how much help I can possibly be because I am a hysterical mess over here. But maybe somehow we will perform magic for each other. I'm going to sit here and tell you every-thing that's going on in work. I just know how much you miss it. I must say, though, I would rather be with you at our favorite little place. By the way, everyone's rooting for you, Heather. So you have to get better." So Jenny talked, about new patients and some of the maintenance patients and what's going on with staff at the Center. And while she talked, she held Heather's hand in hers. But no matter what she had told her there was not even a peep out of Heather. It was painful to sit there and pretend as you watched her stare lifelessly. But she loved Heather and was determined to make sure Heather knew it. It was six o'clock by the time Jenny decided to leave. She kissed Heather good-bye, collected her pocketbook and coat and walked out the door. Dr. Stein was waiting for her.

"Are you doing okay?" he asked.

"Yes, I guess so. I had hoped that I would have been able to see some type of response from her. It is hard to see some-one that is normally so full of life, with so much spirit and zest, just sitting there like that. I'll be home tomorrow and Sunday. If you need me for anything, please call. Do you think I should come down and see her?"

"Well, that's entirely up to you. You live some distance from the hospital, and it is the weekend. Why don't you get some rest and catch your breath. You can call the hospital for an update. I promise to call you if there are any developments."

"Thanks, Dr. Stein. I think I needed to hear that because I am drained, and yet I don't want to stop if it will help Heather."

"Yes, but you have to keep healthy yourself. You have your own life, with a husband, home and a job. This is an extremely stressful situation for you."

So Jenny was off to her husband and her home, hoping and praying with all her heart that Heather would start to improve, somehow, over the weekend. Frank had been away on a business trip and she had not mentioned anything more to him. He would be home tonight and she would fill him in.

Stein stood at the viewing station and decided again to go in the room and sit with Heather for a while. She had already had several doses of medication and he was hoping it would elicit some type of response. But he knew he had to wait. He didn't want to miss anything.

It was fortunate that the private-duty nurses were there. He told the nurse he would sit with her until nine o'clock and then he would go home. He leaned forward and talked to Heather for a while, then sat wearily back and watched her breathing, slowly and regularly.

He must have dozed. The nurse gently shook him and told him it was time to leave. There was nothing more he could do for the evening. He left, reluctantly. Heather had had a full day with several visitors; Sutter and Stein had taken turns throughout the day working with her as well as observing her with visitors. The only exciting moment was the tear. He felt bad for the friend, Jenny. She wanted to help and she probably has and doesn't even realize it. Only Heather would be able to answer that. Maybe tomorrow . . . well, he would have to wait.

Chapter Twenty-Two

$\mathcal{A}$lec rang Brian's doorbell. He wondered what he was up to. He had been pretty invisible for the last several days and Alec knew that something was going on. Maybe he would be able to find out. Once again, Brian opened the door in surprise.

"Why, Alec, this is becoming a habit. Come on in. Is everything okay with Mother? You look kind of tired."

"Yes, your mother is quite fine. I thought I would stop by and have a little talk with you."

"Really? What about?"

"Well, I had lunch today with Ralph Duprey." Alec watched Brian closely for some type of reaction, but Brian turned away from him as he spoke. Alec's statement put Brian instantly on guard; he told himself to be careful and calm down.

"Well, that's nothing new. You always have lunch with Duprey. How is he, anyway?"

"Quite well. In fact, he shared with me how you've been keeping him busy, of late."

Brian knew now. Duprey must have told him everything. What was he going to do? "Oh, really? That's interesting."

"Yes, Brian I found it quite interesting myself. So interesting in fact that I had to come over and see you, to find out why you're so involved in the welfare of an employee's wife." Alec's words shot through Brian and rang in his ears. He couldn't believe that Alec had been able to find out what he was up to. Then again, maybe he was just fishing. But Alec caught the tension in Brian's jaw. He knew he'd hit a nerve so he pressed his advantage.

"In fact, I just came from the hospital, where I saw Mrs. Langdon." Brian shot him a look and Alec knew he had him.

"So what if I decided to help out an employee's wife? What's the big deal?" Brian stated flatly. He knew he was caught, but he wasn't ready to give in.

"It is a big deal when you're paying all of someone's hospital expenses. I'm not here to criticize you. I'm here to see if I can help you. Is there anything wrong?"

"No, nothing's wrong. I just wanted to help this person. That's all."

"Well, might it have something to do with the fact that she was offered a job as your administrative assistant?"

Damn him, Brian thought. How did he find out about that? What else did he know? There still was the chance that he had bits and pieces but didn't completely know what was going on or why . . . Brian sat down. Alec watched him intently. So Alec felt his suspicions were confirmed. Brian must be in love with this woman. Whether anything happened between the two of them, he didn't know, but there was no doubt about Brian's feelings. Alec felt he had dug enough. He didn't want to get into an argument. He wanted Brian to know that he loved him and that he was there for him. He didn't want to see Brian make any mistakes that he might regret for the rest of his life. He softened his tone from somewhat aggressive and inquisitive to one of compassion.

"Have you been to the hospital to see this woman?"

Brian shot his stepfather a look. He knew now that Alec at least suspected something between him and Heather. "No, I haven't been over to the hospital to see her. I didn't feel it was my place."

"Well, maybe you should go."

Brian couldn't believe what he had heard Alec say. He was telling him to go and see Heather. Brian was speechless.

"Brian, no one can tell us who we should and who we should not love. Our feelings don't work that way. But the woman is married. Her husband is one of our employees."

Brian couldn't help himself. He blurted out, "No, not any more, he isn't."

"What do you mean?"

"I cancelled his transfer here and, after checking with the foreman, I fired him in writing for failure to report to work the last few days."

Alec stood there and looked at Brian in amazement. He didn't know what to think because he wasn't involved with the husband's problems at all. But he wanted to find out. He decided to play it cool so Brian wouldn't heat up. "Okay, whatever has happened, I understand that to be your good judgment and business decision. I'm not going to pressure you into giving me any explanations. Brian, I'm here because I want to help you, because your mother and I love you. With that, I'm going to leave. Think about what I have said to you: I am here for you. If you want me to go with you to the hospital, for whatever reasons, I'll go with you, though I will be away as of tonight and won't be back for two days. But think about what I said."

Brian nodded his head in reply. He felt it safer at this point not to say anything and not to admit to anything else.

Alec walked over and hugged Brian before he left. He had only been guessing and had no idea about what Brian was attempting to do for Heather. Brian sat down in a chair as the door closed and wept. He couldn't live with himself knowing that he had literally set the stage for the lethal scene that took place between Heather and John. He wept because he loved that woman so much yet he couldn't do anything more than he had. Suddenly the phone rang. Shakily, trying to steady his voice, he picked up the receiver. It was Chris Hurley.

"Mr. Hargrove, I'm sorry it took me so long to get back to you. I've just come from the hospital. It's more difficult to see Mrs. Langdon now because they moved her to the twelfth floor, the Psychiatric Unit." Brian sat up straight and cleared his throat. Alec already knew, he thought. That's why he had offered to go to the hospital with him. He took a deep breath and wondered why it was so impossible for him to reach out to people – even his own family. "Yes, go on."

"Well, there is a viewing station outside her room and I'm telling you that Mrs. Langdon just sits there and doesn't move. I heard the doctors talking inside the room and they don't know how long she's going to be like this." Hurley went on to explain where her husband was. "Oh, by the way, Langdon's parents brought the notifications from Hargrove. Well, that's about all I have, but I'll continue to keep you posted."

"Thanks, Chris," Brian managed and hung up. He wanted to get his hands on Langdon but he wasn't ready to see Heather yet. He wanted a firm foundation for his plan before he went to see her. The timing wasn't right just yet. He didn't want to see her like that. He wanted her the way she was. He grabbed his jacket and was out the door to a meeting. He needed time to think.

While Alec and Alicea were having dinner, he filled her in on Brian. Alicea sat listening to every word. It wasn't that she didn't want to believe him but it was difficult to believe that he was talking about Brian. "Alec, you do realize that you're talking about *our* Brian, who doesn't like to spend a penny if he doesn't have to? It makes no sense, unless he's deeply in love with this woman. Why was he trying to keep this from us? Is he up to something else? Is it possible that the child this woman was carrying was Brian's?"

"I haven't a clue. I only wish I had the answers. Alicea, I didn't want to provoke an argument. I wanted to open the doors of communication for him, hoping that he would come to us. Whatever it is he needs, I want him to know we are here for him."

"Yes, of course, darling. I guess I find it difficult to understand because Brian has always been careful not to let anyone into his heart. It amazes me to hear this now. Do you think I should call him and try to talk to him?"

"I don't know if that would do any good at this point. I think I've given him enough food for thought. I wanted to let him know that we know what's going on, but that we want to hear it from him."

"I realize that, and it makes a lot of sense. But this woman is married, and to not such a nice man! What can *she* be like? I'm worried about Brian for the type of woman he may be getting himself involved with – or maybe he's already too involved with her? What do you think, Alec?" Alec's words danced around in her head. Alicea was mortified at the thought of Brian making a big mistake and throwing his life away. She remembered her own first marriage and how unhappy she had been, except for the boys.

"I don't know, Alicea. I know that we cannot push Brian or we'll end up pushing him further away." They finished dinner, each deep in thought about what all of this meant for Brian and his future. After dinner, Alec went to make a few phone calls. He was scheduled to fly out that night for a meeting but called the pilot to let him know he was postponing until the morning. The very next call was to Leo Martucci. He had a bit of a different assignment for him now.

"Hello, Martucci at your service."

"Hello, Leo. It's Alec Hargrove. I need you to do some more investigative work for me. I want you to look into the background of Mrs. Heather Langdon. I want you to get me everything you can on her. I realize it may take some time, so just be in touch with me.

"That's no problem, sir. I'll try to find out whatever I can."

Alec hung up and suddenly realized how tired he was. He decided not to make any other calls until the next day. He could think of nothing better than getting upstairs and holding the woman he loved. And there she was as he entered their massive bedroom suite. He could see Alicea lying across the bed waiting for him to come up. With her hair loose and flowing down around her shoulders, she was wrapped up in the sheets. He walked over to her and engulfed her in his arms. He felt he was the most fortunate man in the world to have a woman like this, and he showed her how much he loved and needed her. After, they nestled in each other's arms until they fell asleep.

Chapter Twenty-Three

$\mathcal{T}$he weekend brought John's parents to the hospital to see Heather. They arrived just as Stein was helping the nurse get Heather out of bed. Meredith Langdon walked right into the room and lashed out, "Well, Heather; I'm glad you're up and about, because I have quite a message for you. Why don't you two step outside for a moment?"

Stein turned to face Meredith Langdon with a questioning look. He wasn't sure who these people were. He stood up and extended his hand to the Langdons and said, "Good morning. My name is Dr. Stein. May I help you?" He waited for a response from either of them, and finally Tom Langdon spoke.

"Hello, there, Doctor. I'm Tom Langdon and this is my wife, Meredith. We wanted to stop by and see how Heather is coming along. We meant to get here earlier, but our son was put in Hillsworth and we've been over there trying to get him out of that place." Tom stared at Heather, wondering what was wrong with her and why she hadn't even greeted them at all.

"Yes, you heard what my husband said. Our son is suffering because of that lump of crap and I've come to tell her just what I think of her."

Stein was expecting anything from this woman and his guard was up. "Yes. Well, I'm Mrs. Langdon's psychiatrist and this is her private-duty nurse, Stella. As you can see, and I know it must come as a shock to you, Heather has had such trauma that she has been unable to cope; she appears to have withdrawn from life. But it's good to have someone she knows speak to her. In fact, why don't you two visit and I'll be at the viewing station, just outside the door, if you have any questions." Stein felt this might be an interesting visit. He wanted to go into more detail, but he could see that they weren't really interested in what Heather's condition was. They came for their own reasons. Stein turned to walk toward the door as Meredith spoke up.

"Well, what good is it going to do if we talk to her and she sits there staring into space? We need to speak with her about our son. That's why we're here."

Stein could feel this woman's coldness. Apparently they had no interest in Heather whatsoever. This might be the provocation Heather needed to stimulate a response.

But Meredith was not done with the doctor yet. "You see, if our son hadn't married this poor excuse for a woman, he wouldn't be where he is today. He doesn't belong at that place. This is *her* fault." She pointed to Heather.

"I see. Mrs. Langdon, if you don't have any interest in Heather, I must strongly suggest that you leave. Heather needs to be surrounded by people who love and support her. She doesn't need anyone else's anger . . ." Stein was finishing his sentence when he heard moaning from Heather. In disbelief he rushed to Heather and held her arm. He decided to try and provoke Mrs. Langdon a bit to see if he could get more of a reaction from Heather. "You see, Mrs. Langdon, there is a reason Heather ended up in this hospital to begin with. She didn't walk in the door with no place else to go. She was brought here in critical condition, a condition that was brought about by an assault – by her husband." Melodramatically, Meredith Langdon put her hand to her chest.

"Well, that may be your side of the story, but I'm sure there is more to this than meets the eye. My son would never strike a woman, no less his own wife." Once again, Heather moaned. Stein gently held her shoulder while Stella, on the other side of the bed, stroked her head. The moans were as if Heather were trying to speak. Stein took her pulse and respiration; each was racing. This couple had somehow reached Heather. She was still not ready to speak but she was surely communicating in the only way she was capable of at the moment.

Stein continued, "Surely you must understand the trauma that this woman has been faced with?" Mr. Langdon spoke this time.

"Of course we do. You must forgive my wife, Dr. Stein. She has only one thing on her mind." Meredith Langdon could not control herself and jumped into the conversation with both feet.

"That's right! I do have one thing on my mind, and that is getting this woman out of my son's life so that he can live normally!"

"Well, Mrs. Langdon, then maybe it wouldn't be such a bad idea for us to sit down privately and discuss just how badly Heather has behaved toward your son. Maybe you can shed some light on all Heather's bad behavior patterns." Mrs. Langdon stepped back in shock that this doctor would dare confront her. She knew deep down that she was wrong, and she was absolutely mortified at coming to the hospital to face Heather and then seeing with her own eyes what her son had done. But she would never let anyone else know that.

"You're the professional, Doctor. I'll leave that to you. But I will see to it that after John's sixty days in Hillsworth, he will never set eyes on this woman again! In fact, I'm going to contact a lawyer for him to start divorce proceedings." Once again, Heather moaned. Stella comforted her as best she could.

Stein now understood why Heather had the problems she had. Just from speaking to the Langdons, he had learned a great deal about John. Now, if he could only get a few more pieces of the puzzle to Heather's past to find out why she ended up in this situation to begin with.

Heather sat quietly, but Stein noted that tears were coming from both eyes. Stella was gently rubbing Heather's forehead and patting the tears from her face. Stein spoke softly to Heather, "Don't worry, Heather. I'm here with you and I'll protect you, as your doctor, to make sure that you are going to make a complete recovery."

"I think it would be best if we leave her for the moment." Stein said to the Langdons. "I think she's had enough stimulation from your visit. I would like to sit down with you both and discuss Heather and John."

"Not on your life, Doctor! Exactly what part of my comments did you *not* understand?" Mrs. Langdon seemed to be threatened by Stein and wanted to make sure that he understood that they wanted no part of him. "I have had enough. I am only concerned with getting my son out of that place and making sure that he never sees this woman again!" And with that, she turned and stormed out the door. Mr. Langdon looked over at Stein, shrugged his shoulders and followed his wife. Well, he certainly had learned a lot about John's side of the family today. He didn't think this marriage had a chance anyway, but that had to be Heather's decision. And that was down the road. Right now, she had her hands full and that was all he was concerned about.

Chapter Twenty-four

The realtor called Brian's lawyer, setting a closing date for Tuesday. Brian was pleased that the deal was arranged so quickly. He was paying cash for the house so he wouldn't have to wait for the mortgage papers. He wanted the deal pushed through; so far, everyone was cooperating. He never dreamed that he would have the house in less than a week. But he wouldn't have the house fully furnished. He would shop with Heather and she could buy whatever she wanted. He sat back as he imagined that day. He wanted to be close to her. He wanted to do this for her. He wanted her to like him. He knew that he loved her but also knew she would never love him. But he was willing to settle for her liking him enough to spend time with him.

His thoughts drifted to the day he would see Heather in the hospital. Maybe Alec was right. Maybe it was time to see Heather and talk to this Dr. Stein. It was Sunday and the hospital wouldn't be that busy. He fought with himself until he decided that he would take the leap and visit Heather. It was eleven now; he could be at the hospital by one. As he prepared for his shower, he felt his excitement build at the thought of seeing her.

* * *

Dr. Stein filled Tracey and Vito in on the Langdons' visit and Heather's reaction. The couple explained how John's parents had treated Heather so poorly. To Meredith, John was the only thing in the world: no woman could be good enough for him and he could do no wrong. She could be vicious, and had been on several occasions when Heather had gone to John's parents for help and support for their son. Even then, Meredith blamed everything on Heather. She explained further that one of the last times Heather had spoken to John's mother she had slammed the door in Heather's face. Tom was quiet; he never had much to say. But it was well-noted that he would never go against his wife.

Stein explained to them that he had been elated when he walked into Heather's room this morning. She was moving her eyes. She still seemed to be asleep with her eyes open, but they were moving. He tried not to be too optimistic because she could stay that way for a long time. But it was progress and seeing John's parents had helped to provoke this new development. He thought Heather's moans could be expressions of anger, and that moaning wordlessly was the only way she felt safe enough and capable of communicating. Yes, he thought, she was making progress.

Tracey walked over to the chair, said hello to Stella, and kissed Heather on the cheek. "Hi there, Toots, I'm here again. I bet you thought you were rid of me on Friday, right? Well, think again, honey. I'm back to bother you. It's beautiful out there today, Heather. The sun is out and the air feels so good. I wish you could come for a walk with me. The fresh air would do you good. Maybe soon." She patted Heather's arm and then started to tell her about the boys and what they were up to. She knew how much Heather enjoyed them. But nothing she said caused Heather to react. She was disappointed.

Stein stepped out of the room into the viewing station. It had become his second home, but he didn't want to miss anything. His wife teased him and told him that he was on a mission. She was probably right.

The Perillis' visit was uneventful. They stayed for about two hours and spoke with Stein on their way out. Tracey was dumbfounded by Heather's condition. She hated all those tubes. But Dr. Holden said that she was healing well and the tubes would be coming out within a couple of days.

Josh looked out the window; what a beautiful day. The weatherman was forecasting a Nor'easter by Thursday. He was thinking of staying at the hospital if it snowed. He didn't want to be separated from this patient for any long period of time.

Brian took the elevator up to the twelfth floor. He was nervous about seeing Heather. Dr. Stein was at the desk when Brian stopped and asked the nurse what room Mrs. Langdon was in. Dr. Stein stood and extended his hand.

"Hi, I'm Dr. Josh Stein, Mrs. Langdon's psychiatrist."

"Brian Hargrove. Glad to meet you. I have heard a great deal about the work you're doing with Heather."

Stein had met the Hargroves on several different occasions. He knew they were big contributors to the hospital and many other community causes. But what was Brian's connection to Heather?

Brian continued, "I wanted to stop by and see how Mrs. Langdon is doing. Of course, you know that her husband worked for Hargrove Electronics. He had just taken a transfer to Manhattan Headquarters and I had offered Mrs. Langdon a job as an administrative assistant. She was reluctant, but I wanted her to seriously think about it. I must tell you that her husband no longer has a job with Hargrove Electronics. His behavior and his failing to report to work without any notification after several days are grounds for automatic dismissal." Stein listened carefully; what were Brian's motives for disclosing all this unsolicited information? Why was he here and why was he taking such an interest in Heather?

"So, how is she doing, Josh – if I may call you Josh?"

"I prefer that, Brian. Up here we have close dealings with family members and friends and it seems less threatening on a first-name basis. As for Heather, I don't know how much you do know, but her condition remains, for the most part, unchanged. Her expression remains fixed and blank." He looked pensive for a moment and turned back to Brian. "Sorry, had a thought there for a moment. Did you want to see her?"

"Uh, yes," Brian replied, almost laughing to himself at how uncomfortable he felt. Stein picked up on Brian's apprehension.

"I want you to be prepared to see a woman different from the one you offered that job to. Although she is still the same person inside, you are only seeing the outer protective shell at the moment. Now, if you like, you can stand at this viewing station and look in on her if you are not quite sure you want to go into the room. How do you feel about this?"

Brian was speechless. He was not prepared to see Heather any other way than the way he knew and remembered her. They walked to the viewing station. Heather sat motionless in a chair with the private-duty nurse next to her. The nurse had a magazine in Heather's lap and was turning the pages for Heather and talking about what was on each page. Shocked, Brian grabbed hold of the window frame, fighting to catch his breath. He could feel himself breaking into a sweat. He didn't know what was wrong with him and if he was feeling this way because it was such a shock or because of the anger in him for what had happened to her. He fought to keep himself under control and for words to answer.

"No, I think I would rather see her from here. I don't want to intrude on her privacy at this stage." He was overwhelmed at her appearance and it took everything he had not to show what he was feeling. But Stein could see from Brian's stance, braced against the viewing window frame, his knuckles white and tight, he was trying to hide the fact that there was a lot more emotion here than he was willing to show.

"Okay, that's up to you. If you have any questions, stop by the desk before you leave. I need as much background information as possible in order to help this woman. She has had an awful time of it and her nightmare is not yet over. So the more information I can get about her, the better." Stein left Brian struggling with his emotions.

"I see," Brian managed. "Thanks, Josh. I'll probably stop by on the way out," he added. Brian didn't know what to think. His eyes were riveted to her image of stillness. He watched Heather intently; waiting to catch her in a sudden unexpected movement. He wanted to see her smile that beautiful smile of hers. He wondered how long she was going to be this way. He knew there was no way that he could help her because he didn't know anything about her background. In fact, he knew little about Heather at all. He stood there for about an hour before he even had the thought to leave. He hated to leave her. She looked so vulnerable sitting there, unable to do anything for herself. He concentrated on her being until it became so painful that he had to turn away to leave. He would have to make an agreement with Josh to keep him posted on her progress.

He joined Stein at the front desk and asked if he could speak to him privately. Stein took him to the small waiting area, which was empty. Brian was fighting with himself; should he open up to Stein? Was it safe? Definitely not! But maybe he needed to risk opening up a little bit in order to get Stein to share information with him on a regular basis. Before he knew it, he was talking to Stein without further heed.

"Josh, I want to let you know that I am the one who is paying for Heather's care and for the private-duty nurses. I had spoken with Ralph Duprey when she was admitted to make sure that Heather would not want for anything. Is there any-thing else I can do to help her in her recovery?"

"No, I don't think so," Stein replied. He wondered what else, if anything, Hargrove would reveal now. He had already learned that this man was extremely cautious.

Brian looked at the psychiatrist for a moment, then added, "I would appreciate it if you would keep me posted every couple of days on how she is doing."

"I guess I can do that. After all, you are assuming all the medical expenses. But is there something more you would like to share with me, Brian?" Stein returned Brian's regard gently.

"No, I don't think so." Brian wasn't about to let his guard down. "But I appreciate your efforts to keep me informed. In the meantime, if there's anything she needs, please do not hesitate to call me." Brian handed his card to the psychiatrist. Then, "How long do you think she'll be in the hospital?"

Stein studied the card and carefully answered, "That is difficult to say, Brian. At this moment, the surgeon feels that she will be physically ready to go home in about five days but, of course, we will be keeping her longer because of her emotional condition."

"I see. Well, I want to know if there are any changes in her whatsoever." Brian perfunctorily shook Stein's hand and was out the door.

To see Heather like that was more than he could deal with. He was shaken to the core. He was surprised with himself that he had told the doctor as much as he did. He thought about it and realized that Heather meant so much to him that he wouldn't hold anything back that might jeopardize her recovery. He decided to take a ride out to the house – to Heather's new house. He had a camera in the car; he would take pictures so he could show her when the time was right.

Chapter Twenty-five

$\mathcal{M}$eredith Langdon was beside herself. She couldn't believe the rudeness of that doctor! She did not see that any of this was his concern anyway. She wanted to get John moved out of that house. She fixed herself a cup of coffee and sat down in the small kitchen trying to think what she should do next. She could take the dog over to her daughter, Mindy. But she needed help emptying John's belongings out of the house. She needed to contact an attorney. But for now, she decided to call Mindy because it was only Sunday and she would have to wait for a weekday to call a lawyer. Mindy answered the phone.

"Hi, Mom. I thought it might be you. How did your visit go over at the hospital? Was Heather in good spirits?"

"Mindy, that doctor is mean. He tried to get me and your father to say bad things about your brother. Can you imagine?"

"Mom, I told you to stay out of it. You're going to do no good going on the way you do. John is in that place right now and there is nothing you can do about it. You know that and yet you insist on trying to get him out. Apparently things must have happened that you don't want to hear about." Mindy had always liked Heather, and they had had some good times together. But Meredith Langdon had quite a hold on both of her children.

"Now, you listen here, Mindy. John does not belong with that woman and he never has. Why do you think he was never home? He didn't want to be with her! So, I've been thinking about it and I think that we should move out all of his belongings, now! I have decided to call a lawyer so that he can be in touch with John at that place."

"Mom, you're not listening to me. Stay out of it. What is it that you think you can do? What exactly is it that you are trying to accomplish?"

"I am trying to protect my son. It is not fair what has happened to him. But that's not what's most important right now: getting him out of that house is. Now, are you going to help me or not?"

"Mom, I don't want to do this. I don't think it's right." Mindy tried to make her mother see reality, but with no real expectation at success. It was no use trying to argue with Meredith Langdon. Mindy learned that a long time ago. She not only had to have the last word but she had to win, at whatever cost!

"What do you mean it's not right? How can you say that? This way, when John gets out he'll be coming home. That's what's important. The sooner we get started, the sooner we'll be done. So will you help me and your father?"

"Well, I guess I will but we're going to need the truck. I'll have to ask Alan for it. He's not going to like this one bit." Mindy felt like she'd sold out.

"There's nothing we can do about that, is there? Why don't you call me back and let's plan to start tomorrow." Mindy agreed and hung up. She called her mother back later that evening to let her know that she had the truck and she would meet her and Dad at the house at eleven o'clock. Meredith was satisfied. For the first time since this whole mess began, she felt like she was getting somewhere.

The Perilli couple had arrived at Heather's house around a quarter to eleven. They had planned to spend some time with the dog, check the phone for messages and check the mail, which was certainly piling up. They were outside in the backyard playing with the dog when Meredith, Mindy and Tom showed up. The Langdons had seen the couple's car when they pulled up, so they walked right into the house and looked out the back door into the backyard. Meredith was already huffy and puffy and ready for a confrontation with them. She stuck her head outside and said a challenging hello. Tracey and Vito looked at each other and cautiously went into the house. Meredith started immediately.

"I'm glad that you both are here so that you know what is going on. Mindy is going to be taking the dog home with her."

"Oh, that's great, Mrs. Langdon. Of course, Tracey and I don't mind at all watching over the dog and the house for Heather."

"Well, also while we're here, we are going to be moving John's belongings out of the house."

Tracey and Vito looked at each other and then back at Meredith. "Why are you doing that? Heather will be home soon, we hope, and John is going to be gone for sixty days. Don't you think it should be their decision what they want to do?"

"Under normal circumstances, maybe. But I feel it's best this way, and that's the way it's going to be. Now, I know that you are good friends to both my son and to Heather, but I am John's mother and I have to do what is right for him."

"Did you speak to John about this? Maybe someone should," offered Vito. This woman definitely had a way of irritating people.

"This is no concern of yours. You can continue to watch after Heather and I will take care of my son. Now is that a problem?"

Tracey and Vito again exchanged glances and shrugged their shoulders. After all, what could they say? It wasn't their home or their lives; they weren't even family. They loved Heather and John and wanted to see that they could make their own decisions and not have someone else doing it for them, but this was out of their hands.

Vito asked, "Do you want us to keep looking after the house?"

"Yes, I think that's a good idea. After all, I'm sure the house will have to go on the market before too long."

"Okay, sure, we have no problem doing that. But I still think that John should know what's going on here," Vito tried again.

Mrs. Langdon bridled and lowered her head, regarding Vito from beneath threatening brows. "Look, I thought I made myself perfectly clear. Don't you dare go near my son and start to poison him with visions of that woman in the hospital. Do you hear me?" Vito shook his head and decided it wasn't worth it to say another word to her. He would have loved to kick her out of the house, but he knew he had no right. So he and Tracey left without saying another thing. Vito wanted to get out of there before anything else could be said or before he said something that he would regret. But Meredith had to have the last word, and she yelled out the door, "And don't go telling that bitch everything, either! She's getting exactly what she deserves!" Then she slammed the door shut.

On the way to the hospital, they discussed what they should do. Vito realized that he had never had the chance to check the answering machine. He figured they'd stop on the way home. They hadn't checked it since that first day.

Vito thought they should talk with Dr. Stein and let him know what was going on behind the scenes. Maybe Dr. Stein would be able to speak to the counselor at Hillsworth and tell John about it. They knew there wasn't much they could do, but they didn't feel what Meredith was doing was right and they didn't know how this would eventually affect Heather, either. Tracey stared out the window of the car and thought about how miserable John's mother was. How could anyone be so cruel? She had marched right in and taken over the entire situation with no thought about Heather – or even about her own son's wishes. She did not want to get in the middle of this, but they knew they had to tell the doctor. Vito suggested they stop at the diner before heading up to the hospital.

When they arrived, Dr. Stein was in his usual position seated next to Heather. He got up when he saw them come in.

"I'm glad to see the two of you today. How is everything?"

"Okay, Dr. Stein. How is Heather today?"

"The same. There's no change, I'm sorry to say."

"Well, do you think we can talk to you outside for a minute?"

"Sure thing. Let's step outside right now." The concerned couple followed Stein into the hallway. He turned to them. "So, what's up?"

Tracey and Vito started to talk at the same time. Tracey backed down so Vito could continue. He filled the physician in on their confrontation with Meredith Langdon. Dr. Stein listened intently as Vito relayed the details.

"Well, thank you for sharing this information with me. I need as clear a picture as possible about the present because, once Heather is ready, it will be my job to help prepare her for what she is going to face. I have also found out that John no longer has a job."

"You mean John's been fired?" Vito asked incredulously.

"Yes. So there is no income at the present time for either."

"What can we do?"

"I'm not sure at the moment. I have no idea what their financial situation is, but someone must know. Let's take it one step at a time. Let me think about this and I'll let you know if I come up with any ideas. By the way, you wouldn't happen to know the name of the Hilton's attorney, would you?" Tracey and Vito looked at each other and shook their heads no. Stein was thinking of getting in touch with Brian since he was handling Heather's medical bills. He wasn't sure what Brian's intentions were and what his connection was with Heather. Although he had told Stein about offering Heather a job, he also appeared somewhat evasive, and Stein felt there was a lot hidden between the lines.

Tracey and Vito spent their usual two hours with Heather. They discussed the possibility of bringing up lunch the next time they came up. Vito teased Heather about tantalizing her taste buds. "After all," Tracey added, "they still have to be in there somewhere."

Chapter Twenty-six

$\mathscr{B}$rian decided to stop off and see his mother since Alec was out of town until Wednesday. Besides, after seeing Heather at the hospital, he somehow needed to see his mother. She was on the veranda getting ready to have tea. She jumped up when she saw her son and gave him a big hug.

"Brian, darling, I am so glad to see you. Are you hungry? Why don't you sit down and keep me company?"

"Sure, Mom. Now that you mention it, I guess I am kind of hungry." The housekeeper placed a setting for him at the table and left the room to get the lunch.

"So, dear, tell me, how are you?"

"I'm okay, Mother." She looked at him closely. He sure didn't look like he was okay; in fact, he looked down in the dumps. She thought about what Alec had told her but she wasn't quite sure whether she should bring up the subject.

"Is there something specific you have on your mind, Brian? You know, I am your mother, you can talk to me about anything, dear."

Brian wasn't sure what he wanted to say, but he knew he was with his mother for a reason. Before he knew it, he was telling her that he had just come from the hospital. She put her hand on his as if she understood what he was feeling, but that made him uncomfortable. After all, he didn't know if Alec had told his mother everything.

"Mom, I don't know how to help her. You see, I don't know her that well. I had offered her a job as my administrative assistant. She didn't want to take it and I told her to think it over. She has a horrible marriage but she has stayed faithful to it. I don't know how anyone so special could get hooked up with someone so evil. She is *very* special, Mother. I know that she could probably never love me, but I want her to like me and to be my friend."

Alicea listened to Brian. He sounded like the little boy that she remembered when he would come into the house and pour his heart out to her about this or that. She was pleased that he was talking to her. It was something that Brian wasn't very good at. So she let him continue without interruption. He told her how Heather had no family now and she was alone except for a couple of friends. While Brian talked on, Alicea realized how much in love Brian was. He was even willing to sacrifice being loved just to be near this woman. Brian broke down as he was relaying the story.

Alicea got up and put her arms around Brian. She told him that everything would be all right. She reminded him that this woman had the best working with her. Brian calmed down. Sniffling, dazed, he could not believe he had told his mother everything. In a way, it was a relief to tell her about it. She never judged him or tried to talk him into anything. She listened and comforted and then would always ask him what he felt. She never made demands of him and never tried to make him change. That was one of the reasons he loved her so much. He smiled at her.

"Thanks, Mother, for listening. It means the world to me.

I didn't intend to blurt out my story to you like that; it just came out."

"Well, Brian, what are you going to do next?"

"I wasn't going to tell you this, but I bought Heather a house. I'm closing on it on Thursday. I bought it for her in her name. You must think I'm crazy because I never spend my money at all, much less on someone else. But mother, I had to do something for her."

Alicea sat still and listened. She was shocked but tried not to show it. She could not believe that Brian had bought this woman a home. Surely, Alec knew nothing of this or he would have told her. She was worried for Brian, but she also realized that there was nothing she could say or do to persuade him to do differently. Any comment from her could very well push him away from her.

"What do you expect to do with this house, Brian?"

"You know, Mother, that's the strangest part. I don't even know. Of course I envision Heather living in it, but I'm not sure. At this point, they don't even know when she'll start to come out of this state she's in. Right now she's a wax statue that I really care about. You can't talk with her, you can only sit there and watch her, as still as can be. I have never wanted to do anything like this for anyone else in my life. Maybe I'm going crazy but I know one thing for sure: I find myself walking in unfamiliar territory, and yet I keep going as if I know what I'm doing. And as we all know, Mother, that is totally out of character for me. I can't seem to help myself." But as much as he talked, he could not find a sense of relief because he could never share with his mother the position he had placed Heather in.

"Brian, I wish there were some words of wisdom that I could tell you at this moment to help you through this, but I can only tell you to take it one step at a time. This woman – Heather is her name?" Brian nodded. "Well, Heather has quite a bumpy road to travel yet. Give it time and give her space as she gets better. Don't crowd her or try to push her into anything. Apparently, from what you've told me, she's going to have to learn to build trust in people and to start to feel secure in her life. That is not easy and cannot be done overnight."

Brian got up and went over to his mother, put his arms around her and hugged her tight. "Thanks for being there for me, Mother." Alicea was touched beyond words and could only manage gently patting his hand over hers. They finished eating and went outside into the gardens. As they strolled arm-in-arm, Alicea filled Brian in on what was going on with his brothers. Brian realized that he had been so busy lately he had neglected everyone. He had never been close to any of them, but he did keep in touch and they all got along fairly well.

He left the house feeling somewhat better; he was happy that he had told his mother everything . . . almost. He thought that it was stupid of him to have been so secretive in the first place. But the way he had treated Heather, backing her into a corner, bothered him. It was on his mind constantly. He still felt he might have been the cause of the beating she had received. He tried to brush the feelings aside and stay in the relief of the moment. He arrived home more relaxed than he had felt in over a week. But he left his mother in a state of shock and horror. She had no doubt that Brian was head over heels in love with this woman. So much so, in fact, he had become humbled . . .! But not for long. She knew her son well and that's what scared her.

*   *   *

Leo Martucci was busy trying to get a trail on Heather. It was difficult because he needed to gain access into the Hilton residence. He had been out to the house and checked the neighborhood. It was an exclusive area and many of the homes were far apart and gated. He came in the dark to break into a back window where no one would see him. Once he was inside the house, he searched for some paperwork, anything. He wasn't sure what he was looking for. He found picture albums and sat down on the sofa to look for pictures of Heather. He took several pictures from several different stages of her life. He found it strange that they began at age five; it said so on the back of the pictures. In fact, the back of the first picture he pulled out read, "Heather arrives at our home and joins our family." There were no earlier pictures anywhere. He decided to check the bedrooms.

The first bedroom he looked in must have been Heather's; it was decorated in pink and lace. He walked around the room and looked at the pictures from her school years. There was a bulletin board filled with pictures from France.

He left her room and found the master bedroom. In it was a small office area with a roll top desk. He hoped it wasn't locked; it wasn't. He rolled back the top. There were papers in each of several compartments. There were as many drawers which he opened and scanned through. One was filled with drawings from Heather's childhood. The next was filled with bills and miscellaneous documents. The third drawer was locked. He looked around for a key but there were none in sight. He hadn't brought his master keys but he didn't want to break the lock or damage the wood. He decided that he would have to come back. He certainly found it strange that there were no baby pictures. There didn't seem to be anything he could find about Heather before that first picture. He would keep the pictures and not even mention them to Alec Hargrove until he could find an answer. He placed a piece of clear plastic in the window he had broken so nothing would look disturbed and he cleaned up the glass. He looked back to make sure everything was okay and then calmly and casually took off down the road to where he had left his vehicle. He was anxious to get out of there before anyone saw him. It was already three o'clock in the morning and he wanted to get home and get a couple hours sleep before he started his day.

Meredith Langdon was waiting for Mindy to pick her up in the truck. Alan had agreed to let them have the truck all week, so Mindy would routinely pick up her mother and they would head out to the house to do more packing. It was Wednesday morning already and there was a big storm coming on Thursday.

Meredith felt she was racing the clock. She wanted to get John's belongings out of that house as quickly as possible. It wasn't as if John would come home or that Heather was going to be discharged. She was just determined that this be done quickly. She fretted, wondering what was taking Mindy so long!

Finally Mindy pulled up in the pickup and Meredith got in. Tom was not going over with them today. He knew his wife and he knew there was nothing he could do to deter her but he felt bad about what she was doing. He just did not feel like being a part of her crazy venture today.

They had packed all of John's clothing from the drawers as well as the closet, and all of it was sitting in John's bedroom in their apartment. Now they were going to pack up all of his tools, stereo equipment, records and anything else that Meredith decided to claim as his. She shut the answering machine off, unplugged it and put it into a box. She didn't care if John couldn't even walk into his own room as long as all of his stuff was there. Meredith had stayed true to her word and called a lawyer on Tuesday. She contacted Andrew Price, the lawyer that was representing John, and explained why she had called and John's present condition at Hillsworth. She told him that she wanted him to go to there to speak with him. Price was reluctant, but Meredith pleaded with him. She told him that John would want to get this divorce over quickly if someone just confronted him with it. Price finally agreed and told her that he would be out there to see John on the following Monday. Meredith felt satisfied; she was determined and felt that unless she did it herself, it wouldn't get done.

They had so much stuff that they ended up making two trips back to the house. Meredith had decided to take the television, dishes and kitchenware as well as the sofa. She justified her actions by telling herself that they were by right John's as the husband and head of the household, and that he would be able to use them at their apartment. They needed a new sofa anyway. She figured that they would need to go back to the house at least one more time to pick up any other items she felt John would need. The house looked pretty empty.

* * *

At Hillsworth, John was not making any progress. He was belligerent and wouldn't speak to any of the counselors. When he did speak out in a session with his counselor, Bobby Brighton, he explained that it was his mother who was trying to do everything for him and his wife was still not trying to do anything to help him. He was furious when Brighton gave him the envelope that his mother had left for him from Hargrove. He had lost his job. Now, how could that possibly be his fault? He had worked there for fourteen years. It was that bitch's fault because she should have called them and told them he wouldn't be in. He still couldn't remember anything that happened the night he was arrested. The counselors told him he probably wouldn't.

He was in denial about his wife's condition and how she got that way. He refused to understand that she was in the hospital.

He was enraged at her. Brighton tried many times to explain the situation to him but John would not listen. He had closed his mind to everything and did not want to cooperate. Brighton explained that as long as John refused to open up to him and accept help, it could be the court's decision to extend his stay at Hillsworth. But all of Brighton's explanations did not seem to affect how John saw things. He was not willing to give even one inch. He was consumed by anger and hatred. Each day and each session brought the same reaction. He fought going to the mandatory meetings during the day and scoffed at the other participants every time he was forced to attend and listen to the different stories each speaker told. It didn't matter to John. No one seemed able to reach him.

John had made up his mind that he was not going to give in to what those sick bastards wanted him to do. He would continue to remain in a hell of his own making. He would only talk to one person, a woman. Suzy was about thirty years old, with blonde hair and brown eyes, and seemed a lot older than her years, probably due to her alcohol and drug abuse. They started to spend a lot of time together. But Suzy was no help to John, because her attitude was as bad as his. So they were miserable together. They were known as an item among the other clients, but no one wanted anything to do with them. John had gone as far as to tell Brighton, in session, that Suzy was the best thing that could've happened to him. He knew they were made for each other and would end up together once this terrible mess was all cleared up.

Chapter Twenty-seven

It was Thursday morning. The snow was already coming down. Visibility was poor because of the blowing winds. The snow was heavy and accumulating quickly. Carlton Marlo was sitting at his desk reviewing his mail and newspapers. He had been away for seven weeks on vacation and was trying to catch up. His secretary had cut out the article about the bus crash that listed all the victims. She had advised him during a telephone conversation about the Hiltons, who he had represented. He was shocked and, as he sat and reviewed the article, it wouldn't sink in that they were gone. He buzzed his secretary and told her to contact Heather Langdon immediately. The secretary explained that she had left a couple of messages on Mrs. Langdon's answering machine but she had not returned the calls. Marlo told her to try again. The secretary buzzed back and told him that there was no answer. He told her to keep trying but to put him in touch with the medical examiner's office.

"Mr. Marlo? I'm Peter Albright. I understand that you are calling about the Hiltons?"

"Yes, I'm their attorney. I've been in Australia for several weeks so I'm trying to catch up now."

"Well, I'm fortunate to be speaking to someone with authority." Albright let the story unfold.

"She's in the hospital? Do you know what's wrong with her? I have been trying to reach her this morning on the phone and I can't get hold of her. Did she identify the bodies? That poor girl, it must have been horrendous for her."

"It was a nasty scene, Mr. Marlo. But I must refer you over to Brookville Central Hospital. I don't know any details about her surgery or what happened to her, but I do know that her husband had been arrested the same night she was admitted to the hospital."

Carlton Marlo was beside himself. His clients' child was in trouble and he hadn't been there to help. He had to contact the hospital immediately and get in touch with Heather. "Do you know what room she's in? Oh, never mind, I'll just call the administrator's office. Thanks for the information. I'll let you know when the bodies will be picked up."

Marlo beeped his secretary and asked her to get him Ralph Duprey at Brookville Central Hospital and in the same breath told her to stop trying to contact Mrs. Langdon. Marlo was on the line as she signaled back to him. "Ralph I haven't spoken with you in some time. I just found out that two of my clients were killed in that bus crash and that their daughter is in your hospital."

"I don't believe this, Carl. I can't believe you're involved in this, also. Yes, Heather is here with us."

"Well, how's she doing? I think I had better get over there and talk with her. She must be very upset."

"Carl, it's worse than that. I won't fill you in on the details at the moment, but I will transfer you over to her physician. His name is Josh Stein and he is with her practically all the time; he's working with another psychiatrist, Abe Sutter, who oversees her care. Her surgeon is Bruce Holden. Don't feel bad, Carl. But I don'tt think that today is going to be the day for you to come here unless you want to end up spending the night."

"Yes. I guess you're right. But I must speak with Heather and make sure that she's all right."

"All right. I'll transfer you right now. If you want to talk with me after, ask Dr. Stein to transfer you right back."

"Thanks, Ralph." Marlo wondered why Ralph did not want to get into details of the case with him. How bad could it be? But he had no idea what was waiting for him as Stein picked up the phone.

"Dr. Stein, how can I help you?" Stein was wondering who was trying to reach him through Duprey's office.

"Yes, Dr. Stein, my name is Carlton Marlo. I am an attorney and I represent the Hiltons. I don't know if you are familiar with the name, but they were Heather Langdon's parents."

"Mr. Marlo, I am somewhat relieved that you have contacted me. Do you know what has been going on here?"

"No. I just got in from Australia late last night. My secretary had advised me prior to my trip home. I spoke with the medical examiner this morning, and Peter Albright told me that Heather was in the hospital. I then spoke with Duprey and he put me through to you. How is she doing? Can I speak with her?"

"Well, I'm sorry but you can't. Heather suffered a tremendous shock post-operatively." Carlton Marlo listened intently as Stein unfolded Heather's story.

"Oh, my God! What can I do to help?"

"Well, it might be helpful if you were able to fill us in on Heather's early history." Stein mentally crossed his fingers.

"I wish I could. I know that the Hiltons adopted her when she was about five. They went to some agency. I can't remember the name of it, but I can look it up in my records. I know it was in the city. They didn't know much at all. I can't believe this. I am in a state of shock. I'll make the arrangements for her parents and then I'll delve into the personal affairs to make sure everything is taken care of."

"I think that's best. Heather's husband was released from jail, but he came to the hospital and made a scene. Duprey offered him a chance at Hillsworth instead of jail. He took the rehab program for sixty days."

Marlo reeled from all that Stein relayed to him. He made notes of what had to be done as he was talking. He wasn't sure what he needed to do first. His office had already received telephone messages inquiring if there would be services for the Hiltons. He knew he had to contact Heather's husband. He thought about Langdon's parents and asked Stein, "Has anyone been in contact with Langdon's parents? Have they been up to see Heather?"

"Carlton, you don't even want to go there. They came up to the hospital to see Heather and to get rid of her. That woman is determined to get her son away from Heather. There's no talking to her. She has her mind set."

"I see." Carlton remembered the elder Langdons vaguely, but he had no reason to deal with them. "Thanks for filling me in."

"Oh, one more thing," Stein interjected. "I have been informed by Heather's friends that John's mother has contacted an attorney to try and get John to start divorce proceedings. She's already moved him out of their house."

Marlo sighed. "Okay, that's one more thing on my list. If you need me for anything until I can get up there, here's my number. By the way, does Heather need anything like private nurses or anything like that?"

"No, she already has them."

"She does? Do you know who made those arrangements?"

"Well, Langdon's employer is Hargrove Electronics; I'm sure you know that. Brian Hargrove is paying all of Heather's medical bills, including the private nursing services."

"Brian Hargrove? You mean Alec Hargrove's son?"

"Yes."

"Why would he do a thing like that?"

"I'm not sure. He came to see Heather and he explained to me that he had offered her a job at Hargrove since her husband had accepted a transfer to corporate headquarters in Manhattan. Heather will have to make up her mind once she's able to. As far as John goes, it's my understanding that he's been fired and notified in writing."

"Do you know who's taking care of their home at the present?"

"Yes, some good friends; Tracey and Vito Perilli. Uh, let me see. I have their number… ah, yes. Here it is." Stein ran off their address and telephone number. "I think it's a good idea that you contact this couple. They have been with Heather from the beginning of this fiasco. I'm sure they'll be able to help you. They were at the house when Langdon's mother came over to move everything out. I think you should know that, especially if you will be taking care of Heather's affairs."

"Thanks, Josh, for taking the time to fill me in. I surely have my work cut out for me. I'll be in touch. Please tell Heather, whether she can hear it or not, that I'm taking care of things and that she is not to worry about anything."

"I'll do that. Every bit helps. I trust you will come over to see her as soon as the weather permits and tell her this yourself?"

Stein was relieved that Carlton Marlo was in the picture now. Heather had someone backing her whom she knew well and who represented her family.

Chapter Twenty-eight

Stein met with Abe Sutter. They compared notes on Heather's condition and reviewed their plan of action. While they were in Sutter's office, the storm continued its rage; the lights flickered from the lightning. It was strange to see a blizzard and experience thunder and lightning.

The loudspeaker paged Sutter and Stein for an emergency code on the floor. They ran out of the office immediately. The nurses were at Heather's door with the cart ready. As the two doctors reached Heather's door, they could hear her screams. Heather was screaming, "Momma! Momma!" As they entered the room, she was sitting in the chair screaming, her arms flailing in front of her, her face flushed and her hair in complete disarray. A nurse was trying to comfort her but it was no use. She continued screaming, her arms striking out around her. Sutter turned, took Stella's elbow and gently backed her away as Stein tried to comfort and restrain Heather.

"What happened here?" Sutter demanded of the distraught nurse.

"Dr. Sutter, she was silent until the thunder and lightning got worse and all of a sudden she started screaming! We called for you immediately." Stella was trying to catch her breath.

Stein tried to get Heather's attention focused on him. He soothed in rational terms, trying to hold her arms and talking to the visibly distraught woman. "Heather, it's okay. You're in the hospital and you are safe. Dr. Sutter and I are here with you. You are all right. There's a big storm outside. You are safe." Stein kept repeating it and slowly Heather calmed down until she finally returned to her despondent state. She was perspiring profusely and the nurse automatically went to fill the basin to freshen her up.

Sutter and Stein did not want to sedate her. Instead they agreed on monitoring her closely. It took everyone a while to calm down. The doctors exchanged occasional glances while keeping their eyes on the patient. Once Heather seemed stable, everyone left the room except Stella. The doctors stepped around to the viewing station and discussed what had transpired.

"Abe, I don't think she was experiencing thoughts of her parents' death. I think there's something else locked up in there. What do you think?"

"I'm not quite sure. But I distinctly heard her scream out 'Momma.'"

"Yes, several times. That's why I thought about her parents. But it doesn't seem right, somehow. Why would she be throwing her arms up in the air and in front of her face?"

"Good point. Is it possible that she's reliving the abuse from her husband?"

"That's a possibility, but why would she call for her mother? Is it possible that the trauma brought back the accident where Heather's natural mother died?"

"Hmm . . . could Heather have been in the car with her mother?"

"You know, Abe, you might have something there. It definitely would explain the arm movements and her screaming out to her mother. But then there's also the possibility that she might have incidents mixed up in her mind at this point and she is thinking about her mother but could also be protecting herself from her husband."

"No, I don't think so. I think you had it right the first time. I don't feel she would mix up incidents in this state."

"Yes, I guess so. That makes a lot of sense. Remember how her friend stated that Heather was having nightmares and then they were reduced to a recurring dream? It is very possible that she *was* in that car with her mother but she was too young to be able to recall the accident. I wish we knew for sure. But we must consider it a distinct possibility."

"Well, Heather may have given us another piece to the puzzle. Thank you, Heather. You are doing better than you think you are," Sutter remarked, almost under his breath.

Tracey called the hospital to let Stein know that they weren't going to be able to visit, it was snowing so badly. Newscasters advised everyone to stay at home and it would not be long before a state of emergency would be declared. Then no one except the police, firemen and state workers would be allowed on the roads.

The ward clerk put the call through to Stein and Sutter's office.

"Hello, Tracey, I hope you're not going to try and venture out in this weather."

"That's why I'm calling. I wanted to know how Heather is. I know that I won't be able to come up, but I am worried about her."

"Everything's going to be all right. We did have a scare with Heather this morning." He explained Heather's outburst. "Now Tracey, is there anything else you can think of that she has said to lead you to believe that Heather may have been in that car with her mother?"

Tracey thought hard before answering, "No. She said she wished she could remember. But she did say that in her dream she heard a loud crashing noise and screams. She never knew if it was her screaming in her sleep or if it was part of the dream."

"That's worth noting. If you can think of anything else, please call me immediately. You know that we are doing everything possible to help Heather, but we know so little about her childhood. So please, no matter how trivial it seems, call me."

"I understand. I'll think about it and see if there's anything more she ever said to me in passing conversation. But you promise to call me if there are any changes?"

"Yes, I will." Stein relayed the little piece of information from Tracey to Sutter. An hour didn't go by before Stein had almost the same telephone conversation with Jenny. The doctor spent the rest of the day with Heather. He read articles to her about her condition so she would have an understanding of what happened to her, he looked through a magazine with her, he played cards with her. The storm continued on and off during the day. Heather had two more episodes that day. Each one occurred when there was lightning and thunder. He talked to Heather a lot, trying to reassure her and let her know that she wasn't alone. He talked to her about her mother's car accident. Stella worked along side the doctor, picking up cues from him and reinforcing what he had to say. Stein liked Stella. She was a compassionate person. She had volunteered to stay at the hospital with Heather and work a double shift to make sure she wouldn't be alone. She said it was easier for her because she wasn't married and didn't have to worry about getting home to kids or a husband. Besides, she told Stein, she felt close to Heather and wanted to be a part of her recovery. Stein trusted her nursing judgments and left her with Heather to get something to eat.

Chapter Twenty-nine

Alec arrived home late Wednesday night. He was tired from traveling and glad to have gotten home before the storm hit. Alicea had tried to wait up for him, but had fallen asleep reading a book in bed. He walked over to her side of the bed and gazed at her. She looked beautiful and was sleeping peacefully. How he wanted to take her in his arms and hold her. But he didn't want to wake her. He showered and got ready for bed. It had been a long day of traveling and he was weary and in need of feeling those covers over him.

Alicea awoke early the next morning realizing that her husband was next to her. She quietly slid off the bed so that she wouldn't disturb him. From the sitting room off the bedroom suite, she called downstairs to the housekeeper and ordered breakfast for the two of them to be served in their suite. She thought it would be fun since it was already snowing and it was warm and cozy. She walked back into the bedroom, sat down at her dressing table and started to brush her hair. Her thoughts wandered to the conversation she had with Brian at lunch. She had never dreamed that he could be so honest with her about what was going on in his life. This woman must be special to have stolen his heart the way she had. And she had believed him when he told her that nothing happened between them. She was relieved about that. She felt that affairs do not necessarily lead to a happy relationship. She had always hoped that Brian would find someone someday who would love him totally, as she loved Alec. As she brushed her hair she felt two strong arms gently embrace her from behind.

"Alec, darling. I missed you. Why didn't you wake me up when you arrived home last night?"

He grabbed her up into his arms and carried her over to the bed, "Later for talk, my love. I want to show you how much I love you and how much I have missed being near you."

"Why, Alec Hargrove, you wouldn't try to take advantage of a poor, lonely woman, would you?"

"No, I would never take advantage of a poor, lonely woman, but you, my dear, yes. The gorgeous and enchanting creature that you are makes it difficult for me to keep my hands off you." Alicea laughed as Alec muffled her with kisses and engulfed her in his love. They were in each other's arms when the housekeeper knocked on the sitting room door to announce that breakfast had arrived.

"Why, Alicea, you had breakfast brought up this morning. What a wonderful idea."

"Yes, it seemed so warm and cozy up here, and I didn't think you would be leaving the house today with the storm. So I thought it would be romantic to have a quiet and intimate little breakfast for two in our sitting room." Alicea got up, went to the sitting room poured two cups of coffee and brought them back into the bedroom.

"How was your trip home, darling?"

"I'd say it was rather bumpy and it was quite a relief to open that front door to our home. It was a long day of traveling,

Alicea, but well worth it. Was everything quiet here while I was gone?"

"Yes, it was, except I had a surprise visit from Brian."

By this time they had changed and were sitting at the table in the sitting room. The table was placed near a wall-to-wall atrium door. It was like sitting and watching a gigantic movie screen as they looked outside at the fierce, blizzard-like storm.

"Did Brian have anything to say?"

"Alec, I could not believe how much he had to say. He actually admitted to me that he was in love with this woman. He even admitted to me that he bought her a house."

"He did what?!" He did not want Alicea to know that he had been checking up on Brian, so the surprised tone was a necessary one.

Alicea explained further what Brian had said. Alec sat in complete silence as he listened to Alicea's tale unfold.

"He started to cry and said that he wanted to be able to help her. That he knew she would never love him, but he wanted her to like him and to like being around him. Isn't that very unlike Brian?"

"I'll say it is. This woman seems to have stolen his heart. I wonder how much time they've spent together."

"Well, I wondered that part, too, but Brian said that nothing had ever happened between them. You know, I was relieved to hear that. He said that Heather was faithful to her marriage. She was miserable, but faithful."

"Good heavens, what does he plan on doing with that house, then?"

"You know, he even admitted to me that he doesn't know. That's when I realized how much in love he is. Brian never does anything without a plan and he never spends money on anyone if he doesn't have to."

"Well, this is quite the story. I'm pleased that he came to

you and confided in you. You are his mother and it should be that way."

Alec almost told her about the private investigator he had working for him, but decided against it. He wondered if Martucci had come across anything new. He thought about Heather and wondered whether there were any changes in her condition. But it was just a matter of time before he would receive an update. Alec and Alicea enjoyed talking about the last couple of days apart as they finished breakfast.

Brian awakened early Thursday morning to attend the closing for the house. But when he looked outside and saw the storm he was disappointed because he knew the closing would be postponed. There was nothing he could do. He poured himself a cup of coffee, sat by the picture window and watched the fury of the storm. The snow was coming down hard; you could hardly see anything at times.

*   *   *

Carlton Marlo had his work cut out for him. He called the medical examiner's office and spoke with Albright again. The ME said he needed to have the bodies picked up as soon as possible, especially since an ID had already been made. Marlo called Lofton's Funeral Home and made the appropriate arrangements for the pick up, but he knew in this weather it wouldn't be before Monday. He quickly wrote an obituary and gave it to his secretary to fax over to the newspapers. He announced that visitation for Craig and Peggy Hilton would be on Tuesday, Wednesday and Thursday, with services on Friday morning, followed by burial at Hillcrest on Long Island. He hated to do this because he knew that Heather would want to be there more than anything, but he couldn't wait any longer. He dictated the completion of papers necessary for the burial, probate and reading of the wills. He knew from the preparation of the wills that Heather was the sole heir. She wouldn't have to worry about her budget anymore.

He had to make changes in his schedule so that he would be available to the funeral home. He was the only representative of the family. He would miss Peggy and Craig. They had shared a lot over the years. He called his wife at home and let her know and asked her to be with him during visitation and burial. She was upset over the news and affirmed she would do anything to help. He told her about Heather and everything that had happened to her. Louise wanted to be with Heather but because of the storm could not get to the hospital. Marlo told her to sit tight and as soon as he finished up the paperwork he was coming home because he didn't feel like spending the night at the office. Louise said she would call the florist and make all the arrangements for the flowers for them and for Heather. She said she would also set up the luncheon reception for Friday after the burial.

Marlo then called the Perillis. He introduced himself and asked them to brief him on what was going on. He told them he had already spoken with Dr. Stein and was aware of Heather's condition.

"Mr. Marlo, I'm glad you called." Vito said, genuinely relieved. "I didn't even think of the legal end of this mess. But things are becoming more complicated because John has lost his job and is in Hillsworth for sixty days. The mail is piling up. We had a confrontation with John's mother at the house because she emptied it out."

"What do you mean she emptied it out?"

"Well, we were there at the house when she first came and then yesterday as she was finishing up. We left to go to the hospital but when we came back even the answering machine was gone and I didn't even have a chance to check if there were any messages for Heather. I mean, the sofa is gone and, of course, anything that belonged to John is gone. But the dishes, silverware, television, stereo, bed. All the major stuff is gone."

"I see. When you said you had a confrontation with her what did she indicate she was doing?"

"She said she was making sure that John would never set eyes on Heather again. But without any income on both their parts, they will surely lose the house. We continue to check on the house. We were going daily because of the dog, but Mrs. Langdon also took the dog. So we go to pick up the mail and make sure everything is okay."

"Well, I must say Heather is fortunate to have the two of you."

"We love Heather and we will do anything to help her. My wife and I were upset with what was going on over at the house because it wasn't Mrs. Langdon's decision to make."

Marlo listened and tried to reassure Vito that Heather would no longer have any financial worries. He went over the arrangements he had made with the funeral home and asked if they could help out greeting visitors. He explained that he expected a large turn out because of the nature of the Hilton's business; they had been in the garment industry and knew a multitude of people. Vito assured him that they were available to help.

"By the way, do you know Heather's connection with Brian Hargrove?"

"No, none at all to my knowledge," Vito replied, puzzled.

"Okay, here's my number. Please call me at any time either at home or in the office. Of course I'm trying to get out of this office now before I get snowed in. Remember, please call me any time."

"We will, and thank you, Mr. Marlo, for calling and letting us know. Oh, what do you want me to do with the mail?"

"Uh, I think I had better get that from you. I'll call you when I plan to get over to the hospital to see Heather and maybe you can meet me. If not, I'll send a messenger service out to pick it up, but not before Monday."

Marlo felt better after he spoke with the Perillis. They sounded like a nice couple and he was pleased that someone had been looking out for Heather's interests. If they hadn't been there Heather would have been alone.

The storm continued throughout the day. It was still lightly snowing on Friday. Everything was snowed in. The news reported at least twenty-two inches of snow had fallen, but it was expected to be cleared by evening. Stein had remained true to his word and stayed at the hospital to be close to Heather. Brian was locked away in his condominium, dry and warm. John continued to be a problem at Hillsworth. It looked like no one was going to get anywhere until the road was plowed.

Marlo managed to drive to his office to check with his secretary and sign some papers, and then he was off to the hospital to see Heather. He had anticipated this visit since he first spoke with Stein. He could not imagine what he would find.

Even though Josh had explained it to him, when he saw Heather, his heart went out to her. He put his arms around her and rocked her gently, telling her everything would be all right. He found himself holding her and thinking of her as the little girl he used to know. He was devastated that there was no response from her at all. He found that difficult to accept. He explained to Stein that he was moving ahead and taking care of Heather's personal affairs. He advised the psychiatrist that he was on his way over to see John Langdon's counselor at Hillsworth.

Bobby Brighton was in the lobby when Marlo walked through the door. It was clear and sunny but very cold. Any snow that remained on the roads or sidewalks had turned to ice. He hoped that this was the last of the snow for this year.

"Mr. Marlo? I'm Bobby Brighton, John Langdon's counselor."

"Yes, how nice to meet you." As Marlo answered him, he heard a voice from behind.

"Carlton Marlo. I never expected to see you here."

"Why, Andy Price! I haven't seen you in a dog's age. How are you?"

"I'm doing all right. I'm here on business and I take it you are, too. I'm here to see John Langdon."

"Well, isn't that a coincidence. So am I."

"Really. I would take it that you are counsel for Langdon's wife, Heather?"

"Well, it all depends on what you mean. I was in Australia and just got back. I returned to find out that Mrs. Langdon's parents, my clients, were killed in that bus crash. I came to see John because there is no one else."

"I'm here to represent John in possible divorce proceedings against your client."

"Is that so? I didn't know Heather and John were getting divorced. Is this something that's been going on and you're following up on it?"

"Carl, I represented John when he was arrested recently. His mother insisted that he wants to get a divorce, and I am here to speak with him about it."

"That's interesting. I don't know what to say. I think the best thing to do is let you have your appointment with John and you can be in touch with me after."

"Well, considering the fact that we both don't know what is going on yet, that sounds fine to me. I'll buzz you later."

"Mr. Brighton, I will pick up on my appointment at another time and leave this time available for Mr. Price to speak with his client, unless you have anything you would like to discuss with me right now?"

"No, that will be fine. Thank you for coming, Mr. Marlo."

"Mr. Brighton, I'm Andy Price. I represent John Langdon. Do you have a couple of minutes for me before I see my client?"

"I was hoping you would ask." Brighton showed him to his office and asked him to sit down. "We're having a difficult time with John. He's getting nowhere fast and has become friendly with a female resident, who is not helping the situation. John's resisting treatment. He is bitterly angry and is furious with his wife. He refuses to believe that she is ill. At this point, I do not feel his decisions would be competent ones. I have even warned him that the court could extend his time if he doesn't start to get serious about his problem."

"I see. Well, I have to see John and be the judge of that. I am not here to see John about his court order to stay at Hillsworth. The courts will notify me of any action to be taken when the time comes. But that's not why I was retained. His mother has retained me to follow through with a divorce for John She said that he would want this. Until I speak with him, I will not know if this is true."

"Okay. Well, I tried to talk to John's mother while she was here, but she wouldn't listen. She is determined to get John away from his wife for good. But that will have to be John's decision. I told her as much, but she doesn't want to hear that. Why don't I go and get John for you? You can take a seat in that office directly across the hall from mine. It was nice to meet you and if you have any questions after your session with John, please come right into my office."

"Thank you." Andrew Price left Brighton's office and made himself comfortable in the office across the hall. In minutes John walked through the door. Andy could see from his appearance that this was going to be a difficult interview.

"Well, look what the cat dragged in. I thought that we were finished when I got out. Now I have to sit with you again. What is it this time?" Langdon plopped insolently into a chair across from Price.

"Hello, John. You look like you're doing all right. I came here because I had a discussion with your mother. She asked me to speak with you about your relationship with your wife."

"Oh, yeah, well fuck my wife! As far as I'm concerned that bitch can go to hell." Langdon snarled, his right index finger pointed and jabbing menacingly in Price's face.

"John. Why do you have to be so nasty? I'm trying to talk to you, to help you. Can't we have a decent conversation?"

"I guess we can't. So let's get to the bottom of this. What exactly do you want? Let's not beat around the bush. I'm living with enough bullshit already!" Langdon threw a hate-filled glance in the direction of Brighton's office.

"Okay. Your mother said that you would be interested in divorcing your wife. Is that the truth?" Price eased back in his chair, studying Langdon.

"What if it is? She's a worthless little whore anyway. I don't need her around me. She wants a divorce? Is that what this is all about? Well, fine, she can have a divorce! Just draw up the fuckin' papers and show me where to sign." Langdon's nose wrinkled and he trembled so much at the intensity of his declaration that his hair was shaking onto his angry forehead.

"John, is that what you want? I'm asking you. I am not trying to railroad you into anything."

"I don't give a shit." Langdon bolted forward toward Price. "I told you, just draw up the papers and I'll sign." Price kept his eyes on Langdon and nodded.

"If that's what you want, then, fine. But I am talking to you as your attorney, John. I want you to be sure of your decision."

"Yeah, well that's what I want. I don't need that bitch any-more. I found someone that knows just what I need!" Langdon sat back and folded his arms across his chest, his chin elevated smugly.

"Okay, John. I'll draw up the papers and have Heather served. But you know that she is incapable of answering at this time." He watched Langdon's face. Shrewd hatefulness set his eyes dancing. He felt he was getting the jump on Heather.

"I'm divorcing her. She isn't divorcing me. This is the perfect way for me to get rid of her!"

"So, your choice would be irreconcilable differences?" Price crossed his arms.

"Yeah, whatever you think. That sounds good to me." Langdon lost his intensity, looking away absently as he waved a hand in annoyance at Price.

"Well, that would be the least troublesome. Now, what about property?"

"We sell the house and split any money that we make on it." Langdon was ready with his answer, greed gleaming in his eyes.

"Okay. Now, I want you to know that your mother has already moved you out of the house, taking all your belongings...let me see my list here, the stereo, the television, kitchenware, sofa . . ."

"Good. I hope she fuckin' took everything. That bitch doesn't deserve shit from me!" Again Langdon sat back with his arms crossed in triumph and defiance.

"All right, John. I'll draw up the papers and file with the court and have Heather served. I'll be in touch with you in a few days, as soon as the papers are served." Langdon smirked at Price. He wouldn't even shake his hand, so Price left. He stopped off at Brighton's office.

"Mr. Brighton, do you have a minute?" Price walked into Brighton's office as he waved him in. "You were right. You can't talk to him. But he insists on starting divorce proceedings. So I have no choice but to do so. I'll have his wife served before the week is out."

"Wow. I have nothing to say. Langdon will have to live with the decisions he makes, good or bad. But maybe it's the best thing that could happen to her."

"Well, I wanted you to know what was going on," Price said. "He sure has a bad attitude, to say the least. I'll be in touch. Here's my card, in case you need to call me for anything." They shook hands and Price was off to his office. While driving, he called Carlton Marlo.

"Mr. Marlo's office. May I help you?"

"Yes. This is Andy Price for Carl. Is he in?"

"Is he expecting your call, Mr. Price?"

"I spoke with him earlier and told him if I had any information, I'd call."

"Hold on one moment and I'll connect you."

"Andy. How did your meeting go with your client?"

"Don't even ask. We do what we have to do. My client wants to divorce Heather. He is agreeable to irreconcilable differences. The only property he said they have is the house, so sell it and they will split any profit. He really wants this divorce."

"I will have to put in for power of attorney to represent Heather while she is unable to respond herself. But since Langdon is filing for divorce, there is nothing to be done. It's your ball game. What do you want me to do? Shall I call a realtor and put the house up for sale?"

"Sounds reasonable to me. You can fax me the information. Let's hope it's a quick sale and the divorce goes right through without a hitch. I guess I will have to serve the papers at the hospital?"

"Yes. I'll advise her physician so that he expects the papers this week. Thanks, Andy; be in touch." He hung up the phone and shook his head. It was probably the best thing that could happen to Heather, whether she was ready for it or not. He knew that her parents would have been elated that she would be free of Langdon shortly. But when she comes back to reality, she will have many changes to contend with. It was like sleeping for a long time and awakening to a whole new world. Well, no use prolonging it. He asked his secretary to get Dr. Josh Stein on the phone.

"Dr. Stein."

"Josh Stein, it's Carlton Marlo. How's it going?"

"Hi, Carlton. There's no change here. We've been working with her and her friends have been up here. She has another friend that works with her at the clinic. Her name is Jenny Trafarri. She's been here and we've been trying to provoke reactions from Heather; it's like she knows we want her to respond but won't because she isn't ready."

"Well, I have another development that you should be aware of. I spoke to Langdon's attorney, Andrew Price. He had an appointment to see Langdon, who is filing for divorce. Now he's planning to have Heather served at the hospital. When the papers are served, please call me and I will come down myself and pick them up. Also, the house is going up for sale. I'm calling the realtors to have them place it on the market. I'm tied up with the funeral but I have petitioned with the court for power of attorney while Heather is in this condition."

"Wow. You're certainly getting clobbered from all sides at once. I'll try to prepare Heather for what is going to happen, if that is at all possible."

"Okay, then. I had better go and get things moving along with the house." He hung up and spent the next half-hour on the phone with the realtor. They were going to call Vito and Tracey and make arrangements with them to meet at the house to review it and finalize a selling price.

Tracey was home when the realtor called and agreed to meet them at ten o'clock the next morning. When Vito came home she told him about the appointment. They both wondered where Heather was going to go after she was able to leave the hospital. It seemed so unfair. They would have loved to have Heather stay with them, but they had no room. Besides, Vito had been making plans to move the family south, possibly to Georgia. Tracey knew that Heather needed to start fresh with her own place. They thought she might take over her parents' home, but that remains to be seen. It looked like the most logical choice for the moment. They talked about the sale of the house and how much money Heather and John might realize from it. They finally talked themselves out and decided to wait until the next day to see what would happen.

Chapter Thirty

$\mathcal{L}$eo Martucci planned to return to the Hiltons' as soon as the weather permitted. He wanted to pull into the driveway without leaving any tire tracks. His vehicle was still in the shop being repaired so he was using a loaner from the dealership. He figured for sure that the driveway would have been plowed, and it was. He didn't have to break any glass because he had placed that hard plastic where he had broken the window the last time. He noted with amused alarm that someone had been in the house. The master bedroom was mussed, with clothes all over the bed. Since she didn't have any other family, it had probably been the daughter's attorney getting clothes for the funeral. The desk had been left open and the drawer that had been locked was slightly open. Well, he thought to himself, how lucky. If their attorney had been there, he hoped he hadn't taken any papers. He opened the drawer all the way.

It was filled with all kinds of documents. He noticed two Will envelopes, but the wills were gone. He sifted further through the drawer and found copies of the house deed and lots of insurance papers. At the bottom was an envelope marked "Adoption." He pulled it out and looked through it. There was an adoption certificate and several other court papers. He thought he had better take pictures of some of the documents and review them at home. He headed back to Heather's bedroom and took pictures of her walls and the bulletin board devoted to France. Guess everyone has a special place, he thought. He went back into the master bedroom to make sure he left everything exactly as he had found it. He thought about something else he had seen in Heather's room as he started for the back…a child's locket. He went back to get it then decided to take a picture of it instead. He snapped two close-ups and figured he would have a look once he blew them up. He placed the plastic back in the window pane and sealed it.

He was on his way home now before anyone noticed his vehicle. He was anxious to review his find of documents and the locket. Deep in thought about what he had found, he didn't see the car coming down the entrance ramp. He was able to swerve off the road, but rolled down the embankment and into a tree.

* * *

Carlton Marlo had to run in to the office Tuesday morning. He planned to stay two hours. That would give him time to change and get ready for the first day of visitation. While he was in his office dictating, his secretary buzzed him and announced that Alec Hargrove was on the phone for him. He quickly picked up the receiver, but answered conservatively.

"Alec Hargrove, it's been some time since I've heard from you. How are you?"

"Hello, Carlton. I'm doing all right. I guess I can't complain. Alicea and I have been traveling a lot. I saw the obituary in the newspaper and when I saw that you were the contact, I wanted to give you a call."

"Well, Louise and I just returned from Australia last week, you know, just in time for that wonderful blizzard. It's quite a shock coming from ninety degree weather to that. My secretary had buzzed me in Sydney and let me know about the Hiltons. I was, and still am, upset that I was not here for their daughter. She is having a rough time of it in the hospital."

"Yes, I know. I had lunch with Duprey the week before and he filled me in because Brian had taken a special interest in Heather."

"Yes, I mean to ask you about that. I spoke with Dr. Stein and he told me that Brian was paying all her medical expenses?"

"Yes, that's right. He felt bad because he had offered her a position with Hargrove as his administrative assistant the day she ended up in the hospital. He had told her to think about it because her husband had already accepted the transfer to headquarters."

"I see. Well, I don't know what to expect at this point. In fact, I have a couple of her friends going over to her home today to meet with a realtor to place the house on the market. Apparently, her husband is suing her for divorce. He is really something. And I know Peggy and Craig would have been thrilled that Heather will finally be free of him. They were upset when she married him and they continued to worry because of the way he treated her. But Heather wouldn't leave him because she felt it was her duty as a wife to stay with her husband and see the marriage through. Apparently, that was a while ago."

"Yes, I only witnessed his disorderly behavior at the last Christmas party when he created a disaster. There were portable bars knocked down and he started fights with everyone. I felt bad for her then, although I didn't know who she was. I never even knew she was the Hilton's daughter."

"Well, why would you? Your company is huge and you aren't involved in day to day anymore. Anyway, I hated to make the funeral arrangements while Heather was still in this state, but I have no choice. We could be looking at a long-term problem with her and this has to be done."

"Yes, that's a tough decision. I wouldn't want to be in your shoes right now."

"It's easier now that I have the power of attorney for her. In fact, it came in first thing this morning from the Court."

"Well, Carl, I don't want to hold you up because I know you have a lot on your plate, but I wanted to say hello and let you know that Alicea and I will be at Lofton's one of the three days."

"Thanks, Alec. I appreciate it and I know that Heather would appreciate it. I'll see you there and please keep in touch. Maybe the four of us can have dinner one night. It's been a long time. In fact, once this is over, I'll have Louise call Alicea and make arrangements."

"Sounds great. Take care, Carlton." Alec hung up the phone. He couldn't believe that the Hiltons were Heather's parents. He had showed Alicea the obituary when he saw it on Monday morning. It certainly is a small world, he thought. Well, at least Brian took interest in a female who had a good upbringing and came from a good family. Come to think of it, she wouldn't even need Brian to help her out anymore, if that were the case.

* * *

Brian sat reading the paper Monday morning and saw the obituary for Heather's parents. They were very well-known throughout the city and Europe, for that matter. Brian remembered the horrible experience of his own father's funeral. It had been so painful. But he had wanted to be there and he was always glad he had been. He felt bad that Heather would not have the memory of her parents' funeral to carry with her. He definitely planned to attend (although he hadn't made up his mind which day). He would also go to Hillcrest for the burial. He wanted to do it for Heather. He had not seen her since the time he had attempted to visit her in the hospital and had been so shaken at her condition. He hadn't heard from Dr. Stein either, which meant there was no change. The house closing had been rescheduled that Monday afternoon and he had hoped that Heather would be back to normal by then. She now owned a home and didn't even know it.

Chris Hurley had been busy. It was getting more difficult to accumulate information because the subjects were spread out all over the place. He had passed the Langdon house and saw the 'For Sale' sign up. He had been at the hospital when Stein was talking to a lawyer, Carlton Marlo, from which he had gotten some information about Langdon. He contacted Brian, bringing him up-to-date.

Brian thought about Langdon divorcing Heather. What a joke that was! But no matter how it happened, she would be free of him! Yes, he thought, she would be free! He felt his heart jump. The best part was he didn't have anything to do with it; he had sat back and watched the scene play out. That was the best news he had heard in quite some time. Now, if only Heather's condition would improve. How he wished he could talk to her, spend some time with her. Maybe soon.

Chapter Thirty-one

$\mathscr{J}$osh Stein fell asleep in the chair in Heather's room. He had been reading to her and must have drifted off. Stella was sitting by the bed looking out the window. She heard a whisper. She turned and saw that Heather was mumbling to herself. She ran quickly to the other side of the bed and shook Stein gently but urgently to awaken him.

"Dr. Stein, please wake up. It's Heather. Can you hear her? She's mumbling but I can't understand what she's saying."

Stein literally jumped right out of his chair and tried to get as close to Heather as he could to hear. He listened closely and it sounded as if she were saying, "Mommy hurt. I want my Mommy. Where is my Mommy?" He turned to Stella, "Get Dr. Sutter, stat!"

She ran out of the room. Stein continued to lean as close as he could to Heather's face, straining to hear what she was trying to say, "Car fall. I want my Mommy. Where is she? Mommy, I can't see you!" It sounded to him as if she were a child. Then she stopped. Stein stroked her hair and told her everything was all right.

Jenny walked into the room and saw Stein practically on the bed. Wrenched with panic and fear, she stood paralyzed in the doorway. "Dr. Stein, what's wrong? Heather isn't dying, is she?" Jenny put her hand to her mouth, gasping for breath. She clutched at her chest as she leaned against the door, trying to catch her breath, sobs catching in her throat. Stein turned and, realizing Jenny was in a panic, rushed to her side to assist her to a chair.

"Jenny, Heather is fine. Do you hear me? Heather is fine. Look at me and tell me you understand what I said." No longer sobbing, but with tears flowing down her cheeks, she acknowledged by nodding.

"I'm sorry, Dr. Stein." Jenny began, still trying to calm herself. "But the thought of losing Heather . . . I guess I've held on to the fear of something like this happening to her for so long. I'm sorry. I'm so embarrassed. Please forgive me."

"Heather is okay. I must have dozed and the nurse woke me up because she was mumbling. It was difficult to understand what she was saying because she sounded like a child and kept calling for her mommy. So I tried to get as close as possible to hear what she was saying. I guess that's when you walked into the room."

"What do you think all that mumbling was about?"

"I'm not sure. It's a theory, but it's possible that Heather was in the car crash that killed her mother."

"Excuse me, Dr. Stein, but Dr. Sutter is unavailable at the moment. He's in an emergency consultation," Stella explained.

"Thanks, Stella. I'll have to wait. Jenny, why don't you sit here close to Heather? I'm going to get a cup of coffee then I'll be at the viewing station. Talk to her and see if there's any response."

"I would love that more than anything. I would love to be able to jolt her back into reality." Stein left the room. Jenny took a deep breath, went to Heather's bedside and sat on the bed. She stroked her hair as she began to talk.

"Hello, sweetie. It's me. I sure miss you and our talks. I don't even feel like going to lunch anymore because we're not together. We always shared so much. I wish that I could help you and share all that you're going through right now." Jenny talked for about an hour straight before giving up. She started to read the Center's newspaper to Heather and keep her abreast of all that was going on. She must have read for another hour and a half. When finally she looked at her watch she realized she had to get going. She kissed Heather good-bye, gazing at her for a little bit, hoping to see some response. Nothing. She collected her coat and pocketbook and headed out the door.

Stein could see Jenny's disappointment and stopped her on the way out. "I'm sorry you feel so bad, Jenny. You have no idea of the effect you're having on her when you're talking to her and spending time with her. You're more of a comfort than you know."

"Thanks, Doc, I guess I have to look at it that way. I'll see you tomorrow. I better get home and fix some dinner for my husband." Jenny was gone. She thought about her visit with Heather on her ride home. She wished she could get inside her friend's head and figure out what was going on.

Tracey called the hospital and told Stein that they wouldn't be up to see Heather because one of the kids had come down with a fever. He relayed the latest to her and she got excited. Stein expressed good wishes for a speedy recovery for the child.

Leo Martucci was a lucky man. He got banged up in his accident but finally had his vehicle back. He was hurting like hell, but developing film just the same. He couldn't wait to get some of the pictures blown up. He wanted to see what the inscription inside the locket read. While the film was developing, he made himself something to eat and let Skipper out. Then he headed for his darkroom. He was anxious to collect the photographs and sit down to take a look at his find. The locket pictures were the first he grabbed for. It was a dainty locket, child-sized. The back of it read, "To My Princess" and then the initials, 'A.H'. The front of the locket was designed with tiny roses in pink gold. He put those pictures aside and concentrated on the adoption papers. Most of it was legal jargon, but as he glanced onto the next page it read, "Origin of Availability: France." That was interesting. Martucci noted a couple of names. He would try to locate these people and find out more about the agency.

He was pleased with what he had found but was still not ready to advise Alec Hargrove of his findings. He wanted to get as much information together as possible. Who knows, he thought, it all might come up a dead end. Well, he would know the answer to that in a few days.

Brian woke up with the thought that he must go and see Heather. He couldn't shake the feeling that he must see her and explain to her what he'd been doing. So he got up, showered and dressed. While he finished his coffee, he thought about what he was going to say to her. Why did he feel so compelled to see her?

When Brian arrived at the hospital, Stein was at the desk speaking with Carlton Marlo. They both watched as he approached. Marlo was the first to speak.

"Why, Brian Hargrove, how are you?" Marlo extended his hand in greeting. Brian nonchalantly reached out his hand but was not really interested. He didn't particularly care for Marlo. There was nothing specific but something about him he didn't like or trust. "I was speaking with Alec the other day and we were talking about you."

"Oh, really. I sure hope it was all good." Brian couldn't keep his mind on the conversation. He needed to get into

Heather's room and see her as soon as possible. But apparently something had happened that morning. "Is everything all right? With Heather, I mean?"

"Well, Brian, she was served with divorce papers. In fact, you just missed the server. I was having copies made to keep here so Carlton can take the originals."

"You see, Brian, this would have been a day of celebration for Heather's parents. They never approved of the marriage to Langdon and fought her all the way. I don't know how Heather is going to feel about it, though."

"I see. Have you told her yet? I mean, I know she isn't responding, but have you shown them to her and told her anyway?"

"Yes, we were both in there, but Carlton felt it would be better if I was the one to go through it with her. There was no reaction."

"May I see her?"

"Of course. Go right on in and when I'm done here I'll be at the viewing station. If you need me for anything, just speak normally. I can hear everything that is said. The nurse, of course, is still with Heather. Her name is Stella and she is a very attentive to Heather's needs."

"Thanks." Brian shook Carlton's hand, exchanged goodbyes and he was off to see Heather. He didn't want anyone listening in on what he had to say, but at this point he didn't care. He wanted to sit next to her and tell her everything. Stella acknowledged Brian entering the room by getting up off the chair and moving back.

"Good morning, Stella. My name is Brian Hargrove and I would like to have a word with Heather, if I may."

"Of course, Mr. Hargrove. I'll be at the viewing station if you need me."

"Thank you." He walked over to the bed and looked down

at Heather. She was so beautiful, even in her condition. Her long hair was brushed back and looked like spun silk. Her large blue eyes were bluer than ever and seemed to take over her face. He wanted to touch her but instead commanded every ounce of strength to refrain from any such movement. He felt clumsy and awkward as he pulled the chair over to the bed and sat down. Okay, he thought, you are here, now what are you going to do?

He was in awe of the fact that Heather never moved. Her stillness was unnerving, but maybe, he thought, it would be a blessing.

"Heather, it's Brian Hargrove. I know that I'm probably the last person you'd want to see but I came because I must talk to you."

Stein watched Brian from the viewing station, wondering what he was up to. He appeared to be on edge. Stein thought maybe business was on his mind, but as he spoke to Heather his anxiety seemed to increase. Suddenly Brian bolted out of the room.

"Heather, I'll be right back," Brian said as he turned in the doorway and then looked at Stein. "I think I have to talk with you."

"Brian, what's wrong?"

"I need to know whether you've told Heather that I'm paying her bills."

"No, I haven't said anything, but I think it's a good idea that you explain this to her. Relax, Brian, she isn't going to eat you alive. Is there any other reason you feel that she might become upset if you are speaking to her?"

"Well, maybe. I mean, I have . . . I want . . . I, uh, yes, I guess so."

Stein listened to Brian stuttering and stammering and tried to calm him down. "Brian, listen to me. No matter what you have to say to Heather, it can't be worse than what she's been through already. Don't you agree?"

"Oh, absolutely. It's nothing like that."

"Well, then go back inside and say what you want to say and look at Heather as you're talking to her. Don't be afraid of her condition. We need to bring her back. Now, if there's no huge crisis, I think you should go inside and talk to her, okay?"

Brian was angry with himself for losing his cool and having to be calmed by a professional. After all, he was Brian Hargrove and he could handle anything . . . except this. "Thanks, Josh. I feel somewhat awkward." With that, Brian was around the doorway and back in Heather's room. Stein wondered what Brian was so afraid of saying to Heather but, whatever it was, he hoped it would elicit some kind of response from her.

Brian sat down again in the chair, rearranging himself, then looked at Heather and started to speak again. "I'm sorry, Heather, that I walked out like that, but I'm nervous being here with you. I hope you find that amusing, especially after that little stunt I pulled with you on the telephone. Well, regardless, I deserve it. I don't care what your condition is now. I want to start out by apologizing to you about what I did to you during and after that Christmas party and then for the phone call I made to you just before all this happened. I'm so sorry, Heather." He hesitated, searching for the right words. "I guess at times I can be a real dick. Sorry about that, but I can't express my behavior any other way." Stein was definitely intrigued.

"You see, Heather, I've never met anyone like you before in my life. For some reason, I felt as if I knew you. I don't know how to explain it, and it doesn't excuse my deplorable behavior toward you in the past. I think you are so special. It drove me crazy that someone as special as you were stuck with someone like John. He did not deserve you. I know that it's none of my business and that I don't have the right to be saying that. You are such a wonderful, beautiful and intelligent woman. You are so full of love and life and have so much to give to this world, but you were wasting a lot of energy giving it to the wrong person. Now, I'm not saying that I'm the person you should be giving it to, although it would make me the happiest man in the world, but it would make me happy if you accepted me as your friend. I hope someday you will be able to forgive me. I am having a terrible time dealing with how I treated you on the phone and hoping that it was not the direct cause of John's rage upon you that evening. I cannot stand living with that secret.

"When I found out about your admission to the hospital, I arranged for you to have the best of care, including the nurses. I wanted you to have the best because you are the best," Brian took a deep breath. He could feel himself starting to lose control. She was so lifeless. He put his head down for a minute to wipe his eyes and to fight back the building lump in his throat, wondering how he was going to go on. Suddenly he felt a hand. Stein watched in complete amazement as Heather, looking directly at Brian, started to stroke the side of his head.

"It's okay, Brian," Heather barely managed to get out. He looked up at her with tears in his eyes. Stein came running but stayed at the doorway. He didn't want to interrupt this scene. Heather was awake and alive! He wondered if it would last.

"Heather, I can't . . . it's you . . . you're talking to me. Oh my, God! I can't believe it. Oh, Heather, welcome back!" He took her hand and they regarded each other in silence before Stein rushed in. Stein held Stella back allowing Heather and Brian to have their moment. Stella looked at Stein and he finally let go of her arm, eagerly following her into the room. Stella fussed about Heather and Stein came over to the bedside and smiled.

"Well, welcome back, young lady. We have missed you around here and we hope you plan on staying with us." He checked her heart and pulse and made a few mental notes.

Brian left the room and waited outside for Stein. Stein told Heather he would be right back. He asked Stella to have Sutter paged and walked outside to the viewing station to have a word with Brian.

"I'm sorry to cut your visit short, Brian, but I need to work with Heather right now."

"Of course, doctor. No problem at all. Please tell her I'll be back in to see her as soon as I am allowed."

"Give it a few days, Brian. If you want I'll call you with the green light."

"That would be good. Thank you, doctor." Stein could see that Brian was still shook up. Who would have thought that it would have been Brian that brought Heather back? Then again, maybe he happened to be here when she was ready to return to the land of the living. He walked back into the room.

"Where's Brian, Doctor?"

"Heather, Brian had to leave because we need to spend some time together and slowly discuss a lot of things. I told him I would be in touch with him when you're ready. Does that sound acceptable to you?"

"Well, sure."

"Good, then." He took Heather's hand and patted it gently, continuing to hold it in his own. "You have no idea how wonderful it is to talk with you. Maybe you were getting tired of all the magazine articles we were reading you?" Heather laughed, weakly.

"It's all so weird. In fact, I'm aware of everyone that visited and what they said to me, but it's like being in a tunnel where I couldn't respond. I can't believe how much time you and my friends have spent with me. I don't know exactly where to begin."

"Well, why don't we do a brief summary of what you remember last and let's take it from there. By the way, are you hungry?"

"I think so, but maybe only for some chicken broth and crackers. That sounds good to me. Dr. Stein, thank you for being with me all this time. Whether you believe it or not, you were quite a comfort to me. I never felt alone. I always felt someone was watching over me. Your wife must be a very special lady to part with you for such long periods of time."

"I'm glad you feel that way. I tried to be here for you. It was important that I be with you as much as possible because I wanted to be here at the very moment that you were ready to return. I tried to keep you informed about everything that was going on around you and in your life while you were incapable of living it."

"Is it true that I'm on the way to a divorce?"

"Yes, you were served with papers this morning." Stein was amazed how clear her mind seemed and she didn't seem shaken or confused. But she seemed very weak and her voice showed this. "But we will talk about that and anything else you want to talk about starting tomorrow. Right now I want you to eat what Stella is bringing you and then get some rest, maybe even get up and sit on the side of the bed, later. I'll be keeping an eye on you, young lady."

"That does sound kind of good. Thanks, doctor, for everything. But you're right, I am feeling tired." He nodded his head in agreement, squeezed her shoulder gently and walked out the door. He stood at the viewing station for a few more minutes and then he went to find Sutter. He wanted to call Heather's friends as well as Carlton Marlo and her surgeon to let them in on the good news. He was also hoping to get some of his paperwork done now. Yes, Heather was definitely on the mend now.

Stein wouldn't let anyone near her for at least three days. They had a lot of ground to cover and he didn't want any outside interference during this period of time. He couldn't wait to start working with her. His next step, once she was better, would be to hypnotize her and see what caused her nightmares. Was she actually in the car with her mother at the time of the accident? But for this moment it was enough that his patient had returned to the living. As he thought about it, his wife would be happy, too, because she would have him home again.

Heather smiled at Stella. "Stella, I'm so grateful that you are here with me. It's strange that I never met you, and yet I know that you've been with me the entire time."

"Yes, my dear. And we will have the opportunity to share a lot more now that you're back with us and talking."

Chapter Thirty-two

*J*ohn was creating absolute havoc at Hillsworth. His counselors were losing patience with him. All he wanted to do was "hang out" with Suzy and not go to meetings or counseling sessions. He refused to get involved in any activities. He constantly tried to bribe the aides into bringing up some booze and a "few lines" to hold him over. He was more interested in making sure that Heather had been served with the divorce papers than anything else. He told everyone that he and Suzy were getting hitched as soon as they got out of that hell hole.

Bobby Brighton called Andrew Price on several different occasions, advising Price that there were no changes in John's attitudes. Price had to make an appeal to the court on the ruling that John's stay be extended at Hillsworth, as recommended by the counselors. But Langdon didn't seem to care about anything except having a good time, all the time. Price knew his client was headed for a crash landing and nothing would save him until he hit rock bottom. So Price went through the motions, but the appeal was denied and John was looking at an additional sixty days inside.

One day John lost it completely. He picked up chairs and threw them as hard as he could into anything he could, then threw everything else he could get his hands on. They put him on the third floor where the "Thorazine shuffle" patients were isolated. The center would not tolerate such behavior. It was certainly going to be a long and painful journey for him.

*　*　*

Heather progressed well over the next couple of weeks. Of course, the first week dealing with the death of her parents was the most painful. So much so that Stein extended her "no visitor" status for a full week. She was anguished that she was unable to attend their funeral. With so much to deal with, part of her therapy was screaming and beating a bean bag chair with a badminton racket. She became angry with Dr. Stein at times because he kept pushing her when she didn't want to deal with all her emotions. But he kept pushing, and she kept going through the pain and was no longer stuck in it. It had been a long and intense seven days but Stein felt they had covered a lot of ground and she was finally ready to receive visitors.

Tracey and Vito were the first to arrive. Jenny was miserable because she came down with the flu and knew she would be home for the week. But she promised to call Heather everyday. Brian was anxious to return and resume the conversation they unexpectedly started the day she returned to normal. But he called her first and asked if he could come up. She told him to come whenever he felt like it. And when he did Heather didn't waste any time getting to the point.

"Brian, I never could understand why you wanted to treat me the way you did. I had never done anything to encourage you."

"Yes, you're right, but I guess my behavior was so intense because of the person you married and the way he treated you. I felt that you deserved one hundred percent better than that. That's why I'm so sorry. I didn't mean to hurt you in any way. That would be the last thing I would want to do. I guess I figured that if I could control you, then you would love me. That's sick, I know it is. I understand that now. I think the threat of having caused this situation for you combined with the thought that I might never be able to speak to you again made me take another look at what I was doing. It's important to me to have you as a friend. I don't expect an answer from you. With everything you've been through it's probably the least important thing on your mind right now. In fact, there have to be many important things on your mind right now, and that's what you should use your energy for."

"Brian, I like the idea of being your friend, as long as I can trust you. You see, I have close friends and I know they would do anything for me. It works both ways. My friends are everything to me and I would do anything for them. They don't try to influence my thinking or make up my mind for me about anything. But they are always there to listen and talk. Do you understand that?"

"Yes, I do Heather. I certainly will try to be the best friend you have ever had."

"Brian, you don't have to do that. Just be yourself, but remember that everyone has their own life and has to feel free to make their own decisions."

"I can't believe you're talking to me!"

"Well, a lot has certainly happened," Heather responded as she took in a deep breath. Brian could see the tears beginning to fill her eyes. His discomfort grew.

"Heather, maybe I should go. You need rest and time to reflect on all the changes."

"Well, okay, maybe you're right, but only if you promise to return as soon as you can. You know, Brian, I would like to talk with you, also. Thank you for coming to see me. I really appreciate it." Heather extended her hand to Brian. He gently took her hand and squeezed it.

"You take care of yourself, Heather, and if you need anything, make sure you make it known and it will be done. Okay?" With that he grabbed his coat and left the room.

Jenny was shocked when Heather told her about Brian's visits. She couldn't believe that they were becoming friends. She was afraid of Brian's need to control.

Brian still had not mentioned anything about the house. He wanted to wait until they had talked discharge before he mentioned anything. He didn't want to frighten her off and she had many things to consider. She knew that she was well on her way to being divorced; she was aware that her house had been on the market and had been sold, even though the deal wouldn't close for another two months.

Carlton Marlo had come one day for the reading of the wills. It was difficult to face, even though her parents had left her everything. That wasn't a surprise. Her parents had always talked to her about it. But it was so painful to realize that that was all she had left of them. She would have to make a decision about the business, but Marlo felt she should take it slowly and, when she was able, attend a board meeting. She would also have to decide where she was going to live. Marlo had suggested that she wait until she got out of the hospital and back on her feet before she decided what she wanted to do with her parents' home and all of its contents. He also had to tell her that John's family had taken almost everything from their house before it was sold. She was hurt when Marlo told her that. But Heather was growing and she was learning. She more readily accepted the idea that John and his parents would never change and that had nothing to do with her. She was beginning to understand that. It certainly seemed to make things easier to take.

Heather spent most of her time in session with Stein and then pondering the things she was learning about herself, her situation and her relationships while she walked around the hospital floor and lounge area. There was so much to think about and consider. So much had happened in such a short time, her life would never be the same. For her, this was the most difficult pill to swallow. As she looked back at her marriage, though, she was glad her life would not be the same. She knew she had been in a terrible mess with no way out. It was painful to think of all the things John and his family had said and done to her. And it was painful to deal with the reality of never seeing her parents again. She was going to leave the hospital a divorced woman, never able to have her own children, with no parents and no family.

She had cried so much over the last several weeks. Yet, none of it seemed any easier to take. She still had to attend anger sessions with Stein, continuing to release bottled-up anger from within her. Just when she thought she had control over the anger, it would unexpectedly well up again. She wondered if it would get any easier with time. She missed the long conversations with her mother. What was she ever going to do without her to ask for advice or just share all her silly stuff with? Her mother loved to spend time with her on the phone. They were never without words and always had something to talk about. But now . . . She tried to take each day as it came now. After all, what else could she do?

She realized she didn't miss John at all. And she found this incredible after the years of worrying about where he was and what he was doing. She saw now how she was driving herself crazy doing that. She was beginning to accept the fact that John had his own path to travel. She understood that it was not her fault that John verbally and physically abused her. She realized that no matter what she had done, it would not have made a difference because the problem was within John.

Although she did not miss him, she found herself thinking about him and wondering what was going on in his life. She would catch herself when she did this, realizing it was a bad and unhealthy habit. She knew it was the codependent part of her and that she had to continue to work on that part of herself. She needed to make sure that she would always come first and not give her self-control and control over her life to anyone else ever again.

But she didn't blame herself for thinking about him. After all, they had shared a life together and she felt it was only natural to think about some of the times they had spent together. Through the help she had received at the hospital, she was able to reflect on both the good and the bad. Before, she would deny the bad and try to hold onto only the good memories.

Heather wondered where she was going to go when she left the hospital. She had been there for so long and felt safe and secure there. But she knew she couldn't – and wouldn't want to – stay there, of course. She thought about going to stay at her parents' home. After all, the property belonged to her. But she didn't feel that strong yet; the house was filled with so many memories, which only triggered her old feelings of abandonment. She felt everyone she had loved had left her, especially her real mother. But what about her father? Where was he and who was he and why was she left all alone for some strangers to take in? And after learning to love these two strangers they leave her in a bus crash. It made no sense. That feeling of terror would rise up in her and she wanted to scream! She wondered if she would ever feel normal. But what was normal? Is there any such thing? Her mind jumped back to the living situation. If she didn't stay at her parents' home, where would she go? She did not feel up to going out and buying a house. And where would she begin to look; in what town or part of the city? If she moved to her parents' she would be close to Manhattan.

She knew she still had the terrible task ahead of emptying out her parents' home. But realistically, she could not see herself doing that for a while yet. She needed time to adjust to their not being there anymore. It was daunting. She knew that she was just feeling the pain of *all* the losses in her life and that she had to go through it then try to get on with her life. She knew that she could make it on her own, but she felt alone and frightened. She also knew that time was closing in on her because Dr. Stein was talking discharge. They had spent time in sessions talking about all of this, and Heather knew she was seeing things much clearer, but it was difficult to control the swing of the pendulum of emotions.

She had missed her job, but she had been out for such a long time she had told her boss to fill the position. She missed Jenny most of all. She missed seeing her every day, working with her, sharing everything with her. There was no relationship compared to theirs. Jenny was always brutally honest and Heather loved and appreciated that about her. Sometimes the honesty was a bit hard to take, but it was the truth, no matter how hard to hear. Her life had changed so drastically, she was still only beginning to accept the changes. Yet to go back to the Center was bringing back a part of her old life and she no longer wanted that. She was also incapable of moving back into a position that would be too demanding. She knew she would have to keep it simple for quite a while and take things slowly. She would miss the hectic pace of her old job but it was time to move on. Where to, was the question.

Then there were Tracey and Vito. Vito had visited some friends in Georgia who hooked him up with some investors looking for a construction company. It was a deal made in heaven and apparently meant to be because everything slipped into place. So, Vito and Tracey were moving. Vito had already started up his construction business and was moving the family to Georgia. He was going to be building a shopping center and condominium complex.

Vito had been traveling between Georgia and New Jersey for some time now. He was involved with setting-up the business and picking up workers. He searched high and low for a suitable place for his family. This had turned out to be an extremely lucrative deal for Vito and he was thrilled with the lifestyle he could present to his loved ones. Heather felt sorry to lose Tracey, but they would be able to have a better life down there. She couldn't imagine her life without Tracey. They had been so close all these years. They had shared so much together that it seemed impossible to go on without them close to her. But she knew it was for the best. It was hard for Vito to keep his business going during the winter months and it would be so much better with a full work load twelve months a year. This was just one more change in her life she was going to have to get used to.

Then there was Brian. He had been such a creepy animal for the longest time and now, she could not believe, he had quickly become a good friend. She had grown close to him in the last three months. She did not find him attractive; not for her, not boyfriend attractive, that is. But she had been able to trust him; when he said he would do something, be there or call her, he always did. She appreciated and welcomed the friendship that had blossomed between the two of them. He constantly brought her gifts and had clothes delivered to her hospital room. Heather was beginning to believe that she was the best-dressed patient in history.

She giggled to herself as she looked down the hallway through the lounge doors and saw Brian popping his head into her room and then looking straight down the hall to the lounge area. He saw her and quickened his pace.

"Well, don't you look pretty this morning, my dear," he announced as he bent over to plant a kiss on her cheek.

"Thank you. I must say you look rather dashing in that three-piece suit. Are you going some place?"

"Yes, I have a meeting across town and I thought I would stop by and see you before I go; this one could prove to be a long one."

"I see. It's funny that you came at this moment, I mean, because I was thinking about you."

"Well, I hope they were good thoughts. But I do have something I would like to discuss with you. I mentioned it to Dr. Stein and he told me that he thinks I should speak with you about it."

"Oh, really? What is it, then?"

"Well, Heather, I don't want you to take this the wrong way, but a few months ago, I wanted to do *something* to help you. I couldn't think of anything and then I realized how I *could* help you. I bought you a house. I bought the house for you. I mean I bought the house for you and in your name."

"Brian, you did what?"

"Heather, please don't get upset with me. You were still despondent when I bought it. Then I was afraid to tell you about it because I didn't want you to get angry with me . . . you know, get the wrong idea. But when I found out about your house being sold and even though I know you have your parents' home to go to, it was already too late because I had bought this house."

Heather was awed. She couldn't believe that Brian had bought her a home. Not just clothes or candy or whatever, he had bought her a home in her name.

"Brian, dear, I don't know what to say. You are always full of surprises, but this one takes the cake. I can't believe that you bought me a house!"

"Well, Heather, I didn't know when to tell you, but I didn't want you to get the wrong idea about you and me. I bought this house for you because I love you. I know and understand how you feel, and realize that there could be nothing more between us, but it doesn't matter. I want you to be happy in this house and decorate it and shop for furniture and get exactly what you want to fill it all up. What do you say?"

"Brian, I'm overwhelmed! You bought me a house! You know, I was thinking about where I was going to live. You see, Dr. Stein is talking discharge. He said that we are far from through yet, but he feels that I am ready to leave the hospital and start my life."

"There, you see? It would be perfect! And I will help you with whatever you want to do. You know that. I would never impose my will on you, Heather. I only want the best for you, and if I can help you in any way starting over, well, then, I'm your man for the job." Brian took a deep breath. He had been so afraid to tell her about the house because he was not sure how she would take it. He didn't want to risk all the progress they had made in their relationship. But now his thoughts of Heather living in this house had become a reality. He had picked it out just for her and she would love it. It was almost too perfect.

"Gee, Brian, I'm really starting over. I think it's more frightening than when I did everything the first time around. I mean, every aspect of my life has changed. I have to start over all alone because even my parents are gone now."

"I know. But remember that you don't have to go the distance alone. I want you to think seriously about the house. Please remember that it's in your name and there are no strings attached. Now, I'm not going to say anything more about it because I want you to have time to digest it. When you're ready, I'll bring up the pictures, blueprints and lay-outs for you to see. But for now, I must run or I'll be late. I'll call you later." He bent over and kissed her hand and told her to take care. He didn't even give her a chance to answer, but turned on his heel and walked away. He wanted her to feel excited. Heather's mouth dropped open, but he was already halfway down the hall.

As Brian rushed from the lounge and from Heather, he congratulated himself on how well the house had gone over. She must never know what was really in his heart but he would do everything he could to try and make her love him, even though he already said he was accepting of the present conditions of their relationship. Yes, indeed, he was pleased with himself. He felt he was another step closer to Heather.

In amazement, Heather watched Brian walk away then burst out laughing. Life is really strange, she thought. Here she was wondering where she was going to live. And then Brian comes along, nervous as anything, to tell her that he had already bought her a house. She couldn't help but wonder what kind of house Brian would buy and what it would look like. She headed back to her room.

Chapter Thirty-three

*H*eather sat, observing Stein and Carlton Marlo exiting the elevator together and heading in her direction. She waved to them smiling broadly. Carlton and his wife had been wonderful! They were both supportive. His wife, Louise, tried to reassure Heather that she would never be without family and that as far as she was concerned, she was family and always would be.

Yet, as they came nearer, Heather studied their faces. "My goodness, we are awfully somber this morning. Maybe I should invite you both to come to my office and tell me what's on your minds. And, in fact, I won't charge either of you for the session!"

Both men laughed as Heather teased them. Stein was thrilled with the recovery that Heather was making. Stein spoke first. "Heather, we need to talk to you about something that has come up."

"Well, all right, but it sounds dreadfully serious. I do hope that you aren't kicking me out of the hospital today. Although I must say I wouldn't feel too bad about it because Brian was here and told me that he had bought me a house a couple of months ago, but he was afraid to tell me. At first, I couldn't believe what he was saying to me, but now I find myself getting excited at the prospect of moving into a new home."

"That is great news, Heather, but of course, you realize that you have your parents' home, also," Marlo reminded her. "By the way, you said Brian *bought* you this home? Would that be Brian Hargrove?"

"Why, yes, Carl, we have become quite good friends. Didn't you tell me that you know his father fairly well?"

"Yes, my dear, we go back quite a few years together. He is a wonderful man. I don't know too much about his son, though." He was not going to mention his discussion with Alec Hargrove about Brian some time back. It wasn't necessary. Besides, he felt he owed it to Heather's parents, and especially to Heather, that he look after her best interests. He had talked to Louise about it and they had both agreed to try and remain in Heather's life and be there for her as long as she wanted.

"Well, I'm glad he finally told you," Stein rejoined. "He's been sweating over this for some time now. I knew there was something he was reluctant to talk to you about, but I had no idea it was a house. We can discuss some of this in session today, if you feel like it."

"Really, Dr. Stein. I can't believe why he was afraid to tell me. I thought we had become good enough friends to share anything without the fear of how the other would take it."

"Well, just remember all you've been through and know that people are not going to be too quick to bring you news, especially if it may be disturbing. Now this kind of sets the stage for why the both of us are here to see you. Come on, let's go inside your room so that we have a little privacy."

"Dr. Stein, what is it? Why are you both acting so strange? Please tell me what is going on?"

"Carlton, why don't you explain what has happened. I think it would be best coming from you," Stein suggested.

"All right." Carlton walked over to the bed and sat down next to Heather. "Heather, something has happened to John. There is no easy way to tell you this, but last night there was a car accident and John was driving. He was seriously injured and did not survive the crash." Carlton went to put his arm around Heather but she shrugged away and stood up. Stein spoke.

"Heather, are you all right? What are you feeling?"

"What am I feeling about this? What do you think?!" Heather was pacing the floor. "It seems like every person that becomes attached to me in one way or another ends up dying or leaving me. I am shocked! I can't believe that John is gone!" Heather started to cry and Carl handed her some tissues.

"Thanks," she said through her tears. "Was he alone in the car? Did he die at the scene?"

Carlton took a deep breath before he spoke. "John was not alone. He was with a woman he was seeing from the rehab. I think her name was Suzy." Heather nodded her head in acknowledgement. "Apparently they borrowed an aide's car from the center. They were intoxicated and John must have lost control of the car and it went over to the opposite side of the road and crashed into the rock wall along Route 8. They were both killed instantly."

Heather struggled to speak. "You know, deep in my heart, I knew it was just a matter of time before something like this was going to happen. It used to be one of my biggest nightmares while we were together. In one way I feel frightened to death to realize how close I came to being in that car last night and not that other woman. In another way I feel the pain of remembering how things were once, a long time ago." Heather sat back down next to him and Marlo held her.

"You know, Heather, you have many people who love you. I think you are a wonderfully loving and caring person; you have no idea how special you are. You must try to feel some comfort in knowing that Louise and I are here for you and love you, dear," Marlo said softly.

"Thanks, Carl. I love you and Louise, too. But if this keeps up there will be nobody left. Everyone close to me eventually leaves. How do you explain that?"

Stein said gently, "Heather, you're upset now. We've covered this in session. Would you like a little medication?"

"No, definitely not! I might be upset and sound confused again, but it's only for the moment. I want no more drugs. I want to know what I am feeling. I need to know what I am feeling. I don't think I'm in any danger of losing control. God is always with me and I do know that I am not alone. I am all right."

Heather was determined to remain in control of her life. She had had enough. Yes, all of this was painful, but all that time in session with Stein was not going to go to waste. She would get her life started again. She was tired of it all; the hospital, doctors, being helpless. It was time for her to move on with her life. Of course, she thought, she felt horrible pain over John's death even though she was furious with him for what he had done to her and to have sentenced her to a life without children; at least her own children.

But she would go on. "I'm trying to sort it all out. This was a tremendous shock to me. But I don't intend on losing it. So you can get that thought right out of your head." Just as she finished her sentence, Jenny walked into the room. She took one look at Heather and realized that she had already been told.

"Heather, I came over as soon as I heard."

"Thanks, Jenny, you're the best friend ever. But I'm all right. I was explaining that it's the shock of the news and also understanding how close I came to being the woman in that car with John. I must say it is a tremendous relief and that emotion is more overwhelming than any grief that I feel for John. He had a death wish and he was an accident waiting to happen."

Being business-oriented, Marlo wanted some details taken care of. "Now, Heather, what about the funeral? As your lawyer, I can make any arrangement you wish if you want to see him"

"No, I don't want to go to the funeral. His mother was always mean to me and I have no desire to see her now or any-time in the future. As far as visitation for John goes, I have no intention of seeing him. There is no reason for me to go there. It was over for us before this happened and I have been trying to put closure to it. I don't even want to send flowers."

Marlo, Jenny and Stein exchanged relieved glances. Stein was amazed at how well she was doing but he knew they had more work to do. He could still hear much anger at John in her voice.

He said, "Heather, you are marvelous. We are *very* proud of you. There is no room for shame in what you feel, you must always remember that. Your feelings are yours and they can-not be taken away from you."

Everyone stayed a while longer. Stein and Marlo were the first to go, leaving Heather and Jenny to talk. Heather told Jenny all about the house that Brian had bought for her.

"What do you mean he bought you a house?" So Heather shared her excitement with Jenny and let her story unfold, explaining how Brian had visited her earlier with the news. "This is a splendid opportunity because there are no memo-ries. It will all be new."

"Yeah, but wait one second. I understand that you said that Brian bought this house in your name. Now, where does *he* sleep?"

"Jenny, it's not like that at all. Brian has made it clear to me that the house is mine free and clear and with no strings attached. He is happy to be friends. I have already told him that I could never be romantically involved with him."

"Oh, really, and what did he say to that? Have you forgotten all the times in the past you told him the same thing?"

"Yes, but it's different now. We're friends and we've shared a lot in the last couple of months. Of course he was disappointed when I told him I only wanted to be friends, but he said he would rather have me as a close friend than not to have me in his life at all."

"Well, isn't Brian Hargrove simply amazing! I'm sorry, Heather, but after all you've been through I don't trust anyone anymore."

"I hear what you're saying, but one thing has changed here. I am in total control of my life now and that will never change. I never plan on giving that to anyone ever again."

"Well, I sure hope so, sweetie, because you are too precious to me and too special a person to go through anything near what you have been through."

"You know, Jenny, I love you to pieces. You are the closest thing I have to a sister on this earth."

"Yeah, well, I'm not too sure about how you're feeling about John. Do you want to talk about that more?"

"Honestly, Jenny, I'm okay with it. Believe me, it came as a tremendous shock and I feel sick to my stomach, but you know that was one of my biggest fears as things got worse between us. I know it was one of yours. You kept warning me but I couldn't see it. It sickens me to think how people waste their lives thinking they can find happiness by drowning their sorrows in liquid. Then I think back about how John and I were and I *really* feel sick."

"Well, one thing's for sure. He was always like that and it was his problem and not yours. You wanted to take it all on and make it all better. I hope you're starting to see that now." Suddenly they heard a woman yelling at the top of her lungs. Heather immediately recognized the voice. It was John's mother. Heather told Jenny who it was in a whisper.

Heather and Jenny peeked out the door. Meredith Langdon had gotten off the elevator and was heading toward Heather's room. A nurse had stopped her and asked her if she needed help. Meredith instantly got loud and nasty, which brought staff running from all directions to the nurse's assistance. Security was called immediately by the ward clerk. Dr. Stein was at the counter and came running. He immediately recognized John's mother. He asked calmly, "Mrs. Langdon, what can I do for you?"

"Never mind what you can do for me! I came up here to tell that bitch that my son is dead and she is the one who killed him!"

Mrs. Langdon, I'm sure you don't mean that. That is your grief talking. I'm so sorry for your loss. Maybe we can go some place and talk?"

"Talk? Talk about what? I only want to talk to one person. That's what I came up here for and that's what I'm going to do. And when I find her I am going to give her exactly what she deserves. I'm going to take from her what was taken from my son."

By this time security had arrived. They escorted Meredith Langdon into the elevator with Dr. Stein. Heather and Jenny watched in amazement as the elevator doors closed behind them. They looked at each other in horror and then, all of a sudden, they started to laugh. They laughed uncontrollably until they couldn't laugh anymore. Several of the staff came to Heather's room to see if she was all right, but she waved them off. They started laughing too when they saw Jenny and Heather rolling on the floor in paroxysms of laughter. Finally sore, the two friends started to calm down just as Dr. Stein walked in.

Amused, he asked the obvious question. "What are you ladies laughing so hard about?"

"You know, Dr. Stein, it must have been a release of emotion once I heard Meredith Langdon's voice. Jenny and I looked at each other and all of a sudden we started laughing. Shall I ask if everything's all right?"

"Yes, everything's fine, Heather." Smiling, he left the room. Sometimes he found it difficult to shut off his own emotions with some of the patients he had become too close to. This situation could have been a potentially dangerous one; Heather had no idea. Once they had Meredith Langdon in the elevator, the two security officers started to search her, just in case, and they found two knives on her. Of course the police had to be called. But Stein did not see the sense of enlightening Heather about it. There was no reason to at the moment. If the investigating detectives find it necessary later on, let it be. But not now.

Jenny stayed a while longer. She was as relieved as everyone else that Heather was doing all right. She was reeling from John's death and how his mother came up to the hospital the way she had. It was so bizarre she was almost afraid to leave, but she knew her friend was in good hands.

Carlton Marlo had a busy afternoon scheduled by the time he got back to his office. As he passed his secretary, he asked her to get Alec Hargrove on the phone before he started anything else. By the time he sat down at his desk, she buzzed him to let him know she had him on the line. She also advised him that Dr. Stein had called and left a message for him to return the call when he had a moment. He thanked her and pushed the button connecting him with Alec.

"Alec, how are you?"

"Carlton, I can't believe I'm getting another call from you within the same year!" He chuckled at his joke. "You know, I'm only kidding. But I enjoy hearing from you. What is going on?"

"Oh, I thought I would give you a holler and see how you're doing. I just got back from visiting Heather Langdon.

"My goodness, that poor thing. Is she still in the hospital?" Alec knew exactly where she was, but wanted to keep his information to himself.

"Yes, it's taken quite some time and I'm sure they want to be sure that she's all right, but they are talking about discharging her within the next week. So it's looking pretty good." He paused. "I also have another reason for calling you, Alec. You know that I am in charge of Heather's affairs. Louise and I feel the closest to her since we have known her since she was five. Anyway, after speaking with Heather, I understand that Brian has been seeing quite a bit of her and they have gotten close."

"Yes, that's my understanding, also. Of course I have spoken to Brian and he said they are just friends."

"Well, I would have to think it's much more than friendship because Dr. Stein, Heather's doctor, told me today that Brian had purchased a home in Heather's name." Hargrove realized what the telephone call had actually been for…Carlton was fishing.

"Yes, he did do that. Some time ago. He said the house belongs to her with no strings attached. I don't know what to tell you, Carlton. I think it might not be a bad idea if you contact him directly. In fact, it might be an excellent idea."

"Well, I wanted to kind of check things out because I am trying to look out for Heather now. In fact, she had another blow today."

"My God, what else could happen to that woman?"

"It really wasn't bad news for her directly anymore, but her ex-husband and another woman were killed in a car crash last night. Of course, it was a shock but he was bad news and she took it fairly well. She did say she was grateful that it wasn't her with him and that they were divorced before this happened."

"Well, it sounds like she's made progress. She is lovely. I would like her to find happiness."

"Listen, I know I told you Louise would call Alicea, but next Friday evening Louise and I are entertaining a few friends. How about it? Why don't you have Alicea call Louise and let them work things out?"

"Sounds good to me, Carl. I'll tell her." After they got off the phone, Alec sat for a few minutes, thinking. Brian had been busy lately and news from him was scarce. If Alicea had heard from him she would have said something. He thought about his conversation with Carlton Marlo. He never cared much for the man; never trusted him. Their prior business dealings, years before, had left Marlo bitter and angry. Alec tried to stay clear of him and his ruthless business tactics.

Chapter Thirty-four

*L*eo Martucci was pleased with his follow-up work. He had also been busy, and in fact, ended up taking a trip to France to check out the information in Heather's adoption papers. Now he was ready to see Alec Hargrove and present it to him. He had wanted to call Alec since the day he found the locket but he knew he couldn't. He had to make sure that his information was accurate and true, not coincidental. This was a serious situation and a most unbelievable one.

His trip to France had been difficult. At first it seemed all the leads were dead-ends. He couldn't get precise information. But he did find something out that led him to England then back to the States, to Florida. He had a lot of indigestion lately, which he blamed on all the rich food. He chewed an antacid. But he knew he couldn't quit. He was possibly onto something and he had to keep going with it. He was going to type a complete report first but he couldn't wait that long to break the news to Alec. Martucci reached for the phone.

"Hargrove residence, may I help you?" It was the housekeeper.

"Yes, my name is Leo Martucci. I work for Mr. Hargrove and I need to speak with him."

"I'm sorry, but Mr. and Mrs. Hargrove are away for a few days. They are not expected to return until next week."

"Well, I really need to talk with him. Take a message and tell him that I called and I will call back the middle of next week. Thanks." Martucci was disappointed. Well, he thought to himself, it looks as if I will be preparing the written report first after all.

Alec and Alicea had taken a few days to get out of the cold weather and go down to Cabos St. Lucas to bask in the warm sun. It had been so rainy, damp and cold that Alec suggested they fly out for several days to get out of the miserable weather. Alicea was tickled and wasted no time preparing for their immediate departure. With their private jet, they would be in Cabos in a few hours and the thought of that hot sun made her move faster and faster. Alec had filled Alicea in on Carlton's invitation, and so, before they left, Alicea spoke to Louise and accepted Marlo's invitation for the weekend following their return.

Tracey was packing up the house for what they would need to take with them to Georgia. She didn't want to leave. She didn't want to leave Heather and she didn't feel the children wanted to leave their school and friends. But what was she going to do?

Vito had worked so hard to make life better for them. After all, his family meant everything to him. After weeks of looking for a place he was satisfied with a four- bedroom home, situated on six acres, and purchased it.

So there was no choice to be made in a situation like this. Tracey knew that she had to go if she wanted to be with her husband. She was excited over his recent success and was actually looking forward to her new life. But she was reluctant to give up her friendship with Heather.

Now the week was here that she and the children would be leaving. She planned to go to the hospital the next day to say good-bye to Heather. She knew it was going to be tearful. Vito had called her over the weekend and told her to be ready. He was coming up to get her and the children with the truck and take whatever belongings that Tracey had decided to take with them.

Tracey had read about John's car accident in the obituaries but she knew she would be unable to go to the funeral because they would already be on the road. Poor Heather, she thought. She definitely has no past behind her now. Her first inclination was to run right up to the hospital, but she couldn't. She had already taken the children out of school for the move and she knew that this was the beginning of her distant relationship with her dearest friend. But she did call her at the hospital. Tracey was happy that Heather was taking the news in stride and seemed to have moved past that hopeless, helpless stage. She knew Heather would be fine now. She only wished she could remain close to her. She told Heather that she would be up the next day to say good-bye with Vito before they left for Georgia.

It was a dreadfully sad good-bye between Heather and Tracey. They felt they had known each other for centuries. They felt it was the most difficult thing either one of them had ever had to do. They had relied on each other all the time. But each woman knew there was no other way. Heather had to go on and make her new life and Tracey had to go with her family and start hers.

Vito let Tracey have time alone with Heather before he came in to say good-bye. After all, he was the one that was responsible for this entire situation. Heather hated him in one respect because he was taking away from her another special person in her life. But, in reality, she knew that this was an excellent opportunity for them. Vito had everything in place for his family. So she knew it was just the selfish part of her.

She did not want to say good-bye. Heather tried to keep her composure until they turned away. It was one more loss that she could not stand to bear. She knew that she was feeling the worst at this very moment and knew she had to let go.

As the couple walked out the door, Heather felt herself go to a million pieces. She cried and cried some more. She saw that their good-byes symbolized the closing of a chapter in her life. As Tracey and Vito left, she felt alone but said a prayer for them as she wished them good luck...and a new beginning.

Stein said his good-byes to the couple before they left the floor. He explained that he was planning on discharging Heather on Wednesday. He wished them the best of luck and told them to keep in touch with Heather

Stein waited for Brian to come that day. Heather was happy to see him after the tearful morning good-byes. Stein knew that Heather didn't need anyone's help to get started in her life but she just wasn't convinced of it yet. He wanted to give Heather and Brian a little time and then go in and announce his plans to discharge Heather. It had worked out perfectly because Brian had happened to bring in the plans for the house for Heather to see as well as the pictures he had taken, inside and out. They were laughing and talking away when Stein finally walked in the room.

"Look, Dr. Stein! Look at this house I'm going to be moving into! Isn't it beautiful? I am so excited!"

Stein smiled and looked at the photographs. It was a gorgeous house, he thought. "Well, Heather you are lucky to have such a beautiful house. I want to wish you the best of luck in it. And that brings me to an announcement that I would like to make. Ms. Heather . . . uh, Hilton, I believe?"

Heather giggled as Stein addressed her by her maiden name. She was pleased to have the name back again. "Oh, Doctor, really. Please go on."

"I am pleased to announce that you have successfully completed the courses here at Brookville Central Hospital and therefore declare you ready to go on with the rest of your life." There was a moment of silence before Heather spoke.

"But, Dr. Stein, are you sure I'm ready for this? I mean, I feel so insecure and alone. How will I manage?"

"Heather, you are more than ready to go on with the rest of your life. If you like we can get someone to check in on you regularly." As this subject came up, Brian was about to burst with his other secret. But he winked at Stella, giving her the signal to speak up.

"Well, I do have something to tell you, Heather." Stella, started. "Mr. Hargrove had approached me some time ago and asked me if I had a job to go to or any plans once you were discharged from the hospital. I told him I didn't so he offered me a job taking care of you once you were discharged, if that's what you want." She finished slowly, concentrating on Heather.

"Oh, Stella, that's definitely what I want. I feel comfortable with that and so fortunate. We could have such a wonderful time." Then she looked at Brian. "Brian, how can I thank you enough? You are *so* good to me. You have thought of everything." She put her arms out to him and without hesitation he rushed into them, only wishing he could kiss her passionately instead of getting a friendly hug. He felt dizzy from the closeness of her; her scent . . . her warmth . . . the feel of her skin against his cheek. How was he ever going to continue to pull this off? He had fantasized about the moment of her discharge, when he would fold her into his arms and carry her off from the rest of the world to their new little hideaway. He knew he would have to be careful. He didn't want to do anything to jeopardize the ground he had already gained.

Stein watched in amazement. He hadn't known about Stella going home with Heather. Brian had never mentioned it to him. He was a bit concerned about Heather's vulnerability and her relationship with Brian. He would have to continue to stress the consequences of control in her future sessions. That was something he definitely worried about. If Stein had learned anything from this patient, it was that she was extremely open and loving and therefore easy to take advantage of. It had been part of his plan to educate her and cut through that denial so that she would be able to see through this process. There would always be a degree of vulnerability but at least she would have a chance. "Well, you seem to be happy with all the arrangements. How do you feel about your discharge now, Heather?"

"Let's do it. I'm ready to go whenever you're ready to get rid of me. So, when can I go, Dr. Stein?"

"Well, I was going to discharge you on Wednesday, but if you feel you are ready, you can go home tomorrow. How does that sound?" Heather let out a squeal of excitement.

"Great. It sounds weird but great! I feel better knowing that I won't be alone and that Stella will be with me. I feel like I've known her for a million years."

"Well, all right then. We will spend the rest of today getting ready for tomorrow. I am going to advise the desk downstairs that you are to have no visitors because we have a lot of ground to cover before you leave tomorrow."

"Well, maybe I should call Jenny and let her know I'm going to be going home, uh . . . to a new house and life."

"That's fine, Heather. I want to finish up the paperwork and set up a schedule for us to work together after you leave. So I'll leave you for the moment." He smiled at everyone and walked out of the room. He knew he had gotten too involved in this case and he felt a lump in his throat growing at the thought of Heather leaving the hospital and going out into the uncontrolled world. She had become his child and he was afraid to let go. He had to find Sutter and have a few words with him.

"Well, Heather," Brian began. "I can't believe that you're going home! There's so much to be done. I'm going to call a furniture rental place and have them deliver some things you will need. Let's make a list of what you want them to bring. Oh, and Stella, do you have a couple of hours this afternoon for us to do some shopping?"

"Oh, Mr. Hargrove, I'm sure that will be no problem. I'll go and ask Dr. Stein if I can have three hours off this afternoon." Heather had called Jenny and shared the good news. Jenny told her she would call her back later that evening.

As Stella left the room, Heather and Brian were making a list of things that should be rented for the house.

Furniture was the last thing Heather wanted to worry about right now. They also made a list of calls to make. They laughed and talked excitedly.

When Jenny called later that evening Heather rambled excitedly, laying out the details they had covered that afternoon in preparation for her discharge. She promised Jenny she would call her as soon as she had her new telephone number the next evening.

The discharge from the hospital went smoothly. Heather was on cloud nine. She couldn't believe that she was finally getting out of that place. Even though she appreciated the security of knowing that Stein and Sutter were always available, she knew she needed to move along with her life now. She also owed an awful lot to Brian, because without him she wouldn't have a place to live or anyone close to her to help her.

It was good to be outside and in the real world again! Heather was in absolute awe when she saw the house. Brian was so proud as he escorted her up the entry stairs and opened the door, then thought twice and closed it again.

"What's the matter, Brian? Is something wrong?"

"Well, it was just for that instant. This is your home and you should be the one with the key and the one who opens the door for the first time." With that he handed her the keys and stood next to her, waiting.

"Okay. Here goes nothing." The key went into the lock and she pushed the door open. She took a few steps in and then took a step backwards. She gasped. The furniture had already been delivered. The lights were on, making it look warm and cozy!"

Stella was busy bringing her things in from her car. Brian was standing by Heather silently, watching her. Suddenly she turned, and with her arms outstretched she ran over to him and hugged him.

"Brian, thank you for everything. I can't believe that you have done this for me! Come on, let's go look and see the rest of the house!" She took Brian by the hand and then turned to him and unbuttoned his coat, pulling it off. "C'mon, let's go!" She took his hand again and they started to wander through the house. Brian held his breath, trying to get through all this close contact with Heather. This had to be the most difficult thing he had dealt with in his entire life. He didn't know how he was going to manage to keep his hands off her. It would be even harder now that they would be alone and not in the hospital where people were around constantly. He wished there were some kind of pill that would take away what he was feeling; at least the physical symptoms! She was so natural and so easy to love. She was full of life. To be with her, one would find it difficult to believe that she had suffered so much pain and heartache. It seemed as if it was the first time for everything to her. She was definitely a rare treasure.

Heather and Brian went through the whole house together while Stella tried to set up the necessities in the kitchen. Then

Brian ordered some lunch to be delivered. Heather wanted to make a special dinner for the three of them. Stella was concerned that it would be too much for her and suggested they have pizza in front of the fireplace and rent a good movie. They all agreed to that plan and it was a perfect evening. Before the movie began Heather made her daily phone call to Dr. Stein. The rest of the evening flew by. Brian reluctantly left at eleven, saying he would be in touch. He didn't want to wear out his welcome so instead of crowding her into plans he felt it was better to give her some room.

She would have a busy day the next day. Dr. Stein was coming over for a session, and later on Heather and Stella were going shopping for some new clothes. Before retiring, she called Jenny as promised to fill her in on all the details of the house and the evening and invited her to come along the next day. But Jenny was unable to make it and asked for a rain check. They finally said good-bye, promising to be in touch later that week. Heather called Marlo and let him and Louise know her new address and telephone number. He wanted to come over with Louise to see the house; maybe there was something she needed? So they were going to be stopping by early in the evening.

Chapter Thirty-five

$\mathcal{L}$eo Martucci was anxious to get back to Alec Hargrove. It was Wednesday. He planned to call Hargrove in the late afternoon. He had realized he needed more pictures of the locket because he had forgotten to take any of the inside; he hadn't even thought to look inside it. He still hadn't written the report. His indigestion had increased miserably lately. He was feeling more tired than usual but he attributed it to jet lag and his busy schedule of late. He thought about his trip to France and the information he had accumulated. He sat down at his table with his magnifying glass and looked at the picture of the locket. He stared at the initials 'A.H.' and wondered. Was it possible? It was killing him to find out but he had to wait. The dog nudged him to go out so he got up.

They were finally home. Alec and Alicea were greeted at the door by their housekeeper. She advised the couple that tea was set up in the study. Alec stopped talking as he looked over the messages on the table by his chair. Leo Martucci had called. He must give him a call later. There was nothing else of much consequence. He followed his wife upstairs, watching the gentle, flowing motion of her hips as she climbed the stairs. Alicea had gone into the dressing room to prepare for a shower. Alec waited for her to get into the shower and then joined her. There couldn't be a better way to spend an afternoon, he thought.

Brian had spent so much time away from his office that he had to get caught up. He couldn't get Heather off his mind, though. He thought about her and smiled. Just thinking about her and the possibility of spending time with her made him happy. But he didn't dare call. He wanted to give her as much breathing room as possible. Besides, if there was anything going on she would have called him. He had made sure she understood how and where to call and he had given explicit instructions to his secretary in the event that did. It was impossible for him to hide who she was any longer. After all, the press had gotten hold of the story and it had run in the paper for several days. Whether she used her maiden or married name, she was no longer anonymous. He brought his mind back to the task at hand. He had an enormous amount of work to get done, and he plowed right through it. He wanted his weekend wide open for Heather.

Detective Joe Hawkins had followed Heather's story in the newspaper. He was fascinated with it. He had never gotten Heather's image out of his mind. He knew he would have to follow up on the case in order to close it with the district attorney's office. He planned an official visit but wanted to give the former Mrs. Langdon some time and space. He looked forward to meeting her, especially after all this time. Upon his initial attempt to contact her, the operator reported that the number had been disconnected. He asked for the number of the Hiltons' home and rang it, but there wasn't an answer. After research, he came up with her new number and dialed.

"Hi, Hilton residence. May I help you?"

"Yes, Heather Hilton, please."

"May I ask who's calling?"

"My name is Joe Hawkins. I'm a police detective assigned to the Langdon matter. I need to make an appointment with Ms. Hilton."

"Hold on one moment, please." Stella ran to the family room, where Heather was sitting in front of the fire with Carlton and Louise.

Heather caught Stella's urgency. "What is it, Stella?"

"It's a Detective Joe Hawkins from the police department. He'd like to speak with you."

Heather shot a glance at Marlo, who immediately got up. "I'll take the call, Stella. Which phone?"

"You can use the one in the study or the one in the living room." Within minutes, Marlo called Heather to the living room. She jumped up and headed towards him. "What is it, Carlton?"

"The detective insists on speaking with you in person and wants to set up an appointment to do so. There is nothing wrong and no more surprises, believe me. It's a formality for the police department."

"Okay, then. Tell him to come to the house tomorrow around noon. Will that be okay?" She listened to Marlo relay the message to Hawkins. He looked at Heather and nodded his head yes. When Marlo got off the phone he hugged Heather and reassured her that everything was all right and this would be a simple interview. He escorted her back into the family room.

"Of course, if you'd like, I'll come over to be with you."

"Oh, no. That won't be necessary. But I appreciate the offer. If it's nothing, like you said, then it shouldn't take that long."

"All right. But I want you to promise to call me at the office as soon as he leaves. If you can't reach me I want you to call Louise and let her know, is that understood?"

"Yes, sir. I promise." The Marlos left soon after since he had an early day in court the next day. Heather hugged and kissed them both and thanked them for being there for her. Louise told her she would be in touch later in the week to make a date for lunch.

Alec left Alicea sleeping peacefully and came downstairs to his office. He picked up Martucci's message and called him.

"Martucci here. How can I help you?"

"Hello, Leo. It's Alec Hargrove. I have a message that you tried to get in touch with me."

"Yes. It's good to hear from you, Mr. Hargrove. I trust you had a pleasant trip?"

"We most certainly did. Any place warmer than here would definitely be a comfort. So, what do you have for me?"

"Well, I seem to have quite a bit, sir. I went to the Hilton home and took pictures of documents and personal items belonging to Ms. Hilton. I think you will find them interesting. But before I get to that I want you to know that I found her adoption papers. She apparently was adopted at the age of five by the Hiltons. I tried to run down the adoption agency but it is no longer in business. But I did find a couple of the people who worked for them. Only one woman had a slight recollection of the case. She said it was a strange one because the child came from France but only spoke English. It stayed in her memory because overseas adoptions usually brought children that only spoke in their native tongue." He paused for a moment.

Alec was all ears. He sat frozen in his chair as he listened to Martucci. He went on to explain his trip to France and how he had come across a couple who finally admitted to knowing people who had an American little girl they were nursing back to health. They weren't able to be specific as to the problem or whether it was an accident. Of course, it was many years ago and they couldn't remember all the details but those people no longer lived in France.

Alec felt an old familiar sensation creeping up into his chest. The anticipation he would feel each time he received a note or a phone call insisting someone had seen his daughter. He sat very still, unable to speak. "Please go on, Leo," he managed.

"Well, there's quite a bit more, Mr. Hargrove, but there is an interesting item that I found in Ms. Hilton's room. It is a gold locket with pink and gold flowers on the front..." Alec interrupted, his hand to his chest. He was almost breathless. He could not believe what he was hearing, and didn't know how he could respond.

"The initials are 'A.H.' and the back says, 'To my Princess.'"

"You are absolutely correct, Mr. Hargrove."

"It doesn't seem possible, but I gave my little girl a locket like that once. A long time ago. She went away with her mother to France where they were both killed in a car crash. They never found my daughter's body, though. For a while I used to get phone calls and letters, but there were so many reward seekers and nothing ever developed. I don't know what to think now. This seems like too much of a coincidence. But I want to see the pictures. Can we meet tomorrow?"

"Absolutely. How about Chelsea's at noon?"

"That will be fine. Thank you, Leo."

"You're welcome, Mr. Hargrove." Alec hung up the phone and felt the greatest tugging at his heart. He put his head down toward his chest and thought about his darling little girl. What was happening here?

He was deep in his thoughts and he didn't hear Alicea come into the study. She hurried over to him and put her arms around him. "Alec, darling, is everything all right? Who were you talking to?"

When Alec looked at Alicea she could see the tears in his eyes and the torment that she had seen there many years ago in his face. "Darling, please tell me." She knelt beside him and looked up into his eyes, pleading with him to confide in her. And he did. He told her about the telephone call, Martucci's trip to France, the adoption agency and the little gold locket with the inscription and the initials. He wept as Alicea held him. There were years of pain locked within him, streaming out now. Alicea comforted him until he was ready to stop. They sat quietly in each other's arms. Alec was the first to break the silence.

"I'm going to meet with Martucci tomorrow at noon. He took pictures and I have to see them"

"Well, maybe I should go with you. What do you think?"

"My sweet, precious Alicea. I think it would be absolutely comforting if you were to be with me. Thank you for wanting to be with me. I love you so much."

"I know you do, Alec. And I love you with all my heart and soul. I have shared in your happiness and I will share in your pain."

They sat for a long time before, arm-in-arm, climbing the stairs to their bedroom.

They were up early the next morning. Alec couldn't keep his mind on anything; it was just about all he could do to sit and read the paper. Alicea wanted to be able to help him cope with this situation. He didn't explain what he was feeling or what he might be afraid of finding out. She knew that he was in pain and she couldn't do anything to make it better. But she was relieved that he wanted her to go with him today.

Their limousine pulled up around eleven-thirty. This would give them more than enough time to get to Chelsea's. Once they were on their way, Alec informed his wife that they would not be going in but he wanted Martucci to come into the limousine. But Alicea would not hear of it. "Let's at least sit down and see what the man has in pictures. Let's remain calm about this. Besides, I think a small glass of wine will do you some good, Mr. Hargrove."

Alec turned to look at his wife and then smiled. "I don't know what I would do without you."

"Well, thank goodness that's something you don't have to worry about." She leaned over and gave him a peck on the cheek. He sank back into the seat and relaxed a little, but held onto Alicea's hand like a scared child.

Chapter Thirty-six

$\mathcal{M}$artucci was waiting for them. The restaurant was crowded and there was a festive atmosphere to the place. The hostess approached the table, followed by Alec and his wife. He stood up and shook hands with both of them. Alec looked strained. Martucci turned to Alicea and asked if she had enjoyed her vacation.

"Oh, yes, it was wonderful to get away. Do you travel very much, Mr. Martucci?"

"Leo, ma'am. And yes, I do travel a lot. But in this line of work you never know where you'll end up next." There was small chatter throughout lunch and the meal moved right along. Finally Alec could not stand it any longer and began the conversation.

"Okay, Leo. I'd like to see some of those pictures you have. But before we start I want to say something to the both of you." He looked deliberately from Leo to his wife. "I do not want Brian to know anything about this, for any reason. Is that understood?" Both Martucci and Alicea nodded in agreement.

Martucci pulled out some pictures from an envelope. They cleared the middle of the table. Martucci explained the pictures as they went along. He showed them some from France, then of the adoption papers, Heather's room and finally the locket. The first one was of the front of the locket with the pink and gold flowers. Alec was taken aback when he saw it. But with the second…the last thing he remembered was Alicea's exclamation at the initials 'A.H.' Suddenly Alec couldn't breathe. He grabbed at his shirt collar. Martucci yelled out to the hostess to call 911 for an ambulance. Martucci held him as, pale and limp, he slid to the floor. Almost hysterical, Alicea held her husband's head in her arms. He looked up at her with terror in his eyes and then they closed.

The ambulance was there in no time, intravenous going. They put Alec onto the stretcher and out he went. Alicea followed with Martucci supporting her. They would take the limousine to the hospital. Once on the way, Martucci asked Alicea, "Is there anyone that you want to call?"

"Yes, please call my son, Brian. I can't remember his number . . ."

"Don't worry, I have Brian's number." He picked up the car phone and dialed.

"Brian Hargrove's office, may I help you?"

"Yes. I need to speak with Brian Hargrove. I am with his mother and there's been an emergency."

"Just a moment, I'll put you right through."

"Brian Hargrove."

"Yes, Mr. Hargrove, I work for your stepfather and I am presently with your mother on the way to the hospital. Your stepfather collapsed . . ."

"Let me speak to my mother." Martucci handed the phone to Alicea. As soon as she heard Brian's voice she started sobbing.

"Mom, it's going to be all right. Alec is very healthy. Now put that man back on the phone." Alicea handed the phone back to Martucci.

"Mr. Hargrove?"

"Yes. I want you to stay with my mother. Do you know what hospital they're taking him to?"

"Yes. Brookville Central."

"Good. I'll be in touch with the administrator. Try to shield my mother from the press until I get there. All right?"

"You can count on it."

"Thanks." Brian was out the door. On the way to the hospital he called his brothers to let them know. They would all meet at the hospital. Then he called Duprey.

"Ralph Duprey's office. How may I help you?"

"It's Brian Hargrove, Lisa. Do me a favor and let Ralph know that they're bringing Alec in by ambulance. I have no details but he collapsed at Chelsea's."

"Of course, Mr. Hargrove. Is there anything else I can do?" Duprey was standing in the doorway and turned to listen to what Lisa was saying.

"No, thanks. I'm on my way and will be there shortly. Please watch after my mother until I get there." He hung up the phone, not believing what was happening. He had his problems with Alec but he didn't want anything to happen to him. He knew how much his mother loved him and how well he took care of her.

"Lisa, what's going on?" Duprey inquired.

"They're bringing Alec Hargrove in by ambulance. It appears he collapsed at Chelsea's. That was his son. He wants us to look after Mrs. Hargrove until he gets here."

"Okay. Call down to cardiology and tell Mack Cauley we have a priority coming in for a possible cardiac." Duprey went flying out of the office to Emergency. The ER staff advised him they had been in contact with the ambulance and its ETA was approximately fifteen minutes.

*   *   *

"Remember, Stella, when this detective comes, just be close by, promise?"

"Heather, stop worrying your pretty little head. I am right here and I'm not going anywhere." Heather popped her head out of the closet and gave Stella a big smile.

"Thanks," she said. "You have no idea how much I appreciate it. I thought I was done with all the ugly police business. After today I hope it's over." With that she stepped out of the closet.

"Wow, you look great, Heather! You'd definitely stop a clock!"

"Thanks for your words of encouragement, Stella. I need to hear them. But you have no idea how great it feels to be out of those hospital clothes! That's why I can't wait until we go shopping this afternoon. And it's not only me who's going to be shopping. I insist that you buy yourself a bunch of new things, too."

"That's so thoughtful of you." But before Stella could say another word the doorbell chimed. "Well, this is it, Heather. I'm going to show him into the family room."

Stella opened the front door and immediately liked what she saw.

"I'm Detective Joe Hawkins. I have an appointment to see Ms. Hilton." He extended his hand to Stella in greeting and then showed her his badge and identification.

"Hello, Detective. Ms. Hilton is expecting you. Won't you please come in? Right this way." She showed him into the family room. The fireplace was lit and there were candles burning everywhere.

"Well, this certainly looks cozy," Hawkins observed. He couldn't wait to see what this woman looked like in a living state.

"Ah, Detective. I hope I didn't keep you waiting."

Hawkins was speechless for a moment as he extended his hand to her and then showed her his badge and identification as he had to Stella. He couldn't take his eyes off of her. What a contrast to the first time he had ever seen her. She was gorgeous. Heather was wearing a pair of chocolate merino wool slacks and a camel cashmere sweater with a leopard scarf tied loosely around her shoulders. So well put together. Was this the same woman? "How do you do, Ms. Hilton? It's a pleasure to meet you, although I must say I'm sorry that we had to meet under these circumstances. But if you bear with me I promise I won't take much of your time."

"That's kind of you, Detective. Would you care for anything to drink?" Heather looked him over. He was attractive. She suddenly felt self-conscious in front of him. He had the most beautiful green eyes she had ever seen. She tried to gain control of herself.

"I'll have a diet soda." Stella went to the kitchen and came back with a diet root beer for him and a cup of coffee for Heather.

"Thank you, Stella. You have already met Stella. She is my nurse and companion and takes care of me. I don't know what I would do without her. Anyway, Detective, shall we get down to business?"

"Yes, I suppose we must. I want you to understand that the case against your husband in your assault was being handled by the district attorney's office. They were going to press charges against him, even if you weren't. But it is my job, as part of the investigation and follow-up, and since we never had the chance to question you, to tie up all loose ends so we can close the case."

"Okay. Well, go right ahead and ask me whatever you have to."

"I would like to go back to the night of your assault. Can you tell me what happened that night?" Heather bravely recounted everything she could remember. "Well, that pretty much covers it and answers all my questions. I'm sorry that this had to be brought up to you again, but unless I had the answers I could not close the case. You understand that, don't you?"

"Yes, of course I do. But Detective, don't be afraid. I am not made of glass and won't break." She found herself attracted to this man and she didn't even know him. She didn't know what it was about him that mesmerized her.

"Well, in that case, since my business with you is over and the case is officially closed, maybe we could go out to dinner and sort of celebrate?" He couldn't believe he had asked her, that those words had come out of his mouth!

"Why, Detective. You have taken me by surprise with your lovely invitation. But I am sorry that I can't accept because I have other plans."

"I see. Well, would it be all right if I called you?"

"I think it might be worth a try," she said teasingly and with a sly smile.

"Well, thank you, then. I will be in touch." He turned to leave, and as he walked through the doorway, he turned to look at Heather one more time. He knew he was going to call her – soon! Stella followed him out to the front door and said good-bye but she couldn't close the door fast enough. She ran back into the family room.

"Heather, you are really something else. You let that gorgeous hunk of man walk right out of this house?"

"He was that and some, don't you think? One could definitely get lost in those green eyes. But I'm not ready."

"Oh is that so? Or are you scared?"

"Oh, Stella, of course I'm scared to death. After all I've been through I'm so afraid to ever give my heart to another man."

"Yes, but he didn't ask you for your heart. He only asked you out to dinner."

"I know that. In due time, Stella. Now, let's go shopping!" And off they went for a fashionable afternoon.

* * *

The ambulance backed into the emergency entrance. Both attendants jumped out, the driver coming around to meet the other at the back to bring the stretcher down.

The triage team rushed through the ER doors and started reviewing the patient as they ran alongside the stretcher into a treatment room. "It looks like he's coming to," one of the nurses remarked. Dr. Mack Cauley, Chief of Cardiology, moved quickly over to the table. He gave several orders for medications to be added to the IV and blurted out different tests to be completed. He also noted that the patient was starting to awaken.

"The patient's vitals are in the high normal range, Doctor," the nurse announced.

"Yes, his heart sounds good, too. I don't think this man has had a heart attack, although let's wait until the blood gases get back before we make any definitive diagnosis."

At that moment Alec groaned as he awakened. "What's . . ." He felt a hand on his shoulder.

"You're all right, Mr. Hargrove. The doctor will be back with you in just a moment. Are you having any pain?"

Alec, completely dazed by all the activity around him, became more aware of his surroundings and realized he was in an emergency room. He tried to answer the question the nurse was asking him. "It's hard to catch my breath."

"Well, we're going to increase the oxygen level a little bit. There; is that better?"

Alec nodded. He felt he had been hit by a Mack truck, and was weak and woozy. He tried to raise his head. The nurse was right by his side. "What is it, Mr. Hargrove, are you having a problem, pain?"

"Where's my wife?" he asked weakly.

"We'll let her come in as soon as the doctor is finished reviewing your tests, all right?"

He nodded and closed his eyes again. Slowly the chain of events came back to him. The locket. That was all he could remember.

"Okay, Mr. Hargrove. I'm Mack Cauley, Chief of Cardiology here at Brookville. We've checked your blood gases and everything seems to be fine. Are you experiencing any chest pain or did you have any chest pain at the beginning of this episode?"

"No. I'm not having pain and I didn't have pain. I just couldn't breathe."

"I see. Were you sitting quietly when these symptoms started or were you active?"

"I was having lunch with my wife and an acquaintance and I got an unexpected shock. All of a sudden I couldn't breathe."

"Well, I don't think you had any type of cardiac episode, Mr. Hargrove. Do you attribute this inability to catch your breath directly to this unexpected news?"

"Yes. I had felt fine earlier and I have no medical problems."

"Well, just to be on the safe side I would like to monitor you for twenty-four hours. I think you suffered a severe anxiety attack, Mr. Hargrove."

"That wouldn't surprise me in the least."

"I think you can rest assured that it is not your heart. But I am going to have Abe Sutter...I think you are familiar with him?" Alec nodded in assent. "I'm going to have Dr. Sutter come down to talk with you."

"Well, if you think it's necessary, then I have no choice, do I?"

"Alec, please do this for me. Everything else checks out fine, but if you are experiencing such shocking news it might be a good idea to be on medication for a little while. That's no problem, is it?"

"No, Mack. I'll do it."

"Okay, then. Let me bring your wife in. I understand she's out there waiting to see you." He walked out the double doors of the triage room and over to a group of people sitting together in the waiting room. They all stood up as he approached them. Brian was the first to come forward to shake the doctor's hand and escort him over to his mother.

"Hello, Dr. Cauley. I'm Brian Hargrove, and this is my mother."

"Yes, it's good to see you again, Brian." He shook Brian's hand. "It's very nice to meet you, Mrs. Hargrove." He directed his attention to Alicea. "Mrs. Hargrove, I know it must be difficult waiting for news about your husband. I want to assure you that I do not feel he had any type of cardiac episode. I think he has suffered a severe anxiety attack. He hasn't had any chest pain and only complains of being unable to catch his breath." Alicea nodded in agreement.

"He went down so quickly I didn't know what happened to him, and then he went out, so I couldn't talk to him to find out what was wrong. It all happened so fast!"

"I understand. But I think you can relax and know that he is doing all right. I did recommend to him that he have Dr. Abe Sutter come down and speak with him. He is Chief of Psychiatry here at Brookville. If he has had any type of a shock recently, it may help him to be on some type of medication for a while." He was careful not to divulge what the patient had told him, even to his family.

Alicea was at first stunned at what the doctor recommended but then thought about the events just prior to Alec's episode. He had been carrying this load by himself for a long time. It would probably do him good to get it off his chest. So she nodded as she listened to the doctor.

"If everything remains as it is now I would say that you can take him home tomorrow." Brian, Bob and Winston surrounded their mother in an effort to comfort her. Brian, as always, was the first one to speak.

"Is there anyway we would be able to take him home today if we have help at home?"

"It's really not even worth it because I don't think you will need any help at home when he is discharged tomorrow. I would suggest that you come in and see him and then go home and get some rest. Tomorrow will be here before you know it. Now, I noticed that there are a bunch of reporters gathering. I would suggest that you have your drivers come around to the back entrance of the hospital and we will also make similar arrangements for the discharge tomorrow morning. Mrs. Hargrove, would you like to come in first?" She nodded and followed the doctor back through the double doors.

Alicea stopped short as she saw Alec lying on the stretcher, still pale and hooked up to machines and bags. "It's all right, Mrs. Hargrove. Your husband is fine. We're taking every precaution possible. Now, come on up to the stretcher and talk to him. Alec, look who I brought in for you."

Alec's expression softened as he saw his wife. He put out his hand to her and she took it gently in hers and smiled at him. A lump in her throat prevented her from speaking and Alec could see the tears starting to form at the corners of her eyes.

"I'm all right Alicea, honestly. I know what you're thinking but the doctor said I'm all right." The doctor smiled and walked away to give them some privacy.

"Oh, Alec, if anything ever happened to you I couldn't go on. We are so happy together. You're my other half. But I can't even begin to imagine what you were thinking when you saw that locket. But please, darling, you must try to calm yourself. Talk to Dr. Sutter. You know that you have carried all your pain and this burden all these years. It would probably be a tremendous relief to talk to someone. Maybe this is your opportunity."

"I guess. But all I can think about is the locket, the pictures; there are too many similarities. How could it all be a coincidence?"

"I don't know, my love. But you are going to have to try to put it out of your mind for a little while and feel better. Then you'll be able to pick up where you left off." They talked for a while longer. Brian, Winston and Bob came in to see their stepfather and wish him a speedy recovery. Brian said he would make all the arrangements to pick him up in the morning with Alicea. Gratefully, Alec hugged Brian when he leaned over to say good-bye.

Before too long, the nurses came in to transfer him to a private room. The three sons left, but Alicea stayed with Alec the rest of the day, only leaving to go home and get some sleep herself.

During the afternoon, Dr. Sutter came down to see Alec. He shook hands with him and told him he was surprised to receive his referral but he hoped that he would be able to help him. Alicea wanted to leave the room in order to give Alec complete privacy, but he wouldn't hear of it. He wanted Alicea to stay and go through it with him.

And so, after twenty-some years, Alec was going to unburden himself and share the details of his painful losses to someone else. Sutter sat listening, only intermittently asking questions and taking notes while Alec's story unfolded. Sutter became uncomfortable when the story started to include Heather Langdon. He could not even begin to imagine what that woman would have to do with Alec Hargrove. But he sat quietly until Alec brought him up-to-date with the day's events leading up to his hospital admission. Alec trembled most of the time as he told his story but when he relayed what had been in the pictures even his voice shook noticeably.

When Alec finished, Sutter sat silently for a few minutes. Then, he began.

"Mr. Hargrove, I don't know how you held out for all these years without sharing this with anyone. I know that you have shared a lot of it with your wife, but I'm sure there are many details you have shared with me today for the first time. I don't know what your investigation is going to lead you to. That has to be your decision. My job is to try to help you function. I don't think you want a repeat performance of today, that's for sure." Alec shook his head in agreement with the doctor. "Good then. I would like to prescribe some medication for you. Let's start you on it and see how you do. It's what we call an anxiolytic and it will assist in preventing a repeat of today's episode. I would like to talk to you in a week and see how you're doing. You can either call me or stop by the office, if you like."

"Thanks, Doctor. I think it did help to tell you about it. I mean, people around you, who know and love you, don't want to see you hurt, and help you to wish it away. But talking to a professional was what I think I needed. Besides, it was what the doctor ordered!" All three laughed. Sutter spent some time explaining the long-term effects of anxiety on an individual and what a person can do to help himself in the future. He went over a couple of things he had taken notes on to make sure he understood Alec's feelings when he discussed certain topics.

"Well, that's good then. I expect to hear from you in a week." He shook Alec's hand and turned to say good-bye to Alicea. "If for any reason you need to get in touch with me, please do not hesitate to call." He handed her and Alec his card. He said good-bye and then left the room, reminding Alec to call him.

Alicea walked over to the bed. "Oh, Darling, how do you feel?"

"You know, not half bad. The picture of the locket 'unlocked' everything." He chuckled ruefully and Alicea hugged him and pecked him on the cheek. They turned as the nurse entered the room with some medication. As the nurse prepared the injection, she explained to Alec that it would make him drowsy.

"Do I have to take it?" He looked at the needle and winced. "I don't want to go to sleep."

"I'm sorry, Mr. Hargrove, but it's the doctor's orders. He wants to make sure that you get as much rest as possible." With that she gave him the shot and was gone. It didn't take long before the medication took effect. Alicea sat with him a while longer and, once she knew he was asleep, wrote him a note and left to get some rest herself. It had been quite a day. She was relieved that Brian didn't have a lot of questions. And she was also relieved that Martucci was able to disappear without too much fuss.

Chapter Thirty-seven

$\mathcal{H}$eather and Stella had a full afternoon of shopping. Heather had insisted on treating Stella to several outfits. She had found a few things herself but she was more in the mood to be out and having fun than seriously shopping. And shopping for Stella was so much fun! They came home with their arms full of bags and boxes. Still, Heather had to admit that she was extremely tired. She quickly changed out of her clothes while Stella prepared a nice herbal tea for her and lit the fireplace and prepared the sofa. She came back downstairs in a robe and slippers, found her niche on the sofa and was asleep in minutes.

The phone woke Heather. "I'll get it, Stella. I'm right here. Hello?"

"Hello there, Ms. Hilton. How are you this evening?"

"Why, I'm fine, thank you." She felt a bit of excitement; it was Joe Hawkins. "And how are you this evening, Mr. Hawkins?"

"I'm fine, now that I'm talking with you. I have to admit, though, I'm nervous. I thought I could do this but when you answered the phone, it threw me."

"I'm sorry that I'm making you nervous. So why don't you go ahead and tell me what you want to tell me?"

"Thanks for that vote of confidence. I was calling to see if you wanted to go to dinner with me on Saturday night?"

"Well, I have to think about that one, Detective."

"Please, call me Joe."

"Well, of course I'd like to go out to dinner with you, Joe." And to herself she added, you have no idea how much I want to.

"Good. I do feel a lot better now that that's out of the way. So, how was your day?"

"It was wonderful. This afternoon Stella and I went on a shopping spree. It wasn't that we bought tons of stuff but it was a lot of fun to go out and kick up our heels."

"Well, I'll remember that for future reference. Shall I pick you up about seven-thirty on Saturday?"

"Sounds perfect."

"Okay, I guess I'll see you then."

"Oh, Joe?"

"Yes?"

"Thank you for the invite."

"You're welcome." He laughed to himself as he hung up the phone. He couldn't wait until Saturday night. He felt like a teenager going out on his first date.

Stella came running into the family room. "Well?"

Heather jumped off the sofa. "He asked me out for Saturday night. Do you believe it? Maybe I should talk with Dr. Stein about this. I wonder where he'll take me for dinner. Ooh, I can't wait, Stella!" Stella laughed along with Heather and hugged her. She was thrilled that this woman was getting some happiness in her life.

Leo Martucci was sitting at his desk at home, looking at the pictures he had shown to Hargrove. What had happened at

Chelsea's still stunned him. He thought there might be a possible connection, but he'd been in the game for so long he'd seen it all. He wondered how long it would be before he'd be able to meet with Hargrove. He thought about going forward with the investigation but he didn't dare unless he got the okay. Nope, he had no alternative but to wait. He wondered how Hargrove was doing. The phone rang.

"Yeah, Martucci here."

"Yes, Mr. Martucci, this is Brian Hargrove. Do you have a few minutes to speak with me?"

"Of course. I hope your stepfather is doing all right?"

"Yes, he is. Thank you. In fact, he'll be discharged tomorrow morning. But in the mean time, I'd like to discuss the job you're doing for him right now." Brian figured he would be able to get away with it. He needed to find out what his stepfather was involved in and why. He wondered if it had anything to do with him. Besides, what could have been such a shock to land his stepfather in an emergency room? He needed to know.

"I'm sorry, sir, but your stepfather has asked me not to speak to anyone about any of the work that I do for him."

"Yes, but I'll have to take over for him while he is laid up. You don't want to have to wait to continue your investigation, do you?" He was hoping that Martucci would slip up but he was too sharp for this ploy. No wonder Alec liked doing business with him.

"I'm sorry, Mr. Hargrove. I am not at liberty to discuss anything with you. Is there anything else I can do for you?"

"No. Thanks." Brian hung up. Martucci's reticence had piqued him. Maybe his mother knew what Alec was up to. But he knew she would not tell him anything. It was worth a try anyway. Maybe it was nothing important. It's possible he could be investigating a new company or investment. That was more than likely with Alec. He was always looking, always searching for new avenues.

He wondered how Heather was doing and decided to give her a call. Stella answered the phone and cheerfully greeted him. She told him to hang on while she got Heather.

"Hello?"

"Hey there, Heather. How's my girl?"

"Brian, I've missed you. What have you been up to? I thought I would have heard from you already."

"Well, normally you would have, my dear, but my stepfather was rushed to the emergency room today." He went on to explain everything that happened.

"Oh, Brian. You poor sweetheart. But he is doing better?"

"Yes. He'll be coming home tomorrow and the doctors don't anticipate any problems. Thank God it wasn't his heart. I felt sorry for my mother. She looked lost; there was no consoling her. I've had my problems with Alec. Not because of who he is but because he is another man in my mother's life. I guess for many years I had this notion that my mother should be faithful to my father's memory, even if they were divorced. Maybe I was jealous in my own stupid way. Anyway, I don't know why I'm going on about this to you."

"Brian, you've got to be kidding. After where I was? Who was always listening and there for me? Huh? Anyway, not to change the subject, but why don't you come over to the house tomorrow night for dinner? We'll have a nice fireplace-picnic dinner while watching a great horror movie. What do you say?"

"Sounds ghostly to me!" He could hear Heather giggling. "Want me to bring anything? How about a bottle of wine?"

"Definitely. By the way, Stella and I went out shopping today and we had a wonderful time. It felt terrific to get out. I'll show you what I bought when you come over tomorrow. I even picked up something for you. See you tomorrow about sevenish?"

"Try and keep me away, you little vixen."

"Really, Brian. Don't forget the wine." She hung up the phone. Stella came into the bedroom and they began discussing what to make for dinner the next night. Then the conversation switched to Joe Hawkins. Heather was excited about their date. She didn't know what to expect and she was rather nervous about going out on a date . . . her first date after being a married woman for all those years. Stella finally had to ask her.

"Did you tell Brian about Joe?"

"No. I didn't see the need to. Besides, I don't know how Brian would react. I know how he feels about me, but I don't feel that way about him. I think of him as family but nothing else. He said he understands that. But at this point nothing may happen . . . I mean it's only our first date and there may never be a second."

* * *

The limousine picked up Brian by nine and then picked up Alicea. They arrived at the hospital at ten in the morning. Brian escorted his mother up to Alec's room and then took off to meet with Duprey, who informed Brian that he would handle the arrangements for Alec's discharge.

Alicea was anxious about Alec and wanted to see him herself to determine how well he felt. It didn't take much convincing. He was in great spirits. Alicea was delighted.

"Alicea, my love. How I missed having you next to me last night. Those nurses aren't good substitutes."

"Why, Alec Hargrove, how dare you." He grabbed her onto the bed with him and gave her a big hug.

He felt so good next to her. How she had missed him just that one night. She never wanted to let him go. He looked good, although a little groggy from the medication. But the doctor had explained that he might feel drowsy for a few days until his body got used to the medication. Yesterday had certainly been a shock and she never wanted to have to face that again.

"Why so serious this morning, my love?"

"Oh, Alec, I was thinking about yesterday and how you looked and I can't believe how well you look today. Please promise you'll never scare me like that again?"

"Okay, I promise. Now where are my clothes so I can get dressed and we can get out of here? Don't you think that's a good idea?"

"That's the best idea I've heard today." Alec grabbed his clothes and got dressed while the nurse talked to Alicea about ordering his medication and making sure that he took it and didn't skip any pills. There were no other restrictions. He could resume his normal lifestyle and check back with Dr. Sutter in one week. She insisted that Alec ride in the wheelchair, but she explained she was taking them downstairs to one of the back entrances because the reporters were aching to get some kind of story. The morning's paper had only a small article but the reporters didn't miss a trick and had run an article about Alec's collapse. It was really ridiculous. But unfortunately, that's what sells newspapers.

Within fifteen minutes they were packed into the limousine and on their way home. Alicea and Alec snuggled.

Chapter Thirty-eight

*H*eather's plans included going to the video store and picking up the latest horror flick out. Brian had ordered her a thirty-two inch television and it was magnificent to watch movies on. She planned a Mexican-style dinner with three different kinds of enchiladas to be served with rice and refried beans. She prepared them ahead of time. She had included Stella in the evening, but Stella declined, saying she had other things to do.

Even though she was happy Brian was coming over, she could not get her mind off dinner with Joe. She couldn't wait! She found herself attracted to this man. It was so sudden. Life was truly weird. She wished Brian would find someone to spend his life with. He didn't realize how lonely he was, and he would never admit it. Her daydreaming was interrupted by the telephone. She ran to pick it up.

"Hello?" she answered breathlessly.

"Hello, my little sweet! How are you doing today?"

"Carlton! I'm glad you called. How's Louise?"

"Oh, she's fine. Busy as always with this club and that club and this function and that one. But there is a reason that I called you right now. Did I catch you at a bad time?"

"No, not at all. What's up?"

"Well, I wanted to set a date for you to meet the board of directors of your parents' company. They are a bit concerned. You see, the spring collection is being prepared for a show in Paris soon. There are many plans and preparations yet to be made and they are afraid that the company will fold or change hands. They don't know what to expect. I think it would be a good idea to let them meet you."

"But Carlton, I wouldn't know what to say."

"My dear, that's why you have me. You're in a different ballgame now. That's if you want to be. I didn't want to fling this at you while you were in the hospital but I think you must address this issue as quickly as possible."

"I wouldn't want to sell the business, at least not now." She thought for a minute and then shook her head. "All right. You know I have trust and confidence in you to lead me in the right direction, Carl. I feel like a dummy because I don't know anything."

"Well, how about this? I'll get last year's board meeting minutes over to you to review and I'll set up an appointment with the board for Wednesday."

"That's a great idea. I'll have a great synopsis of the company's activities over a period of time by reviewing them so I don't go in there stone cold. Thanks, Carl."

"You are welcome, my dear. I want to be able to help you in any way I can. Now, I'll send them over by messenger so they should be there in a while. By the way, what have you been doing since Louise and I saw you the other night?"

"Oh, I've been busy. Stella and I went clothes shopping and that felt great. But you're not going to believe this, Carl. I have a date tomorrow night."

"How could you already have a date?"

"I do and you know with whom."

"You don't mean Brian Hargrove?"

"No. I care about Brian, but only as a friend. Remember when you were here the other night and that detective called to come over?"

"Yes."

"Well, he called and asked me out on a date. I like him. I'm looking forward to this."

"Oh, you mean Joe Hawkins. Well, isn't it a small world. I've known of Joe for quite some time. He has an excellent reputation in the department and is well-liked. I haven't had any dealings with him myself, but I know many who have and like him. He comes from a good family. I'm surprised that he worked up the nerve to ask you out. He must really like you."

"Well, I hope so because I feel like a teenager going out on my first date. We're just going to dinner, by the way."

"I hope you have a good time, Heather. Please call us on Sunday and let us know how your date was, all right? Oh, and before I hang up, I'll pick you up at ten o'clock on Wednesday morning."

"Yes, I promise. Thanks for calling, Carl." She hung up the phone and then realized that she had actually told family, or almost family, that she had a date. It was so strange.

She had called Jenny and told her all about it and Jenny was excited for her but concerned. She wanted Heather to find happiness more than anything in the world! But she was so afraid for Heather. She was at such a vulnerable point in her life. She could only tell Heather to take it easy and take things slow.

Heather felt bad because they lived a good distance from each other now. It wasn't hours of distance, but far enough so they could no longer spend lunch hour together or stop home to have coffee. But she tried to keep Jenny posted on every-thing that was going on. Besides, Jenny was experiencing her own problems at home with her husband possibly accepting a transfer to Arizona.

Heather ran upstairs to shower and dress before Brian got there. She came downstairs all ready for the evening minutes before Brian arrived. He walked into the kitchen where he found her, apron on and preparing their dinner. What a sight, he thought. How he wished he could come home to this scenario every night. He would be the happiest man on earth.

"Heather, look at you!"

"Hi, Brian." She held her hands up in the air and ran over to Brian and gave him a hug and a peck on the cheek hello. "You smell good tonight. What is it that you've got on?"

"I don't remember. It's some new stuff I picked up."

"Well, I like it, Brian. The scent must agree with your chemistry, my dear, because you smell like a million bucks. I hope you're hungry?"

"Yes, I'm starving."

"Good. Do you want to open the bottle of wine and Stella will help me bring the food inside? Stella has other plans for the evening but wants to help us get settled. Show time is about to begin."

They talked, joked and laughed all through dinner and then watched the movie together. It was a nice evening. Heather was delighted it turned out so well. This is what it must be like to have a brother, she thought.

Brian, on the other hand, was in so much pain being so close to Heather and not able to touch her in the way he would have liked to. It seemed so unfair! But he was there having dinner with her and that was more than he had hoped for even a year ago. Yes, now that he was here with Heather, it didn't seem like enough anymore. He wondered if this was how he would feel forever if Heather didn't give him a chance. But her words rang in his ears about how she felt about him. He sighed and wondered if the pain he felt being close to her would go away or only get worse with time. If that were the case, would there come a time when he would find it too painful to be close to her?

Brian left around eleven. He was playing golf the next day with some clients and had to be up early. He promised to call her. He actually felt stiff from pain as he kissed her gently on her cheeks, trying to linger for one second more than necessary. Heather noticed that Brian seemed distant or stiff. She didn't want to think about Brian; she wanted to go to bed and dream about her date the next day! But she was worried about Brian. Something was going on with him but she didn't feel she should ask.

*   *   *

Alec was up early on Saturday. He and Alicea had spent a quiet Friday and he was feeling like a new man. Although he couldn't get the locket off his mind, he knew he had to build his strength and rest. He wanted to call Martucci, but he didn't dare; at least not yet. Alicea would be furious with him that he was jumping right back into the frying pan and risking his health for what could very well turn out to be another wild goose chase. No, he would have to wait – but he wasn't going to wait any longer than Monday! He had to find out as soon as possible.

Heather was ready ahead of time, in a long, royal blue skirt and matching silk scarf worn over a white angora sweater and royal blue suede ballet slippers. She swept her hair up on each side with flowered clips. She was taking the final look in the mirror when the doorbell rang. She felt little butterflies in her stomach and then calmed herself with Dr. Stein's stern reminder to "not let go of your power." She smiled as she thought of him. Stella answered the door. Sure enough, it was Joe Hawkins.

"Good evening, Stella, I hope I'm not too early."

"No, you're doing fine, Mr. Hawkins. Please, won't you come in?"

"Thank you." Stella could tell that he was nervous by his walk. She smiled to herself and thought the two of them were a comedy team. One was upstairs a wreck and the other one just walked stiffly through the door. But as Heather came down the stairs and Hawkins saw her, neither one seemed nervous anymore. Heather tingled with excitement as she saw the delight on Joe's face. He walked over to await her at the bottom of the stairs. He took her hand, held it and then kissed it. "You look absolutely magnificent tonight, Heather."

Heather was pleased at his appearance. She thought he looked smashing in his camel sports coat over a green shirt that made his green eyes all the more vivid. "You look quite dashing yourself, Mr. Hawkins."

"Have a great time, you two," Stella called to them as they walked to the car hand in hand. Stella closed the door behind her and leaned up against it. It was nice to see two people together, feeling the way they did about each other. As long as Heather was happy, that was all that mattered. She curled up on the sofa in her bedroom and turned on the television.

Heather still felt a little uncomfortable. But Joe seemed to sense it and started talking about his job and how he started in police work to get the flow of conversation going. She was fascinated with everything he had to tell her. Before she knew it they were laughing and joking as if they'd known each other forever. As he drove, she watched him. He had such big, strong shoulders and arms in contrast to the gentle features of his face. She couldn't help but wonder what it would be like to be held in those arms and kissed by those lips. She felt herself blushing and looked out her car window, hoping Joe hadn't seen her. By that time they had arrived at the restaurant. He hadn't told her where they were going because he wanted it to be a surprise. It was an elegant city restaurant serving French cuisine, and it had a beautiful view of the water.

The hostess showed them to their table. Each table had its own private area, a booth partially enclosed in glass. It was like being in your own dining room. The chairs were huge, high-backed and plush. They reminded Heather of chairs for royalty. There was a delicate crystal chandelier hanging in the center of the table. They had a picturesque view of the harbor where they could see that, despite the cold air, there was quite a bit of activity on the docks around the restaurant.

"Heather, I'm happy that you accepted my invitation to dinner." I would like to lean over and kiss her right now, Joe thought. How was he going to get through the meal? He was excited to be with her. She took his breath away. Heather was having similar thoughts, only Heather wanted this feeling to last and was afraid to kiss him because it might disappear.

"Well, I must say, you definitely took me by surprise when you called so quickly."

"Why shouldn't I? And let someone beat me to the punch?" They both laughed and Joe took Heather's hand. "You are a special lady. I am so fortunate to have met you. I hope we can see a lot of each other." Heather was tickled. She felt the same way. She was scared but she didn't want him to know that. She smiled at him and felt herself getting lost in those green eyes.

Their evening was magical. They lingered, oblivious, until the restaurant's closing time. They seemed so comfortable with one another. And yet, on the way home, Heather began to feel anxious, not knowing what to expect. Was he going to kiss her? Did she want him to kiss her? But they were at her front door before she knew it and that moment had come.

"Heather, I've had to fight with myself all night to keep myself from taking you in my arms and kissing you." Heather couldn't believe that he was having similar thoughts to hers. But that comment made her feel more at ease. He kept looking at her for a sign or an answer but she just looked up at him. Finally, he couldn't help himself any longer and took her gently by the shoulders and kissed her. Heather felt dizzy, like she was drowning. No one had ever kissed her like that before. He raised her face up to his and looked into her eyes.

"Heather, will you see me again?"

"Yes."

"Tomorrow?"

"Yes." It was about all she could get out. With that he kissed her again and she felt herself melt in his arms. She felt safe with this man. But she was shaken to the core with emotion. He then took her keys and opened the front door for her and helped her inside.

As he turned back out into the night he said, "I'll pick you up tomorrow at seven. Is that all right?"

"Oh, yes. Tomorrow at seven will be fine." He whistled all the way to his car. Heather stood at the door watching him in utter amazement, her heart still racing. She had walked out of the house earlier in the evening feeling one way and had walked back in several hours later overwhelmed. He was the most amazing man she had ever met. She couldn't wait to tell Stella in the morning. But right now all she wanted to do was get into bed and think about how wonderful the evening had been, how great it was to spend time with him and to have that dynamic chemistry. She couldn't wait to call Jenny and tell her all about it. As she walked up the stairs she laughed gently to herself as she thought how nervous Jenny would be about how she felt. She went over the evening bit by bit until she fell into a peaceful sleep.

Chapter Thirty-nine

*A*be Sutter was pondering over the Alec Hargrove situation. He could ask Stein to come in as a consult, then he would be able to discuss the details with him. That was the only way to handle it. He needed to have Stein involved because there was a lot more to this. There were too many similarities between the Langdon case and the Hargrove case. He decided to give Alec Hargrove a call and discuss how he felt about having a consult on the case. He was a reasonable man and Sutter was sure there wouldn't be a problem.

When he did reach Alec, just as he thought, there was no problem whatsoever with a consult. In fact, Alec wanted to make sure all the bases were covered. He wanted some answers. So Sutter felt comfortable getting in touch with Stein. But when he called he was informed that Stein and his wife were gone for the weekend and wouldn't be back before Tuesday. The answering service assured him that the message would be given.

"Brian Hargrove, please. It's Chris Hurley."

"I'm glad you got back to me, Chris. I hope you have something for me?"

"In fact, I do, sir. I've been watching over the Langdon house as you've requested. There hasn't been too much activity but I have something."

"Oh, really. And what is that?"

"I saw Mrs. Langdon leave with a detective, Joe Hawkins."

"Don't tell me they went back to the precinct?"

"No. This was a pleasure trip. They went to that fancy French restaurant on the water, uh, Grande Maison. They were there until two o'clock in the morning. Then they went back to Mrs. Langdon's. He didn't go inside with her, but he did kiss her at the door." Brian didn't want to hear anymore. He wanted to be alone. He was angry and could feel his fingernails digging into the palm of his hand.

Brian hung up the phone but he couldn't sit still. He wanted to break something, throw something! He couldn't stand the thought of another man kissing her. She was supposed to belong to him – at least eventually. No one else was supposed to come into the picture. He knew only too well how Heather felt about him, but he still felt he could change her mind. The phone rang. He snatched the receiver and barked into it.

"Brian? I'm sorry. Did I catch you at a bad time?" It was Heather. His tone immediately softened as he heard her voice.

"Why, Heather, no. I'm sorry. I didn't mean to snap, but it hasn't been a good day."

"I'm sorry to hear that. I hope your stepfather is doing all right?"

"Oh, yes. Everything there is fine. I'm all right. I'd rather not talk about it. Let's talk about you instead. What have you been up to?" He wanted to squeeze the information out of her, figuring she wouldn't say anything to him about this detective. It hurt just to hear her voice.

"Oh, nothing much. I went out to dinner Saturday night with a friend. A new friend, in fact. But that's not the reason I called."

"Okay. So what's up?" He was surprised that she mentioned it so casually.

"Well, I spoke with Carlton Marlo, my attorney. He's set up a meeting with the board of directors of my parents' company. He wants me to meet with them and get a feel for what's been going on. But, Brian, I don't know if I can pull it off. You know all about things like that. What should I be prepared to say?"

"Do you want to meet for lunch today? The beginning of the week is always light for me."

"Oh, Brian, would you? It would mean so much to me if you could go over a few things with me."

"Sure." His heart was pounding. He couldn't wait to see her, but wondered if she would tell him more about her new "friend." "Why don't we meet at the Blue Dove at one o'clock? It that convenient?"

"Thanks, Brian. You're a sweetheart. I'll see you in a little while." And she was gone.

Brian didn't know what to do with all of this emotion building up inside him. He would never force himself on her but it was becoming more and more difficult to refrain from taking her in his arms. That's all he wanted to do. Well, he thought, that wasn't *all* he wanted to do but that was a good start. But he felt he wasn't going to get to that point; not with this detective around. But, he reminded himself; Heather had called him, needed him. That had to mean something.

Over lunch Brian explained the order of the board meeting and what to pay attention to and what was general comment. She was like a sponge, absorbing as much as possible, taking notes covering areas that were less familiar to her. It was hard for him to maintain any other focus but her.

He made his luncheon crash course stretch to three hours, admittedly inventing ways to keep Heather with him. But the time came when he had nothing to add, and he did have to get back to the office for a meeting. Heather, it seemed to him, was a little too eager to rush home to review her notes and prepare for the board meeting. He knew it was his jealousy coloring his perceptions now. But he couldn't help feeling let down when they parted.

Heather had been spending as much time as possible with Joe. She felt comfortable with him. She was aware that he knew a lot about her and about everything that had happened recently, which would ordinarily have put her on guard, but she didn't feel that way with him. She seemed to know this was a good, decent man, who would never use any privileged knowledge against her. He made her feel special. She knew she should probably not get involved with him right now, but she didn't care; she wanted to. He never invaded her psychic privacy by asking her personal questions. Joe was not pushy, in any way.

Hawkins's job took a lot of his time. He was on call quite often. She smiled as she thought about him on the way home from her meeting with Brian. She missed Joe. She couldn't believe it! They hadn't known each other long enough to have this kind of feeling, had they? But there it was, explainable or not. She couldn't see enough of him, kiss him enough or talk with him enough.

*   *   *

Josh Stein checked with his answering service upon his return. His first call was to Sutter, who was still in the hospital when the call came through.

"Josh, thanks for getting back to me. I hope you had a great vacation?"

"Abe, you have no idea. You ought to try it some time. It was easy to get away from it all for a couple of days. So, what's going on?"

"Well, I had something come up. It's a new case I took on through an emergency admission. I've given it much thought and the only way I can include you is to ask you to be a consult. I have already checked with the patient and received his permission, so there's a green light. That is, if you accept."

"Of course I do. I would do anything to help you with any of your cases."

"Well, this is one you are already familiar with. I think you're going to be pretty surprised, but not shocked."

"Okay. You got my curiosity up. So fire away."

Sutter let the details unfold, making sure he didn't forget a single word of his interview with Alec Hargrove. Stein fired questions at him regarding the locket, the private investigator and France.

"Josh, it turns out that this locket is the same as the one Alec bought his little girl. It has the same inscription of the initials 'A.H.' on the back."

"Hmmm. But . . . that's still no proof, because the locket could have been bought at a jeweler's or flea market. You can never be sure about these things. But I will admit this is an interesting coincidence."

"What's even more interesting is that your patient, according to the detective, has a keen interest in France and has pictures from there all over her room." As Sutter continued to explain, Stein thought about his discussions with Heather about France. This was not new to him. He wondered if there was a legitimate connection. He and Sutter set up a meeting with Alec Hargrove.

Heather spent the rest of Monday afternoon and all of Tuesday getting ready for the board meeting. Of course, she went out with Joe each evening for dinner, but these were short dates compared to their first one. Joe was working a case and squeezing these brief dinners in was the only way they could get to see each other. But they enjoyed every minute they had together. She marveled at how fast she was growing to trust and depend on him. She loved all the notes and flowers he sent to her. There was always something from him, and it kept him near to her heart.

Heather checked in with Dr. Stein on the phone on Tuesday and filled him in on her activities. He reminded her of their previous discussion regarding Joe and cautioned her to take things slowly. She told him she agreed with him but the feelings were so intense that they were getting involved quickly. But she explained this was different than with John. She felt her relationship with Joe was a healthy one. He told her they would discuss it further if she liked in her next session, which was scheduled for the following Monday.

Heather was nervous and psyched at the same time about the board meeting. She would wear a navy blue fitted suit with heels and a matching navy hat. She wanted to look smart without the overkill; after all, she was entering the world of fashion. She did her nails and gave herself a facial. She was going to wear her hair partially up under the hat so she didn't fuss with it. It would fall down around her shoulders gracefully if she took off her hat. She practically memorized the minutes from the meetings; she was impressed with what she read and started to look forward to this meeting. She called Brian and thanked him for all the help. It was another new beginning . . .

Abe Sutter and Alec Hargrove agreed to meet on Wednesday at one o'clock in the afternoon. Alec was feeling well and anxious to get back to his own investigative work. But Alicea had made him promise that he would relax until his visit with Sutter, so he had reluctantly given in and had taken it easy for the last week. And now he was ready to roll! This meeting with Sutter would probably be the confirmation that he was doing all right and was ready to go back to his full-time activities.

Yet by the time he got to Sutter's office at the hospital he was all keyed up. He knew he would be meeting with Stein also and the three of them were going to delve into his painful loss in order to get more details.

Alec was relieved and surprised that their meeting went quite well. Sutter and Stein interviewed him and asked him questions about the smallest details of the accident in France all those years ago, and they wanted to know more about his daughter, Melissa. By the time the session was over he felt completely drained and couldn't wait to get home and relax. He was beginning to find out that this was going to be one emotional ride. Dr. Stein explained that there was only one way they could solve the mystery of the coincidences, but he was afraid to do it with Heather at this point in her recovery. He felt doing hypnosis so soon after her episode might upset her. Alec Hargrove was horrified that they would think of putting Heather under hypnosis to see if they could get any definitive information from her. If there was any chance that she . . .he couldn't let them take a risk with her. But Stein felt he would have to follow his normal sequence of therapy to ensure Heather's complete recovery. He explained that he had talked about hypnosis with Heather while she was in the hospital and she had agreed to it. It was just a matter of timing.

"Mr. Hargrove," Stein began, "in therapy nothing happens to any patient that they do not want to happen. I want you to understand that as part of Heather's normal treatment, once I feel she is on stable ground, we are going to begin hypnosis. I can see how you reacted to the word 'hypnosis' but please understand that we would do nothing to jeopardize a patient's recovery or stability."

"Thank you for that explanation, Dr. Stein. I agree with you one hundred percent and will leave it in your capable hands." Their session concluded. Sutter explained to Alec that he wanted to keep in touch with him, especially during this period of investigation.

On the way home, Alec reviewed what had transpired at the meeting. He was afraid even to think about the implications. After all this time, would he be given a second chance? But he knew one thing for sure; he didn't want Heather's health and well-being to be jeopardized in any way. At this point, if the evidence led them to the conclusion that Heather was his daughter, he would be satisfied to know that she was alive and well and within viewing distance. He didn't want to make the connection, or the reconnection, in his life yet, if this were the truth. Besides, he wouldn't want Heather to know that he had had a private investigator going into her home, into her own bedroom. Yet, as he had learned in the past, things have a way of working themselves out.

Chapter Forty

$\mathcal{L}$adies and Gentlemen, I would like to introduce to you, Ms. Heather Hilton." Carlton Marlo proudly looked toward Heather. He was ready to carry the ball for Heather but she had a big surprise in store for him. She hesitated and then slowly rose, using the tips of her three middle fingers to support herself. She could feel all eyes on her but, especially since they were all in the fashion business, she could feel all eyes on her clothes. Strangely enough, Heather felt completely at home as she stood up and represented the company that her mother and father had worked so hard to build. She could sense respect from the members around the table. They nodded their heads in welcome.

She began, "I'm happy to be here this morning, and most importantly, representing an enterprise that both of my parents worked hard to develop. I feel it would be in the company's best interest if I heard from each of you in your area of expertise rather than for me to fill this room with words." Looking to the woman sitting on her right, Heather extended her hand. "I'm Heather, please call me that. I'm pleased to meet you. Won't you summarize your responsibilities and what your department is trying to accomplish?" There were looks of approval as Heather followed suit with each member in turn around the table. In fact, she hadn't been sure of how she was going to handle the situation until she stood up and started to speak. It had just seemed like the right thing to do.

Marlo relaxed back in his chair as he saw Heather successfully take command of the situation. He was pleased with the young woman's ability with the board, and proud of the way she'd done it. He watched each of the members; they appeared pleased with the opportunity to be able to speak up at this first meeting.

Once in the limousine, Heather turned to Marlo, "Well, how do you think I did?"

"I think you were a smash hit. I think you answered all of their questions about the future of the company without saying one word. I am so *very* proud of you, Heather." He hugged her, and for a moment Heather put her head on her attorney's shoulder.

"Thanks, Carlton. You have no idea how much that means to me coming from you. After all, you were with Mom and Dad all the way building this company."

"Yes. It was quite an ordeal. But I never thought I would be sitting next to you, my dear, and continuing down the same path." They smiled at each other and Marlo patted her hand. "Louise is going to be thrilled for you. In fact, I can't wait to tell her."

The limousine pulled up to Heather's house. "Won't you come in for some coffee, Carlton?"

"I'd love to but I can't. I have to prepare for court tomorrow. You take care of yourself. I hope you know that we will be doing this once a month. Then you will have to decide how involved in the daily operations you want to be. But let's take it one step at a time. For the moment, the board knows they have an interested and capable leader. That means everything to them. You have a pretty dedicated crew."

"Thanks, Carlton. I'll be in touch." Heather was out of the car and running up to her door. Stella was anxiously awaiting her arrival.

Heather couldn't wait to tell Stella all about the meeting. And Stella was excited for Heather, listening intently to every word she said. Stella wondered what all the booklets were that Heather carried into the house. She helped Heather put them down on the table. Heather explained that it was material each director had prepared for her to read. She certainly had her work cut out for her. But she was proud of herself and pleased at how things had turned out. She thought about Brian and how much he had helped her. After she changed out of her business clothes she would call him to tell him all about it.

On Monday, Heather rushed into Dr. Stein's office; there were no other patients. She took a deep breath and sat down. His secretary was not at her desk so Heather picked up a magazine and started to look through it. But she wasn't looking at the pages. She was thinking about today's session and what she wanted to share. She had grown fond of Dr. Stein; he was more of a friend than a doctor, but as a doctor she was happy that he had been hers when she really needed him.

"Heather, my dear. I hope I didn't keep you waiting for too long?"

"No, not at all, Dr. Stein!" She smiled at him and he seemed pleased to see her looking so well. They walked down the hall to his office. Heather followed him in and sat down in one of the leather chairs in front of the desk.

"So, tell me, Heather, how is the world treating you lately?" He listened intently as Heather talked to him about Joe, Brian and the latest development in her life, taking the reins of her parents' company. He smiled to himself as he listened. He was pleased to see how full of life she was. He was ecstatic with her progress. He discussed her relationship with Joe and was relieved that she had found someone good to attempt a new relationship with. He was somewhat worried about her relationship with Brian but she adamantly reassured him that Brian understood what their relationship was. They went into some detail about the meeting with the board of directors, the feelings she experienced during the meeting, how she felt about working in the company right away, if at all, and even about Brian's standing offer as his administrative assistant. She seemed sure that she wanted a slow entry into the business to ensure herself she was doing the right thing.

Pleased with the session, Stein laid the groundwork for their next sessions. This meant discussing what they had originally spoken about in the hospital . . . hypnosis.

"Heather, I know it has been quite some time since we discussed it, but remember I asked you to think about hypnosis and taking you back to your childhood?"

"Of course I do. It's been on my mind ever since. I guess to me it's like handing me a key and unlocking the answers to my nightmares and my fears and my insecurities. You see, Dr. Stein, I realize where I've been and I don't want to go back there. I want to move ahead in my life to new experiences. I want to feel good about myself and my relationships and the work that I do. So, yes, I have given it a lot of thought."

"Well, would you have any objection if we start to work on it during our next session?"

"I guess we could. But only if you tell me right now exactly what I can expect. I want to do it but I am also afraid."

"And most understandably so." Stein went on to explain what Heather could expect and how long it would take to get her back to her childhood. He warned her that she still had a lot of repressed anger and traumatic situations she had possibly never told anyone that could make the sessions take longer, but that was the name of the game. He reassured her that she had nothing to worry about and that he would be with her every step of the way. And if she felt more comfortable, she could have someone close to her present during the sessions. He also asked her if it would be all right to have Dr. Sutter as a consult.

"Dr. Stein, after all we have been through together do you think I have anything to hide from any of you?" Stein stopped for a moment, smiling.

"Of course not, Heather. But you do understand that no one is going to force you into doing anything you do not want to do or feel uncomfortable doing. Is that clear?"

"Yes. But I think I am ready for the next step. I want to move along with my life and I feel that there are still things holding me back."

"All right, then. Let's schedule your next session for this Friday. Is that a problem?"

"No, not at all. Let's go for it!" And the session ended. As she pulled into her driveway she saw Joe getting out of his car. Her heart skipped a beat as she slowly pulled up behind his car. He heard the car coming and turned to look. When he realized it was Heather he stopped and leaned up against his car to wait for her. Heather jumped out and ran to him. He sure looked good leaning up against the car like that, she thought.

"How's my woman doing? How did your session go?"

"Good, and your woman is just fine! Somehow I like the way that sounds!" He put his arms around her and kissed her. Heather's head still spun when he kissed her. He was too much to take! She loved to stare at him and wonder what it would feel like to make love to him. But that was a commitment she wasn't ready to make. She was still afraid to totally give herself to any man, even Joe. She knew that before too long she would have to come to terms with those feelings. But for now she didn't have to think about it. Joe wasn't pushing her for an answer like that. It was something that was on her mind because she knew it was inevitable. But she loved to kiss him and she loved for him to hold her and touch her. It was magic!

They went into the house and Heather told him about her session with Stein and what they were going to do. He put his arm around her and held her as they sat on the sofa. She felt so "at home" with Joe. He didn't ask any questions. She already knew that he respected her space and that if she wanted him to know something she would tell him. She leaned against him as they sat together quietly looking into the fire.

*   *   *

"Hello? Mr. Hargrove? It's Leo Martucci."

"Yes, Leo. I must say the last time we got together was not the best."

"It sure wasn't, Mr. Hargrove. I trust you are feeling better now?"

"Oh, yes, Leo. Thanks for asking. I wanted to call you but I promised my wife that I would catch my breath before we proceed with this investigation any further."

"Oh, no problem, sir. I had a bout with my stomach and it finally sent me off to the doctor. Nothing serious, unless I don't take care of it."

"Well, Leo, I'm glad to hear you have the sense to take care of yourself. Now, I think I'm ready to move ahead. I must say you came up with some interesting information. I guess I was unprepared for it."

"Mr. Hargrove, I'm sorry it had such an effect on you. But I'm ready whenever you are to go ahead with this. Just tell me what it is you want me to do."

"Well, the first thing I would like to do is see those photographs again. I don't think I saw them all. Please bring any information you have when you come. I think it would be best if you come to the house and we'll go through everything here in my office."

"Fine. When do you want to get together?"

"Tomorrow's good. What's it like for you?"

"I have no problem with tomorrow. What time?"

"Oh, let's meet around eleven o'clock."

"All right, Mr. Hargrove. I'll see you then." When he got off the phone, Alec sat thinking about the pictures and the meeting the next day. Finally, he thought. He wanted some answers. He didn't know what he was going to do with the answers, but he needed to know them nevertheless.

Brian was surprised to hear from Heather. Each time they talked he hoped she would come out with some kind of declaration of her love for him. He thought it was pretty stupid of him to think that; especially him, Brian Hargrove, the ladies' man. He could have any woman he wanted. They threw themselves at him as a rule and of course he took advantage of it. With the exception of his mother, he had always thought of all women in the same category, until Heather. He was groveling on his knees for the love of this woman! But he was losing ground with her and he didn't know if he could make it up without losing her totally. He had never been in a spot like this. But he knew one thing for sure; the whole situation was driving him crazy.

*   *   *

Alicea and Alec were having dinner with Carlton and Louise Marlo. They had been to the Marlo home for dinner and now Alec and Alicea wanted to take them out for the evening. They had never been friends but knew each other socially. The

Marlos traveled in totally different circles from the Hargroves. But suddenly, for some strange reason, Alec felt it important to keep in touch with Carlton. He had never really liked Carlton after he tried to play hardball during prior business negotiations. But now, in light of Heather's situation, he wanted to keep Marlo close.

"So, how's Brian doing?" Carlton started the conversation.

"He's been busy lately. As I'm sure you already know."

"The house he bought for Heather is very nice. I must say, he has good taste. And she loves it. She told me she had him over for dinner and a movie one evening. She said they had a great time."

"Well, I haven't spoken to Brian, so I don't know what he's been up to."

"Alec, he seems to be carrying quite a torch for Heather. I hope he isn't going to get hurt."

"Why would you think that he would get hurt?" Alec found that statement about his stepson rather amusing but quite irritating at the same time. He knew Brian's reputation with women. Alicea was absolutely mortified by his reputation and always hoped he would find someone to love one day. But there was also something cocky in Carlton's voice and it continued to irritate Alec. His smile slowly disappeared as Carlton filled him in on the latest news.

"Heather's been dating a detective, Joe Hawkins, and they seem to have quite a thing going." As Alicea heard the words, she thought about the son she knew so well. What was he capable of if he couldn't get what he wanted? She didn't know what was going on with the investigation her husband was pursuing but she didn't want her son to get hurt or get caught in the middle of a no-win situation. She sat quietly, as Louise did, and listened intently. Only Louise and Alicea exchanged knowing glances.

"No kidding." That was all Alec could manage. He knew that this news would crush Brian. But there was nothing he would do to protect Brian from the truth; Brian would have to deal with it. But he wondered why Carlton was sharing this with him and Alicea; it wasn't like they were friends. So he listened to Carlton and tucked his uneasy feeling away. He couldn't put his finger on why, but it was as if Carlton was gloating.

"How long has she known this detective?" Alec wondered why he was even asking the question.

"Oh, not long at all. In fact, she only met him because they were closing the Langdon case and he needed to ask her a few questions. I've heard a lot of good stuff about him. Heather seems to be happy and they're seeing each other every day."

"Well, I wish the woman a lot of happiness. She deserves it. She's gone through hell and back."

"That she has, Alec. But I'm telling you she looks wonderful. It's good to see her coming back to life."

Louise added, "She is a lovely person. She is thoughtful and kind. I only wish for good things in her life. And she seems to be off to a good start."

Marlo filled them in on Heather's first board meeting. He felt like a proud father bragging about his daughter's achievements. He was now the closest thing she had to anyone paternal.

They chatted away the rest of the evening and enjoyed good food and wine together. But Alec was anxious for the evening to come an end.

* * *

"Stella, do you still plan on coming with me today?"

"Well, that depends on where you're going." She smiled and hesitated teasingly. "Of course I'm with you all the way, you must know that by now."

Heather had filled Stella in on her last session with Dr. Stein, and had already asked Stella if she would come with her to her session on Friday and stay with her during the hypnosis, and of course Stella had agreed. The only thing that made her feel more comfortable was the fact that both Stein and Sutter would be there. She had grown to trust them completely. But she was afraid of what this session would reveal. It was a horrible feeling wondering what part would reveal itself that you had tucked away inside of you all this time.

They left early for the session because Heather wanted to drop by her parents' home. There was something she wanted to get. She showed Stella around the house she had grown up in. Things were much the way she remembered except for some clothes lying around from the time Carlton Marlo came to get clothes for her parents' burial. It felt strange to be in their home without them. She felt the stone silence and emptiness of the house now. She walked into her old bedroom and looked around. It had been awhile since she had spent any time in that room. She wandered over to her bulletin boards and touched the pictures of France she had pasted up so long ago. She turned around and suddenly she saw what she had come for . . . her locket. She grabbed it and held it close to her heart. She needed this to get through the session today. Overwhelmed, she sat down on the bed and began to cry. Stella tried to comfort her but she knew she had to do this. It was all a part of the healing process. But Heather could never have imagined life without her parents; they had served as her lifeline. She was so frightened to face what existed before them. She suddenly realized her life seemed so empty without them. And now she had to go and face who knew what. It was time to get going or they'd be late. Stella rushed Heather along. Reluctantly, she followed with a last glance around the house before she closed the door behind her.

Chapter Forty-one

With mounting anxiety, Martucci pulled into the long driveway headed for the Hargrove home. He wondered what was going to happen today. So far he had only shown the pictures to Alec but he had so much more to tell him.

The housekeeper showed Martucci into the study and told him that Alec Hargrove would be with him shortly.

"Alicea, do you want to come downstairs with me and sit in on this meeting with the investigator?"

"Of course I do, Alec. I wouldn't miss it for the world. I want to go through this with you every step of the way. I only wish there were a way I could be of more help to you."

"Just knowing that you are with me is more than I could wish for." He hugged her and then grabbed her by the hand.

"Come on, let's go. Time is a-wasting." They flew down the stairs into the study where they found Martucci setting up on the round conference table.

"Mrs. Hargrove, Mr. Hargrove, it's good to see you. I have been setting things up over here." He walked them over to the table and explained how he laid out the pictures. Alec and Alicea took their time and carefully examined each one.

Martucci stood back quietly and gave them time to absorb what was in the pictures. Afterwards, they all sat down at the table and went over the pictures one by one. Of course, Alec was extremely interested in the pictures of the locket, but he also found the ones of France intriguing.

Alec was the first to speak. "Leo, I've had some time to think a lot of this over. First, we don't seem to have any proof that this locket wasn't purchased at a flea market or a jewelers."

"That's true, Mr. Hargrove. But I do have some bewildering information. You see, my clues led me to France. While I was over there I tried to speak to as many people involved in this case as possible. I visited the scene of the accident and tried to find people who were there or lived in the immediate area at the time it happened. That was difficult. I don't know if you are familiar with the family's attorney, but his name keeps coming up. It's Carlton Marlo."

"Wait a minute." Alec held up his hand and Alicea took in a deep breath. "What do you mean, his name kept coming up?"

"Well, I spoke to an elderly woman, who must remain anonymous. She told me to look for someone by the name of Françoise DuBois. She said that I could probably find him in Miami, Florida. She said that if I found Françoise he would be able to explain things. She did remember that the child was found with this locket around her neck. But by the time I got to Florida he was gone. So I had to fly back to France because I figured for sure that was where he would go. I don't know what the relationship is between this woman and DuBois, but I'm sure she called him and told him I was on my way to see him. He's a real sleaze, if you know what I mean. I had a hard time trying to catch up with him. I guess he figured I would come back to France and try to locate him. But he had good reason. He had been ordered to take the little girl to Florida one year after the accident. He said that she had been injured in the accident and had been taken to Switzerland for whatever medical treatments she needed. When I checked with this hospital in Switzerland the name Carlton Marlo came up in connection with other children treated there. Anyway, when DuBois entered the picture he was taking her to Florida to get ready for an adoption. That's where Carlton Marlo comes in again. I didn't know if you wanted me to follow up with this Carlton Marlo. So I stopped there until I got further orders from you."

"I see." Alec was deep in thought as Martucci stopped and waited for an answer. He held up his hand for Martucci to wait a moment.

"Alec, are you all right?" Alicea got up and went over to him.

"Yes, I'm fine. I'm thinking, trying to piece this thing together. I guess my biggest question is when did Carlton Marlo become involved in this and, if he was involved from the beginning, what was he doing? I mean, I hate to think of what he was doing, if I am right.

"Leo, I'd like you to investigate Marlo. I think we might come up with some interesting information. Now, I dare say that I cannot comprehend the possibility that my daughter Melissa is alive today." He leaned back in his chair and sighed deeply. "After all this time, how do I begin to make it up to her? I have so many questions. I would like to know what she was doing in Switzerland."

"Well," Martucci said, "I think I can answer that. DuBois said that the little girl had amnesia and they had special treatments in Switzerland for that. But it's my guess that they took her there to be sure her memory didn't return. I could be wrong. Apparently this Marlo character had a pretty lucrative illegal adoption operation going on. It could have been a kidnapping gone bad, but I don't think so."

"Those are both strong possibilities. Now, Leo, I want you to continue but you need to know a few things. I know Carlton Marlo. Not well, but my wife and I had dinner with him and his wife the other night. Almost thirty years ago, in fact, before the accident, I had some dealings with Marlo. The client he was representing was battling with me over an electronics company. This guy was trying to turn the screws but I got his company. Marlo had put up the money for his client and ended up losing everything when I got the company. I don't know if that has anything to do with all of this. I would be in a state of shock to find out now . . ." Alec paused for a moment. "I wanted you to have a little background to help you."

Leo Martucci started to collect everything he had placed on the table. "Okay, whatever you want me to do. I will get right on it. Now, do you want to hold onto any of these pictures?"

"Are these your only copies?"

"No, Mr. Hargrove. I made more and have them at my office."

"Fine. Then why don't you leave these with me.?"

"Okay. Well, I'll be in touch with you, then. It was nice to see you again, Mrs. Hargrove." Alicea smiled as he left the room.

"Alec, I can't believe all of this! What are we going to do?"

"Well, I know exactly what I have to do. It's time to call Alan Switter. I think I had better set up a meeting with him. I don't know where all of this will take us, Alicea, but I am always prepared." So he punched in their attorney's number and set up an appointment for the next day. Then he sat down next to Alicea and leaned his head back. Alicea could see the pain in his face.

"I can't believe. . ." That was all Alec got out before he broke down sobbing. Alicea put her arms around her husband, comforting him. It was years of pain still crying out and there was no stopping it. She hugged him and let him cry. No one could have been prepared for news like this, she thought.

ChapterForty-two

Stein and Sutter were going over a few strategies before they met with Heather. They already knew that Stella would accompany her and were pleased with her choice. Stein had worried that Heather might ask the detective she was seeing. Sutter had agreed that he would take a back seat and would not ask any questions; he would be there on a consult basis only.

They heard Heather and Stella coming through the outer office door and Stein opened his door to welcome and show them into his office. He could tell by the look on Heather's face that she was tense. He decided it would be better to start off by catching up a bit and getting her to relax.

Once everyone greeted one another, Stein began. "Heather, why don't you sit down and relax and bring me up to date on what's been going on in your life since I last saw you?" He could see Heather begin to relax a bit and a smile came over her face. He knew she was thinking about the new love in her life. She chattered casually on, telling him about her visit to her parents' home before coming to the session.

"How did it feel to be in your parents' home and in your old bedroom?" Stein asked.

"Everything was pretty much the way it was the last time I visited except the house felt empty and that in turn made me feel extremely hollow. I felt a void I didn't know how to fill. I walked into my bedroom and looked around at all my pictures. I didn't want to be there. I only went home because I wanted my good luck charm."

"Really? And what is your good luck charm?" Heather got up and walked over to Stein. Her hand was gently grasping at a delicate chain.

"See? This is my good luck locket." Heather replied, showing it to Stein and then to Sutter. "I don't think I could have gotten through today unless I had it with me."

"It's a beautiful locket, Heather. Did your parents give it to you?"

"No. As far as I know it has always been with me. I don't know whose initials are on the back but I love the message inside." She took the locket off and showed it to everyone, including Stella. "I assumed it was my mother's initials because my father was never in the picture, but I don't really remember. I guess that's why we're all here, aren't we?" She asked nervously.

"Of course, Heather. But we have been through so much together already that going over another hurdle doesn't seem that bad, does it?"

"No . . . well, at least not the hypnosis part. I mean, I have grown to trust the three of you completely. I am just afraid of what my past holds."

"Heather, your past is like a bad dream that keeps haunting you. If we hold the key to unlocking that door then the ghosts behind it will disappear," Sutter explained.

"I realize that. My intellectual self understands that. It's my fearful self that I'm trying to deal with. But I must admit that I'm not as fearful now that I am here." Heather sat back down in the easy chair, putting her locket back on. Sutter was darkening the room so they could get started. Stein was testing the tape recorder to make sure it was working properly. He explained everything to Heather again and then went to work on the hypnosis.

Stella could feel herself tense up; this was all new to her. She couldn't believe how quickly Stein went to work and how quickly Heather went into a hypnotic state. Heather began answering questions. Sutter sat quietly nearby observing and taking notes. Stein asked Heather questions for about two hours with Stella and Sutter observing.

They had gotten to the core of what they needed to know. Several times during the session, Stein had to reassure Heather that she was all right and safe. Other than that, there were no complications. He then brought Heather back and they all listened to the tape.

"Heather, how are you feeling?"

"I feel like I took a hard test. Very tired."

"Do you want to stop at this point or do you want to hear what happened during your session?"

"I don't care how tired I am, I have to know what happened and what I said." Stella moved over and sat on the sofa next to Heather. "Did I say anything . . . do you know now about my past . . . what happened?" "Yes, the session was productive. I think you're going to be surprised. Now listen to me, Heather. I need to talk with you for a few minutes before we start the tape. Okay?"

"All right, all right!" Heather said impatiently.

"Come on. Let's take a little walk outside and take a break while I talk to you." Stein looked around and nodded to Stella and Sutter to stay behind.

Once outside he gave Heather a hug. "I want you to know how proud I am of you. You did wonderfully today. You were very brave. I know it was a horrible experience for you but you did it. You've been through the worst."

"Thank you, Dr. Stein, for the compliments. I must have revealed some lulus in there for you to be spending this time with me buttering me up. Isn't that what you're doing?"

"No, not exactly. Don't forget you've been through a tremendously traumatic experience. I want you to catch your breath before we continue on and deal with what you have revealed. Now, Heather, look at me." He put his hands on her shoulders. "Heather, look at me." Heather looked up into Stein's face.

"We've gone through a lot together, haven't we?"

"Yes, we have." Heather was nodding her head in agreement.

"Well, you have to go on trusting me for just a while longer, okay? Now listen to me. I want you to sit on the sofa and listen quietly to everything on that tape. If you feel you want to speak up we'll stop the tape and talk about it. Is that acceptable to you?"

"Yes, now let's go!" Stein shook his head at the impatience and followed her back into the office.

Stein turned on the tape. Heather sat and listened. At first she nervously giggled. All her most private thoughts during her marriage came out. Her true feelings. She felt self-conscious in front of everyone all of a sudden. But at the end of the questions about her marriage Stein shut the tape off and they had a discussion. He wanted to give Heather every opportunity to express herself and get used to being on tape from hypnosis. Then they went on to the next section covering her school years. Stein didn't feel the need to delve into her past academically. But he wanted to make sure that he didn't skip around. After that section he stopped and once again let Heather talk it out.

His anxiety level rose as he started the tape this time. Heather was talking to someone on the tape. Her voice had changed to a child's about the age of five. Heather was completely taken aback and couldn't believe that it was she. Stein had to stop the tape for a minute until she could get used to the idea. When he started it again she seemed to be in conversation with someone by the name of Françoise. She was apparently going somewhere with him. Stein's next question to Heather was, "Where is Françoise taking you?"

"He's taking me to my new Mommy and Daddy. I don't want to go. I'm afraid. I want my Mommy." Heather was whimpering like a child. "Oh, mon dieu. Ma mer. Ma mer!" Stein stopped the tape. Heather couldn't believe she was speaking in French. She didn't speak French; only what she had learned in school. Stein calmed her and they talked a bit more before he put the tape on again. This section covered Heather meeting her adoptive parents and beginning her life with them and the start of the horrible nightmares. At this point, Stein did not question Heather about her nightmares. He wanted to press on because he felt, as he had felt from the first day he started to work with her, that her problem went way back. So he took her back further. He knew she had been five years old when she came to live with the Hiltons. So he took her back to when she was four years old. And he knew he had hit the jackpot.

"Where are you, Heather?"

Heather answered in an even more childlike manner, "I'm with Mommy. We're gonna have a birthday party in France. I'm gonna be four years old!"

"Where is your father, Heather?"

"Daddy can't come. He has to go to work." She started whimpering again.

"What does your Daddy call you?"

"I'm Daddy's little princess but my name is Melissa."

"Stop that tape!" Heather was trying to catch her breath. "That can't be me. It must be someone else. Are you sure that's me on the tape?" Heather held onto her locket for dear life. "Please, Dr. Stein, tell me that's not me."

"It's all right, Heather. It is difficult to accept what your past has been. Let's take another minute and take a walk outside and get some fresh air."

"No! I want to stay here and finish this now, no matter how difficult it is! Even if you have to sedate me, I want to know everything now! It's too late to turn back!" She sobbed. She was terrified to find out more than she had remembered about her past. She hadn't even thought she had ever known a father or that he might still be alive. Now she was sitting on this sofa in a shrink's office listening to herself talk about her father as if it were an everyday occurrence to see him. It was too much! But she felt driven to go on. She had to find out the truth. Stella tried to relax Heather and calm her down. She tried to take Heather's hands from the locket. Suddenly it hit Heather. The locket! She started to take the locket off. Stella helped because her hands were shaking. "This must be the locket that my real father gave me! If what I just said on the tape is the truth, the same thing is inscribed on this locket!" She stared at the locket in utter disbelief, and then she handed it to Stella to confirm. "This is absolutely unbelievable. So then . . ." Heather stopped as she began her next sentence. "Who is my father? Is it on that tape?" She looked at Stein.

"Heather, I want to continue this with you. I can only begin to imagine the anguish you feel at this moment. Yes, this tape is very revealing. I want you to sit back and take a deep breath. Are you listening to me?" Heather nodded her head. "Good, then. Now, I want to know if you feel you are ready to continue."

"Are you kidding?! You couldn't haul me out of here! I know that the three of you already know what I need to know!" She looked at each of them in turn and they all nodded their heads. "Well, then. Let's get on with the show." She shakily dabbed at the corners of her eyes and touched her nose with a tissue. Stein shot a glance at Sutter and they both nodded in agreement to continue.

In questioning Heather during hypnosis, it had been agreed upon by the two doctors to establish if Heather was with her mother during the accident before having her identify who her father was. Stein turned the tape on and the session continued.

"Heather, can you tell me if you went to France with your Mommy?"

"Yes, we did."

"What is your mother's name?"

"Mommy. But Daddy calls her Monica."

"Did you drive in a car with Mommy while you were in France?"

"Uh-huh."

"Did anything happen while you were in the car with Mommy?"

"We were in the car. Crash! I went to sleep. When I woke up I was in bed but I can't find Mommy. Someone told me I was sick and had to go away. I wanted Daddy but he never came." At this point, the little girl, Melissa, was crying hysterically, and it took some time for Stein to reassure her that she was fine, safe and in no danger whatsoever.

"Do you remember what happened after that?"

"I had to go to a hospital and get better. The doctor had to operate three times. Then he said I was all better so I thought I was going home, but I didn't see Mommy and Daddy."

"Where did you go?"

"We went to Florida."

"Who went with you?"

"Nanny, who took care of me and Françoise."

"Now, I'm going to ask you a question, Melissa. Listen carefully and see if you know the answer. All right?"

"Okay."

"Do you remember what your Daddy's name was?"

"Mommy calls Daddy Alec."

"That's very good, Melissa. Now do you know what Daddy's last name was?"

"Yes. It's the same as mine. Melissa Hargrove." Heather screamed and passed out on the sofa. Stella caught her to prevent her from falling onto the floor. Stein shut the tape recorder off and Sutter jumped up and came running. But Heather was out only for a minute. Stein gave her a tranquilizer and some water.

"Heather, dear, you are all right. Everything is going to be fine. You are safe and with people who care about you. Now I want you to take a couple of deep breaths and lie down on this sofa for a few minutes.

Heather didn't fight him; she felt dizzy. The last statement on the tape recorder rang in her ears . . . Melissa Hargrove, Melissa Hargrove, Melissa Hargrove! It was intense but slowly faded as she looked around her and saw Stella, Stein and Sutter standing over her.

"I don't believe this. I can't comprehend . . . did I say I was Melissa Hargrove? If I'm Melissa Hargrove, then who the hell is Heather Hilton?" She looked at the initials on the locket in her hand. "A.H.: that's Alec Hargrove. Oh my God, that's Alec Hargrove of Hargrove Electronics. He's the owner of John's company! He's Brian's stepfather!" She tried to get up but started laughing. She was laughing so hard. Stella, Stein and Sutter just let her go. She looked at the three of them. "Don't you think this is funny?"

"No, Heather," Stein answered. "And after you get over the shock of it, you won't think it's funny, either. Your past is now out in the open for you to deal with. It is going to take time." Heather stopped laughing as she listened to what Stein was saying to her. She was starting to feel drowsy from the medication he had given her.

"Well, I think it's a mess!" Heather answered, but her speech was becoming slurred. "I don't know what to do now. I don't know who I am anymore!"

"Sure you do, Heather. I'm not going to say much more to you today because you're getting drowsy, but after what you went through in that hospital you definitely know who you are. Of course it feels like deception to find out your name is different than you knew all these years. But it does not change the wonderful person that you are. Do you hear me?" Heather nodded, drifting off to sleep.

"Stella, I'll help you home with her. We'll get her into the car and I'll follow you to the house. I will be staying with Heather tonight to make sure everything is all right. I don't anticipate any problems but I want to be sure." Stein looked at Sutter. "What do you think Abe?"

"I think that's a good idea. She has had a very big shock today. I know she had plenty of them in the hospital, but this is different. We are dealing with real core issues now." They loaded Heather into the car and Stein followed Stella home, where he carried Heather upstairs to her bedroom. Stella went to make coffee and then came upstairs to fuss over Heather.

"Dr. Stein, why don't you go downstairs and take a break. I made a fresh pot of coffee and put out some sandwiches. I thought you might want a little something before dinner. I started a nice fire in the fireplace. Please, go downstairs and take a break."

"Thank you, Stella. I don't think I'll fight you on that. In fact, I'll make a few phone calls while I'm down there and check in with my wife." He left the room. Heather was sound asleep. Stella covered her with a down quilt and sat and watched her for a while. She looked peaceful sleeping there, she thought. Heather had a rough day, probably the roughest one anyone could have in their life. She hoped Heather would sleep clear through to morning. She needed it. The phone rang. Stella picked it up.

"Hilton residence."

"Hello there, Stella, how's my girl doing tonight?"

"Oh, not too well, Mr. Hawkins. She had a rough session today. In fact, we arrived home about twenty minutes ago. The doctor is here and will be staying over tonight just in case Heather has any problems."

"Well, how about if I come over, then? I could be around in case she needs help."

"That's very kind of you, Mr. Hawkins, but I think if you keep in touch tonight that would be good enough. The doctor has tranquilized her and she should sleep through the night. I don't anticipate any problems. If there are any changes, I can call you."

"Thank you, Stella. I will take you advice, then. But in case Heather wakes up please tell her that I called and that I love her, okay?"

"I promise." Stella hung up the phone with a deep sigh. They were so much in love. With a man like that by your side, how could any woman go wrong? Heather was lucky to have him. But she had told Stella that her recovery was a road she wanted to travel alone, without getting Joe all twisted into it. She said she had to close this chapter in her life before getting on with the next. But she had thought she had done this with John Langdon; she never anticipated having to close another chapter. She had told Stella that Joe was a goal for her. But she had many steps to go before she could feel free to be with him completely. Those steps not yet taken would be another new beginning.

Chapter Forty-three

Normally a cool and composed captain of industry, Alec was going crazy. He knew that the doctors were planning to see Heather and yet he would be unable to get any information because of patient confidentiality. He would have to wait and continue with his investigation and hope to uncover something. He wanted to find out why Carlton Marlo's name was involved in this. The telephone rang and Alec could hear Hilda speaking. She came into the study.

"Phone for you, sir. It's Mr. Switter."

"Thank you, Hilda." He waited until she walked out of the room and then picked up. "Hello, Alan. I hope you're getting back to me with some news or advice. I'm slightly going out of my mind here."

"I don't have anything for you yet, Alec. I wanted to let you know that we are working hard on this. I do know that both the woman and Françoise DuBois are gone. There is not a trace of them. I don't know much about this Carlton Marlo. We're trying to get some info on him, too. By the way, I would suggest searching through old records to see if you can find Melissa's birth certificate and her blood type. This young lady will need to take a blood test. Do you still have any old records?"

"I'd have to search for them. I know I have them some place."

"And please do not speak to Marlo under any circumstances. I don't know what his involvement is, so it is best for you not to have any contact. It doesn't look good for him right now. So you have to protect yourself in every way possible. I might even suggest that you have security keep a watch on your house, just to be on the safe side."

"All right, Alan. I'll do whatever you say. But I know that is going to make Alicea very nervous."

"Tell her it's just a precaution. I don't think you have anything to worry about. If Marlo had anything to do with this thing he might be long gone before we get the evidence. Well, that's about it for the moment."

After the call, Alec sat for a long while, wondering what was going to happen. Sometimes the anticipation of finding his daughter overwhelmed him. It would be beyond his wildest dreams! But for now he would have to wait. He remembered what Alan had told him and got up and started looking for those papers.

Leo Martucci was trying to get into Carlton Marlo's office, but security was tight. He kept sitting outside, waiting for the opportunity to present itself, but luck wasn't with him. He figured that there must be a safe in the office someplace and that would be the best place to look. If Marlo was somehow involved in this matter, he definitely would not leave any paperwork around, even from quite some time ago. Martucci would have to sit and wait for that perfect moment.

*   *   *

The week following her initial hypnosis session was a rough one for Heather. She refused to see Joe that entire week, and he was sick over it. She had talked with him over the phone and explained why, but he didn't want to take no for an answer. He kept telling her that he wanted to help her to get through this. She told him she would call as soon as she had sorted things out. She was careful not to share anything that had happened in the sessions. She tried to explain to him that she did not want any memories of this cropping up in the middle of their relationship, and he knew she meant it. So, in resignation, he told her he would be there if she needed him. Of course she needed him; she needed him desperately, probably now more than ever! But that was the point: she was the one who had to make things happen in her life . . . no one else. In fact, everything else was a plus! It was a tough lesson to learn but she was hell bent on learning it.

She felt so angry and didn't know how to get rid of it all. One life was stolen from her and it had been replaced by another. Her emotions were running wild and so she stayed away from everyone, trying to vent this anger. Alec Hargrove, her father? She refused to speak with Brian and got into an argument with Stella when she refused to take Joe's calls. She was hiding from everyone.

On Saturday she asked Stella to go with her to her parents' home again. Somehow she needed to be there. She needed to search for something. Maybe, if she were lucky, she would find . . . something.

Heather needed to be close to her roots. She was trying to make sense of what had happened to her. She had had a session with Stein every day since the hypnosis but nothing seemed any easier to take. She dropped onto her old bed and stared at the pictures of France on her wall. As she concentrated on them it made no sense that part of her had remembered all along and the conscious part of her chose to repress so much of who she was all this time. She didn't dare think about

Alec Hargrove. How could that man be her father? She could not comprehend it. She knew nothing about him except for what the other wives talked about at the Hargrove Electronics functions she and John had gone to. It still seemed like a horrible nightmare that she was waking up to. Outside of sessions she had tried for hours on end to remember something, but nothing seemed familiar to her. Stein had explained that she might never remember more than what she had revealed in hypnosis. But she didn't have a sense of reality anymore. Was she Heather or was she Melissa? She was trying to put all the pieces of the puzzle together but didn't feel she was getting anywhere. Dr. Stein told her it was going to take lots of time for her to understand this. She got up and looked outside of her old bedroom door.

Stella was busy in the kitchen making coffee and sandwiches. She had been hovering over Heather all week, making sure she was all right, that she was eating and keeping her appointments with Stein.

Then there was Joe. Heather was so in love with him but couldn't face him after everything she had been through. She didn't know if he would feel the same about Melissa as he did about Heather. Maybe it was better to forget the entire romance and start fresh where nobody knew anything about her. But she realized she couldn't continue to deny herself because she had to face up to this if it were going to be her reality. She just wasn't ready yet. But at the same time she didn't want to lose him. Stein had said she would have mood swings like a pendulum. He explained that as she became sure of herself and all the dust settled, the pendulum would slow down.

She wandered down the hallway and found herself in her parents' bedroom. She looked over at their bed and, for a fleeting moment, could see both of their forms under the covers, sound asleep. But as she moved closer the images disappeared and there was nothing but emptiness. She sat on the bed; gazing around the room. She missed them both so much. They had been her life all these years and then suddenly they were taken away from her. Just like that! Tears stung her eyes; a catch rose in her throat. Everything seemed so quiet; almost as if time were standing still. She took a quavering, deep breath. Dust was starting to collect everywhere in a room where she remembered so much life. Then she saw her father's desk and went over to it to look through it. Maybe she could find something that would help her understand. But she knew deep in her heart that her parents would have told her the truth. They loved her and they would never have done anything to hurt her like this.

In the bottom drawer she found her adoption papers. She looked at the dates and saw she was five years old when she came to the Hiltons. The rest of the papers were legal adoption documents. But there was a stamp indicating that the origin of adoption was in France. How odd, she thought. Then again, she had never seen those papers and she also realized that children are adopted from all around the world, so that really meant nothing. Everything else in that drawer was legal documents and the empty will envelopes, the contents of which Carlton must have taken when he came to collect the clothes for her parents.

All the way on the bottom of the drawer, hidden underneath a piece of wood, like a false drawer bottom, was another envelope. Heather pulled it out. Her name was written on it and also "Just in Case." Heather opened it. It looked like some type of an agreement between her parents and Carlton Marlo. It stated that Carlton would have forty percent of the business as a silent partner. What?

Heather thought for a moment. Her parents would never have agreed to anything like that. Besides, it was her understanding that she was the sole heir of her parents' estate, which meant the business, also. If Carlton had such an agreement with them, why hadn't he mentioned it to her?

She thought about calling Brian but she couldn't face him. If all of this were true, then Brian would be her stepbrother. She thought back to her dinner with Brian by the fireplace. She remembered wondering if that's what it felt like to have a brother.

She felt something terribly wrong here but didn't understand enough to make any sense of it. She needed to get legal counsel. The person in the world whom she most trusted and wanted by her side right now was Joe. Still holding the papers in her hand, she went to the kitchen and picked up the phone to page him.

"Heather, is everything all right?" Stella turned to see what she was doing.

"I'm not sure, Stella. Look at these papers I found in my parents' desk. They're addressed to me. They say that my parents' attorney was to get forty percent of the company. But it doesn't look like a legal document. It only looks like an agreement, but it doesn't state the reason at all." Stella took the papers and looked at them. The telephone interrupted their conversation. Stella quickly picked up the phone.

"Hilton residence. May I help you?"

"Stella, is that you? It's Joe Hawkins. I've been paged but I didn't know from whom until I heard your voice. How is she?"

"She's fine and she's right here, Mr. Hawkins. Hold on." Stella handed the phone to Heather.

"Hi, Joe. I'm sorry that I haven't called you before."

"Heather, I'm so happy you called. I have been miserable and worried about you. Is everything all right?"

"Well, something has come up that is quite troublesome. I'm at my parents' home right now. Joe, this has made me realize that I want you to be by my side. I wanted you to be there all along but I didn't feel this was your problem. I had to stand on my own and try to solve it. Do you understand what I mean?"

"My dearest, sweet Heather, I would climb mountains for you, don't you know that?"

"Yes, I do. But that wasn't my point. You shouldn't have to. But I am trying hard to deal with this situation and I can't do it by myself." Then Heather asked the hardest question for her to ask anyone in the world. "Joe, will you help me?" she started to cry.

"My darling, please don't cry. I'll do whatever I can to help you. Now, if you stop crying and listen to me, I'll make a bargain with you, all right?"

"Okay." Heather wiped her eyes with a tissue Stella handed her.

"Good girl. Would it be all right if I came over around seven tonight?"

"Oh, absolutely, Joe. I can't wait to see you!"

"Good. But only on one condition. You have to make me dinner because I am famished and I don't have time to stop for lunch today. Is that a deal?"

"You bet it is! Thanks, Joe. I can't wait to see you. I'm sorry that I was so mean."

"Heather, you weren't mean. You needed space and I prayed that you would call me and that you would need me."

"Oh, I do, Joe. I really do. I realize how much now."

"Well, I want you to know that works both ways. Now make sure you have something good for dinner or else!"

Heather laughed despite herself. "I promise. Bye, Joe." As she hung up the phone, Stella could see a little bit of peace in Heather's expression. That was a good thing, she thought. Heather needs Joe to be with her and help her through this.

Heather smiled at Stella as she sat down at the kitchen table where lunch was set.

After lunch, Stella helped Heather look through the rest of the house but they found nothing more. So they closed up the house and went to Stein's office. Heather couldn't wait to tell him about what she had found. Her mind was all over the place, even thinking about what she should make for dinner. She couldn't wait to see Joe. She thought about how she had pushed him away. Stella pulled up in front of Stein's office and Heather got out and ran in. Stella parked the car and then sat outside on a bench in the sun. It was chilly but spring was definitely in the air.

Heather reviewed the day's events with Stein. He was interested in her telephone conversation with Joe. Something had happened there that she was not aware of. She had reached out. They discussed that for a while. Then Stein concentrated on the agreement Heather had found at her parents' home.

It was a good session and Heather felt better and a bit clearer about things when she left his office. She greeted Stella at the bench and they took off for home. Stella had talked Heather into letting her prepare dinner for the two of them. "Why don't you go upstairs when we get home and take a nice bath?"

"You know, that doesn't sound half bad. Thanks, Stella, I think I'll do that."

Chapter Forty-four

$\mathcal{L}$eo Martucci had waited and waited. Now his patience would pay off. His golden opportunity had come and he made the most of it.

Once inside he quickly sifted through the papers but didn't find what he was looking for. There must be another place, he thought. He went back into Marlo's inner office and checked behind all the walls but there was no safe.

He sat down at the desk and leaned back and thought. Where would he put a safe so it wouldn't be noticeable? He kept staring at the wall unit and finally got up and walked over to it and started opening the cabinet doors. Bingo! Now, he thought, this should be the jackpot. And it was. In it he found an agreement between the Hiltons and Marlo, Heather's adoption papers and a bunch of letters from France. He opened them. They were instructions to Françoise DuBois. There were also notes to the woman Martucci had met in France. He laid the letters on the desk and took pictures of them, as well as of the agreement between Marlo and the Hiltons. This was it. But he knew that Alec Hargrove would never be able to use the pictures he was taking in a court of law. They would have to enter legal action and start from scratch with a search warrant. He carefully put everything back into the safe and closed it. He had to get these pictures developed and get them to Hargrove quickly. Apparently, this Marlo character was a real mover and he might pick up and high-tail it out of town.

Martucci closed the door behind him and beat feet out of there. He made a beeline into his darkroom to develop the pictures.

*   *   *

As Brian sat at his office desk, trying to read his mail, his thoughts kept wandering to Heather. Why hadn't he heard from her? It was already over a week – and the longest he had gone without talking with or seeing her. It was too painful to hear her voice, so he'd stopped actively pursuing her but still expected a call from her. He knew she was involved with that detective and that really pissed him off! But there was nothing he could do about it. He was starting to realize that he was never going to have Heather. He had wanted her of her own free will or not at all, he'd thought. He wasn't really a monster, just selfish. He laughed at the mental picture of himself. Well, he had nothing to lose. He dialed her number. But there was only the answering machine to talk to.

"Hello, Heather, my love. I'm checking in with you to see how you're doing. I haven't heard from you and am starting to worry. Please call me and let me know that you're all right. Bye."

"Mr. Hargrove, it's for you on line three," his secretary buzzed. Well, he thought, so much for that right now. And he answered the call.

Alicea and Alec were sitting down to dinner when Hilda announced a telephone call for Alec. He excused himself and went into his study to take the call. It was Leo Martucci.

"Gee, I'm sorry to interrupt your dinner, Mr. Hargrove, but I have some important information that I think you should have."

"All right, Joe. Why don't you come right over?"

"You bet. I'll be there in twenty."

"Fine. Maybe you will join us for coffee and dessert."

"Thank you. I'll be right over." Alec hung up the phone and walked back into the dining room where Alicea was waiting for him.

"Is everything all right, darling?" Alicea asked, looking up at her husband as he walked over to the table and sat down.

"Everything is fine, my precious." He took her hand and kissed it. "That was Leo Martucci. Apparently he feels he has some vital information. He's on his way over. I told him he could join us for dessert and coffee."

"Oh, let me tell Hilda to set another place." She rang for Hilda.

Hilda was bringing in dessert when the doorbell sounded. "I'll get that, Hilda," Alec opened the door to a somewhat breathless Leo Martucci.

"Hello, Mr. Hargrove. I got here as quickly as I could."

"Soon enough. Please come in and join us in the dining room."

"Thank you, sir." Martucci followed Hargrove. He greeted Alicea and then sat down at the table. "I'm sorry it's taken me so long to get back to you but I had a difficult time trying to gain access to Marlo's office." Alicea shot a glance at her husband then back at Martucci. She sat quietly, amazed that her husband was including her in his meeting. Alec was too engrossed in what Martucci had to say to notice his wife's glances.

"But I finally got into the offices. He has two safes. The first one I went through and found nothing at all. But the second safe was well-hidden and I hit the jackpot. I want you to know that, though you won't be able to use any of this information in court, you should get it to a lawyer right away. I'm sure that once he sees it he will want to start some type of formal investigation leading to charges. Now," Martucci paused as he pulled the pictures from his briefcase, "these are the documents I found in the second safe." He handed Alec several of the pictures. "The first two you're looking at are pictures of a document signed by both the Hiltons and Marlo. It entitled Marlo to a forty percent take on all dealings in the Hilton business. I found that strange since I read that Heather Langdon was the sole heir. There wasn't any mention of Carlton Marlo getting in on the act.

"The next several pictures I think you will find interesting. These are notes and copies of letters sent to Françoise DuBois and the woman I spoke with in France. She apparently served as the girl's nanny."

"Wait one minute, Leo. I need a minute to absorb what's in these photos." Alec handed some of the pictures to Alicea, who also looked them over.

"I'm leaving you two sets. I figured you would send one to your attorney and you would want to keep a set to review yourself."

"Now, please listen to me, Mr. Hargrove. I know you pay me to investigate and not give advice, but I can't help it in this case. This is going to be one man on the run. I don't know how long it will take him to catch on but it shouldn't be too long. Besides, he might have heard from DuBois by now. It appears that he's one slick dude. In fact, I think he might have become suspicious once Mrs. Langdon was in the hospital. Who knows what could have come out during that time with her, the way she was. Anyway, I'd get those pictures over to your attorney fast. As I said before, there will have to be an investigation. If you ask me, Marlo will be long gone by then. If there is anything else I can help you with, Mr. Hargrove, let me know. In the meantime I will be watching over you and the Missus, here. So, if there's nothing more, please excuse me and let me get to my work."

"Thank you for this information, Leo. You did an excellent job. You have no idea how much I appreciate it. Your money will be in your account as usual in the morning." Alec walked Leo to the door. He shook his hand and let him out. Closing the door, he stood for a moment thinking about the information that had been revealed this evening. If they were able to use it, it would be enough to indict Marlo. But, like Martucci said, it wasn't going to be that easy. He returned to the dining room where Alicea and he spent some time going over the pictures and discussing them. As Alec continued his review, he could feel his anger toward Marlo growing. He had known all along and had arranged this adoption. How could a man like that live with himself? The swell of emotions was so great Hargrove had to sit back for a moment to catch his breath. Alicea, immediately at his side, hugged and comforted him. He vowed to Alicea that he would get this man if it were the last thing he ever did.

Chapter Forty-five

Carlton Marlo had been out playing golf and decided to stop at his office before retiring for the evening. He said hello to the security guard and signed in before going up to his office. "I won't be long, Charles," Marlo advised him. He breezed passed the outer office into his private suite and sat down behind his desk. He noticed that it looked a bit messed up but tossed the thought aside as he looked through his mail and telephone messages. He decided to make himself a drink and walked over to the wall unit to get a glass and some scotch. He noticed that the cabinet holding his safe was slightly open. He never left that cabinet open. In fact, he always checked it before he left every day. His staff had no reason to go anywhere near the cabinet, for any reason whatsoever. He bent down and opened the door. He looked inside and saw that the stack of magazines he had placed directly in front of the safe opening had been moved. Now his suspicions were confirmed. He quickly moved the magazines out of the way and opened the safe. He looked inside and it became obvious that someone had been into it.

This was not good, he thought. He was not in a good position at all. Who had it been? He couldn't take a chance; it was too risky to sit and wait for something to happen. It was obvious someone had found what they were looking for. The papers for Heather Langdon's adoption as well as his correspondence with Françoise DuBois and the nanny were on top when previously they had been on the bottom. At least he thought they were. He never referred to them anymore, but now he couldn't remember. But he couldn't take the chance. Suddenly he saw the document between the Hiltons and himself. "Oh my God!" he exclaimed.

He had made a lot of money off the Hiltons; this was his insurance policy and his ticket out if he had to run. He had never believed he would have to but his discovery tonight made it a necessity. He knew he had to get out of the country. He would have to take Louise with him. Nobody could know where they were going. He had to make arrangements. He would have to tell Louise that something had happened and they had to leave for their own protection.

He removed all the documents out of the safe and decided to burn them. He stuffed them into his briefcase. He would burn them at home in the fireplace while Louise was fixing dinner. He had a large stash of money in Australia. Maybe they should go back and hide in a mountain village. He finished what was in his glass and then poured more as his thoughts raced on. How could he possibly get caught after getting away with everything for so long? He closed the safe and put the magazines back in front of the safe door and closed the cabinet. He had to get out of here and get home. He finished his second drink and put the bottle away. He turned off the office light on the way out.

He was perspiring profusely as he stepped into the elevator. He tried to catch his breath but couldn't. His shirt suddenly seemed tight around his neck and the pain in his chest radiating down his left arm was excruciating. He dropped the briefcase that he had been carrying in his right hand, struggling to loosen his collar. He tried to reach for the main floor button but never got to push it.

*   *   *

"Joe, I'm so happy to see you." Heather had been waiting by the door and opened it as she saw him walking up the driveway. She ran to meet him, flung her arms around him and kissed him soundly.

"Now, that's the kind of welcome I could live with all the time! Oh, Heather, I have missed you!" He said it between planting kisses on her face, cheeks and neck. Finally he took her face in his hands and looked deep into her eyes. He felt he was the luckiest man in the world to be in that spot at that very moment.

"Joe, oh, Joe, I feel it's been years since I last saw you! I couldn't wait for you to get here. And Stella has insisted on preparing dinner. Isn't that nice of her?"

"It most certainly is, and I hope it's almost ready because I'm so hungry I could eat a bear!"

"Well, come on then!" And she took Joe by the hand and led him into the house. She took his jacket and hung it in the coat closet and yelled into the kitchen to Stella. "Stella, Joe's here and he said he's mighty hungry!"

Stella had set up the dining room for them so they would feel like they were in a private restaurant. She was tickled for the both of them. They were truly a couple made in heaven. She had a good feeling about them and knew they would have a happy life together.

"Good evening, Stella." Joe greeted her as he followed Heather into the kitchen. "I understand that you're cooking up a storm tonight! I want you to know how much I appreciate that because I'm starving!" He looked around the kitchen to see if he could get a peek at what they were having. But nothing was in sight. It sure smells good, he thought.

"Well, time's a-wasting and everything's ready, so why don't you two go on inside and sit down and I'll start serving."

Heather and Joe walked into the dining room hand in hand. Joe pulled the chair out for Heather and then sat down himself. "So, you have something pretty heavy on your mind, Heather?"

"I most certainly do, and I can't wait to show you! Excuse me for a moment." She got up and ran upstairs to her closet where she put all the papers she found. As she came back into the dining room she handed them to Joe as she settled into her chair. "Now, I want you to understand something first. This document is signed by the attorney and my parents, and it states that I am sole heir to their estate, but this document, see here?" She looked up into Joe's face to make sure he was following, finishing slowly, with emphasis. "It seems to entitle Carlton Marlo to forty percent of everything."

Joe reviewed the document closely. The first thing he thought of was blackmail. But for what? He didn't say anything to Heather. He could be wrong, but he didn't think so. "Heather, I think we need to get these papers to an attorney. Now, since you don't have one, I know someone who is good. He's about forty-five minutes from here. He's expensive, but he's the best."

"Well, then, let's go for it! I don't care how much it costs. I have to get to the bottom of this."

"It's late, so he won't be in his office tonight, but I'll give him a call tomorrow morning and ask him to call you."

"Thanks, Joe. I appreciate it. It's amazing how one can be deceived by people's seeming kindness and caring. What is this attorney's name?"

"Oh, that would help. It's Alan Switter. Write it down so you don't forget. I know he will call you right away. He was my family's attorney. I haven't had cause to use him but we've remained in touch."

Heather felt comfortable now and was able to enjoy her dinner. She hadn't realized how hungry she was until she started eating. Sitting in her dining room and having dinner with Joe was the best medicine in the world. She felt almost complete.

Leo Martucci got up and let the dog out. He walked down the driveway to get the morning paper. He was still half-asleep and waiting for his morning coffee to brew. He took the rubber band off the paper and opened it to reveal the front page. He did a double take fully awake now. The headline read, 'MANHATTAN ATTORNEY FOUND DEAD." He couldn't believe his eyes. The first several words of the story said, "Prominent attorney Carlton Marlo was found dead in his office building elevator by a security guard early last evening."

Martucci ran into the house and picked up the phone, punching in Alec Hargrove's number.

"Good morning, Hargrove residence."

"Yes, this is Leo Martucci. I need to speak with Mr. Hargrove right away."

"I'm sorry, but he hasn't come downstairs yet."

"Well, did you get the morning paper yet?"

"Yes, I did, Mr. Martucci."

"Then do me a favor and take that paper right upstairs to Mr. Hargrove and tell him to be in touch with me. All right?"

"Of course, sir." Hilda hung up and went into the study to retrieve the paper. As she headed toward the stairs she heard the Hargrove bedroom door open as Alec came out.

"Good morning, Hilda. It's going to be a busy day. Is breakfast ready yet?"

"Yes, Mr. Hargrove. But Mr. Martucci called for you and requested I bring this morning's newspaper to you immediately."

"Really?" He took the newspaper from Hilda as he reached the bottom of the stairs. "Did he say anything else?"

"No, but he sounded as if it were urgent. I'll go and put your breakfast on the table." Alec was already taking the rubber band off the paper, opening to the front page. He stared in utter disbelief at the headline then read the first paragraph of the story.

This is unbelievable, he thought. Carlton Marlo, dead! He sat down in his study chair, reading on. Well, he thought, this certainly puts a different light on things. He still had to get to his attorney's office this morning and give him the paperwork. He called him at home last night and let him know he would be stopping by with it. Alicea walked into the study and saw Alec engrossed in the front page of the paper.

"Good morning, darling. Is there anything interesting in the paper this morning?" She was walking around to the back of his chair, and putting her arms around Alec's neck when she saw the headline. She read on. "Good gracious, Alec. This is unbelievable."

"That's exactly what I said."

"Well, will this make it more difficult to pursue?"

"I really don't know, but as soon as we finish breakfast we should get over to Alan's office. I've already called for the car to be brought up so it's waiting in front for us."

"I'm all ready, dear. Come on, Alec, let's go have breakfast before we start this day. I think it's going to be a full one.

"Hilton residence." Stella managed breathlessly. She had been in the back of the house and hadn't heard the phone. Heather was in the shower and hadn't heard it, either.

"Stella, this is Louise Marlo."

"Well, good morning, Mrs. Marlo. Is everything all right? You're calling mighty early this morning."

"Well, actually it's not. Have you or Heather seen the morning paper yet?"

"No."

"Well, thank goodness. I wanted Heather to hear this from me before she reads it in the paper. Stella, Carlton is dead." Stella could hear Louise's voice shaking. Shocked, Stella struggled for words. She was about to answer Louise Marlo when Heather yelled down the stairs.

"Stella, who's that on the phone? It couldn't be Joe calling this morning with indigestion?" Stella rolled her eyes. There didn't seem to be an end to the surprises. Before she could answer, the doorbell rang.

"Mrs. Marlo, I'm sorry. Please hold on one moment. Can you do that?"

"Yes."

"I want to go get Heather so she can speak with you herself."

Stella opened the front door to find Joe standing there with the paper.

"Where's Heather?"

"Well, she's still . . ." But Heather was coming downstairs and saw Joe at the front door. "Stella, why didn't you tell me Joe was here? Then, for Pete's sake, who is on the telephone?"

Joe closed the door and Stella went over to Heather. "Heather, Louise Marlo is waiting on the phone. She needs to speak with you."

"Wow, it must be important for her to call this early." She walked over to the phone and picked up the receiver. "Louise? Is everything all right?" Heather was pleased that it wasn't Carlton after what she had discovered in her parents' home. She didn't think she ever wanted to speak to him again, though she knew she would have to eventually. But no one was going to pull the wool over her eyes again and get away with it!

"Oh, Heather, nothing is all right. I'm glad I got to you before you saw the morning paper!" Heather turned to look at Joe, who was holding the newspaper.

"Heather, Carlton is dead!" Louise was crying as she explained. "The security guard found him in the elevator last evening. They think he must have had a heart attack." Heather heard Louise sobbing.

"I can't believe this! Oh, my God! Louise, is there anything we can do for you?"

"No, thank you. The kids are coming in today. I never thought I would have to face anything like this. I don't know what to do!" She sobbed. "I'm sorry, Heather. You have had more than your share of pain and I don't mean to burden you with this. I will call you or one of the kids will call you with the times once the arrangements are made. Carlton was proud of you. I think he would have wanted you to know that."

"Thank you, Louise. Remember, if there is anything I can do, get in touch, okay?" She hung up the phone and looked at Joe. "I can't believe it! And as I started to talk to Louise I had such nasty thoughts of Carlton for what he had done to my parents. Of course I don't want anyone to die, but I can't help feeling furious at the moment."

Joe walked over to Heather and put his arm around her. "Heather, it's perfectly understandable why you feel the way you do. You're too hard on yourself."

"Well, I can't get it out of my mind that he thought he was going to screw me like he was screwing my parents all these years; and with looks of admiration and pride, no less."

Stella ushered Heather and Joe into the kitchen where she had fresh coffee and bacon waffles. "Why don't you come inside the kitchen and have some breakfast?"

"Sounds good to me, Stella," Joe responded. "After last night's dinner I will never refuse another meal you prepare! But there's something I need to do first. If you both will excuse me for a moment, I want to call Alan Switter's office." Switter's secretary answered. She told Hawkins that Switter was not yet in the office but she would give him the message as soon as he got in. Hawkins stressed that it was extremely important and that time was of the essence. Joe came back into the kitchen and sat down to enjoy his breakfast. He looked over at Heather and winked. He had never wanted to have breakfast with any woman before, but now he was looking forward to the day when they would be having breakfast together every morning.

Chapter Forty-six

$\mathscr{A}$lec couldn't wait to get started. His mind was going a mile a minute. He couldn't believe this turn of events but he wanted to have legal counsel in on this. It was much too complicated. Alicea and Alec reviewed the pictures again on the way to Switter's office. Alec told her that he wondered if they would ever find out the truth now.

"But, Alec, don't the documents in these pictures prove what he was involved with?"

"Yes, but we can't use them. I think we have to be able to get hold of the originals. I don't know, but that's why we need an attorney." The ride to Switter's office seemed endless, but finally Alec caught sight of the office building up ahead.

"Good morning, Mr. Hargrove, Mrs. Hargrove," the secretary greeted them. "Please come this way and Mr. Switter will be right with you." Switter was talking on the telephone and waved them to come in and sit down.

"Joe, I'll be back in touch with her later. But if you can fax me a copy of those documents Ms. Hilton has, I'll be able to review them right away. Thanks, Joe." Alec's interest was piqued when he heard Heather's name mentioned but thought better of asking the attorney about it. They had enough on their plate to deal with at the moment.

Switter stood up and came around the desk to shake their hands. "Alec, how are you? It's been some time since I last saw you. And how are you, Mrs. Hargrove?" They exchanged pleasantries. "Now, let's get down to business. I understand you are in possession of some pictures that you want me to see. While I am looking at them, please fill me in on what's been going on. Apparently, you have not been leading a quiet life, of late."

"No, I think not," Alec replied. He glanced at Alicea and then began his story, careful not to forget one detail. He told about the private investigator and the work he had done for Alec, about Brian and his relationship with Heather Hilton, his episode at Chelsea's, everything that had happened up to the present.

"So, there is a good chance that Heather Hilton is going to turn out to be your daughter, am I correct in assuming that?" Alec Hargrove opened his mouth to speak but hesitated. He nervously ran his fingers through his hair and sat up straight in his chair, clearing his throat, before any reasonable words came to him.

"Well, it certainly looks that way. It's difficult for me to comprehend yet, after so many years of having no hope."

"I can't even begin to imagine what it has been like for you." Now he was starting to put two and two together. Joe Hawkins had called him about his girlfriend. She was in possession of documents that needed to be reviewed and might even involve criminal actions on the part of Carlton Marlo. Now Alec Hargrove is sitting in his office explaining to him that this Heather Hilton may be his long lost daughter.

"Alec, I think you know that if we enter any legal action against the estate of Carlton Marlo, it would only be in order to recover any monies, because that's all we would be able to recover at this time. We would have to be in possession of the documents. Do you have knowledge of where they are?"

"Yes. They are in a safe in Marlo's office."

"I see. I would assume that your private investigator found them?"

"Yes."

"Now, when I spoke with you on the phone, you did mention Heather to me and I asked you to search for her paperwork. Were you successful?"

"Yes." Alec opened his briefcase and took out several envelopes. "This is Melissa's, my daughter's, birth certificate, and this is the information you requested including her blood type." He realized his hands were shaking as he handed the information to Switter. Switter looked over his glasses at Alec and could see how emotional this was for him.

"Would you folks like a cup of coffee?"

"I could go for some coffee, Alan. How about you, Alicea?"

"That sounds good. Thank you." Switter buzzed his secretary to prepare coffee for them and bring it into his office.

"Alec, I know this is difficult for you but I am going to need some time with this. Is that a problem? Were expecting something different?"

"As of last night I was because I thought we would have to move quickly since Marlo might decide to leave the country if he became suspicious. I wanted him to get caught so that he could pay the price for what he has done to me . . . to my daughter." Alec began to choke on his words. "But as of this morning, with Marlo deceased, I don't know what it means. I know that I have to find out if this is my daughter and then figure out a way to make it all right."

"Okay, Alec. I will review what I have and take some investigative action of my own. I will be in touch with you as soon as possible."

"Thanks, Alan. Knowing that this mess is in your capable hands makes me feel better."

"Well, thanks for the vote of confidence. I assure you we will do our best to get to the bottom of this." The Hargroves left their lawyer's office and Alec put his arm around his wife as they got into the elevator. They didn't speak to each other on the way down, but once in the car they had a lot to discuss. Things would start to move now. Alec had the utmost confidence in Switter's ability.

"Allison, did that fax come over yet from Joe Hawkins?" Switter asked over the intercom.

"It's coming through now, Mr. Switter. As soon as the transmission is completed I'll bring it in to you." Allison got up from her desk and went over to the fax machine. She took the pages that had already come through and quickly ran them through the copy machine and then made a file, did the same with the remainder of the fax and brought the file in to Switter.

Switter sat back in his chair and reviewed the documents while sipping another cup of coffee. He looked at his cup and decided it would be his last cup for the day. He was drinking far too much coffee.

Looking back at the documents he saw a written agreement between three people: Mr. and Mrs. Hilton and Carlton Marlo. It appeared to be the same document that Alec Hargrove had left with him. Now he wondered if Heather Hilton had an original. It appeared the court was not involved in this at all. Why would someone sign over forty percent of their assets? He also remembered Joe mentioning that Heather Hilton was sole heir to her parents' estate. There had to be a reason and it sure wasn't going to turn out to be an honest one on the part of Carlton Marlo. Switter put down those papers and picked up the copies that the Hargroves had left with him. He looked over the pictures of the documents. He was right.

The agreement was exactly the same. But that was all Heather had faxed over. She did not have the other documents that Hargrove's pictures reflected. He picked up the photos of those documents and, with a magnifying glass went over them for validity. They appeared to be valid. Well, he thought, as valid as an agreement could be between three people. But it was an agreement between three deceased people. He would have to have an assistant go over all the information from public records. He felt there was much more to this than met the eye.

Alan Switter was waiting for the reports regarding Heather's blood type to be faxed over from the hospital. Things were beginning to take shape, but he had taught himself long ago in his practice never to jump to any conclusions. Nevertheless, he had a strong hunch. He called in his assistant and went over the paperwork with him.

Brian sat in his office with a fresh cup of coffee. He turned to look out the window as he started his new day and reached for the newspaper, flipping through it before all hell broke loose and he wouldn't have a minute. Why was that name so familiar? Then it came to him. Marlo was Heather's attorney! He picked up the phone and called her to make sure everything was all right. Stella answered.

"Hilton residence."

"Hello, Stella, it's Brian Hargrove. I just read the morning paper. Is Heather around?"

"Sure, Brian. Hold on one minute." Joe had already left, and Heather and Stella were sitting around the kitchen table talking about Carlton Marlo and what had happened. "Heather, it's Brian." Heather was feeling guilty that she hadn't called him, after all he had done for her. She had grown to care deeply about Brian and the way things seemed to be turning out that brotherly thing she felt might actually come about.

"Hi, Brian. I got your message and I'm sorry that I never got back to you. Are you all right?" She asked him partly out of guilt, but there was something else in his voice. She didn't quite know what it was but it was definitely there.

"Yes, I'm fine. But I saw the morning paper and at first I didn't recognize the name, then all of a sudden it came to me."

"I know, but that's not all. I can't talk about it at the moment. I had to retain another attorney to help me with some papers that I found in my parents' home."

"It sounds serious."

"It's very serious but I won't know more until the lawyer has a chance to review them, but I promise I'll keep you posted."

"Just remember, if you need any help I'll do everything I can."

"Brian, I just love you to death. But you have done so much for me already. How can I ever repay you for all you've done?"

Well, to start, you can marry me, he thought. But instead he said, "Don't worry about it. That's what friends are for. Just keep in touch and let me know that you're all right. By the way, how's that detective of yours doing?"

"Joe is doing all right. With everything that's been going on around here I even pushed him away, but now I realize that I was wrong. I don't know, Brian. But one thing's for sure, if I didn't have all of you I don't think I could get through all I have. Now, are you sure everything's all right with you? You sound kind of funny."

"I'm fine. But please don't forget to call me." He hung up the phone and realized that he was losing her forever. He wasn't going to lose her as a friend but he would never have Heather as he wanted to have her. He knew he had to get out of that office, out of town, even out of the state, and the sooner the better. He asked his secretary to book him a flight to Los Angeles.

"Let's see, preferably tonight if we can get the tickets. I want two and both in first class." He couldn't believe he had said that. Who was he planning to take? Then he thought of Jessica. He hadn't seen her in at least six months because she had become so serious about their relationship. She was hurt and angry when he stopped calling her. He had special feelings for her but at the time he was not willing to get tied down. But he was positive she would drop everything to go with him.

"I'll need the name of the other passenger."

"Of course, I'm sorry. It's Jessica Hillbrook. Now I'll also need a penthouse suite at that hotel you always book me at . . . uh, oh I'll leave that to you."

"Thank you, Mr. Hargrove." She left the room. Brian quickly dialed Jessica. Yet he put the phone back down and thought about what he was about to do. Jessica, he thought. He had had some good times with her. But she was *very* serious about marriage, and that had been the furthest thing from his mind. She was extremely attractive with long curly red hair, deep green eyes and a body that didn't stop. He thought about her lips, those pouty lips . . . what they were meant for. Thinking about those lips made him aware of what he had to do. He had to do something and this was the best solution. He realized that he could no longer wait for Heather. He had to move along with his life now.

He picked up the phone again and dialed her number. He knew she would be at home – unless she was at the spa or the beauty parlor. He had to be with someone. At least with Jessica he could carry on a conversation, not like the other mannequins he had dated. She was delightfully intelligent and well-informed so they could talk when they were together. But there wasn't that chemistry he felt when he was near Heather. What difference did it make anymore? Without Heather to share his bed, his life, it didn't make a difference.

"Jessica? It's Brian Hargrove."

"Brian, darling, how are you? It's so good of you to call. I was just on my way out to the beauty parlor." Jessica glanced at her reflection in the mirror as she smoothed her suit around her hips. Hearing his voice again made her think of all the time they had spent together in the past and how much she had missed him. She had hoped Brian would have asked her to marry him. But he hadn't and her heart was broken. She had fallen hard for Brian and wanted to be his wife, his lover: oh, his everything. He had made it clear to her that he did not want marriage at the time and, in fact, told her that he was satisfied with the arrangement they had, which in Jessica's opinion was no relationship at all. She had to be there for him when he wanted her. It made her wonder why he was calling her after all this time. But her heart skipped a beat. After all, he could have changed his mind.

"Well, then I'm fortunate that I got hold of you. How have you been?"

"Very well, thank you. I have been busy with hospital benefits for this year and actually dying to get away, but I haven't had the time." She listened closely, hearing something different in his voice.

"I see. Well, I called because I have to take off for Los Angeles on some business and I thought you might like to take a ride."

"Why, Brian, it's such short notice!"

"Yes, it is. But I found out fifteen minutes ago that I had to go. So I thought I would give you a call and see if you were free to come with me. I know what you must be thinking and I didn't call hoping you would be at my beck and call. In fact, I called hoping that you would like to get away and spend some time with me. I want you to know that." Brian put his hand over the receiver because he felt he was going to choke on those last words. He felt like a real jerk, but he knew he had to turn his life around somehow and this seemed the best way.

"Well, of course I would. You know I love spending time with you. How long will we be gone?"

"Oh, probably a couple of weeks. So bring enough clothes so you won't have to spend that much time shopping, although I know that's where you'll be headed."

"You are so right, my dear. All right then, what time shall I be ready?"

"My car will pick you up at eight o'clock. I'll see you then. And Jessica?"

"Yes, Brian?"

"Thanks." And he was gone. Jessica sat for a moment before hanging up the phone, wondering what had gotten into Brian. He never thanked anyone for anything. She leaned back on her bed, her head sinking into the pillows as she thought about what he had said to her. Maybe he has changed, she thought. Then she quickly jumped up with thoughts of what she was going to pack. She didn't have much time and she had to be perfect!

Brian turned around in his desk chair and looked out the window of his office at the Manhattan skyline. It wasn't a dull day but it seemed awful gray to him. He thought about Heather and how he wished she had been the one he had called. But he knew what his reality was now. He could go no farther than friends with her. He still wanted her in his life. His life would seem empty if he never saw her again. In fact, it would be intolerable. It would be difficult but he would settle for a hug and a kiss on the cheek from Heather any day rather than nothing. He kept seeing that same picture of her in the kitchen preparing their dinner the night he went over for the first time. He thought that was truly the happiest moment in his entire life. But now it was gone. Gone, gone forever, he thought.

There was absolutely no way he was going to win her over, not with this other guy in the picture. He knew she was extremely happy; when he had seen her she glowed. He felt such pain in his heart for what she had gone through in the last year, but his heartfelt pain throbbed for his own need to be fulfilled and he knew now it never would. He turned away from the window, sighing deeply.

He had several calls to make a few letters to dictate. He tried to finish up as quickly as possible. He wanted to get out of there and get ready to go. He called his housekeeper, advising him to prepare his things for a trip. He did not want to chance a meeting with any of his brothers or especially Alec. He thought about calling his mother and then realized that was the worst thing he could do. He would call her from the hotel, if he had time. He grabbed for his briefcase, gave his office a sweeping glance, turned and left.

Chapter Forty-seven

Louise Marlo had returned home from the funeral. The house would soon be filled with friends and family and well wishers. She wished they would all go away. She didn't feel like seeing or talking to anyone. She looked out the window and thought about this most unfortunate turn of events in her life. She never would have expected Carlton to die from a heart attack. He had been healthy, at least as far as she knew.

She turned and looked at the bag holding her husband's personal effects as well as his famed briefcase. She slowly walked over to it, picked it up and took it over to the table. She sat in the chair and stared at it. She felt she would betray Carlton if she opened it. He had always instructed her that he never wanted her in his briefcase. But he was dead now, wasn't he? She slowly reached up toward the push lock. She hesitated and then pushed it. The top flipped open. She pulled out a bunch of papers that looked as if they had been quickly stuffed into the briefcase. She leaned back in her chair and started to review them. But what she found made her gasp for air. What had Carlton been up to? She saw her good friends Craig and Peggy Hilton's signatures on an agreement between them and Carlton. The next page was regarding some adoption. Then she realized that it must have been about Heather. But why from France? Then it all struck her. Something was horribly wrong and she didn't know what to do about it. He must have been blackmailing the Hiltons regarding the adoption and they didn't even know why. There was another piece of paper with Alec Hargrove's name all over it. What could this possibly be about? What child's adoption was this? She looked over all the paper work again and started to understand. Yes, that was it. What had Carlton been involved with? Who were the other children mentioned in other agreements?

Louise stood up suddenly, papers fluttering to the floor, gasping and holding her chest in shock. She bent down to pick them up as the door opened and her children came in. She assured them she was fine and quickly stuffed the papers back into the briefcase and placed it in the closet before going downstairs with them to join the others congregating in the living room. She was reeling from the information she had seen. She felt a horrifying tingling sensation up and down her spine. She was too scared to even think about it. She would have to think about it later. How she was going to get through the next few hours?!

Two weeks later, Louise got up the nerve to look again at the contents of the briefcase. Her husband had been involved in something evil and illegal. She wished that she had never opened that briefcase. But she had always loved Heather ever since she came to the Hiltons. Louise felt she owed it to her to come out with the truth, but how? There was bound to be publicity over this. Then another thought struck her. Was it possible that anyone else knew about this? She needed more time to think about what to do. She cupped her face in her hands and wept.

The housekeeper knocked on Louise's bedroom door and announced that Heather was downstairs waiting to see her.

With a start Louise was jolted out of her contemplation and, dabbing at her eyes, dashed to the mirror to fix her face and hair. She was scared to death. How in heaven's name was she going to keep this to herself? She would try to hold the pieces together, she told herself as she went downstairs and into the living room. Heather rose from the sofa as soon as she saw Louise burst into tears. In two strides Heather went over to her and wrapped her arms around the distraught woman to comfort her.

"It's okay, Louise. I know what you're going through. It's horrible, but believe me you'll get through it." That made Louise cry even harder. Heather held onto her and guided her over to the sofa to sit down. "You don't have to say anything if you don't want to. I wanted to make sure that you were all right. I know that your children keep checking on you but I wanted to see with my own eyes that you are all right."

Louise realized that no matter how bad it might be, she had to tell Heather. She gently pushed away from Heather, stood up and walked to the window, sniffling into her handkerchief.

Surprised and concerned, Heather asked, "Louise, what is it? Something seems to have upset you terribly. Are you all right?"

"No. I am not all right. You are very right, Heather. Something is wrong. I just found out about it and I don't know how to tell you, but I feel that I must." The way Louise's voice sounded made Heather's heart begin to pound.

"You see," Louise began, "a few weeks ago I went through Carlton's briefcase. I . . ." Louise started to cry. "I'm sorry to have to do this to you, Heather, but I would much rather you hear it from me than from anyone else."

"Oh, Louise. It's okay. Tell me." Heather went to Louise and gently touched her arm. She could see how much pain she was in.

"Well, I went through Carlton's briefcase, and the first papers I picked up and looked at were all about you, your parents and," she lowered her voice, "your false adoption."

"What?" Heather could not believe what she was hearing. Although she realized that Carlton had done something horrible and her attorney was working on it, she wasn't ready to hear this from Louise.

"Heather, I know this has to sound crazy to you, and you probably don't even know what I'm talking about. But I have all the papers. Rather, they are all in Carlton's briefcase."

"Louise, please don't say any more. I want to call my attorney before you say another word. Please, go and get that briefcase right now. May I use that phone over there?" Louise nodded mechanically and went upstairs to get the briefcase.

Chapter Forty-eight

*H*eather dialed Switter's number and breathlessly waited for him to pick up. After what seemed an eternity, she heard the receiver at the other end complete the connection. She blurted out, "Alan Switter and hurry! It's Heather Hilton."

"Heather, what can I do for you?"

"Mr. Switter, I am in the middle of a most unbelievable situation and I need your help now!"

"Heather, calm down and tell me, what has happened?"

"I came over to see how Louise Marlo was doing and she broke down crying and told me that she found some papers in her husband's briefcase regarding the agreement between my parents and Carlton as well as fraudulent adoption papers. I asked her to get Carlton's briefcase so that I can see the papers with my own eyes. What should I do?"

"Calm down, Heather. Let me see. I think it would be in everyone's best interest if we could meet in this office. If she wants to have an attorney present that's fine. Do you think she knew anything before?"

"I would have to say no. I would find it hard to believe that she did from the way she's acting. She seems like she is in as much of a state of shock as I am."

"Okay. You and Mrs. Marlo come over to the office as soon as you can. I want you to know that I must include Mr. and Mrs. Hargrove at this meeting. Do you have a problem with that?" There was a prolonged pause as Switter waited.

"I guess I don't because I can see where all of this is going to go."

"I think you can, too, Heather, and it's just as well because everyone needs answers and needs to get on with their lives. I'm proud of your courage. Now, let's meet here in two hours, all right?"

"Hold on a minute, Mr. Switter." Heather covered the receiver as Louise came into the room. "Louise, I have my attorney, Mr. Switter, on the line, and he wants us to go to his office. Do you feel you can do that?" Louise nodded in agreement. She didn't care anymore what would happen or about the shame over what her husband had been doing all these years.

Heather confirmed their meeting with Switter and hung up the phone. She walked over to Louise and put her arms around her and held her while Louise sobbed uncontrollably. Heather knew, for sure, that Louise had never known what her husband had been up to. She felt sorry for Louise; she had not only lost her husband but his legend along with it. She also knew that Louise would have to explain all of this to her children before it got out in the news.

Louise slowly gained control of herself and stepped back to face Heather. "Heather, I want you to know that I am doing this because I have always loved you and would have done anything for you. I had no idea . . . all these years . . . I don't know what to say except that I could never keep anything like this from you." A lump formed in Heather's throat and she found herself fighting back the tears.

"Thank you, Louise. I want you to know that I will be with you no matter what and help you see this nightmare through." They hugged each other for a while before Louise got up the courage to open up the briefcase and show Heather what she had found.

* * *

"Allison?"

"Yes, Mr. Switter?"

"See if you can get Alec Hargrove on the phone. If you can't reach him by phone then try his beeper, anything." Alan paced his office wondering what would unfold in this meeting. He had concluded that this was going to be, in part, a family reunion. He wanted to get his hands on those documents.

"Mr. Hargrove on the line, Mr. Switter." Alan ran over to his phone and slapped the speaker button.

"Alec, I'm happy to get hold of you."

"Why? What's up, Alan?"

"Well, first of all, are you and your wife available to get to this office within two hours?" Hargrove looked at his watch dubiously.

"It's going to be a close call, if we do."

"Well, I highly recommend that the two of you try to be in my office as close to that as possible. There's been a big break-through in this case."

"Please, tell me about it."

"There's no time, Alec. Just get Alicea and get in here as quickly as possible."

"All right. I'll contact the airport and have a helicopter waiting. That should bring me there in about one hour."

"Great. See you then." It would be great if Alec could make it in earlier, because Switter wanted to brief him and

Alicea on the developments, and tell him that Heather, along with Louise Marlo, would be there. He immediately buzzed his secretary in to prepare for this meeting.

"Mrs. Hargrove, it's Brian on the telephone." Hilda buzzed the intercom upstairs in the study.

"Thank you, Hilda." Mildly surprised, Alicea picked up the extension. "Brian, darling, what a wonderful surprise! How . . ."

"Alicea, Alicea, where are you?" Alec shouted as he ran into the hallway downstairs from his study.

"Brian, hold on one moment, dear. Alec is calling frantically from downstairs." She called out. "I'm up here, Alec." Alicea returned her attention to her son. "Where have you been, Brian? I've missed you and I've been somewhat worried about you."

"I'm okay, Mom. I didn't mean to worry you, but a lot has been on my mind and I didn't want to upset you." Alec had already reached her and was sitting in a chair, catching his breath and listening to what was going on but, all the time, dying to pull Alicea right out of the house. "But there have been some developments," Brian said heavily. From looking quizzically at Alec, Alicea's alarmed gaze dropped to the coiled cord in her hand.

"What do you mean? What developments?" Alicea questioned as she threw an alarming glance at Alec.

"Well, right now I'm in Los Angeles. I got here about two weeks ago."

"No wonder I haven't heard from you. What in heaven's name are you doing in Los Angeles?"

"I'm getting married, Mom!" Alicea jumped up out of her chair when she heard that.

"You're getting what?! Did I hear you right, Brian? Who are you going to marry?" Now she had Alec's full attention.

He was signing to her to give him the phone but she pulled away.

"Mom, please calm down and don't get so excited. It's not like I already eloped. I am calling you first to let you know what my intentions are. I'm planning to marry Jessica Hillbrook."

"How did this all come about?"

"I'm glad you're so pleased, Mother." Brian could hear the slight tone of disapproval in his mother's voice. She did not like surprises. But he decided to push it all the way. "In fact, Jessica is right here if you would like to speak with her. Hold on a sec."

"Brian . . .!" Alicea was beside herself and did not want to speak with Jessica or any other woman at the moment. But what was she going to do? Her son had called her and told her that he was getting married. There was nothing she could do. She only knew that he did not love this woman and that was what upset her so much. She did not want him to sacrifice for the sake of getting married. She had always wished that some-day Brian would find the woman of his dreams, even though in his mind it was Heather. But he also had no idea what was going on back home, which, she knew, would also change his life and feelings. Maybe it was best not to say anything. A female voice broke through her thoughts.

"Mrs. Hargrove? This is Jessica Hillbrook. I don't know if you remember me, but we met about a year and a half ago at the Memorial Hospital fashion show in Manhattan." She had jolted Alicea's memory. Yes, she remembered her, the redhead. She certainly was gorgeous, and she hadn't hid the fact that she had been head over heels in love with her son at that time. Maybe this wasn't such a bad idea. She did remember asking Brian about her and he had said that he enjoyed her company because he could talk with her, and that there wasn't an empty space under all that red hair.

"Why, of course I remember you, Jessica. How have you been? I hope Brian didn't kidnap you and is forcing you into anything you don't want to do?" Jessica laughed.

"By all means, no, Mrs. Hargrove. To be quite honest with you I was as shocked as you were, I'm sure! But I couldn't be happier. Are you and Mr. Hargrove going to come out for the ceremony?"

"What?" Brian grabbed the phone away from Jessica before she could say anything else.

"Mom? Jessica beat me to the punch. That's the reason we called. We wanted to see if you guys would be able to come out for the wedding. Jessica already called her parents and they will be coming out to join us, along with her brother. What do you say, Mom?"

"Well, Brian, I don't know. I have to run this by Alec. When are you and Jessica planning to get married?"

"In about two weeks. We're staying out here until we do, kind of a 'test honeymoon,' you know, Mom?"

"Brian, all kidding aside, I want to come more than anything else in the world and I know Alec would feel the same way. What's the date?"

"The first Saturday in June, Mom. That's two weeks and two days away." He gave her the telephone number of the hotel where they were staying. She told him she would call him back in the evening. Alec was ready to pounce on her as she hung up the phone.

"Well? What's going on? Who's getting married?"

"Well, our Brian has taken off with that red head he was seeing a year and a half ago. They are in Los Angeles right now and plan to stay there until they get married in exactly two weeks and two days, and they want us to be there."

"What? Are you sure about this, Alicea?"

"My darling, Alec, you know our Brian. Once he has made up his mind, that's it. The only thing we can do is to be there to support him. And come to think of it, he could have chosen worse. Jessica comes from a good family, is lovely and is madly in love with Brian. Not bad for a start, don't you think?"

"Of course, but is he in love with Jessica?"

"I know. I thought of that, too, but remember, darling, Brian is going to have a tough time getting used to the idea that Heather is possibly his sister – stepsister. Now, what did you come bounding up those stairs for?"

"We have to leave immediately! I have a helicopter waiting to take us right into Manhattan. We have to be at Alan Switter's office within two hours, and time is ticking away."

"But why? What has happened?"

"All Alan would say is that there are some developments in the case and he needs to have us there."

"Oh. Let's go, then. Let me get my purse and I'm ready to leave right now." They were quiet as they traveled to Switter's office. They were anxious but also excited that there was such an important breakthrough that warranted their presence.

Chapter Forty-nine

$\mathcal{A}$s they opened the door to Switter's suite, Allison smiled and immediately ushered them into a conference room. She asked them if they would like refreshments and told them that Alan would be in shortly.

Heather, Louise and Joe Hawkins were in the office with Switter. He thought it would be better if he had the opportunity to brief the Hargroves first and then bring everyone in together. He wanted to be sure that Heather was up to this and that she understood how things looked. But she assured him that she was open and would try to deal with anything she had to. With that Alan Switter left his office and went to the conference suite.

"Alec, Mrs. Hargrove. Thank you for getting here as quickly as you did, especially on such short notice." He walked around to the other side of the table and opened up a file. "Now, I need to go over a few things with you before we start this meeting. First, I have Heather's tests back from the hospital." He handed Alec the blood test results and then the original blood test on Melissa. They matched. Alec was speechless as he looked at the papers. His heart began to pound and he could feel his eyes well up with emotion. He cleared his throat. He squeezed Alicea's hand the whole time. "Any questions thus far?"

"No." It was all Alec could manage to get out. He was literally holding his breath.

"Good. Then let's go on to the next test, which is the paternity test. It's also a match." He paused, watching Hargrove's reaction. Then, "Congratulations, Mr. Hargrove, I think you have your daughter back." Alec sat back and tried to comprehend it. The emotion he felt was overwhelming. He couldn't say a word; his hands were shaking and beads of perspiration had formed at his temples. He fought with his emotions realizing that the moment was here that he never dared to dream about. He started to cry and Alicea held him as he sobbed in her arms. Finally he looked up at Alan.

"How can I ever thank you?"

"Well, we're not quite done yet, Alec. There have been more developments in the case. I need to know how you feel about this before I continue."

"What do you mean?"

"I had been retained by Heather Hilton to review some original documents she found in her parents' home – her adoptive parents' – home. To complicate matters even more, but at the same time making it easier for me to pursue this case, we have yet another amazing development. Heather went to visit Louise Marlo today. It seems that Louise had opened her husband's briefcase a few weeks ago, after his death, and found all the documents that had been in his safe at the office. That's why we didn't come up with anything when we finally got a search warrant. I didn't want to tell you at the time because there were a few other angles that we were trying to work on. But now we don't have to.

"Now, I have Heather and her detective Joe Hawkins, as well as Louise Marlo, waiting in another conference room.

Would you feel comfortable if I brought them in and we all sort through this together and decide what to do?"

Alec was initially speechless. Then, "Well . . . I . . . yes, of course. Whatever you think is best. But may I ask you, does Heather know yet?"

"Alec, I have already explained everything to Heather. This is the perfect time for a meeting. I would like to send her in first before I bring everyone else in. I think you need a little time together."

"I agree, Mr. Switter," Alicea spoke up. "I would like to leave the room, as well. I feel this is a very private moment between a father and a daughter. They need to be alone and they shouldn't be rushed." With that Alicea stood up and kissed her husband, walked out to the waiting area and took a seat. Alan nodded and went back to his office.

Alec felt his hands getting cold and clammy. His heart was racing so fast he felt like he couldn't breathe. He still could not believe, for the life of him, that he was about to see his daughter again. He turned as he heard the door open and saw Heather standing in the doorway.

Heather knew this was right; she knew it in her very soul. She was home at last. All her fears seemed to vanish as she caught sight of Alec standing and waiting for her. It was as if she knew this had been her father all along. But how would this man, whom she hadn't seen since she was four, react? What would he call her? She reached up and touched her good luck locket. Alec saw the locket. All her questions were answered as this man, her father, slowly came toward her with tears in his eyes and apparently the same lump as hers in his throat. And she suddenly moved toward him and said in a small, scared voice, "Daddy? I've finally come home Daddy." They embraced, weeping, in each other's arms. Heather could hear him say "Melissa" repeatedly.

Alec was the first to break away to take a look at Heather. He pointed to her locket. She held it up for him to see. He turned it over to find the message he had inscribed many years ago and said, "I gave you this locket on your second birthday, my little Princess." He took her by the hands and said, "Now, let me have a look at you. I cannot believe that you are standing in front of me like this. I never want to let you go again! I have so much that I want to tell you about everything. But most of all how much I love you and how much I have missed you." Heather clung to him, sobbing like a little girl, not wanting to let go. She felt something inside of her ease and she knew how right it was and how silly her fear of this moment had been. But she had never felt such deep emotion. For perhaps the first time, she felt "normal," as she knew she should, and like she would have all her life if it hadn't been interrupted. "Heather, we have a lifetime to make up for. This is the beginning . . . a new beginning for the both of us."

"Yes, it is and I'll never let you go again, either! You know, it's really amazing. I was so afraid to come into this room and see you. I did not know how you would react to me. Now it's like I've known you all my life and we were never apart, but at the same time, I have so much to share with you."

"And we will share it all, my little princess! But for the moment, I want you to meet your stepmother, Alicea. You know, I loved your mother like I could love no other woman. It was quite some time before Alicea came into my life. She is a wonderful person and I think you will like her. But I will leave that up to you and her and then you can tell me about it. All right?"

"Okay." He kissed Heather on the cheek and went to the waiting room where Alicea was anxiously sitting. Seeing Alec open the door, she was instantly on her feet. He waved at her to come in. She came haltingly to the door and peeked in. She saw Heather and smiled. She could see why her son had fallen in love with this woman. She was absolutely lovely.

Alec attempted to clear the constricting emotion in his throat as he reached for Heather with one hand and held onto Alicea with the other. "Alicea, I would like to introduce you to my daughter, Heather."

"Oh, Heather, I have heard so much about you, especially when you were a little girl. I certainly look forward to your filling me in on the rest." Heather smiled as Alicea hugged her. "Welcome home, dear. You are absolutely lovely and I am so pleased to finally meet you." Heather wept again. It was amazing that her father and his wife had been so close all this time and she never knew it! "Why don't you come and sit between your father and me. I understand we have some material we have to discuss at this meeting?"

Heather composed herself with effort. "Yes, there are some documents that you both need to see. Also I want you to meet the man I love, police detective Joe Hawkins." She looked at them both teasingly. "And I think you will both approve." The three of them laughed and hugged into each other.

There was a knock on the door and Alan Switter stuck his head in. "Is everything all right in here?" He saw all three smiling broadly and nodding. "Well, maybe we should get started?"

Switter returned with Louise Marlo and Joe Hawkins. Heather, Alec and Alicea stood and everyone shook hands as the attorney conducted introductions. Then he got down to business as everyone took a seat.

"Now, Mrs. Marlo found some documents in her husband's briefcase. These are the same documents that Mr. Hargrove's detective found in Carlton Marlo's safe. My office has already verified that. Although we may never know what

Mr. Marlo was doing and with what frequency, we do know for a fact that he knowingly processed a fraudulent adoption. In fact, according to these records, he was directly involved with all the plastic surgery that the child received due to injuries sustained in the car accident in which her mother died and in changing her appearance so that she could not be readily identified.

"The next item is the agreement between the Hiltons and Carlton Marlo. We are not sure why he was blackmailing them. We may never know, but Heather Hilton was listed as sole heir to her parents' estate and yet Mr. Marlo had forty per cent of the business for himself. We will be working with the district attorney's office until we either find an answer or we cannot and close the case.

"Now, Carlton has a bank account in Australia of over twenty-five million dollars. Mrs. Marlo, until the district attorney has finished his investigation, you will not be entitled to any of that money. That will all be decided later."

Louise Marlo raised her hand to stop Switter. She cleared her throat and took a deep breath. "Mr. Switter, I would like to speak, if I may."

"But of course, Mrs. Marlo, please go right ahead."

"Thank you. I want to apologize to you, Alec, for what my husband has done to you and your family. I never knew anything about it until I found the papers in Carlton's briefcase. But I do want you to know that I have loved your daughter since the first day I met her at the Hiltons. She was a little angel. I am so sorry." She stopped for a moment to maintain her composure before going on. "I would like it noted at this meeting that Heather be the recipient of all monies to be recovered from Australia. I think that it is only fair for the damages that Carlton caused as well as reimbursement of monies he seemed to have taken from her adoptive parents.

That's all I would like to say at this time." She looked down into her lap. A weight had been lifted off her shoulders.

Alan acknowledged Louise's offer, then continued. "Now, I would like everyone present to sign this affidavit. It indicates your presence at this meeting and your acknowledgement of reviewing the documents set forth today. With that concluded, I will have a document drawn up to submit to the courts stating Louise Marlo settled her husband's debt with the twenty-five million dollars in an Australian account and same to be given to Heather Hilton. Now before we bring this meeting to a close, I have documents bringing Heather to life that have to be filed with the court. But, before I can have you sign these documents, I need to know from you, Alec and you, Heather, what name to type in. Melissa Hargrove was the deceased and we must bring her back to life first. Heather, I need to know if you wish to resume your name or . . ."

Alec interrupted. "I think Heather needs time to think this through. Is it at all possible to wait on the name change, if there is to be one?"

"Sure, we can wait. But we can't wait too long because we have to show proof that Heather Hilton Langdon is one and the same as Melissa Hargrove. It would be much simpler to file everything at once."

"That's okay, Mr. Switter. I would like to talk it over with my . . . uh, my father . . ." Her voice trailed off as she looked over at Alec with weepy eyes.

"Of course, call me as soon as you are ready. Okay, with that concluded, I want to thank everyone for taking the time to meet here today, especially you, Mrs. Marlo. We are all grateful for your honesty and willingness to help in this case." Louise nodded her head without looking up. They saw a tear fall into her lap, and she dabbed at her eyes with her handkerchief. Then sweeping his gaze to include Alec and Alicea, he offered with gusto, "Congratulations to all of you upon your reunion!" Louise and Joe joined in and there was clapping and well-wishes and lots of hugs for the happy family. Alec invited everyone to dinner in celebration of the rejoining of his family, but Louise gently declined. She felt she had intruded on this family too much already and had no right to further invade their lives. Sensing Louise's discomfort, Heather had her driver take her home, taking time to walk the broken and distraught woman out and offer her comfort, gratitude and friendship. When she returned to the company in the conference room, she and Joe, along with Alan Switter, gladly joined the Hargroves for dinner.

Chapter Fifty

$\mathcal{D}$inner proved to be a celebration to match all celebrations. Alec took them to his favorite private place in Little Italy in Manhattan. Everyone was talking excitedly as they walked down the flight of outdoor stairs leading to the illusion of sidewalk cafes painted on the walls in bright colors. There were red and white checked tablecloths with Chianti wine bottles as candleholders, the wax melted down the bottles forming a waxy vase. The owners knew the Hargroves well and catered to their every whim. Alec introduced everyone to his daughter and Joe. Heather truly felt like she had a family now and felt dizzy with the realization. There was no doubt about it. While they ate dinner, Alicea told Heather and Joe about her sons. Heather and Alicea discussed Brian, but it wasn't until dessert and cappuccino that Alicea and Alec announced that Brian was getting married in two weeks. Heather almost spilled her cappuccino.

"He's what?!" Heather sputtered. Alicea laughed at Heather's reaction and told her it was similar to her own.

"Yes, he called us before we left for Alan's office today and informed us of his wedding plans."

"Really? Whom is he marrying?" Heather asked.

"Well, he met his fiancé about a year and a half ago and they dated on and off for a while. Her name is Jessica Hillbrook. Of course, Brian wants us to fly out and attend the ceremony, and of course we will. I don't know about his brothers at the moment, but how about you, Heather, and you, Joe?"

Heather sat thinking for a moment. Alicea knew why Heather hesitated. "Well," Heather began, "Maybe Brian wouldn't want me to be there. But we do have some unfinished business, and I need to speak with him. Maybe even if I didn't attend the wedding but went out there to talk to him, you know, about being family now? I don't know exactly what to do. What do you think . . . Dad? Alicea?" Alec smiled. He couldn't believe she had called him Dad. He lifted his eyebrows and shook his head. But Alicea answered.

"You know, Heather, we will be speaking with Brian this evening. We plan to explain what happened today and who you are. That will break the ice. But you are the only one who knows your relationship with Brian."

"Yes. You're right. I think I had better sleep on it. But will you tell me his reaction after you speak with him tonight?"

"Of course we will, dear. I'll call you tomorrow morning after breakfast and tell you. Right, Alec?"

"Absolutely." Alec found himself without words once again. He was so happy to have his daughter back. He couldn't take his eyes off of her. He didn't want to let her out of his sight. They had an eternity to catch up on. With that thought he asked her, "How about lunch tomorrow? Do you have time for your dear old Dad?"

"Are you kidding? Try and keep me away! I would love it!"

"Good. I'll pick you up around noon. How's that?"

"Great! I can hardly wait!" She smiled at Joe and he hugged her. There shone a peace in her eyes that he had never seen before.

In the parking lot Heather invited her new parents over to the house for yet more visiting. It was late, though, and they declined, saying they would another evening. They wanted to get home and call Brian. So they hugged and kissed and said good night several times before Alec found himself able to let Heather go for the evening.

"I'm going upstairs to call Brian now," Alicea announced to Alec. "Do you want to talk to him yourself?"

"Well, I think I should be the one to tell him about Heather, don't you?" Alec felt uncharacteristically unsure of himself. Alicea hesitated thoughtfully, too.

"I guess so. I'm afraid of what his reaction will be. I think Heather was worried about that, too."

"I think you're right," Alec agreed. "It appears she knows how he feels about her. But it did not look as if she had encouraged him any. Thank goodness!" They both jumped as the phone rang.

"Brian? Hello, dear. We were going to call you! We just came in from dinner. How are you, sweetheart?"

"I'm fine, Mom. You sound like you're worried about me. But trust me, I'm all right. So what's the good word? Are you and Alec coming?"

"Brian, of course you knew we would come. We wouldn't miss it for the world. But we've had a lot going on here and Alec wants to talk to you about some things. I'll put him on and I'll talk to you again when he's done." She handed the phone to Alec. She began to pace nervously around the bedroom as he started to talk.

"Hey, Brian, what's this I hear? You're getting ready to take the big step?"

"Yes, that's right, Alec. I surprised myself as well! But here we are, getting ready for the big event. But Mom said you've had a lot going on, too. Any problems I should know about in the office?"

"No, Brian. But we have had a lot of excitement here and when I explain it to you, you will know what's been going on here now for some time." Alec paused, gathering himself for what was sure to be Brian's shock. Alicea kept pacing. "You remember when I told you about my wife and daughter dying in a car accident in France?"

"Of course I do."

"Well, there's been the most unbelievable chain of events here. I have my daughter back. She survived the accident but somehow Carlton Marlo was involved in an illegal adoption scheme and she was adopted while she was in France."

"What?"

"That's what we said at the very beginning of this investigation. You see Brian . . . I don't know quite how to tell you this."

"Oh, Alec, come on. Just blurt it out. It can't be that bad."

"Oh, Brian, it's not bad at all but it's going to come as a shock to you because my daughter is none other than Heather Hilton." There was silence from the other end. "Brian, are you still there?"

"I'm here, but you have to run this by me one more time. Heather Hilton is who?"

"She's my daughter."

"How's that possible?!" Brian exclaimed, with disbelief strangling his voice.

Alec explained the whole story to Brian, who did not say one word until he finished. Then, without warning, Brian said, "I have to go now. Tell Mom I'll call her tomorrow," and he hung up. Alec stood with his mouth open in incredulity, gaping at the phone, as Alicea grabbed the receiver from him, calling Brian's name into it.

"It's no use, Alicea. He hung up on me. I'm sorry, sweetheart, but there was nothing I could do. He said he had to go and hung up." He put his arm around Alicea and sat down with her on the sofa. "Listen, darling, you knew he wasn't going to take the news well, no matter what. We have to give him some time to adjust to this. But I'll tell you, we have to tell the other boys and let them know exactly what is going on. I think the best way to do this is to have them over for dinner. What do you think?" Alicea looked at him in panic.

"Alec, I don't know what to think. They all have to accept this and that's final. This is your daughter we're talking about, not some stranger you are deciding to adopt off the street. I apologize to you for Brian's sake. There's no excuse for his behavior, but he has no idea of the pain you were in all these years. But you are right: I think a dinner at the house this weekend will be the best thing. Why don't you call the boys and set it up with them for Saturday night?"

"Okay. But I'm going down to my study to do this. I'll be back in a while." When Alec returned with everything set for Saturday night, he found Alicea stretched out across the bed sound asleep. He watched her sleeping for a while. He loved her so much. She knew him so well. He left her there while he got ready for bed. Then he lifted her into his arms and placed her under the covers, but she responded to his touch.

Heather had so much to tell Stella when she and Joe walked in after dinner! Stella had never seen her this excited and Joe sat back and laughed. She was quite a sight. She finally plopped down on the sofa, having exhausted herself. The telephone rang. Stella answered it.

"Hilton residence, good evening."

"Yes, good evening. This is Alec Hargrove and I would like to speak with my daughter."

"Of course, Mr. Hargrove. Just one moment please and I'll get her for you." Stella ran into the living room with the phone, her hand over the receiver. "It's your father!" Joe laughed again, seeing Heather get excited all over again.

"Oh, my God! Hello, Dad?"

"Hello, sweetheart. I wanted to call you and check to see what you and Joe are doing on Saturday night. Are you both free?" She knew Joe was because they were talking about what to do this weekend.

"Why, of course we are. Why? What do you have planned?"

"Well, I don't want you to get nervous or anything but Alicea and I want you to meet the rest of the family. We'd like you and Joe to come for dinner here on Saturday night."

"Are you sure you want to do this? I mean, it's so much work and maybe they don't want to meet me."

"Heather, I've already called everyone, and they can't wait to meet you. You will have to get used to the idea that I introduced you to this family many years ago, after the accident. I kept your pictures and your memory alive. So they know all about you, and now they want to meet you. It's your family, too, dear and we all belong together."

"Thanks, Dad. We'll both be there. Oh, can I bring anything?"

"Absolutely. That gorgeous, drop-dead smile of yours! Good night, my little princess, and I'll see you for lunch tomorrow." He was gone.

Heather was smiling from ear to ear when she returned to the living room. She sat on the sofa next to Joe just as Stella got up and excused herself, saying good night. Heather turned to Joe when she left. "My father has invited us to dinner on Saturday night to meet the rest of the family. Are you game? Do you want to be with me?"

"Heather, when are you going to get it through your head that I want to be with you no matter what? I don't care what we do or when we do it, as long as we're together. And of all things, of course I want to be by your side when you meet the entire family." Heather rose up on her knees on the sofa beside Joe and threw her arms around him, smothering him. He gladly responded but, in sudden gravity, Heather pulled away.

"Joe, there's something else, and I don't know if you'll be able to do it."

"Well, come clean. Let's hear it."

"I've been thinking about it this evening and I want to attend Brian's wedding." Heather told Joe all about Brian, even about his feelings for her. Joe wasn't jealous but he was worried about Heather's reaction to Brian's probable animosity now. His instincts, honed by his experience as a detective, led him to believe that Brian's reaction to the news that Heather was now his stepsister would be hostile. After all, she was his love object and this development would put a different light on his obsession. He would either accept it or he would act out and Joe did not want Heather alone in the line of fire. "Joe, are you listening to me?"

"Heather, I'd love to go with you. As long as a case isn't breaking at the office I have quite a bit of lost time I can take." He kissed her gently on the forehead. "Now, set up the plans and let me know, okay?"

"Oh, thank you, Joe! I have so much to do. I have to shop for clothes and make reservations. Maybe I'll wait until tomorrow and talk to Dad." She stopped and grinned at Joe, relishing the way that sounded. They finished off the evening talking about the coming weekend and the trip out west. They were both looking forward to getting away together. It was exhilarating to be so much in love.

It was already the next morning. Brian hadn't returned to his hotel room. Jessica was beside herself. He was screaming in incoherent and angry exclamation when he had left the suite the night before. She didn't know whether she should go out and look for him or just stay put. She finally decided to stay at the hotel and take a relaxing bath. What could his parents have said to him to get him that upset? It surely wasn't about the wedding because he said they were all right with that. What if he didn't return to the hotel room? She finally fell asleep across the bed, catnapping after her bath, waiting for Brian's return. She didn't even turn on the television. She napped fitfully, worried.

She rolled over in bed and looked at the clock. It was already ten in the morning. She had a spa appointment at ten thirty and she was determined to keep it. After all, there was nothing she could do here. She had never been the type to pine or fret. If Brian was going to marry her it would be of his own free will and he would be there to do it. She had waited all this time for this to happen and had never even dared to dream that Brian would ask her to marry him. She would continue to be patient. She giggled as she caught herself humming the wedding march. Whatever was bugging Brian was his problem to work out. But he had asked her to marry him and that's all that mattered!

Brian was out cold in a rented car. He had been out all night drinking himself into oblivion. In his agony the irony only made it worse: he was surrounded by women but could only think of one! He didn't want anyone near him. He only wanted to keep drinking until his head stopped thinking. Finally, around three in the morning, he staggered his way out to the car, managed to clamber in and fell over on the front seat, where he remained, unconscious, the rest of the night.

The heat and the sun beating down on the car, making it insufferably stifling, finally caused Brian to stir. He grabbed his head with an agonized moan as he tried to sit up. He felt awful. He groped in his pocket for his sunglasses and put them on. His mouth felt like there had been a war going on. He was extremely thirsty but he had such a bad headache he couldn't even think about drinking anything. He sat all the way up by painful degrees and caught a glimpse of himself in the rear view mirror. What a sight, he thought. Well, he had definitely drunk himself blind last night. But the inescapable realization came to him, and as he started to focus again, that nothing had changed. Heather was his sister by marriage. How could that be?! He felt sick thinking about it. How could he love her the way he did? He shook his head ruefully, knowing that even though he had planned to marry Jessica, he had still been hoping that one of these days Heather would fall in love with him. He knew it! He knew himself too well to fool himself. But now what really mattered? Maybe it would be better to stay drunk so that he wouldn't have to think about it anymore. But he knew better than that, too.

He got out of the car, straightened himself out the best he could, headed for a hotel coffee shop and ordered coffee: strong, black. Lots of it. As he sipped on the brew, he looked out the window to figure out where he was. He had no idea. After a while he walked over to the cashier and asked for directions to get back to his hotel. He was informed that he had quite a drive ahead of him. He was in San Francisco.

He made his way unsteadily to his booth in the coffee shop and ordered still more coffee. The waitress glanced at him knowingly. He gulped his coffee hard and tried to remember but couldn't. Well, only one thing to do. He asked the concierge to get him a helicopter to take him back to his hotel in Los Angeles. He tipped him a fifty. The concierge was more than pleased and would have moved oceans with that kind of tip. Brian also handed him the keys to the rental car and asked him to return it to the rental company.

"No problem, Mr. Hargrove!"

On the way to Los Angeles, Brian tried to call Jessica but there was no answer in their suite. He had reserved a two-bedroom penthouse suite so that Jessica wouldn't feel like she was on the spot. He tried both rooms but there was no answer. He looked at his watch; it was already noon. Well, he thought, she's probably at the beauty parlor or the spa. He rested his head back and closed his eyes. He tried to stop thinking about Heather but couldn't. She was in his head and he couldn't get her out. He didn't want to get her out; that was the problem. He had to get through this wedding. Then things would quiet down and he would try to live with it. But until then . . . Jessica. That's what he had to think now. He had made a good choice, after all. She was fun to be with, gorgeous, and came from a good family with lots of money. He had to keep selling himself on that idea. After a while he would buy it. In fact, he thought, he might grow to love her one day. Regardless, he was going to do this no matter what!

In his hotel bedroom at last, Brian found a note from Jessica. He read,

> *"Darling, I know you were very upset last night and I'm sorry for whatever is troubling you. I hope I can help. I'm at the spa right now and then I'm going shopping on Rodeo Drive. If you feel like it, meet me for cocktails at Jimmy's. Love you."*

He stared at the note, realization dawning in him that she was a jewel, considerate; another woman would have been hysterical and all over him as soon as he walked in the door! At least she knew when he needed space. He didn't feel like meeting her for cocktails but he knew he had to. He had written the script for this drama and had promoted it. The other players were fulfilling their assigned roles. Now, of course, he had to star in it.

Heather saw the limousine pull into her driveway. She ran out the front door to greet her father. She couldn't believe how natural it felt when she saw or spoke with him. They walked back to the house together, arm in arm. Heather couldn't wait to take him on a tour of the house, her home, the house that Brian had given her as a gift. Her brother, she thought with delight and amazement, had bought her this house! It sure was starting to sound good! Alec, of course, loved the house and couldn't wait for Alicea to see it. Then father and daughter were on their way to lunch.

Alec had selected another family favorite but at least this time it was close by. They were so engrossed in conversation; it seemed like only a few seconds passed until they arrived. After they were shown to their table, Heather asked about Brian.

"Heather, Alicea was going to call you this morning but she is quite upset with Brian. So I told her that I would talk to you over lunch. She sincerely apologizes."

Heather had been pretty upset with Brian herself, in the past, and understood. She was elated that she was meeting her father today. Nothing else mattered!

"Why? What did Brian have to say? What did he have to say about me?"

"Well, I tried to prepare him because I knew it was going to be a shock to him. But he wasn't listening. When I finally told him you were his sister by marriage, he gave me a chance to explain but then hung up on me!"

"Oh, Dad, I'm sorry! I can see it would be difficult for Alicea. After all, you found your daughter and now Alicea's son is running away. I feel awful. I knew he was not going to take the news well. But you know I have to see him. I have to talk to him before the wedding."

"Are you telling me that you and possibly Joe will be coming with us to L.A.?"

"Definitely. Joe has a lot of time coming to him so he just needs to know when we're leaving."

"Heather, nothing could have made me happier. But are you sure you should talk with Brian?"

"Dad, he came to see me all the time in the hospital. Most of the time I couldn't even talk."

"I know."

"You do?"

"Yes." He explained to her how he had come up with Duprey. "That was the second time I laid eyes on you. The first time was at that Christmas party when Brian had you up against a wall. He seems to like to do that to people; you know, back them up against a wall?" They both laughed. But Heather was embarrassed and Alec could sense it.

"Heather, listen to me. I can see that you are sensitive about how Brian feels about you."

"But, Dad, believe me, I never encouraged him. He just wouldn't take no for an answer and continued to pursue me."

"I don't doubt it for one moment. But, remember, you are of no relation to Brian. You didn't even grow up together as brother and sister. He is no relation to you except by marriage. It's up to the both of you to make this work."

"That's why I must see him before the wedding. When were you and Alicea planning to leave for L.A.?"

"I really don't know for certain yet. So much has happened in the last twenty-four hours that we haven't even discussed it. But we will discuss it tonight, and then we'll call you." They exchanged warm smiles. The rest of lunch went by in a flurry of conversation. They enjoyed being with each other and spent about four hours at the table before leaving. It was a magical lunch for Heather and one she never dreamed of having. Heather shared her happiness with Joe and Stella that evening.

As Alec had promised, Alicea called Heather and let her know that they were planning to fly out in the corporate jet if they could get the family to leave on Wednesday of next week.

Heather told her it was no problem for her but she would check with Joe and they could confirm things at dinner Saturday night.

The next day, Friday, Heather went shopping for something to wear to that dinner. She wanted to look special when she met her family. She went into the city to her favorite boutique and let them cater to her. Of course, Stella was of no help because she loved every outfit Heather tried on. She must have tried on at least a dozen and finally settled on a creamy satin dinner suit with shoes and handbag to match. It fit her like a glove and was perfect for the occasion. She purchased several other outfits and accessories for the trip to L.A. She called Alicea when she returned home and told her all about her successful shopping venture. Alicea was excited for her and told her she would be going shopping on Monday if Heather wanted to join her. She would have loved to but she had a board meeting at eleven that morning. Alicea said that wasn't a problem; they could plan to leave at one. Alicea would make the arrangements to pick her up. Heather was tickled that she was going to spend time with Alicea. And Alicea was equally elated because she never had a daughter and looked forward to their growing close.

After her conversation with Alicea, she tried to call Jenny at work but she was told that Jenny took a few days off and wouldn't be back until Monday. Heather reached her at home. Jenny was thrilled that things were going along so well with her. She filled Heather in on the news that Frank was being transferred to Arizona and they were leaving in two weeks to look for a home out there. She asked Heather if she was continuing to write to Tracey. Heather explained she had just received another letter and filled her in on what they were up to. Jenny ended the conversation by telling Heather she would call her when they returned from Arizona. Heather noticed something strange in Jenny's voice. She sounded somewhat strained and Heather wondered if everything was all right. But she knew better than to ask because Jenny would not say a word unless she wanted her to know something.

Heather spent the rest of the afternoon getting ready for her board meeting on Monday then turned her attention to getting ready for the big event the next day. She had huge butterflies in her stomach over this dinner. She looked forward to meeting the rest of the family but was relieved that she would have Joe by her side. It was a wonderful feeling! She thought about her adoptive parents and how much they would have liked Joe. They would have liked her father and Alicea, too. She did miss them. If only everyone could be together. She thought about John and her life with him and how distant it all seemed. She knew she was moving ahead now. She was happy and looking forward to Saturday night.

Chapter Fifty-one

$\mathcal{A}$licea was busily adding the last-minute touches to her dining room table. She enjoyed catering to her family and tonight would be extra special. There was a glow about her as she rushed around fixing this and that. She had planned a simple menu of spinach and mushroom salad, tornadoes of beef with mushroom caps, twice-baked potatoes and a chocolate cherry cheesecake for dessert. She heard Alec whistling as he came downstairs. She turned to look at him, her hand straightening her hair. He took one look at her and let out a long whistle. "Alicea, darling, you look sensational!" Alicea could feel her excitement show in her cheeks as she blushed at her husband's compliment.

"Well, thank you, Mr. Hargrove. I must say you are looking quite striking in your Armani suit." They turned and looked in the hallway mirror. "Yes, Alec, we make a very handsome couple." Alicea had on a flowing, black-sequined, floor-length gown, with the neckline extending down the sleeves into black mesh. When Alec saw her in it, he saw her for the first time all over again. She was as breathtakingly beautiful tonight.

"Alicea, what time is everyone coming?"

"I told them to be here around seven o'clock. It's almost that now. They should be here any moment. I can't wait! It's been a while since we've had the family together. I know that we still don't have Brian and Jessica with us but, hopefully soon, we'll all be together."

"You know, you're right. I think the last time together was Christmas. I guess we've all been busy. Alicea, how do you want to handle Brian's situation?"

"Well, I think we have to introduce everyone to Heather and Joe and let them talk and then by dessert we should be able to announce Brian's coming marriage."

"Sounds like a plan to me. I will then stand up with the champagne glass and make a toast to Brian and Jessica and announce their marriage next Saturday. Do you think any of them will want to attend?"

"I haven't the slightest idea, Alec. But we'll know for certain shortly, because here they come!" Alec joined Alicea at the dining room window as they watched their children pull down the long driveway. "Who knows? Maybe Winston will have an announcement to make! They've been living together for quite some time now," Alicea observed. They walked to the entrance. Alec opened the door and they walked outside onto the front porch to greet everyone. Bob and his wife were the first ones up the stairs to embrace the Hargrove couple. Alec and Alicea asked about the three grandchildren and wanted to see the latest pictures. They motioned Bob and his wife inside, where Hilda stood waiting to take their wraps. When Alec and Alicea caught a glimpse of Winston, they noticed sadly that he was alone. Another car came into sight and they watched as Winston waved the car in. Alicea smiled up at her husband.

"I know, you thought that Winston was alone for a second." He hugged her shoulder. The last to arrive were Heather and Joe. Bob and Winston, wondering what was keeping their parents and when Brian was coming, joined their parents on the porch.

Alec covered the bases. "Oh, Brian won't be able to join us tonight. I'll explain later. But we do have another surprise for you!" They all stood on the porch and watched as Heather and Joe got out of the limousine.

"Bob, Winston, why don't you go and get everyone seated at the dining room table. I think that might be the easiest way to do this" They turned and headed for the dining room to seat their ladies. But they found them looking out the dining room window at Heather and her escort. They saw the little party on the porch head for the front door so they scooted to their seats and sat down quickly. Alicea entered first, followed by Heather and Joe, with Alec bringing up the rear.

"May I have your attention, my wonderful family? I am very proud – and lucky and fortunate – to be able to introduce my daughter to you!" Turning to Heather and taking her arm, Alec presented her to the gathered assembly around the table. "This is Heather Hilton Hargrove. And this is her boyfriend Joe Hawkins. Joe is a police detective." He brought Heather and Joe in and introduced them around the table to each individual. Once the introductions were over, he escorted Heather and Joe to their seats. Dinner began. Heather was seated next to Winston and his girlfriend and across from Bob and his wife. Alicea had arranged the seating so that conversation would flow easily and they could get to know each other over dinner. Alicea and Alec watched in utter amazement. It was as if Heather and Joe had been a part of the family from the beginning. Conversation and laughter flowed. Alicea and Alec exchanged glances and held hands tightly under the table. They were ecstatic. By the end of the main course, everyone was comfortable and enjoying each other.

As Hilda cleared the table, Alec opened the champagne. He stood up and moved around the table. No one said anything but happily watched him as he completed his rounds. He knew everyone thought they were going to toast to Heather, but the actuality would be a big surprise.

Back at his place, Alec tapped his spoon against his champagne glass. "Okay, everyone – and yes, I can get away with hitting the glass with my spoon because this is not a wedding – I have a wonderful announcement to make. I am only sorry that Brian is not here to join in these festivities." Holding his glass up in the air he said, "I would like to announce the coming marriage of my son, Brian, to Miss Jessica Hillbrook, next Saturday in Los Angeles."

A loud silence hung over the table. Then everyone broke out with a flurry of questions and shocked glances. Alec once more tapped his glass for quiet and attention.

"Everybody listen, please. Brian called us, from Los Angeles, and we spoke to both him and Jessica. Now, he wants everyone to come to Los Angeles, to attend the wedding, if possible. You do not have to worry about reservations because I will take care of everything. So, what do you think?"

"Dad, we'd love to come. We'll bring the kids and make a vacation out of it," Bob announced. Winston followed with, "We wouldn't miss this for the world! It's big brother taking the vows! Somehow it has a sweet ring to it!"

Alec smiled and let out a deep sigh, briefly exchanging glances with his wife. They were relieved that everyone wanted to be at the wedding ceremony. Alec continued, "We plan to leave Wednesday morning around eight o'clock. That should get us into L.A. by eleven o'clock west coast time. Since we're traveling in the corporate jet you will enjoy casual dress."

The rest of the evening flew by. Everyone had a good time. The conversation was constant with Heather and Joe. Alicea and Alec were exhausted by the time everyone left. And by the time they rolled into bed it was past two in the morning. Alec held Alicea in his arms and they both fell asleep instantly.

*   *   *

Brian woke up to knocking at his door. "Brian, are you in there? It's me, Jessica."

"Yeah, I'm in here. Give me a couple of minutes. I want to jump in the shower so I feel human."

"Okay," was all Jessica replied. Disappointed, but relieved he was back, she walked across the suite to her own bedroom. She lay down on the bed and thought about what Brian was going to say to her. She was interrupted by a knock on their suite door. Reluctantly she got up and opened it. To her shocked delight the room service attendant was standing there with a huge vase of long-stem red roses.

"I have a delivery for Ms. Jessica Hillbrook."

"Well, yes, that's me. Why don't you place them on the table, over there." She was pointing to a table by the window. "Thank you." As the door closed behind the attendant, she hurried over to the roses and pulled out the card. It was from Brian. She gasped with delight as she read the card.

> *"Jessica, I'm so sorry about last night. I hope that you will forgive me and forgive me and forgive me, and that I will have a lifetime with you to make it up and make it up and make it up some more! Love, Brian"*

She read the card over and over. She was startled by the sound of Brian's door opening quickly. Looking up, she stood, suddenly conscious about her own presence and feeling her face flush. "I received your roses, Brian. They're absolutely beautiful, but the card is beyond words. Thank you so much." Her voice was a quavering whisper at the end. As he started to come toward her she nervously moved back and fell onto the sofa. Brian moved closer and engulfed her in his arms. "Ah," he said. "This is more like it!" He nuzzled her fragrant, silky neck, and then kissed her. She felt she would melt in his arms. He gathered her up and carried her into his bedroom, where he sealed his fate with more than a kiss.

*   *   *

On Wednesday morning, Alec and Alicea picked up Heather and Joe then headed straight for the airport. Excitement reigned as they all spoke at once. Alec had reserved four large suites for the family at the same hotel as Brian. They were the first to arrive at the airport and their pilot and crew were waiting for them.

As they started to board the plane, the rest of the family showed up. Amid another flurry of excitement everyone picked seats and got comfortable and ready for take off. Alicea smiled, thinking it was only a matter of hours before she would see her other son and become acquainted with her future daughter-in-law.

Brian awoke to the sound of the telephone ringing but it took him a minute or so to realize what the noise was. As he picked up the receiver, he looked behind him and saw Jessica sleeping peacefully. He quickly walked out of the room as he answered. "Hello?"

"Brian, this is Alec and I'm calling to let you know that we are on our way. We should be arriving at L.A. International by noon or a bit earlier. I'm sorry to call you so early."

"You know, I can tell you have the entire family with you; I can hear them in the background."

"Well, you know our family, a bit of a noisy bunch. But all kidding aside, everyone is excited about the wedding and looking forward to seeing you."

Brian wished he could be as excited as they were. But he would never let on. He knew, no matter what, he had made a good choice. Jessica could be everything a man might want. He had to get used to the idea and settle himself into a married lifestyle. "Thanks, Alec. I can't wait to see the family and introduce them to Jessica. Do you want us to meet you at the airport?"

"No, I don't think that's necessary. We'll have a couple of cars waiting for us."

"Well, why don't we plan for all of you to come to my suite by two o'clock? I'll have food brought and we can catch up. Jessica's parents won't be coming in until Friday. So that gives us some time together."

"Sounds good. We'll see you in a few hours." Brian clicked off the phone. Just as he walked back into the bedroom, there was a knock at the door.

"Breakfast, Mr. Hargrove." He unlocked the door and told the attendant to come in. He ran back into the bedroom to rouse Jessica.

By that time, Jessica was rolling over to see what the commotion was. "I took the liberty of ordering our breakfast."

"Well, that's thoughtful, Brian. What time is it?"

"It's six o'clock. That was my father on the phone. The entire family is already on the way here. They should be arriving at the hotel around noontime."

"Oh, my goodness. I have to get ready." Brian laughed as Jessica tried to unwind herself from the covers in a hurry to get up and get going. Brian slid across the bed and pulled her back down.

"Relax. You have lots of time to get ready." He laughed again at the sight of her fighting with the sheets. "We don't have to go to the airport so we have some time to . . . well, let me show you." Jessica didn't resist. She was starting to see another side of Brian. She certainly had no problem getting used to that side! Yet as Brian held Jessica in his arms he thought of Heather and what he had wanted this to be. She seemed further from him now than ever. He did not know how he was going to ever accept her as his sister. It seemed totally impossible to him. The next time he would see her or speak with her, he would be a married man. He fought his thoughts to get back to the moment. But Jessica was very good. It was no problem at all getting back into the moment.

Later, Brian called to schedule a reception in their suite. He wanted everything set and ready to go for two o'clock. Jessica disappeared and said she would be back by one from the beauty parlor. He laughed to himself because he had never seen anyone spend as much time at the beauty parlor. But it didn't bother him. He didn't care how she spent her time.

He found he was excited about the family coming out. He hadn't mentioned the plans they were working on for the wedding so that they could announce it at this afternoon's reception. He sat at the desk in the living room and made a few more phone calls to confirm orders for the wedding reception. Brian and Jessica had discussed everything but she left the arranging for him to do. He was glad he had something to keep him busy. He even had thoughts of calling Heather, just to hear her voice. But he knew he couldn't do that. In a way he was furious with Heather. He felt betrayed when he found out she was to be his stepsister. But he knew he was being irrational when it came to Heather. He was afraid of how he might react to her if he heard her voice. Well, he thought, I don't have to worry about that because I'm not going to call her. With that he finally picked up the phone and started to make his calls.

Alec directed his family off the plane and into the waiting limousines. One great thing about traveling with your own jet is the convenience of the cars pulling right up to the plane and not waiting for luggage. They were soon packed into the waiting cars and off they went to the hotel. It was only a twenty-minute ride.

Heather was becoming anxious at the thought of talking to Brian. This was the final hurdle and then she would be literally home free. Alec had announced on the plane that Brian was planning a reception in his suite at two. Heather had already told her father she would not be attending the reception. She spoke to Bob and Winston and asked them not to mention the fact that she was in L.A. for the wedding. She would leave a message at the desk for him to meet her in the bar later in the evening. Joe knew exactly what she was planning and agreed that she had to do this. He wanted to be with her but she had told him it was better that she do this alone. Joe told her that he had the utmost faith in her, but warned her about getting caught in Brian's web.

* * *

Jessica and Brian were ready and waiting as the first knock on the door came. Brian found his entire family waiting to come in – nieces, nephews, everyone. He ushered them all in and then started the introductions. He hugged his mother. She could feel the tears start to sting her eyes. She looked at her son and knew that he was making a sacrifice, but nothing could be done about it. She could see it in his eyes. Oh, she thought, he's definitely a pro when it comes to hiding his feelings; but she knew, and her heart ached.

She liked Jessica immediately. She found her somewhat self-centered but attentive. She would make a good wife for Brian. She was used to meetings, dinners and all sorts of affairs and knew her place by Brian's side; in fact, she already appeared confident in the position. Alicea could only hope that they would be happy.

Brian was pouring the champagne and handing it to everyone. He had ordered some sparkling cider for the three children so they wouldn't feel left out. With his arm around Jessica, he held up his glass and called everyone to attention.

"Now that you have met Jessica I would like to make the formal announcement of our marriage on Saturday." He stopped and everyone took a sip of champagne. "We would like you to know that the wedding and reception will be held on Warren Tornock's eighty-foot yacht. I happened to run across him the other day. I didn't know he was in town. He offered the use of his yacht because he would not believe that Brian Hargrove was getting married unless it was in front of his own eyes!" Everyone laughed and even Brian had to chuckle because he had always been so careful not to get hooked! He continued, "The wedding ceremony is scheduled for one o'clock, with a full reception to follow on the yacht."

Alec now held up his glass and said, "I would like to propose a toast to Brian and Jessica. Your mother and I wish you both a life of happiness. It's yours; all you have to do is take it. We love you very much!"

The rest of the reception was filled with lots of food, laughter and planning. Brian had asked both of his brothers to share the position of best man because he couldn't choose between them. By eight o'clock everyone was finally talked out and ready for bed, tired from a day's travel. Plans had been made for the next day so that tuxedos and accessories could be arranged for. The ladies planned to go shopping together. Brian wondered why there was no mention of Heather. He couldn't understand why no one even mentioned the fact that they had a new member in the family.

After everyone left, Jessica ran to answer the telephone in her bedroom and Brian went to his room to see if he had any messages. The light was flashing on his phone so he called the front desk.

"Good evening, Mr. Hargrove. Yes, there is one message for you. Someone asks that you, and you alone, meet in the lounge at nine o'clock."

"That's it? The person didn't leave a name?"

"I'm sorry, Mr. Hargrove. I did not take the message. It only says what I read to you."

"Okay, then thank you." Brian sat back a bit and wondered who it was. Maybe Warren and his wife had come over to the hotel and wanted to have a drink with him. But then the message would have been for both him and Jessica. He shook his head, not able to think who it might be. He went from his bedroom to Jessica's. She had just gotten off the phone with her parents and was bubbling with excitement. Brian put his arms around her, caressed her and asked her how she was feeling.

"Brian, I am numb. I can't believe everything that's going on. I am *so* happy, but I am *so* tired. All I want to do is climb into a nice hot sauna and relax with one more glass of champagne. Why?"

"I'm going to meet with my father for a little while. That is, if you don't mind."

"Brian, you go do what you have to do. I'm pooped and want to feel refreshed for our ladies' day of shopping tomorrow." She pecked him on the lips, walked back into her room, peeked around the door and waved as she closed it. Well, he had to hand it to her, if this is the way she always is, life will be easy with Jessica. He headed out the door on his way to the lounge, his mind already on the person who, so mysteriously, wanted to meet with him.

Chapter Fifty-two

Heather was already sitting at the bar waiting for Brian. She looked stunning in a sleek long black dress, black satin sandal heels, her hair piled on top of her head with gentle wisps falling around her neck. Heads turned as she walked through the lounge. She looked well put together but inside there was a war. She was afraid of Brian's reaction. She didn't want to hurt him. She did love Brian, but she loved him like a brother. And that's exactly who he was. It was going to take time for him to get used to the idea.

Suddenly she caught a glimpse of him heading for the lounge. She turned in her seat so that she faced him as he walked into the room. But Brian was looking around at the tables because he was still expecting a couple to be greeting him. Heather was not even a thought in his mind. She started to slide off the stool and walk toward him as he caught sight of her. Up to that moment, she had never caught Brian by surprise. But she could tell that he was totally unprepared for the sight of her. He couldn't take his eyes off her and felt glued to that one spot. He was in a state of shock; he could not believe he was seeing Heather.

He tried to move but couldn't. For a moment he wanted to run; he felt so angry with her! But suddenly seeing her, he found he could do nothing. She looked gorgeous. He had never seen her look this way before. He tried to find something to say as she approached him but couldn't. So Heather took the lead.

"Brian, I'm sorry if I startled you. I was afraid if I left my name you wouldn't come, and I feel we have to talk before you get married."

"Heather, please, you don't understand . . ."

"Brian, I think I do understand, only too well. Please, let me help you. You helped me through so much pain in my life. That must count for something. We have become close and I respect and value your opinion. I couldn't ever imagine my life without you in it anymore."

"Stop. Please, Heather. I can't let you go on. You have no idea how I feel . . ." But he stopped talking because she came right up to him and put her arm through his and started to walk him over to a table in the corner of the room. There was a bottle of champagne already waiting. He could only look at her. He was mortified at his loss of words. But everything was so different now. He couldn't get it straight in his head. He wasn't close to his brothers; they had never really included him in their lives. With Heather it had been different, but he still could not make the change. He was stuck. He felt he could never become "unstuck," especially with her looking so gorgeous tonight.

"Heather, you are the last person I expected to see here. I don't know what to say to you. I'm so angry I could scream and it's like I want to strike out and hurt you because I am hurting so much over you."

"Brian, Brian. I know that. You have to give me a lot more credit than you have. I know how you feel about me. It has made it extremely difficult for me because I do love you, just like I told you in the hospital, but not that way. Now, something has happened that neither one of us can comprehend, but don't you see what that means?"

"Oh, yes, I can see what that means. I will never have a chance to win you. That's all that means." Brian felt himself losing control.

"Brian, what are you saying? What about all the things you have done for me and gone through with me? Doesn't that count for something uniquely special in our lives?"

"Oh, sure it does. At least I thought it did until Joe came into your life. Then I knew it was all over. I could see the difference in you. I knew I was losing you without ever having had you." Suddenly he grabbed her by the shoulders. "Don't you see, Heather? I can't accept you any other way in my life unless I can have you totally to myself." He held her close to him by her shoulders. All he wanted to do was kiss her. He couldn't stand it. The pain was unbearable. He let her go and started to walk away.

"Brian, please don't leave! We have to come to some sort of understanding! That's why I came. I didn't come because I wanted to flaunt myself in front of you. I care too much about you to do that. But you have to get it through your head! Brian, we're family now, whether you like it or not! Do you hear me?" Brian turned to look at her and for a moment Heather thought he would say something but then he turned again and walked toward the front door of the hotel.

Heather ran to the desk and asked for a car. She followed Brian. She didn't know where he was going but she was not going to let him get away. He was running away and he had to stop. She knew that they had to get through this . . . together, she hoped. His car stopped in front of some big bar and Heather told the driver to wait for her until she was ready to leave. She waited about ten minutes and then went in. Brian was at the bar with a line of five shot glasses in front of him. Three of them were already empty. He was unaware of her presence. She continued to stand at the entry and watch him. Finally, she took a deep breath, walked up next to him and said to the bartender, "Line mine up the same."

Brian looked over, shocked to see her standing next to him, but he had heard what she asked for. He started to laugh. "I don't think so, Miss. You have no idea what you're getting yourself into."

"Well, I think I do. Just think of it this way, Brian. If you can do it, I can do it. It must run in the family."

He wanted to slap her every time she made reference to the two of them being family. "Just why did you follow me? Don't you understand that I want to be alone?"

"Yes, I can understand if you wanted to be alone to think things out, but sitting at a bar and drinking yourself to the other side of the moon is not accomplishing anything. What about your future? What about that woman in your room back at the hotel? Aren't you planning to marry her and spend the rest of your life with her?"

"That's none of your business. It's my life and I'll do what I think I have to do to get by."

"Well, I want to be included in that life, Brian. You are the only brother I've ever known and loved. Don't you understand what all of this has meant to me? I've never felt like I've had any roots. Now I understand where my roots are. This has been a tremendous thing for me to accept, too. You know what your problem is?" Heather stopped talking for a moment to down the last two shot glasses. "I'll tell you what your problem is. You're so self-centered, only thinking about how you hurt, what your needs are and what you can get from people. You're so caught up in all of that, that you don't even have a clue when someone actually has genuine feelings toward you, because you have never had them for anyone else in your life; not unless there was a totally selfish motive. I think it's about time you get off that pity pot of yours and move your mother-loving ass!" With that last comment the alcohol hit her and she fell right off the stool. Brian didn't know what to do. He was mortified that she might have hurt herself but she was so funny when she had slipped off the barstool!

He got up and tried to help her up but all she did was try to yank her arms away from him and push him away. Finally he stood up and pulled a bill out to pay the bartender. Then he bent down and gathered Heather up in his arms and over his shoulder. She kicked all the way out of the bar – and some of her kicks really hurt! But he knew he had to get her out of there before something worse happened. Some of her words had reached him but he just wasn't ready to accept them.

His driver opened the backseat passenger door for Brian and his flailing burden, and waved Heather's driver off. This was a potentially serious situation but he couldn't help laughing. Amid a steady stream of expletives, Heather struggled to sit up but the liquor had definitely taken hold of her. Brian kept laughing, which only made her angrier.

Finally Heather managed to slur in exaggerated indignation, "Just what, may I ask, do you think is so funny?"

"You are. The big – shot drinker! Just look at you."

Again Heather tried to sit up and straighten herself out. But the harder she tried the worse she felt. Yet her anger would not let her relent. "Well, let me tell you something, Mr. Brian Hargrove, I am not leaving you until you accept me as who I am: your sister!" Brian knew she meant everything she was saying but she looked so darned funny he couldn't be serious. He had lost track of the number of shots he had had. He dimly realized that he, too, was silly drunk. He continued to laugh uncontrollably and finally Heather had to join him. The driver interrupted for instructions. Between bursts of laughter Brian told him to go to the nearest diner and get them some coffee. Then he went right back to this uncontrollable laughter. Eventually their laughter turned serious and they both found themselves in tears.

"Heather, I don't know what to say. I don't want to lose you and I don't want to be angry with you."

"Then, Brian, you have to let go and accept me for who I am. I can't be what I am not. Just think, we will have a lifetime of closeness as a family. I've never had any brothers or sisters and I don't even know what it's like. But we have shared so much already. Why should it be any different now that we know we are family? I know I will grow to love Jessica and I know that you will, too. But we will always have each other to share everything with." They both cried as Heather hugged him. Heather was relieved that things finally seemed to be under control, and Brian finally knew Heather was right, and that he did want her in his life. He felt closer to Heather than to either of his brothers and that was because she had accepted him just the way he was.

"Heather, I understand everything you have said and deep down I agree. But I need time to get used to this change and the change in my feelings. I know you are shocked that I'm getting married this weekend. But I have to do it. My feelings have been so strong for you, but I knew you would never feel the same way about me. So I reached out to the next best thing. Jessica is a good person and she's easy to get along with. I do have a good feeling about how our life will be. I respect you for what you tried to do here tonight. I know that I would much rather have run and hidden behind a marriage for the rest of my life, in reality only feeling sorry for myself, instead of accepting the changes in my life and really starting to live."

"Brian, the trouble with you is you don't realize how much you mean to your family. You've always pushed everyone away. I'm not saying that's going to change – unless you want it to. But you have to understand that, as your friend all this time, I'm not going to let you push me away. I wouldn't have missed this wedding for all the tea in China. And the reason for this is I love you, Brian. What has come of this is that you're still my friend, but you're also my brother now. That makes us family, kin, related . . . get the picture?"

Brian smiled as he looked at her. He nodded in agreement.

"Now, Mr. Hargrove, don't you think it's time you take your sister home? If you don't, I'll tell on you!"

"Wow, and growing up together, you just would have!" Brian exclaimed trying to choke back the tightening of emotion in his throat. Heather sighed deeply as she felt that she had finally touched Brian. She didn't know if it was totally absorbed, but he was beginning to come around. Maybe after he was married things would be easier for him. But, for now, she knew they had climbed the highest mountain. From here on in it would be much easier. But it wasn't so easy getting Heather out of the car. She had lost her legs to the alcohol. Brian carried her to her room. Joe was anxiously waiting and opened the door to find Brian with Heather over his shoulder.

"Hi, Joe." Heather attempted in slurred speech. "Meet Brian." Joe stood aside and watched Brian carrying Heather over to the sofa.

"Nice to meet you, Joe." Brian held out his hand and Joe, bewildered, shook it. "Just call her 'little miss shot drinker.' Good night."

When Brian returned to the suite, he knocked on Jessica's door. She didn't answer but he entered anyway. He needed to talk to her. He wanted to come clean and tell her about Heather. After all, she was part of the family now and Heather was coming to the wedding. He wanted Jessica to understand this. He walked over to her bed and she stirred. She took one look at him and realized that something serious had happened. She could smell the alcohol on him. "Brian, what's the matter, is something wrong?"

"No, Jessica. Nothing's wrong, but we need to have a talk."

"It sounds very serious." Her heart pounded, so fearful was she that Brian was going to back down and not marry her. She didn't want to hear those words. But she decided to hold her tongue because she had been spending time with a different Brian lately. Maybe he needed to get something off his chest.

Brian explained his new sister to Jessica and then let the entire story unfold. But he didn't tell her how much in love he was with her. After all, he didn't want to hurt her but he did want to be as open as he could be in his relationship with his future wife. Jessica was so relieved and pleased with herself that she had held her tongue and listened. She intuitively realized there was more to this story than what Brian was telling her, but she let him continue. He was confiding in her, and that was the important thing. When he finished she held him tenderly until they eventually fell asleep.

Chapter Fifty-three

The next morning, Jessica left a message for Heather to join her for lunch. It was a crazy morning of shopping for all of them but Jessica was intent on doing this. She rushed back to the hotel and told everyone she had an important errand to run and that she would meet them back at the bridal boutique.

Heather was late getting to the restaurant at the hotel where Jessica asked to meet her, and she didn't know what Jessica looked like. But Jessica recognized Heather as soon as she walked through the doors. Jessica could see Heather looking at other patrons and not finding recognition. She signaled. Heather reached the table somewhat breathless.

"Heather, I'm Jessica Hillbrook and I'm happy to meet you. I must say you definitely look better than your brother does today."

Heather blushed at the mention of last night. She liked Jessica instantly and shook her hand, congratulating her on her upcoming marriage.

"Heather, there's a reason I asked you to lunch today. I'm sorry you weren't at the reception yesterday, but I have something to ask you."

Heather held her breath. She liked Jessica so far, but she didn't know anything about her. Was she going to tell her to stay away from Brian? How much had Brian told her? "Of course, Jessica. Ask me anything."

"Well, I guess it was kind of meant to be. But if you say no I will understand. Would you consider being my maid of honor?"

Heather was so taken by what Jessica was asking; Jessica could see tears forming at the corners of Heather's eyes. Jessica knew she had surprised her, so she sat for a moment while Heather collected herself. "Jessica, I'm touched beyond words. It would be an honor to be your maid of honor. But I don't even have a dress!"

"Oh, don't worry about that. I have that all taken care of. After we finish lunch we'll go back to the boutique. I'm supposed to meet the rest of the girls there. I'll announce you as my maid of honor and you can be fitted right then and there."

"Sounds like a plan to me! Thank you so, Jessica. I think this is so thoughtful of you! I appreciate your wanting to include me in your wedding. I wouldn't have missed it for anything!"

"Oh, Heather, thank you. I think we're going to be good friends." She squeezed Heather's hand and they talked about all the plans for the wedding.

The rest of the day was a flurry of activity, in a wonderful and exciting world of picking out dresses and accessories and all the things the bride would need. But Jessica wasn't quite so sure about being prepared for the honeymoon. Brian had planned a surprise honeymoon. He wouldn't tell her anything except that she wouldn't need many clothes, and that the clothes she did bring should be light and brief. Everyone laughed as Jessica repeated his instructions. They all concluded the honeymooning would be in a hot climate.

The entire family met for dinner that night where plans were set for dinner with Jessica's parents the following night. Then there would be the wedding rehearsal on Warren Tornock's yacht, followed by a special rehearsal dinner given by the Tornocks, again on the yacht.

Heather was excited about all the plans; but, most of all, she felt more comfortable with Brian. He seemed a bit distant, but that was to be expected. But he did not avoid her or her glances. He met Heather and Joe and fully acknowledged them from across the table. Joe was happy for Heather. He wanted for her to feel like she had her feet firmly planted on the ground at last. To know where she came from was important and would take time for her to absorb fully. He loved her beyond words and he had already made up his mind that this was the woman he wanted to spend the rest of his life with and to grow old with. But there was plenty of time for that. To add to the magic of the evening, Joe had slipped a diamond ring on Heather's finger. They belonged to each other but had a lifetime ahead. She was just beginning to understand who she was and where she was coming from. He was pleased that the entire family welcomed her with open arms. He had seen a lot as a detective and not all families were that open or accepting.

Time raced by, full of joy and celebration. Before they all knew it they were dressing for the main event. Joe and Brian shared a suite. Winston and Bob joined them the morning of the wedding and they all got ready in Joe's suite. Heather dressed in Jessica's suite along with both Alicea and Jessica's mother.

There were four limousines to take them to the yacht club where Tornock's yacht was docked. As they pulled up to the dock they could see that the yacht was decorated and had become a sailing bridal vessel. It was beautiful and there were people everywhere, including the news media, who had gotten wind of the upcoming marriage and other events in the Hargrove clan and were out in droves, taking pictures and pushing their microphones into everyone's face.

Winston and Bob escorted Alicea down the aisle and then came back to get Jessica's mother, Mrs. Hillbrook, just before the procession began.

Heather was trying to straighten out the train of Jessica's dress and primping her veil. "Jessica, you look absolutely gorgeous!"

"Oh, Heather thanks for everything! I feel like I've known you all my life already."

"It's true. I feel the same way!" Fighting back tears, they gently hugged each other, fearful to muss themselves. They heard the Wedding March begin.

"Daddy," Jessica called. "I think we have to go now." Mr. Hillbrook took one last look at his daughter and took her arm.

"I'm so proud of you, Jessica, my dearest daughter." She could only smile at him because her heart was beating too fast to get a word out.

Heather walked down the aisle in front of the bride and her father. With her first step she felt like she was on a new path; the long walk down the aisle symbolized her dramatic and difficult journey. There was no looking back. She didn't want to look back. She only wanted to concentrate on her future, beginning with this very moment. It was beyond comprehension that she had become a part of this family and was there, participating in this wedding. She smiled at each person as she paced down the aisle. She focused on Alec and Alicea, then the rest of her family. Then she found her Joe standing at the end of the first row. So much had happened to her in such a brief period of time. And yet, everything else seemed so distant now. Finally she had found all the pieces to the puzzle and it had become a complete picture. She watched as Brian and

Jessica were joined in marriage and managed a glance at Joe, catching his wink. She smiled and winked back. She knew her life would be full and happy from this moment on. She had found her way home. For not only was it the beginning of a new life for Brian and Jessica, it was yet another *new beginning* . . .

THE END